CV

THE NIGHT VILLA

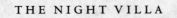

BALLANTINE BOOKS

NEW YORK

The

Night Villa

A NOVEL

CAROL GOODMAN

A Ballantine Books Trade Paperback Original

Copyright © 2008 by Carol Goodman
Reading group guide copyright © 2008 by Random House, Inc.

Published in the United States by Ballantine Books,
an imprint of The Random House Publishing Group,
a division of Random House, Inc., New York.

BALLANTINE and colophon are registered trademarks of Random House, Inc.
RANDOM HOUSE READER'S CIRCLE and colophon
are trademarks of Random House, Inc.

LIBRARY OF CONGRESS CATALOGING-IN-PUBLICATION DATA

Goodman, Carol.
The night villa : a novel / Carol Goodman.
p.   cm.
ISBN 978-0-345-47960-0 (pbk.)
1. College teachers—Fiction.   2. Women classicists—Fiction.
3. Excavations (Archaeology)—Fiction.   4. Cults—Fiction.   5. Pythagoras—Fiction.
6. Herculaneum (Extinct city)—Fiction.   7. Italy—Fiction   I. Title.
PS3607.O566N54   2008
813'.6—dc22   2008008519

Printed in the United States of America

www.randomhousereaderscircle.com

2 4 6 8 9 7 5 3 1

Book design by Dana Leigh Blanchette

For Nora

There also stands the gloomy house of Night;
ghastly clouds shroud it in darkness.
Before it Atlas stands erect and on his head
and unwearying arms firmly supports the broad sky,
where Night and Day cross a bronze threshold
and then come close and greet each other.

—HESIOD, *Theogony*

Acknowledgments

I'd like to thank my editor, Linda Marrow, for her always insightful editing and my agent, Loretta Barrett, for her continued support and encouragement. Thanks, also, to all those at Ballantine whose hard work made this book possible: Gina Centrello, Libby McGuire, Kim Hovey, Brian McLendon, Gene Mydlowski, Lisa Barnes, Dana Isaacson, and Junessa Viloria. Thanks, too, to Nick Mullendore and Gabriel David at Loretta Barrett Books.

As always, I'm grateful to my circle of first readers: Laurie Bower, Gary Feinberg, Marge Goodman, Rick LaFleur, Lauren Lipton, and Scott Silverman and Nora Slonimsky.

I couldn't have written this book without my husband, Lee Slonimsky, who wrote the sonnet to Wilhemina Jashemski and the

"Golden Verse" of Pythagoras. It was Lee's research into the life of Pythagoras that gave me the idea to create the Tetraktys.

Finally, I owe special thanks to the late Ross Scaife, professor of classics at the University of Kentucky, who gave me the idea for the Papyrus Project. To Ross, who died in 2008, and his wife, Cathy Scaife, I owe not only the inspiration for this book but many years of invaluable friendship and encouragement.

THE NIGHT VILLA

CHAPTER I

When the first call came that morning I was with a student, so I didn't answer it.

"Don't worry," I told Agnes Hancock, one of my most promising classics majors, "the machine will get it."

But it stopped after the third ring.

"I guess whoever was calling changed his mind," Agnes said, relacing her fingers to conceal the ragged cuticle on her right thumb. She'd been gnawing on it when I found her waiting outside my door—ten minutes early for my eight o'clock office hours. Most of my students were sound asleep at this hour, which was why I held my office hours so early: to discourage all but the most zealous. Agnes was definitely a zealot. She was on a scholarship, for one thing, and had to maintain a high average, but Agnes was also one of those rare students who seemed to have a genuine passion for the material. She'd gone to a high school with a rigorous Latin program and gotten the highest score on the national Latin exam in the state. Not shabby for a state as big as Texas. She wasn't just good at declensions, though; she had the ability to translate a line of ancient poetry and turn it into poetry again, and the agility of mind to compare the myths from one culture to those of another. She could have a successful academic career in classics or comparative literature. The only problem was that her personal life was often chaotic—a result, I suspected, of her looks.

Agnes was blessed with the kind of classic American beauty that you thought only existed in fashion magazines—until you saw someone like her walking down the street. Long, shiny blond hair, flawless skin, straight teeth she was born with, blue eyes—the kind of Barbie-looks I would have traded my dark hair and olive skin for when I was growing up. I couldn't complain though; the enrollment in my Latin and mythology classes had never been so high before Agnes declared her major. There were always a couple of suitors waiting outside on the quad when we emerged from Parlin Hall, but they had been replaced this year by one in particular: a wild-eyed philosophy major who pursued her relentlessly through the fall and then became so jealously possessive of her when she finally agreed to go out with him that she'd broken up with him over spring break. I hadn't seen him since then and I'd heard that he dropped out. Now I wondered if he was back. I have a feeling the torn cuticles and dark shadows under her eyes are his doing, but I'm afraid that if I ask her about it she'll burst into tears. And that won't do either of us any good. We're both due in Main Building at nine o'clock for the Classics Department's summer internship interviews. Which is why, no doubt, she'd camped out on my doorstep so early this morning.

"It was probably someone calling about the final," I say, reaching toward the phone. "I'll turn the ringer off so we won't be disturbed."

"Oh no, you don't have to do that, Dr. Chase. It wasn't anything that important . . ." She's already half out of her chair. I'd forgotten how easily spooked she gets when attention, good or bad, is directed at her. It surprised me at first because I thought that, with her looks, she'd be used to it, but I've gathered through talks we've had about her childhood that her father, a Baptist minister in a small west Texas town, preached endlessly against the sin of vanity. She seems to think it's her fault when boys fall in love with her, which has made it all the more difficult to deal with her possessive ex-boyfriend.

"Don't be silly, Agnes, I do it all the time. Believe me, they'll just e-mail me instead. My inbox will be filled with a dozen questions designed to ferret out the exact passage that'll be on the exam. Anything to avoid actually reading the whole of *Metamorphoses.*"

"But Ovid writes so beautifully," Agnes says, her eyes widening in genuine disbelief. "Why would anyone not want to read everything he wrote? I especially love his version of the Persephone and Demeter story. I'm using it for my presentation."

I smile, not just because of the pleasure of a shared literary passion, but because my ploy has worked. At the mention of her favorite poet a calm has settled over Agnes. She's sunk back into her chair and her hands, released from the knot she'd wrung them into, fan open, loose and graceful, in her lap, like one of those paper flowers that expand in water.

"Is that what you wanted to see me about? Your proposal to Dr. Lawrence for the Papyrus Project?"

Agnes hesitates and I see her gaze stray out my second-story window toward the quad, where a few students are lounging in patches of shade cast by the live oaks. It's not yet nine, but the temperature is already in the eighties and the forecast predicts it'll break a hundred by noon. The sunlight between the trees is so bright that it's hard to make out anything but amorphous shapes in the shade. So if Agnes is checking to see if her ex-boyfriend is waiting for her, she'll be looking in vain.

"It's on the role of women in mystery rites?" I prompt. Since my specialty is women in the ancient world, I've been coaching Agnes on her proposal.

"Yes," she answers, tearing her eyes away from the window. "I plan to argue that the frescoes in the newly excavated section of the Villa della Notte, which was buried in the eruption of Mount Vesuvius in AD 79, depict a mystery rite similar to the 'little mysteries' of Agrai, which combined Eleusinian and Dionysian elements."

"And can you give a brief definition of mystery rites and of those two in particular?"

"Sure. A mystery rite was a secret form of worship that revealed some kind of 'truth' or doctrine only to those initiated to the rite. They usually had something to do with the afterlife. The most famous were the Eleusinian Mysteries, which got their name because they were originally celebrated in Eleusis, Greece, and although we don't know exactly what went on because they were, well . . ."

"Mysteries?"

"Yes, *secret* mysteries. We know they reenacted the story of Persephone and Demeter. An initiate probably relived the story of the rape of Persephone, her trip to the underworld, and then the wandering of her mother, Demeter, who killed the crops and everything growing because she was so upset at losing her daughter. While she's wandering around she comes to Eleusis, which is why the rites were there, then she goes to Zeus, who sends Hermes to bring Persephone back. Only Persephone had eaten some pomegranate seeds, so she could only spend half the year aboveground and the other half she had to spend in Hell—I mean, Hades . . ."

Agnes blushes at her slip, and I save her by nudging her on to the next topic. "What about the Dionysian rites?"

"We think they reenacted the story of Dionysus Zagreus, a variant of the wine god myth. In this version Dionysus is the son of Zeus and Persephone . . ."

Agnes notices me lifting an eyebrow and a little light of understanding dawns in her face, "Oh, I hadn't thought of that before! Persephone's a link between the two myths! Anyway, Hera, jealous of her husband's illegitimate child, gets the Titans to eat the baby"—here Agnes makes a face and mock shudders—"but Athene rescues the heart and brings it to Zeus, who eats it and proceeds to have another affair—this time with Semele, who gives birth to a new Dionysus. In the rites, a group of women, called maenads, become intoxicated with wine and reenact the dismemberment and consumption of the god—"

"Literally?"

"Oh no—at least we hope not! I mean there is that play by Euripides where Agave, the queen of Thebes, and her women are so frenzied they tear apart Agave's own son, Pentheus, but probably they just tore apart bread meant to represent the god and drank some more wine. Of course, if you believe Livy, the rites turned into this big sex orgy, but I think that was just prejudice because the rites were popular with women and took place at night. Anyway . . ."

As Agnes goes on to describe the Dionysian elements in the frescoes in Herculaneum, such as the presence of the traditional basket (*liknon*) and wand (*thrysus*), I wonder, not for the first time, at a Baptist minister's daughter choosing to study pagan religions. But then, casting off the family religion was no alien concept to me, and I suppose studying Dionysian orgies and blood sacrifices was as harmless an act of rebellion as the piercings and tattoos sported by her contemporaries. Still, her passion for the subject is a little unsettling. Describing the frenzy of the maenads she begins to look like one herself, her cheeks pinking, her blue eyes flashing, and her hair coming loose from its ponytail. She comes abruptly back to herself when she notices, as I do, that another call is coming in on my phone. The light flashes four times and then stops. My caller has apparently gotten slightly more determined to reach me.

"Excellent," I say. "And now tell me why you have to go to Italy to study these frescoes?"

"Well," Agnes says, taking a deep gulp of air and refastening her ponytail, "for one thing, the newly excavated frescoes haven't been photographed yet, but, most important, they've also found charred papyrus rolls in the villa. The little taggie things on them—"

"*Sillyboi,*" I suggest, providing the Greek term for the tags that ancient librarians used to identify papyrus rolls.

"Um, yeah." She giggles nervously. "I guess I should use the Greek name, but it always makes me laugh . . . The *sillyboi* indicate that the library of the villa was dedicated to foreign religions— there are books on Mithraism, Isis worship, the cult of Cybele, Orphism, Pythagoreans—so why wouldn't there be one that described the *little mysteries* that went on right there? And while at one time we wouldn't have been able to read these scrolls because they were all burned on the outside when Vesuvius erupted, Dr. Lawrence is going to use multispectral imaging to see inside them . . . which I think is just so cool. I really think Dr. Lawrence is a genius, don't you?"

Not Agnes, too. She hasn't gotten caught in his web, has she? Elgin Lawrence has a history of seducing his teaching assistants, and Agnes is just his type—and not just because she's beautiful. He preys on young girls who are insecure. Agnes's father might have thought he was doing her a favor by scourging her of vanity, but he would have done better to instill a sense of self-worth in his daughter.

I open my mouth to form some sort of polite but qualified response to Elgin Lawrence's claims to genius, but I am spared such shameless equivocation by the appearance at the door of Barry Biddle, Elgin's grant partner on the Papyrus Project.

"Hadn't you better get over there, Sophie?" Barry asks. He's in a suit and tie and already sweating. Although he left the Northeast eight years ago he still dresses as if he were in Boston instead of Austin. He hasn't realized that no one wears suits after March in Austin. Well, no one who doesn't have to. I'm in a gauzy Mexican blouse I picked up in San Antonio a few years ago and a skirt that's a tad too short, but then I've always thought my legs were my best feature. Right now, they're bare down to my sandals and tanned from spending yesterday swimming at Barton Springs. Agnes, on the other hand, is wearing a crisp seersucker suit, stockings, and navy pumps adorned with silly red and white bows . . . but then, she's the one applying for the job. Barry always looks as if he's on his way to a job interview, and though he may not know that Elgin asked me first to work on the Papyrus Project, I suspect he still feels like a second fiddle in the operation. I imagine he's no happier with Elgin's flamboyant style than I would have been, but then Barry is coming up for tenure next year and he hasn't published anything of significance since his dissertation.

I stare pointedly at the clock, which reads 8:42, and then nod toward the window. "Elgin always walks up through the quad and I haven't seen him go by yet," I say. "You go on ahead. We'll be right behind you." I give Agnes a hard stare to keep her in her seat. "Tell Elgin I'm personally escorting Miss Hancock."

I wait until Barry disappears from my doorway, leaving a damp stain where he'd grasped the wood door frame, and then roll my eyes at Agnes. She's not looking at me, though; she's looking at my phone, which has started to flash again.

"Someone must really want to talk to you," she says. "Maybe you should get it."

"If they really wanted to talk to me they could leave a message," I say, trying not to count the flashes, but doing so anyway. It flashes five times and then stops.

"It's just I'm afraid . . . it might be my fault."

"Your fault?" I ask, sounding angrier than I'd meant to. Agnes's self-deprecation can get on my nerves. Probably because she reminds me of myself at that age. "How in the world—" I stop when I see Agnes's eyes fill with tears. I get up and close the door and hand Agnes a box of tissues on my way back to my chair.

"I think it might be my boyfriend . . . I mean, my ex-boyfriend, Dale Henry," she manages after blowing her nose. "He's back in town and I'm afraid he's going to show up at the interview."

"If he's an ex, how does he know your schedule?" I ask, trying to make my voice kind but firm. It occurs to me that I could teach a course in this subject: How to Separate from Your Crazy Ex.

Agnes blushes and chews on her thumb. "One of my roommates called and told me that Dale came by the house this morning right after I left. Of course they didn't tell him where I was, but apparently he'd seen an announcement about the internship interviews and he was sure I must be going there. I know he's not too happy about me going to Italy . . ."

"You realize he doesn't have a say in your plans, Agnes. He's not even your boyfriend anymore."

"I know, I know, it's just that he gets so jealous and he's gotten this idea about Dr. Lawrence—"

Agnes stops and I see her looking at the phone, which is flashing again. I don't have to count; the three flashes feel like the beat of my heart.

"Well, Dr. Lawrence *does* have quite a reputation, you know," I tell her, hoping to get in a little warning about Agnes's future romantic plans as well as her past ones. I'm afraid it doesn't seem like she has the best track record, but then, with my romantic history, I'm not really in a position to judge.

"Oh," Agnes says, "I know. All the prizes he's won and he was on CSPAN last year! I can't believe I might get a chance to work with someone so famous!"

I don't point out that it wasn't Elgin Lawrence's academic reputation I was referring to. The phone has started to flash again, but Agnes is too busy listing her professor's curriculum vitae to notice. At least she's not crying anymore. When the light fades after the fourth ring I hand her a mirror to fix her lipstick and mascara and grab my briefcase. "Dr. Lawrence would be lucky to get such a bright and competent assistant to work on the project," I say, checking my own lipstick in my reflection in the window—and surveying the quad at the same time. "Come on. Let's go."

Agnes smiles shyly at my praise, her newly glossed lips pink and innocent. I smile back, glad I've managed to reassure her without having to admit that it's not her crazy ex on the phone. It's mine.

*I*t's the number sequence that's clued me in: 3-4-5, the simplest representation of the Pythagorean theorem. Ely was obsessed with it. He heard it in the cawing of the grackles outside our Hyde Park bungalow and claimed the traffic lights on Guadalupe were timed to it. He counted his steps in sequences of 3-4-5 as he walked around the campus, and changed his route if the number of steps from one building to another weren't divisible by twelve. Instead of walking straight from Parlin to Main, as Agnes and I do now, he'd swing around the statue of Robert E. Lee and approach the Main Mall from the east side.

I pause now under the shade of a live oak opposite the statue and scan the mall. It's been five years since I saw Ely, but I'm sure

I'd recognize his tall, rangy figure anywhere—and there's no place to hide on the mall. The expanse of pavement below the University Tower glitters in the morning sun, a burning desert compared to the shady nook we're in now. There are benches on the edges of the mall but no one's sitting on them—it's already too hot to sit in the sun.

Then I glance up at the tower. I can't help but feel I'll be exposed once I step out of the shade and into full view of the tower, but that's as much because of the tower's history as my own. I wasn't born yet when Charles Whitman barricaded himself on the twenty-eighth-floor observation deck and picked off fourteen people with his arsenal of weapons, but I'm enough of an Austinite to think of that August day every time I walk beneath the tower. My aunt M'Lou was working in the emergency room at Brackenridge Hospital then, and she told me that in addition to the gunshot wounds, they treated patients for third-degree burns. That was because when Whitman started shooting, pedestrians on the mall dove for safety under these benches and were pinned there for the next ninety-six minutes. Somehow that detail has always haunted me the most, the thought of feeling your own skin sizzling against the pavement but knowing that a worse fate awaited you if you stood up. It was the kind of choice Dante would have dreamed up for his Inferno.

"Um, don't you think we should go?" Agnes asks me. I turn to her and realize I've made her even more nervous by my hesitation. She's sweating under her seersucker suit, her eyes skittering around the mall like pinballs.

"Sure," I say, squeezing her elbow and leading her quickly across the hot pavement toward Main, "into the lion's den."

A quick blast of heat and light and then we're in the lobby and walking past the security guards, two ex-students whom I've seen around the Drag for as long as I've lived in Austin. The town is full of these underemployed malingerers who fall for the Austin lifestyle during college but who also don't find, or want, anything very challenging in the way of work after graduation. Right now they seem more interested in admiring Agnes's legs than in checking IDs. Besides, the real security in the building is to get up in the elevator to the observation deck, and all we have to do is walk up one flight to the conference suite.

Elgin had said that he'd scheduled the internship interviews here because there wasn't a large enough room available in the Classics Department, but I suspect he just likes the formality of the big boardroom and that the plush swivel chairs and gleaming mahogany table, set behind a wall of polished glass so that the whole room feels like a stage set, make him feel more imposing. I can see Agnes shriveling into herself as we enter the room, so I give her arm another comforting squeeze, steering her toward a chair on the far side of the table, near the head where Elgin is sure to sit, and then go to get us two coffees from the cart that Odette Renfrew, the dean's secretary, has just wheeled in.

"Pretty dress," I say, sidling next to Odette as she sets out cream and sugar. "The color suits you." The orange in her dress and matching head cloth more than suits her, it casts a warm glow on her dark skin that's like a flame burnishing her cheekbones and toned biceps. Odette's a large woman, but she keeps fit by swimming daily at the university pool, where I often share a lane with her and then, afterward, trade school gossip in the sauna. Which is why she looks surprised to see me.

"I thought you'd excused yourself from this particular party," she whispers to me as I pour the coffees.

"I have," I say, "I'm just here to watch the interviews . . . and to lend moral support to Agnes Hancock."

Odette glances over her shoulder at Agnes, who's looking out to the hall where Elgin Lawrence and several students have just appeared at the top of the stairs. I see Agnes's eyes widen and her shoulders relax at the sight of her professor. I can't say I totally blame her, finding my own gaze stuck on Elgin as he stops to talk to someone in the hall. He's in his Indiana Jones mode, as I've come to think of it: rumpled but nicely fitting khakis; soft blue shirt that brings out his blue eyes; sleeves rolled up to reveal muscular fore-arms that I happen to know he keeps toned by rowing on Town Lake but which always make him look as if he's just gotten back from an archaeological dig in Cairo. Agnes is staring through the glass at him as if mesmerized—and so are the cluster of students around him, male and female.

"Shit," I whisper under my breath.

"Yeah," Odette says, shaking her head. "I'm not sure going to Italy with Professor Romeo is the best thing for that girl."

I laugh at Odette's private name for Elgin Lawrence and pour milk in the coffees. "I agree, but what can you do? Kids, right?" Odette smiles and pats me on the shoulder. She's got four sons, all in various stages of advanced education here at UT, thanks to their mother's tuition benefits. Although I imagine their infractions are minor—it's hard to imagine anyone crossing Odette—she's always shaking her head over some new exploit by one or the other of them. "I've got pastries from Cisco's," she tells me before going back to her office. "I'm gonna heat 'em up and bring 'em in if this meeting goes on too long—the dean wants the room cleared by ten-thirty."

I take the coffees back to Agnes, but Barry Biddle has taken the seat next to her so I sit across from them, my back to the glass wall. I hear Elgin come in with his entourage of students but refrain from turning to greet him until I notice he's hovering over me. When I look up I see he's grinning down at me—or possibly my bare legs.

"Dr. Chase, so kind of you to take time out of your busy finals schedule for my little ole Papyrus Project," he says in a southern drawl that sounds like he grew up on a plantation and not the pig farm I know he did. "I hope it's not too *flashy* for you."

Flashy is what I called it when I told Elgin I didn't want in. The truth was I wouldn't have minded being a part of the project if Elgin had a shred of evidence that the multispectral imaging was going to work on the papyrus scrolls from the Villa della Notte, or if he'd framed the project as an experiment, but instead he'd gone around spreading outrageous claims for the technology and promising lost manuscripts to gullible students like Agnes. The project had been turned down by three institutes before Elgin had finally gotten funding from the Pontificia Instituto Sacra Archeologia—PISA—on the grounds that one of the charred scrolls found in the villa might contain an early Christian document. It was one more reason I didn't want anything to do with the project; I'd had my fill of nuns in parochial school.

"I'm here because I'm interested in Agnes's presentation on women's roles in mystery rites," I say primly. Elgin nods, keeping his eyes on me a beat too long for my comfort, and then turns to Agnes.

"Ah, Miss Hancock, punctual as always. A good sign. We'll be getting started early on site this summer to get our work done before the damned *riposo.*"

I try to catch Agnes's eye to say *See, what did I tell you? We had plenty of time!* but she's blushing and stammering something about being an early riser. The other intern candidates are avidly eyeing the coffee urns, wondering if they still have time to get themselves coffees. Elgin settles that by announcing in a booming voice, "Let's get down to it then!" and sitting down at the head of the table. Barry's gotten him coffee and so he's oblivious to the caffeine deprivation of the rest of his little flock.

"Well, as you all know," Elgin begins, "we're here to see which one of you lucky youngsters gets to go to Italy this summer to work on the Papyrus Project. If it were up to me I'd take you all—" There's a murmur of approval at this sentiment, which reminds me how popular Elgin is with his students. "But I'm afraid there's only money enough for us to take one, so that's why we're holding this interview—kinda like cheerleading trials all over again, eh?"

The girls in the group titter—most of them look as if they were cheerleaders not too long ago—and even the boys smile, no doubt reliving their own fond memories of the cheerleaders of their youth. *These Texas boys never get over seeing their first flaming baton toss,* my aunt M'Lou always says. I bet Elgin would like nothing better than to have the girls do flips and straddles to see who gets to go with him to Italy

"Only here the winner gets to dig up ancient charred papyrus scrolls in the hot sun and then stare at them in an un-air-conditioned lab. Y'all still interested?"

The group voice their undaunted enthusiasm for the project—all except Agnes, who is, I notice, still staring blankly over my shoulder out the glass wall behind me. She hardly seems to be paying attention. As the students begin their reports my mind wanders back to the phone calls. Maybe it wasn't Ely. After all, the rings could have been a random occurrence of the 3-4-5 sequence, an argument I was always making to Ely. If you look for the numbers, I told him, of course you're going to find them. He would respond by citing the odds of those specific numbers occurring. He always knew the math. When I met him in my first year of graduate school he was still an undergraduate but already something of a legend on campus as a math genius. He was sitting in on the graduate seminar in Greek philosophy because of his interest in Pythagoras. Although he had no background in ancient languages (except a smattering of Hebrew from his bar mitzvah training), he'd spent the summer teaching himself Greek and could sight-read Heraclitus faster than the Greek majors. So when he asked me to tutor him I suspected he wasn't just interested in my classical background.

We would meet in my house because he was living in an airless triple that smelled of gym socks and greasy wrappers from Dirty's

Hamburgers down on the Drag. My little Hyde Park bungalow, which I shared with an introverted psychology major, was a paradise of space in comparison. For most of that warm Austin autumn we could work outside on the front porch, sitting side by side on an ancient metal glider that Ely kept in constant motion while we translated Heraclitus and Plato. Since it was hot, and he always turned down my offers of beer, we drank a lot of iced tea, glass after glass through torpid September and into still balmy October, when my front yard started filling up with pecans from the trees that lined my street. The pecans would find their way onto the front porch and under the runners of the glider. Ely made a game of seeing how many we could crack during a passage, dividing the number of split shells by lines of Greek.

I collected so many shelled pecans during those tutoring sessions that I started making pies, but Halloween came and went and the cold fronts of November rolled in and broke the back of summer's heat and still he hadn't kissed me. On Thanksgiving Day I was heading out to my aunt's ranch in Pflugerville when I saw his bicycle (a peeling red Huffy with an old orange crate for a basket) parked in front of Luby's Cafeteria. I found him inside nursing a piece of corn bread for the free iced-tea refills, so I brought him back to my house and we ate a whole pecan pie that I had made for M'Lou before he worked up the courage to kiss me. I never made it to Pflugerville that weekend. I can still taste the caramelized sweetness of his mouth and recall the smell of butter and flour on our skin. The smell of butter and pecans has been known to make me weak at the knees, which is exactly what's happening right now. The door behind me has opened and let in a gust of honeyed air, like some enchanted elixir wafting off fabled isles. I swivel in my chair to see Odette with a tray of pecan sticky buns. She winks at me as she sets them on the coffee cart. This is her way of getting Elgin, who has a notorious sweet tooth, to hurry up the meeting. I check my watch and am surprised to see it's nearly ten o'clock. I've lost nearly a whole hour thinking of Ely.

"Hm, perhaps we should take a break—" Elgin says, sniffing the air.

"There's only Miss Hancock left to present," Barry points out. Poor Barry, who's on a perpetual diet, is eyeing the sticky buns as if they were bombs about to explode. I glance at Agnes, who has laid out her neatly printed 3x5 note cards on the table in front of her like a tarot reading, and think it would be cruel to let her suffer any longer.

"Yes," I say, "and I'm sure the dean would like his conference room back."

Odette rewards me by refilling my coffee while pointedly ignoring Elgin's attempts to attract her attention to his empty cup. Agnes clears her throat and launches full speed into her case for secrets of the ancient mystery rites lying in one of the villa's charred papyrus scrolls. Although her delivery is rushed, her passion for the material shines through. Elgin runs her through the requisite drill of questions but the look he exchanges with Barry Biddle clearly indicates his intention to choose Agnes for the internship. The other candidates slump dejectedly during her cross-examination and one even gets up and helps himself to a sticky bun. When Agnes, breathless and damp, answers her last question, Elgin rises and leans over Barry to pat her on the shoulder.

"Excellent work, Miss Hancock, a model for the rest of you."

Agnes starts to smile, but then her gaze drifts over Elgin's shoulder and her big blue eyes widen. I assume she's reacting to one of the other candidates, most of whom have abandoned the conference table en masse to drown their disappointment in sugar and butter, but then I hear something loud explode in the room and Elgin trips over Barry.

My first thought is that one of the urns must have gotten

pushed to the floor and that Odette's going to be furious, but when I swivel in my chair I see that Odette isn't paying any attention to the coffee urns. All her attention is taken up by the slim, dark-haired boy striding purposefully into the room and toward Elgin Lawrence, his right arm stiffly extended as if he'd come expressly to shake Elgin's hand. For half a second I think of Ely because the boy looks a little like him—he's even wearing the same Converse High-Tops Ely always wore—but then I realize Ely hasn't looked like this boy for years. This isn't Ely; it's Agnes's ex-boyfriend, Dale, and he's not trying to shake Elgin's hand, he's holding a revolver pointed directly at Elgin's head.

I want to tell this to Odette because I somehow think it will change things. That the information will stop her from stepping in front of Elgin, a step that pulls her into the blast from the next shot as though she had stepped into the red wave that explodes across her chest and then knocks her back into the coffee cart, splattering sticky buns and terrified students in the wake of her shattered body.

I try to stand, but my legs crumple and my chair slides out from under me. On my way down I have time to notice Barry Biddle grabbing Elgin and pulling him out of the way of Dale's next shot.

Of course, I think as the gun goes off for the third time (why, I wonder, have I been counting?) and I hit the floor, Agnes said that Dale was jealous of her relationship with Professor Lawrence. *That's* why she was so nervous this morning, not because of the internship interview. I should have paid more attention to what she was trying to tell me.

It's dark under the table, like the shade underneath the live oaks we walked beneath this morning. Still, I can make out across the table Agnes's scuffed navy pumps with the little red and white bows that I found so quaint only an hour ago. They strike me now as both heartbreaking and infuriatingly innocent. Hadn't she realized Dale was capable of going on a homicidal rampage? But then, I think, I'd had no idea how far gone Ely was until he shaved his head and went to live with a cult. I remember how all my friends had wondered how I hadn't seen it coming, hadn't noticed that he spent more and more time alone locked in a room chanting, that he'd stopped eating anything but raw nuts, and that the pile of books on his side of the bed were no longer math textbooks but tracts on Eastern mystery religions, reincarnation, and numerology.

Ely. I remember the phone calls and it occurs to me with total irrationality and total conviction that he had been somehow calling to warn me: a warning framed in a numerical code.

Another shot explodes above me, splintering through the table and showering me with sawdust. The fourth shot. The phone was ringing four times when I left my office. I'm suddenly sure there will be five shots in all.

On the other side of the table I see the heels of Agnes's shoes press together as if she thought she was Dorothy and could transport herself back to Kansas, but no, she's standing up. In the silence that still rings with the echo of Dale's last shot I hear her surprisingly firm voice quoting something that sounds like scripture.

"Dale, remember what we talked about. *The evil I flee, the better I find.*"

I see the black sneakers walking toward Agnes's side of the table, making their way around two crumpled bodies—one I recognize from his clothes as Barry Biddle (I can't recognize him from his face because his face is gone) and the other is Elgin. Only Elgin is not crumpled. He's huddled, pretending to be dead, no doubt, his right hand splayed out above his head, his left cupped in front of his face, as if hiding from what is happening above him. I see his face contort as a Converse High-Top steps on his hand, but he doesn't cry out or move. I try to lip-synch a message to him, but he's looking down. I notice that a light is reflected on his face and realize that he's got a cell phone in his hand that he's trying to operate. He must be trying to get help, but I don't believe that anyone is coming in time to help Agnes.

I can feel the rough fiber of the carpet rubbing against my elbows and it reminds me of the pavement that burned those people pinned on the mall while Charles Whitman took potshots at them. There's no shame in trying to save your own life, I can imagine my aunt M'Lou saying. But then there was nothing those people could have done.

I prop myself up on my elbows and start to wiggle myself toward Agnes's shoes. Out of the corner of my eye, I catch Elgin looking at me, his face lit by the light from his cell phone. His lips are forming some silent command to me, but I can't tell what. It's too late, I think; on the other side of the table I can see the black High-Tops approaching Agnes's navy pumps. The white rubber parts of Dale Henry's sneakers are slippery with blood. The last thing I want to do is touch them, but then I hear Agnes scream "No!" and I lurch for the shoes, reaching for an ankle. As soon as my fingers graze the bloodstained canvas I can feel that he's already losing his balance. I hear the weight of his body thud hard against the table, but the fifth shot's already been fired. It goes straight into the table, blasting the wood above my head into pulp, releasing a corona of gold dust that dazzles my dark-accustomed eyes. It's like the sun exploding inside my chest and the sky falling. And then it's like the coldness of deep space as I fall back into the dark.

CHAPTER 3

Once, when Ely had locked himself in his study to meditate and chant, I pressed my ear to the door to listen to what he was chanting. At first all I heard was a low rhythmic hum and then, when I realized there were words beneath the hum, I couldn't recognize their language. I thought for a moment that he'd added speaking in tongues to his repertoire of miracles, but as I listened I realized he was chanting three repeated lines of Greek hexameter verse. It took me another hour to transcribe and translate the three lines. I don't know what I was expecting. A summoning of Satan? A prayer for help? An invocation to the dead? Certainly not these three questions:

Where did I go wrong today?

What did I accomplish?

What obligation did I not perform?

Later I found out that they were a fragment from a Pythagorean text called *The Golden Verses*—reputedly the lost work of Pythagoras, or possibly a third-century-AD forgery. Practitioners of Pythagoreanism were supposed to ask themselves these three questions every night. I never came across a classical reference to using them as a chant. That must have been an innovation of the Tetraktys, the particular Pythagorean cult that Ely had joined.

I hadn't thought about the questions in years, but when I opened my eyes in St. David's Hospital I could have sworn that the sweet red-haired nurse standing over me in her surgical green scrubs asked me, "Where did you go wrong today?"

I tried to answer—I was pretty sure the right answer was "By getting out of bed"—but I discovered that my mouth was taped shut. Two vertical lines, like quotation marks, creased the young woman's brow and, consulting her chart, she tried another question.

"What did you accomplish?"

She smiled at the end of this one as if we were sharing a joke. "Getting myself shot" was one obvious answer, but then the other possibilities—getting Barry Biddle killed and Odette Renfrew shot—pushed up my throat and struggled against the plastic and tape strapped over my mouth until I could feel myself choking.

The nurse reached over my head where a crescent moon gleamed in the pale green light and performed some motion that released a stream of hot molten silver into my veins. I could taste it at the back of my throat. When her face reappeared above me, she looked weary and many years older as she posed the third question.

"What obligation did you not perform?"

Although I couldn't speak I found I could move my head slightly up and down—a motion that caused me great pain but brought a beatific smile to the nurse's face. Yes, I imagined her thinking, you see where you failed! If only you had heeded the portents and signs! The code of rings, the message of the tower, the sign of fire in Odette's skin! Only a blind person could have failed to see what was coming! The nurse turned to summon an audience for my confession. I didn't mind, I was prepared to come clean, it was a relief really, but when a trio of masked men arrived at my bed I found my courage failed me. What good did it do to confess my sins now? What good did it do Odette and Barry? I tried to convey an expression of regret before I sank back into the embrace of darkness that lay like a cave beneath my rib cage. A place I could see, by the tubes attached there, had been hollowed out in a vain attempt to lighten my burden of guilt.

The next time I woke up my aunt M'Lou was there. The tape was gone from my mouth, but tubes still ran from below my ribs to a pump beneath me that gurgled and rasped like a giant mouth sucking in seawater. I told her that a nurse had been there asking me questions.

"Yeah, honey, that's what they're trained to do. They just wanted to see if you knew your name and all. Do you? Remember your name?" She smiled to make a joke of it, but I could see she was dead serious.

"Sophia Anastasia Chase," I told her, surprised my lips could still fit around the syllables. "Who could forget being saddled with a name like that? Thank God you made the nuns just call me Sophie."

"Well, I'd had experience dodging 'Mary Margaret Louise.' " M'Lou stroked my forehead just like she used to brush the hair off my brow when I had a fever. "You were lucky, Sophie. If that bullet hadn't first gone through the back of Dale Henry's head and two inches of mahogany table it would have shattered your chest. As it is, it broke two ribs and punctured one lung. But you're going to be fine. You just have to try a little to get better."

"Dale Henry turned the gun on himself? So Agnes is okay?"

She nodded. "Agnes is fine, but her daddy swooped her on back to Sweetwater—out of the big bad city. She's called me every day to see how you were doing."

I try to ask about the others—Barry and Odette—but the whirlpool beneath my bed is sucking too hard on my chest. M'Lou sees that I'm having to struggle and calls in a nurse. She reaches above my head and I realize what I'd thought was the crescent moon is really an IV bag. She injects something into the tube that runs into my arm and I feel that same rush of silver through my veins and taste the metal at the back of my throat. M'Lou squeezes my hand and locks her eyes on mine, making the same two promises she made to me when I was ten and my mother died and my dour German-Catholic grandparents adopted me. "I'm sticking around," she says. "We're going to get through this together."

I nod, but I still have to ask. I manage just the name. "Odette?"

I see M'Lou's lips move but I can't hear her over the roar of the whirlpool. I can only make out the word *questions.*

I knew then that the Charybdis beneath my bed was sucking me down into Hades and that the three questions were a test to get past the ferryman. If I could answer them correctly I could go down and bring someone back. I hated knowing I might have to choose between Barry and Odette because I knew that Odette would insist I take Barry even if he was an idiot. But still, having to make a hard choice was better than not having a choice at all. I just had to figure out where I had gone wrong.

So I spent whatever time I was conscious—and some time I suspect I wasn't—trying to identify the crucial moment that I started down the wrong path. I thought it might have been when I found Agnes chewing her cuticles outside my office door. I should have sat down right next to her on the dirty linoleum floor and asked her what was wrong. To hell with the interview, I imagined myself saying, we're going to call my lawyer friend Mary Ellen right now and get an order of protection sworn out against this Dale fellow. The details of what would have happened after that remained a little hazy in my head. Each time I thought I had it all figured out a nurse would come in and, mistaking my moans of anguished conscience for pain, give me a shot of morphine.

The whirlpool would open up then, threatening to pull me into its maw. Could I really assign the moment of error to ignoring Agnes's problems with Dale? Wasn't there an underlying reason for my callous disregard of her emotional crisis? A root cause? I could feel the whirlpool pulling me back in time. In the perpetual artificial day of my hospital room, I felt myself slipping back to the last, and only, time I'd been hospitalized before. Only then I had been in the maternity ward.

That first time Ely and I had slept together had come as a surprise. Neither of us had birth control. So I'd counted back the days to my last period and decided it was too late in my cycle to get pregnant. I was wrong. By Christmas I knew I was pregnant. When I told Ely he said that some of the greatest discoveries in the history of math and science had been made through error. Why shouldn't we have a baby conceived in error? That I was in my first year of grad school and he hadn't even graduated college yet weren't good enough reasons not to celebrate the random. He wanted to take some time off before going to grad school anyway. So he got a job at the Harry Ransom Center, the university's rare-book library, and moved into my Hyde Park bungalow. Clare, the psych major, said she'd been thinking of moving to a feminist co-op across town in Clarksville. Before she left she sat me down on the glider on the porch and asked me if I was sure I knew what I was doing. Was it because my grandparents had raised me a Catholic and I thought abortion was a sin? Was it because my mother had me when she was only seventeen and if she hadn't let her parents talk her out of an abortion I wouldn't be here? Or was it because I wanted to relive my mother's story, only *this* time keep the baby and not let some crazy religious fanatics get ahold of it thus rewriting my own childhood crisis of abandonment?

After swearing to myself I'd never tell another soul about my childhood, I asked if she would please make sure she returned M'Lou's truck when she had finished moving her stuff. Then I went inside and translated Horace until she finished packing and left, reassuring myself that Clare had it all wrong. I wasn't trying to relive my mother's story—she'd been seventeen when she got pregnant with me and I was twenty-four. And she'd been sleeping with so many men that she didn't know who my father was. My grandmother believed he was Hispanic because of my coloring, or maybe, she'd add ominously, a Jew. My mother had had no plan beyond dropping me off with friends while she cocktail waitressed at night, which quickly evolved into dropping me off at my grandparents' when she wanted to go to a concert or to Santa Fe to sell jewelry. She left me there more and more until I was ten and she drowned tubing on the San Marcos River during a seven-year flood—an act so silly and frivolous it was as if she didn't even want to be taken seriously in death. I wasn't anything like her. I had a teaching assistantship, a scholarship, and, most of all, Ely. And my grandmother had been dead for three years, my grandfather for two, so there was no question of dumping our baby with them.

Ely and I settled into the little house as though burrowing down for the kind of northeastern weather Ely was used to instead of the brief cold snap that Austin called winter. I had a desk in an alcove off the front porch and Ely took Clare's old room for a study. I traded my creaky old futon for a real bed with a box spring. When the baby came, it would sleep with us. We bought books on attachment parenting and breastfeeding at Starwoman, the New Age bookstore just down the block. The campus shuttle let Ely off right by the store and he often stopped there on his way home and bought me something—a crystal to hang in the window or a scented candle. He poked gentle fun at the lesbians who ran the shop and their Wiccan beliefs.

"You know we're living in a New Age triangle," he pointed out on one of our evening walks. We'd fallen into such routines quickly, as if we were an old married couple who'd been living together for fifty years. "There's Starwoman's on Forty-third Street; that Jungian bookstore, Archetypes, over on Guadalupe; and then this place."

He was pointing to a house on the corner we were passing. It looked like all the other clapboard bungalows in the neighborhood that had been shipped west on railroad cars during the Depression, only this one was a little better cared for than the student rentals— the paint fresh, the grass neatly trimmed—and instead of a street number painted on the front porch there was a triangle made up of ten dots.

"What is that?"

"A tetraktys," Ely told me. "It's a Pythagorean symbol. There's something strange going on here. I think this place is some kind of church."

"Maybe the owner's a math teacher," I said. "What makes you think it's a church?"

"Look at all the cars," he said.

I glanced up and down Avenue H and saw what he meant. The street was lined with cars all the way down to 38th Street, but there was no sound of a party coming from any of the neighboring houses. The double-wide driveway to the Triangle House (as I'd already started to think of it) was packed like a parking lot.

"I'm surprised they can all fit in there," I said, looking toward the house. Then I realized what Ely meant by strange. The windows of the house were completely dark. Not a crack of light seeped out, nor any sound. The Church of the Tetraktys was packed with silent congregants praying in the dark.

The night was mild, but still I shivered. "How creepy," I said, turning away from the darkened house.

"I don't know," Ely said, lingering behind me. "The lack of light and sound probably make it easier to concentrate. Pythagoras said that his disciples should be silent for five years while they absorbed his teaching."

Of course we'd discussed Pythagoras before, but I think this was the first time I heard Ely cite a saying of the philosopher as if he were quoting a prophet. Was that the moment when things began to change? Would I have been able to make a difference if I had paid closer attention to Ely, if I had noticed that the books he brought home from Starwoman were no longer on childbirth and natural parenting but instead were about reincarnation and numerology?

But my focus had turned inward that spring, as if the baby needed all my attention just to grow. Outside the world was bursting with color. Our unmown yard was a riot of evening primrose and bluebonnets, wisteria and coral vine crept over the roof and hung like a curtain in front of the glider, turning the porch into a fragrant grotto. On our evening walks the air was scented with mimosa and night-blooming jasmine. We talked less and less on the walks, a silence I thought of as *companionable*. When we came home I didn't want to disturb that communion, not even with the buzz of electricity. I'd move around the house lighting candles that released their Eastern perfume—sandalwood, pachouli, myrrh—into the southwestern night. I said prayers of thanksgiving to each flame while Ely withdrew into his study. To prep for his finals, I thought. Sometimes I would hear him humming. I thought it was a sign of how intent he was on his work.

One day at the end of the semester I walked to the campus. It was only June but the temperature was already in the eighties. I could have taken the shuttle, but I'd grown a little alarmed at how much weight I'd gained with the pregnancy, so I thought I could use the exercise. I was dropping off a paper at the Classics Department—it was on the lawsuit waged by a Roman slave named Petronia Iusta to regain her freedom, a paper on which I got an A+ and later formed the basis of my thesis—and then I thought I'd surprise Ely at the library. I had just gotten my check for my teaching assistantship and figured we could splurge on lunch out at Les Amis.

The library was blessedly cool after my long walk in the heat. It was built of the same limestone as most buildings on the campus, the thick yellow walls imprinted with the fossils of ancient seashells, and kept dim to protect the valuable manuscripts and photographs in the collection. Ely was lucky to have gotten the job here, I thought as I took the elevator up to the fourth floor, it was the kind of plum university clerical post that Austin slackers kept for decades. Not that he'd need it for that long. I was sure he'd get into the graduate program here at the university and be offered a teaching assistantship, but it was a good job to have in the meantime and in a way I envied him. There had been many days this spring, standing in front of a poorly air-conditioned classroom full of first-year Latin students, that I would have preferred being immured within the library's calcareous carapace.

It was so chilly, in fact, that the receptionist on the fourth floor was wearing a cardigan and drinking a mug of hot tea. It was like I had wandered into the Cotswolds.

"Hey," I said, "Noreen, isn't it? Is Ely in the stacks?"

"Ely gave up his Wednesday hours a month ago," she said, blowing on her tea and looking embarrassed.

I pretended that I'd gotten the wrong day. Then I pretended that he'd told me about the change of schedule but it had slipped my mind.

"Pregnancy hormones," I told Noreen, and then asked to use the bathroom.

I threw up for the first time since my first trimester. The only explanation I could imagine for Ely changing his schedule without telling me was that he was sleeping with someone else. I rifled through the people we knew—the Classics and Math students, neighbors and shopkeepers—and my brain latched on to the checker at our food co-op. I'd noticed lately that she always bagged our groceries when Ely was there—and Wheatsville was a strictly bag-your-own establishment. She never bagged *my* groceries when I went in alone. She also worked at Starwoman. Maybe she was the reason Ely was always lingering there on his way home. In fact, I'd seen her coming and going from an apartment near Ely's shuttle stop on Speedway. It would have been easy for Ely to stop at her place on his way home.

I left the HRC without saying good-bye to the receptionist and without stopping for a sip of water at the cooler even though my mouth was as dry as dust. Outside the day had grown sultry and humid. A green pall hung over the live oak and pecan trees and the air smelled like grackle droppings and sulfur. I got on a shuttle but its swaying made me feel sick so I got off at the first stop and set off walking north at a quick clip. I remembered that Ely had taken his bicycle with him today instead of riding the shuttle. Would he be careless enough to leave it outside the girl's apartment? And if he had would I have the courage to knock on her door? I imagined myself standing there, big-bellied and sweating, and realized what a spectacle I was making of myself. But I couldn't stop. I walked faster and faster, ignoring the first drops of rain and the wind that picked up the fluffy white spores from the cottonwood trees and set them flying around me like snowflakes.

I don't know what kind of scene I would have made at the checker's apartment if I hadn't seen Ely's bicycle leaning against the side of the triangle house first. As on the night Ely first pointed out the place to me, the house was surrounded by cars and half a dozen bikes besides Ely's. The windows were shuttered and lightless even though the storm had now made the air as greenly murky as Texas lake water.

I'm not sure how long I stood there. Long enough to get soaked through to the skin. At one point I thought I could hear a low humming coming from the house, although I didn't so much hear it as feel it, a vibration that needled my skin like an electric current. Its pulsing rhythm was familiar. It had the same cadence as the humming I'd heard coming from behind Ely's study door.

I waited until the service—if that's what they called it—ended and people started to come out. I noticed how quiet they were as a crowd, smiling at one another but not speaking, and how diverse. There were middle-aged housewives who looked as if they belonged over at Hyde Park Baptist, purple-haired teenagers, clean-cut college kids fresh out of towns like Lubbock and Sweetwater, and a couple of elderly black people. And then there was Ely, almost last, his head bowed as he left the building.

As soon as he stepped outside, though, he looked up as though I'd called his name and saw me. I saw then in his face, which had been so radiant and peaceful a moment before, what a fright I must have looked. Other people were staring at me, too: a pregnant woman, standing bareheaded in the rain, soaked to the skin. Looking down at my arms, I saw that my skin was plastered with the cottonwood fluff as though I had grown feathers. At that moment I felt like some hideous monster, a girl transformed by her jealousy into a harpy.

Ely called my name but I turned away and started walking back to our house as fast as I could. I heard him behind me and I broke into a run. I could feel my abdominal muscles contracting to keep the baby from jostling inside me, the ligaments pulling, but I couldn't stop.

Of course, in my condition I couldn't go very fast, either.

Ely caught up with me on the corner of 42nd and Avenue B, only a block from our house. He grabbed my arm from behind. Because the street was wet and because being pregnant had thrown off my balance, I slipped when he grabbed me. He might have been able to hold me up, but my skin was slick with cottonwood spores.

I went down hard on my belly, the pavement sending a shock through my body that felt like a wave hitting me and sucking out my breath as it withdrew. Ely was crouched beside me, his lips moving, but I couldn't hear a word he was saying. My ears roared with the sound of the retreating surf. As he helped me to my feet, I felt water splash against my legs. I remember thinking that we were caught in a rip tide; it was pulling us out to sea and would drown us both.

Then the cramps started.

Perhaps it's the watery gurgle of the pump draining fluids from my chest that's reminded me of that moment, or perhaps it's being back in the same hospital where our baby—a girl we named Cory—was born and lived her brief life. Her lungs hadn't had a chance to develop and on her third day she stopped breathing. The NICU nurses tried to resuscitate her, but her little heart wasn't strong enough. The neonatologist who gave us the news said that it might be for the best. She was born so early that she would have had a multitude of developmental and health issues.

A multitude, he said. I remember thinking that a multitude of anything was better than this nothing. I also remember thinking that even my flaky, scatterbrained mother had done a better job bringing a child into the world.

The hollowness I feel in my chest now feels like the hollowness I felt then. Surely this was the answer to the first Pythagorean question. Waking in the strange half-light of my hospital room I say aloud to the walls, "Haven't I gone far enough back now?"

"It's not the direction you should be going in at all," a voice responds.

I turn my head toward the door and there's Odette sailing into my room, borne through the air like Cleopatra on her perfumed barge. Instead of cupids, she's attended by one tall seraphim disguised as a young man in a navy blue suit who must be her son and who steers her wheelchair to my bedside. She's wearing a fuzzy purple bathrobe embroidered with coffee cups and muffins.

"Honey, I hear you're not making your best effort to get well," she says, leaning over me. The coffee cups on her robe are topped with squiggly lines denoting rising steam.

"I should have warned you about Dale Henry," I say.

"Honey, no one could have known what that poor sick boy was gonna do until he walked into that room with a gun in his hand, and by then any fool could have known what was going to happen next."

"So why'd you have to put yourself between that crazy man and that fool teacher, Mama?" Odette's son asks her.

"Because your mama's a bigger fool than any of us suspected, James. There, I've said it. Happy now?"

The tall young man—he's so tall that it makes me dizzy to look up at him, and when I do his features are blurry in the gloom—looks anything but happy.

"The doctor said not to let you work yourself up—"

"As if you could control what someone else was feeling. That's what I come here to tell this girl," she says, turning from her son to me. "I know you, Sophie Chase. You're lying here brooding on what you could have done different. Well, that and a quarter will get you a ride on a bus to Nowhere. You grabbed that boy's leg so he wouldn't shoot Agnes, didn't you? How were you to know he'd already put that gun in his mouth? At least you tried to do something."

"How did you know I grabbed his leg? You'd been shot—"

"Mama, the doctor said only five minutes—"

"I'm almost done, James. Why don't you go see if you can find me some decent coffee? I'm sick of the swill in this place."

When James has gone, Odette nudges her chair closer to my bed and takes my hand in hers. She leans in close enough so that I can smell the gingery pomade she uses in her hair and whispers something—only the suck and gurgle of the whirlpool beneath my bed make it almost impossible to understand her. It sounds as if she's just said, "Many are the narthex bearers, but few are the Bacchoi."

"Isn't that Plato?" I ask her, "from the *Phaedo*?"

But then James is back, bearing a cup of coffee in a blue paper cup emblazoned with the white columns of the Parthenon. The question of where he found a Greek diner in Austin mingles with the wonder of Odette quoting Plato, but then Odette wafts the cup under my nose and the scent wipes out everything. The coffee smells heavenly. A mixture of cocoa and cinnamon. When I open my eyes, James is wheeling Odette out of the room. I have time only to see the back of her robe, which is embroidered with something written in fancy script. Sure that the words will give a clue to the mystery of her last statement I study them hard.

"Sometimes I wake up grumpy," I read. "And sometimes I let her sleep in."

I wake up the next morning clearheaded and alert. It's as if the whiff of coffee Odette shared with me the night before had finally woken me up. I manage solid food for the first time and the nurses tell me that the tubes can come out of my chest. Even the pain of that procedure feels almost good. Like being alive again. I turn down the offer of painkillers that afternoon. I want to be able to think clearly when I talk to Odette again. It's impossible, I realize, that she was quoting Plato. I must have misheard her. Still, I feel sure that if I can just talk to her again I'll be sorted out.

It's M'Lou, though, who shows up in my room that afternoon bearing flowers and cards from my students and colleagues at the university. She beams when she sees me sitting up with a tray of Jell-O and hard-boiled eggs. "Thank God," she says. "You look a hundred times better. I was afraid . . . well, you seemed like you'd gotten a wee bit lost."

"I think I was," I say, taking a spoon of the ersatz Jell-O (*Schmello,* Ely called it when I was here last). "But Odette knocked some sense into me. Do you think I'm well enough to go visit her? Is she on this floor?"

M'Lou drops the cards to the floor and kneels to pick them up. She spends a long time shuffling them. When she finally looks up, I see tears in her eyes.

"No," I say, "she can't be. She looked fine last night."

M'Lou lets the cards drop to the floor again and takes my hand. "Sweetheart, Dale Henry shot Odette at point-blank range straight in the heart. She never had a chance. She was declared dead on arrival seven days ago."

CHAPTER 4

Only three weeks have passed since the morning of the shooting to this bright afternoon when M'Lou drives me home from the hospital, but it feels like a lifetime. My unmown lawn of wildflowers has turned sere and brown. The coral vine, in which I have always suspected a Julio-Claudian lust for world domination, has sent out feelers that have attached themselves like tiny reptilian feet to the front-door screen.

"I kept meaning to come by," M'Lou says from behind me on the porch, "but I hated to leave you, and then the hospital had me on double shifts."

"It's all right." I brush away the vine, which springs back, smacks me across the face, and then slithers off into the dark rafters. "It's just a house, not a live thing that needs looking after."

When I open the door, though, the house chuffs three weeks worth of stale Texas heat into our faces and moans like a trapped animal. The heavy canvas Roman shades, which I'd drawn against the heat three weeks ago, lift on the outgoing air and then slap back against the windowpanes as the house sucks in new air. The rattle of loose panes sounds like the gurgle the pumps had made sucking fluid out of my chest in the hospital.

"Do you feel any pain there?" M'Lou touches my hand which I'm holding against my chest.

"No, just a little shortness of breath sometimes."

"Well, that's to be expected after losing half your left lung." She walks past me and pulls up a shade. "There's a rehab center out on Bee Caves Road for patients who've had lung surgery. It's called the Oxygym. I'd be happy to take you."

"Sure," I say to M'Lou's retreating back. "Once I'm settled." I'm glad to see that M'Lou's back in brisk, efficient mode. I hear the refrigerator door open and a series of tongue clucks and then the sound of clumpy liquids gurgling down the drain and the snap of a plastic garbage bag being inflated.

The house is being resuscitated while I remain becalmed at its center, unable to move past the living room. I glance at the little desk I still keep in the alcove by the front door for bill-paying and see my desk calendar spread open to May. I've always kept it by the front door to double check appointments on my way out and now I step toward it as though it could tell me what to do next in my own house.

The pressing appointments that I find here have already passed. Final exams, term paper due dates, grade deadlines—all scrawled in emphatic red ink, circled, and appended with exclamation points asserting their importance and urgency—have slipped under the encroaching tide of time without a ripple. My very efficient teaching assistant rooted through my old test files and proctored the exams. She was able to calculate grades for my undergraduate Latin sections and my graduate students were given incompletes. I imagine most of them were happy to get the extra time to finish their papers. My chair called me at the hospital to tell me not to worry about getting in the grades until the fall. He even offered me an extra teaching assistant if I needed one and the fall semester off. The university would of course pay for any medical bills my insurance hadn't covered—rehab and counseling, too. By the end of the conversation I had the impression I could have asked for an all-expenses-paid spa vacation and an in-home Jacuzzi, anything to keep me from suing the university. It was then that I learned that Dale Henry had been seeing a counselor at the Student Health Center in the fall who had responded to his increasingly unhealthy obsession with Agnes with a bizarre cocktail of Ritalin and Prozac. Barry Biddle's parents were already suing. Odette's son—who looked nothing like the tall seraphim who'd appeared in my posthumous vision of Odette—told me that they weren't because "Mama would have hated that."

As for me, I had no intention of suing anyone. I felt at least as responsible for what happened as that counselor.

I turn the calendar page from May to June and find a grid of boxes empty except for one word written across the whole month. VACATION! Although it's my handwriting, I can't, no matter how long I stare at it, evoke the sentiment with which it was written: the delight in freedom from obligation and responsibility I'd clearly been longing for. All it feels like now is emptiness.

M'Lou bustles by me swinging two bulging garbage bags. Did I really have that much rotting food? It's true my refrigerator tended to fill up with cartons of half-eaten take-out toward the end of term, but even so . . .

"I'm going to Whole Foods to get you some supplies. It's important you eat a lot of protein—you're building new tissue. Do you want to go? Or maybe you should stay and rest? Unless you don't want to be alone—"

"I'm fine, M'Lou. Go ahead, but save the receipt and let me pay you back."

M'Lou walks to the curb and tosses the two heavy garbage bags into the back of her turquoise pickup truck as effortlessly as if they were filled with Styrofoam. You wouldn't guess from her thin freckled arms and tiny frame, but M'Lou has a bodybuilder's strength, honed by years of riding the quarter horses she breeds on the ranch in Pflugerville that she inherited from my grandparents. I used to think that if I tried hard enough—ate practically nothing, worked out every day, wore the same brand of jeans—I could attain M'Lou's lean, rangy look. When she realized what I was after, sometime in tenth grade when she caught me trying to fit into her jeans, she sat me down on the edge of her bed and took a picture of my mother out of the night-table drawer. It was a picture I hadn't seen before of the two sisters in front of the ranch, my mother in a checked yellow dress, her hair long and loose around her shoulders, her arm draped indolently over M'Lou's shoulder, one hip playfully bumping against her older sister's. Her eyes looked black in the picture, but I knew that close up they contained sparks of green, just like mine. M'Lou, though, stood ramrod straight, like a pencil next to my mother's soft curves.

"I swear, Lizzy had curves when she was just a baby and she was soft, like a ragdoll. When you picked her up she just molded to your body. I wasted a lot of years wishing I looked like her. Don't you make the same mistake, Sophie. You're beautiful just how you are."

I've made a modicum of peace with my figure since then, but I've never quite gotten over looking for my mother in M'Lou. I realize that even now, watching her climb into her pickup and wave to me, I'm looking for something that isn't there. This leaves me feeling not only empty, but ungrateful: no one could have loved me more or done more for me than M'Lou has. For years she made the long commute from Pflugerville into her nursing job in Austin so that I wouldn't have to absorb the brunt of my grandparents' expectations and regrets alone.

I close the door and quickly cross the living room so I don't get stuck again. The rooms in my house are laid out one after another—a shotgun house, some people call it because you could shoot a gun straight down the middle and it would go out the back door without hitting a wall. I shudder at the image and feel a phantom pain on the left side of my ribs where the lower part of my left lung used to be. When I described the pain to the pulmonologist he said that it was probably an air pocket that had gotten into my chest cavity during surgery and he showed me my chest X-ray. "See," he'd said, pointing to the ghostly white shape lurking beneath my rib cage, "your left lung is stretching to fill the chest cavity. In a month, if you keep doing the breathing exercises I prescribe, it will look nearly the same size as the right one." While I liked the idea that my body was laboring to make itself whole again, I still can't help feeling that there will always be this empty ache there.

I hold my hand over that spot as I cross through the kitchen, which smells like sour milk and bleach, into my bedroom, and stop at the closed door to my study. It's the only room that breaks out of the straight plan—an add-on some earlier tenant built that had been my roommate Clare's room, then Ely's study, and now my study. I know it's this room that I'm dreading. I can feel it crouching like an evil toad at the end of the house and that until I go into it I'll go on feeling like a stranger in my own home.

It's because of that other homecoming when I came back from the hospital after losing the baby. M'Lou had brought me home then, too, because Ely was supposedly taking a final. (I later found out that he'd already dropped out and he was at a meeting instead.) I'd developed an infection after giving birth and stayed in the hospital for two more weeks, so I'd felt that same strangeness coming back to the house after a long absence. I'd shaken it off and set about tidying up, sure that Ely would have let things go while I was away, but he hadn't. The house was spotless. Finally I'd stood at the closed door to his study, like Bluebeard's bride, making excuses for going inside. He'd probably accumulated all his mess in there, I figured. A sickly sweet odor seemed to emanate from the closed door. I pictured rotting food piled up inside. Ely had been so strange since the baby died, hardly talking when he came to the hospital, his eyes bloodshot. At first I'd thought he'd been crying, but I never saw him cry, and then I realized from the dark bruises under his eyes that he'd stopped sleeping. Had he stopped eating, too? He'd tried to explain some complicated dietary laws that the Tetraktys demanded of initiates, but I hadn't wanted to listen to anything about the Tetraktys. As I stood outside that door I began to wonder if the group he'd joined demanded some kind of animal sacrifice.

I opened the door half expecting to find a bloodstained altar, but what I found was somehow more upsetting. The room was completely black. It took me a moment to realize that the walls had been painted black and the one window was covered with a blackout shade, its edges sealed to the window frame with black electrical tape. It was like being inside a cave. When I found the wall switch the bare bulb in the ceiling turned the black into a deep purple. And then, out of that ghostly twilight, silvery images had emerged, as stars appear in the sky at dusk, only this was a sky filled with a thousand stars all bound together by intersecting lines and great arcing ellipses. Looking down I saw that I was standing on a silver triangle painted on the floor. Like a launching pad. I knew at that moment that Ely wasn't off taking his final exams and that I had already lost him to the Tetraktys. For all I knew, I'd already lost him to the reaches of outer space.

Now when I open the study door I half fear that I'll find that black room again. It took five coats of heavy white latex enamel to cover the walls and still when the moonlight comes into this room I can make out the glimmer of stars and planets revolving in their orbits. I see a flash of them now, as if my absence had drawn them out again, as I switch on the overhead light, but then they vanish. Instead I see my mission library table standing under the window, warm sunlight turning the cloth shade gold and striping the Navajo rug with long slanted bars. On the floor-to-ceiling bookshelves my Loeb Classics in their green-and-red bindings, the reassuringly thick spines of lexicons and dictionaries, the leatherbound set of Gibbons's *Decline and Fall of the Roman Empire* that M'Lou gave me when I got my Ph.D., and even the brightly colored modern paperbacks are all arrayed like sentinels against the dark.

I sit down at my desk and touch the pile of printed pages stacked to the left of my laptop and the sheets of handwritten notebook paper pinned beneath a chunk of fossiliferous limestone on the right. I've been writing a book on a first-century woman slave slowly, but steadily, these past five years. Perhaps I'll just do a few pages now, I think, to calm myself and get me into the rhythm of being home. I lean across the desk to draw the shade up—a ritual that starts my workday every morning—but when I look out the window I'm confronted by my overgrown lawn. I can't possibly do any work with that lawn reproaching me. I go back to my bedroom, change into a T-shirt and shorts, and go outside to mow.

I have the feeling right away that this isn't what the pulmonologist meant by light activity. I'm drenched in sweat within minutes and my arms and back feel as if I'm pushing Sisyphus's rock and not a ten-pound manual-reel mower. Still, it feels amazingly good to be doing something physical and to see the results in each freshly mown path I clear. For the first time in weeks—since the sky exploded over my head in the conference room—I feel firmly teth-ered to the earth. Each time I reach the edge of the lawn and turn I can see where I've been and I know what to do next. It's only when I've finished and put the mower back in the shed and set the sprin-kler on that my spirits sag. My lawn is a field of scorched stubble, like the fields of Carthage, which the Romans sowed with salt so that nothing would grow there for a hundred years. Watering it is little more than anointing the dead.

I go in through the back door and open the fridge, leaning gratefully into its cool white depths. M'Lou's not only cleared it, but wiped the whole thing down with bleach. It smells like a swim-ming pool. Thankfully she's left a couple of Shiner Bocks. I open one and roll it across my forehead before taking a long cold drink. When I put the bottle down on the kitchen table it makes a clunk that echoes through the empty house, and I decide to drink the rest of it out on my front porch. Maybe by the time I finish it the house will stop feeling so empty. I take an extra one in case one's not enough.

I realize halfway through the first bottle that I'm not going to need it. Between the pain medication I'm on and the exercise, I'm quickly anesthetized. I let the glider gently sway and watch the gen-tle arc of the sprinkler make rainbows in the late afternoon sun. This will be just fine, I tell myself, a summer nursing the lawn back to life, swimming at Barton Springs, working on my book. . . . By the fall I should be able to walk back onto campus without looking over my shoulder for invisible gunmen.

I've rocked myself into such an agreeable stupor that when the yellow Porsche pulls up in front of my house for a minute I don't realize who it is. But then there's only one person I know in Austin, home of hybrids and rusty old pickup trucks, who drives such a flashy car: Elgin Lawrence.

He unfolds himself from the low-slung car and drapes a jacket over his shoulder in one fluid movement. I have time to wonder why he needs a jacket when it's over ninety in the shade, and also to ponder the leather laptop case he's carrying, while he crosses the short patch of burned grass and looks down to see that he's ruined his delicate-looking loafers in the run-off from the sprinkler. I ought to be wondering what he's doing here, but my beer-and-OxyContin-bathed brain doesn't seem able to wrap itself around the question. Elgin makes a quick dart when he realizes that the sprinkler is heading his way and is up on my porch before I can think of an excuse to get rid of him.

"Sophie!" he exclaims, holding out his arms. "I came as soon as I heard you were discharged from the hospital. Look at you! You're glowing! I knew you'd bounce back from this a hundred percent. You can't keep a good woman down."

I start to smile in spite of myself; Elgin's charm is insidious. "If that were true," I say, suppressing the smile, "Odette Renfrew would still be alive."

Elgin bows his head and shakes it, clucking his tongue just once. "That's exactly what I said at her funeral. I said her memory would stay with us forever. I said"—Elgin lifts his head and lays his right hand over his heart, striking a pose reminiscent of Cicero addressing the Roman Senate—"I will think of her every day of my life and try to make my life worthy of her saving it. I tell you, I'm a changed man." Elgin lowers his head again, this time noticing the unopened beer on the floor. "Mind if I . . . ?"

"Go ahead," I say. "I probably shouldn't be mixing alcohol with my painkillers anyway."

Elgin swoops down on the beer and then seats himself on my porch railing. "That's for sure. Last year after I twisted my ankle playing racquetball I made the mistake of going out drinking with my Tacitus seminar—" Elgin stops himself, no doubt realizing that a ribald drinking story is at odds with the elegiac note he'd struck a moment ago. "But that's another story. I came here to see how you are." He trains the full intensity of his blue eyes on me and—God help me—I feel a little woozy. It must be the drugs, I tell myself, I got over Elgin's charms a long time ago.

"I'll be fine," I say, carefully picking my tense. "I just need some peace and quiet, which I'm sure to get plenty of during the summer in Austin."

"You're going to stay *here*? All summer?" Elgin points his beer bottle at me so suddenly that I flinch. For a second I'd seen Dale Henry lifting up his arm with the gun in it. "What you need," he says, "is to get away. Someplace near the sea, but not some mindless beach resort. You need something to really take your mind off what happened. Something intellectually stimulating . . ."

"Elgin, you're not talking about the Papyrus Project, are you? I mean, are you still even going ahead with it? You had a hard enough time getting funding in the first place. I'm surprised that Catholic organization—"

"PISA."

"Whatever—I'm surprised they haven't pulled out."

Elgin jerks his head back as if I'd thrown something at him. "Why on earth wouldn't we go ahead? What happened had nothing to do with the project. And not only hasn't PISA pulled out, but we have a new benefactor: the Lyrik Foundation."

"Really? I thought the Lyrik Foundation had turned you down, and considering that Barry was half the project—"

"Please. Biddle was a deadweight on the project—no disrespect to the dead intended. You were always my first choice. Admit it, you only turned me down because of our personal history."

Elgin's blue eyes are fixed on mine like a snake transfixing its prey; I find it impossible to look away. I don't generally like to admit even to myself that I had an affair with Elgin Lawrence my second year of graduate school, and when I do think about it I tend to lump it together with that blurry period after I lost the baby and just before Ely left. Blurry because I was crying so much my eyes were perpetually swollen, and blurry because I was drinking a lot. I remember that Elgin's attentions were flattering and that his cynical attitude toward New Age fads, health food, and yoga seemed bracing. He was the perfect antidote to Ely, I thought. Unfortunately, it was an antidote with side effects as toxic as the original poison.

"My decision not to join you on the Papyrus Project had absolutely nothing to do with our . . . personal history. I didn't, and still don't, want to commit to a project that's dependent on technology no one knows will work for sure."

I've delivered this little speech in as cold a voice as I can muster considering I can feel sweat dripping down my back, but Elgin greets it as if it were a declaration of undying love.

"Well, then, if *that's* the only problem, I think you'll be very pleased with what I've got in here." Elgin zips open the soft leather case and spills out a sleek silver laptop. It powers up with a musical chord that sounds like wind chimes. Elgin slides onto the glider next to me and slips the laptop into my lap. Out of the pale gray screen—like an early-morning mist—shapes slowly emerge. It takes me a moment to realize that they're letters. I haven't done that much work with original inscriptions, but the scribe who penned these letters had a beautiful hand. I make out a few words right away.

"Having been tossed across sea and earth . . ." I read aloud, translating the Latin.

"Here." Elgin leans over me, his hand grazing my bare thigh. "There's a higher resolution level available that picks up the metals in this particular ink . . . there, how's that?"

All the letters are momentarily surrounded by a bright red halo, as if they were burning a hole in the screen, and then they sharpen and appear to rise off the page so abruptly that I blink at their brilliance.

"Wow," I say, awed in spite of myself. Out of the corner of my eye I see Elgin smile. "Sounds like you have a bad imitation of Virgil here," I say, scanning the next few lines. "*Having been tossed across sea and earth, a plaything of those on high* . . . Someone's got a hero complex."

"Keep reading," Elgin tells me. "I think you'll be interested in this."

I continue translating the Latin lines and quickly see what he means. "*Having been tossed across sea and earth, a plaything of those on high, and having survived shipwreck, I believe my life has been spared for some divine purpose. Why else would I have been plucked from the sea and borne aloft upon the waves as if held up by the arms of sea nymphs, and brought to not just any shore, but this, the same shore that received the body of that lovestruck unhappy siren, Parthenope. And whereas she met with an unhappy fate, I was rescued by the slaves of a great man and brought, unharmed . . . even my baggage intact . . .*" I skip over an illegible section and pick up again a few lines later. "*. . . . therefore, it seems clear to me that my life has been spared so that I may finish my life project,* The History of Religion, *which I began with my little book,* Athenian Nights. . . ." I look up and see that Elgin is trying to hide his smile by taking a swig of his already finished beer.

"By Phineas Aulus," I say, identifying the first-century Roman historian who wrote two works on mystery religions, *Athenian Nights* and *Alexandrian Nights*. A third book, *Italian Nights,* was lost when Phineas died at sea while sailing from Alexandria to Rome in AD 79. "But this sounds like it was written after the shipwreck . . ."

"Exactly! He didn't die at sea. He escaped in a rowboat and came ashore at Herculaneum. Notice he says his baggage was intact . . ."

"So *Italian Nights* . . ."

"Saved. But not just *Italian Nights*. Do you remember what Pliny said about Phineas Aulus?"

"That he was a thief. He plundered his way through Greece,

Egypt, and the Middle East stealing scrolls from temples and oracles. You think those scrolls were in his trunk . . . but if he was shipwrecked . . ."

"Read the next line."

I scroll down. "*It is indeed another sign of the providence of the gods that I took the precaution of lining the inside of my trunks with wax against the moisture of a long sea journey. Not only have the first volumes of my third book,* Italian Nights, *been preserved, but also several other remarkable sources which I have borrowed to aid in my research . . .* Ha! I've heard that line from students who've plagiarized their term papers. Borrowed my ass! . . . *have also survived completely intact. It is seemly for a historian of religions to be alert to any signs and omens the gods might send and so I dedicate this final volume of* Italian Nights *to the spirits of this bay . . . to Apollo whose prophetess abides here at the Cave of the Sibyl, to Dionysus and Demeter who have so endowed this rich land that it is said they vie over its dominion, and finally to that unlucky nymph whose body was washed ashore here and who is said to haunt these shores. And so in her honor, I name this final volume of my work,* Siren Nights."

I lean back and look at Elgin, who's still grinning at me as if he knew something I didn't—the same look he'd had on his face when he knew I'd gotten the assistant professorship at UT.

"Hey," I say, spurred to generosity by recalling that Elgin probably had a lot to do with me getting my current job, "this is great for you, Elgin. I know Phineas is your specialty and another book of his would be a major discovery. But, as you may remember, I'm not wild about him myself. This isn't my area."

"Uh huh," Elgin says, grinning even wider, "let me show you something else the multispectral imaging can do. You see that line you skipped over? The one you couldn't read?" He drags the cursor to the illegible section and highlights it. Then he pulls down a menu that offers different resolution settings. "This part's water damaged—frustrating, because it would be nice to know whose house Phineas arrived at. The house where this scroll was found is called the Villa della Notte now—"

"Because of the statue of the goddess Nyx in the courtyard, right?" I ask, remembering the austere face of the Roman personification of Night that I saw on my one trip to Naples.

"Right. But no one's been able to say who originally owned it until"—Elgin clicks on a new setting—"now. Ecco! Mystery solved!"

I lean forward to look at the screen. The previously illegible words are now clear. "*. . . not just to any house, but to the house of a man not only renowned for his hospitality but also for his fine library, and his discriminating tastes as a collector of rare works, Gaius Petronius Stephanus.*"

"It may not be the same one," I say, trying hard to keep emotion out of my voice.

"Two Gaius Petronius Stephanuses in Herculaneum at the same time period?" Elgin asks, lifting an eyebrow. "That's what I love about you, Sophie, you're a skeptic. You don't accept any data without proof. It makes you a rigorous scholar. Most people would be jumping up and down right now overjoyed that the subject of their thesis and the book they're working on had just showed up in a lost document, but not you."

"Even if this is the Gaius Petronius Stephanus who owned Petronia Iusta, what are the chances that she'll show up in Phineas's book? I'm sure Phineas Aulus had better things to do than notice a slave girl."

"You underestimate your girl Iusta," Elgin says, clicking on another file. "This portion comes a few pages later. We haven't found the right resolution to make it perfectly legible yet, but a few words stand out . . . here"—he points the cursor to a word in the upper-right-hand corner—"and here"—and to one in the middle of the page—"and here."

Iusta. Iusta. Iusta.

Her name repeated three times like a charm.

"My theory for why her name is clearer is that each time Phineas wrote it he pressed a little harder with his stylus. I bet he was quite taken with her."

"She would have been seventeen . . ." I begin, batting Elgin's hand away from the touchpad and trying to scroll down to the next page, but the cursor blinks stubbornly at the last occurrence of Iusta's name.

"I'm afraid that's all we've got so far. You have to go with me to Italy to read the rest. So what about it? You know you want to."

As usual Elgin overplays his hand. It's unfortunate that he's using the same words he used five years ago to seduce me. I'm tempted to say no outright, but then Iusta's name fades from the screen, replaced by a screensaver of turquoise water, and I find myself frantically tapping the touchpad to bring her back.

"I'll think about it," I tell Elgin.

CHAPTER 5

After Elgin has gone I go back to my study and take out my the-sis and notes on Petronia Iusta. Of course Elgin had known how in-trigued I'd be by the references to Iusta—after all, he'd been my thesis adviser.

I had first encountered her story in Elgin's class on Roman slav-ery. I look for and find the paper I wrote on her—the one I turned in on the day I found Ely at the Tetraktys house and went into pre-mature labor. On top of the first page Elgin had written: "You have a real feel for this material. Petronia Iusta comes alive in your han-dling of her story—come talk to me about expanding this into your thesis. A+" I remember that the paper had been waiting for me when I got home from the hospital and how absurdly grateful I'd been for those few simple words of praise. I'd thrown myself into the research then, finding out all I could about this girl who had lived and died almost two thousand years ago.

There wasn't a lot to go on. What we knew about her came from eighteen wax tablets found in a small house buried in Herculaneum in AD 79. I remember that one of the first details that drew me to the story was the stroke of serendipity that had preserved those tablets—*wax* tablets! It was the nature of the pyroclastic flow that covered Herculaneum that while it instantly killed anyone who hadn't already escaped and buried the city under sixty-five feet of volcanic matter, many fragile things were preserved: a crate of newly purchased wineglasses, eggs, bread, wooden beds and door frames, and delicate papyrus scrolls, charred on the outside but preserved inside, only awaiting a modern technology capable of reading the words within. But Iusta's story hadn't needed multispectral imaging; the bones of her story were in the eighteen law documents.

Her case had first been brought before a Herculean court by Iusta's mother, Petronia Vitalis, a freedwoman who had belonged to Gaius Petronius Stephanus and his wife, Calatoria Vimidis. Vitalis had bought her freedom sometime in the early sixties, but she and her daughter, Iusta, had continued living with the household, the girl being brought up "like a daughter" to Petronius and Calatoria. The living situation was apparently harmonious until Calatoria had her own children, at which time Calatoria and Vitalis began to argue. Vitalis decided to leave the household, taking her daughter with her. The Petronii, however, were not ready to relinquish Iusta and claimed that she belonged to them. Vitalis sued for Iusta's freedom on the basis that Iusta had been born after she had bought her own freedom, and therefore was born free.

Vitalis won her case. She was required to pay back the Petronius household the expenses incurred in Iusta's upbringing, which she was able to do because she had, since her own manumission, made a good living raising and selling oysters. This was my favorite part of the story. I always imagined Calatoria's face when her former slave counted out the gold coins necessary to redeem her child's liberty—and the happiness of mother and daughter leaving that house of slavery together.

The rest of the story wasn't so uplifting. Sometime around AD 77 or 78 both Gaius Petronius and Petronia Vitalis died. Calatoria, newly widowed, decided to sue for the restitution of her property—Iusta, who she claimed was her slave because Iusta had been born *before* her mother's manumission. If she won her suit the money that Vitalis had left to her daughter would become Calatoria's property. According to the court records a slave of Calatoria's, named Telesforus, testified that Iusta had been born *after* Vitalis's manumission. The courts, however, remained undecided and postponed the decision. Most scholars assumed that the case was still undecided in AD 79, when Herculaneum was destroyed, but if Iusta really had been in the Petronius household at the time of the eruption, perhaps the case had gone against her.

I'm surprised at how much this saddens me. After all, if she died in the eruption, what difference does it make if she died a free-woman or a slave? Yet it does. I've always wanted to believe that Iusta died a freewoman—or better, that she won her case and then escaped Herculaneum before the eruption, leaving the grasping Calatoria behind, buried under sixty-five feet of volcanic stone.

"You've romanticized your subject," Elgin had commented on the first draft of my thesis, in which I argued that Vitalis and Iusta represented early feminists. "And overidentified with them."

The remark had stung more than it should have. I had told Elgin about my childhood, my strict German-Catholic grandparents, who probably thought they were doing their best by me but who treated me as if I were a time bomb that at any moment might destroy all our lives *just like your mother had*. That had been the refrain I grew up with—*just like your mother*—whenever I slept too late, ate too many sweets, or giggled in church. I had told Elgin how I had waited and waited for my mother to come back and re-claim me, living for her short visits, and how even after she died I'd dream it had been a lie made up by my grandparents to keep us apart. Someday she'd appear, reformed into a proper mother with a good job and a house, and prove to my grandmother that people *like us* could turn out okay.

"Admit it," Elgin said to me at that thesis conference, "when you describe Vitalis paying off Calatoria you see your mother shoving it to your mean old grandmother, and the little girl—"

"Okay, I get it," I had said to him, taking back the draft. "I'll have a rewrite for you by next week."

I'd been careful in my next draft to stick to the facts, which Elgin had approved.

But even though Elgin had criticized my romantic notions about Petronia Iusta, he wasn't above using them to lure me to Italy. Or maybe he enjoyed seeing those romantic notions dashed by the fact that Iusta was still Calatoria's slave. I find, though, that all that matters less to me than gaining another glimpse of her. For that I might travel as far as Italy—even if it means putting up with Elgin all summer.

Forgetting my fatigue from mowing the lawn and with a mind remarkably cleansed of the effects of OxyContin and Shiner Bock, I reread my thesis and all my notes on the case of Petronia Iusta. I'm so engrossed that I don't hear M'Lou return from Whole Foods or notice her standing in the doorway until a sound like glass wind chimes makes me look up. She's got the two empty Shiner Bocks hooked onto her fingers and she's knocking them together like cas-tanets.

"Please tell me an enterprising teenager came by and was willing to trade lawn work for a couple of beers," she says, tilting her chin toward the mown stubble outside the study window. "Because I know you're not stupid enough to mix alcohol and codeine and then operate heavy machinery."

"I only had one—after mowing—and you know my lawn-mower is a manual."

M'Lou shakes her head and sits down on the edge of my desk. She picks up my hand and turns it over, pressing her thumb to the underside of my wrist.

"I'm not dead yet, M'Lou. I've still got a pulse . . ."

"Shush," she orders. "Hm . . . a little fast. Something's gotten you riled up. Who drank the second beer?"

There's no point lying to M'Lou; she caught me every time I tried it from the time I hid my third-grade report card to the night I told her I was at my girlfriend's house while I was really meeting my boyfriend at the Lonestar Motel. So I tell her about Elgin's visit and the lost Phineas Aulus book, Iusta's appearance in it, and Elgin's invitation to join the Papyrus Project.

"Did you say yes?"

"No," I tell her, "I said I'd think about it. And I am—" I add de-fiantly. I know she's not crazy about Elgin, but she gives me a long level look and a curt nod.

"It might be the best thing—" Oddly it's the same thing she said to me when she'd tracked me and Billy Rackem down at the Lone-star. "—if it'll keep you from brooding."

"I don't brood."

"I've had brood hens less broody than you," she shoots back. "But you've got to promise you'll take care of yourself. Eat right and sleep enough. Where would you be staying? Some fleabag pen-sione?"

"Nah—that's the best part. The excavation of the Villa della Notte is being funded by John Lyros—"

"The software billionaire?"

"The same. Before he made his fortune in computer software he was a classics major here at UT. He's such a fanatic that he's had a replica of the Villa della Notte built on the Island of Capri, a half hour's boatride from the original villa at Herculaneum. Elgin says he's installed a state-of-the-art multispectral imaging lab and now he's invited the whole staff of the Papyrus Project—in other words, Elgin, me, Agnes Hancock, and some tech guy from England—to stay on Capri. So I'd be living in luxury at a villa, soaking in a replica of a real Roman bath, and eating plenty of fresh tomatoes and mozzarella. What more could you want?"

"For Elgin Lawrence not to be there. That man draws trouble to himself like stink draws flies."

I shrug. "That may be true, but how likely is it that someone's going to try to shoot him twice in one year?" I say. "I mean, what are the odds?"

I wake up in the middle of the night thinking about the question I so flippantly posed to M'Lou. What were the odds? It was a question that Ely would have taken literally. I lie awake trying to figure out what the variables would be in such an equation. How many pretty young graduate students has Elgin Lawrence flirted with? How many of them had boyfriends who were mentally unbalanced? Of those mentally unbalanced boyfriends, how many had access to firearms? This being Texas the answer was: most of them. For each variable I imagine Ely writing a letter on a chalkboard: x, y, or z. I can see each letter glowing starkly white against the black and then each letter acquires a halo that flames red in the darkness. I startle fully awake, sniffing the air for smoke. Outside the moonlight has turned my lawn into a scorched landscape. My lungs feel like they're on fire.

I get up to get a glass of cold water from the kitchen but instead find myself standing in my study staring at the faintly glowing symbols that Ely had painted on the walls. When I realize that I'm looking for an equation that would make some sense out of the shooting and predict the future, I go back to my room. It's a long time, though, before I can fall back to sleep.

When I wake up the next morning I still feel unsure about whether I should go to Italy with Elgin. Even the fact that that's how I'm thinking of it—*with Elgin*—sets off alarm bells in my head. I decide to do a little research on the Papyrus Project, to at least pretend that my decision will be based on its strengths and weaknesses. I start off by Googling John Lyros.

I've heard his name bandied about in the Classics Department because he'd been considered one of the most promising Ph.D. candidates before he dropped out in the early eighties, moved to Fremont, California, and invented an encryption program that had made him a millionaire. He'd used the money to found a software company, Lyrik, whose operating system, Lyrik 2.0, made him a billionaire before his thirtieth birthday. He'd gotten an early start. According to his bio he entered college, commuting from his Greek-American family's home in Astoria, Queens, to City College in Manhattan, at sixteen. He'd graduated with a double major in Greek and math and, after taking a year off to go hiking in the Himalayas—"in order to find myself," he mentions impishly in one interview—Lyros entered the Ph.D. program at UT at twenty-one. The picture of him hiking in the Himalayas shows a curly-headed brunet with wide-spaced eyes the same lilac color as the sky above the snowcapped peaks in the background. Instead of finishing the Ph.D., he'd dropped out and within three years was running a multimillion-dollar software company. Another clipping, ten years later, announced the sale of Lyrik for an amount undisclosed but rumored to be in the billions. A photo shows him with shorter hair, the lilac eyes hidden behind square dark-framed glasses. At that point his CV goes blank for about five years. Another trek in the

Himalayas, I wonder? When he resurfaces, it's to announce the establishment of the John Lyros Institute, a foundation intended to aid research in ancient history, philosophy, art, and archaeology. The picture on the Institute's homepage shows a man who looks like he's been whittled down by the elements. His curly locks are gone, shaved to reveal a smooth, elegant cranium. His nose looks as if it had been broken at some point and reset carelessly, leaving a bump that makes him look like a predatory hawk. His eyes are an even more intense violet, as if they had absorbed all the color of all the mountains he'd scaled and all the seas he'd crossed in his travels.

I scroll through the projects that the institute has funded in the last five years: archaeological digs in Greece—in Samos, Delphi, Eleusis, Cape Sounion—and also in the Southwest—the preservation of a Pueblo village in southwest Colorado, a dig in New Mexico—and, most recently, the excavation of the Villa della Notte in Herculaneum.

After an hour spent trolling the Internet for references to John Lyros, I begin to feel like a cyber-stalker and decide to go ahead and e-mail the man. I tell him that Elgin Lawrence has invited me to be part of the team and ask him to tell me a little bit more about the project. And then, because I'm not sure it's a good idea to live in such close proximity to Elgin Lawrence all summer, I ask him for a recommendation for a hotel in Naples. So that I can work closer to the site, I write.

I send off the e-mail and then check my in-box, which turns out to be a mistake. I've got hundreds of messages—from students, colleagues, and administrators. I scroll through the lot of them, checking to see if any look urgent. I decide that none of them do. Perhaps my definition of urgent has changed since Dale Henry burst into the dean's conference room and killed two of my colleagues. With a pang I notice that a number of the messages concern the memorial service for Odette, which I've missed, and a scholarship being started in her name. I check "keep as new" next to those and delete the rest.

I'm just signing off when an Instant Message box opens on the screen displaying an icon of Brad Pitt as Achilles next to a speech bubble that reads: Salve! from LatinLover66. It takes me a minute to remember that this is Agnes's screen name. Before I can reply she adds another line: "Please say you're coming to Italy!" and adds a smiley face emoticon. I can almost hear her breathless inflection.

I type a reply, telling her that I'm still making up my mind, but as usual I'm slow for the pace of instant messaging and before I can finish Agnes has added three more lines of persuasion. "I feel a little nervous being the only girl there," she writes, and then adds, "Isn't it cool the Villa della Notte turns out to be where Petronia Iusta lived!" and then, "Which reminds me, I still have those Phineas Aulus books you lent me. I can drop them off anytime . . ."

I look up on my shelf and realize she's right. I'd lent her my three volumes of *Athenian Nights* two months ago when she started researching her project on mystery rites. I really ought to reread them before going to Italy . . . if I'm going.

I start a reply, but another line from Agnes pops up. "I mean, I'm really just hanging around until it's time to go."

Poor Agnes, I think, she sounds so forlorn. It must have been hard for her to come back to campus after the shooting. In fact, I'm surprised she's done it at all. I would have thought she'd stay in Sweetwater until it was time to leave for Italy. I wonder if she came back to prove to herself she could.

Suddenly I feel like a coward, hiding in my house two miles away from campus while little Agnes Hancock from Sweetwater, who watched her ex-boyfriend shoot himself, braves the campus. I click on the reply box and write: "I was just going out for a walk. I'll drop by to pick them up." And then, before I can change my mind, I grab my keys and go.

CHAPTER 6

1 know where Agnes lives because I've seen her get off the shuttle and walk up her front walk many times. It's a large old yellow Victorian that, if the number of bicycles sprawled on the front lawn is any indication, houses about a dozen students. A young man with sun-streaked blond hair greets me at the door wearing skimpy cut-off shorts and no shirt. He eyes me warily when I ask for Agnes.

"Are you one of her professors?"

"Yes, I'm Dr. Chase."

"Do you have ID?"

"Sam Tyler!" Agnes's voice calls from upstairs. "Would you please lighten up on the security detail?" Agnes appears on the stairs wearing UT sweats and a voluminous sweatshirt that dwarf her tiny frame. UT's burnt orange isn't a flattering color for anyone, but Agnes could have pulled it off a month ago. Now it accentuates her pallor and the dark rings under her eyes. Her once glossy blond hair is done up in two lank braids, one of which she's nervously snaking around her fingers.

"Yeah, well, I'll be down here in the living room." Sam squints at me as if memorizing my face for later identification in a lineup and then retreats to a large messy room just off the foyer and sprawls on a couch. Although he picks up a remote and turns on the TV, his eyes stay glued to us until we turn to head up the stairs.

Agnes rolls her eyes at me. "You'd better come up to my room," she says. "Or the boys will be hovering all over us."

As I follow her upstairs I see what she means. On each floor of the four-story house doors open and scruffy heads peer out, accompanied by blasting rock music and the smell of gym socks, stale beer, and corn chips.

"Are you the only girl in the house?" I ask when we reach the top floor and I've caught my breath from the steep climb.

"Yeah, I know it's weird. I was in a sorority up until the beginning of this year, but then I kind of fell out with some of the girls . . . well, you know how girls can be . . ."

I nod even though Agnes can't see me. I can well imagine that Agnes's looks might have attracted enmity from her sorority sisters.

"It was too late to get housing in the dorms, so Sam said I should move in here. I've known him since high school and he's always been like a big brother to me." Agnes opens the door and waves me into a small room. Every inch of the walls is covered with photos of young people—in prom dresses and tuxes, or bathing suits and floppy hats under beach umbrellas, or huddled together in front of historic monuments. "The guys have all been really great," Agnes says, sitting down on her bed, which is covered with a Little

Mermaid quilt. "Especially Sam. When I moved in he had put up all these pictures."

"It's sweet," I say, taking the desk chair. The only other chair in the room is a bean bag that looks as if it might swallow me whole. "You need friends in times like these." I wince at the triteness of the sentiment, but Agnes is nodding eagerly as though I've said something terribly original. "It's made the biggest difference. I don't know if I could have come back otherwise. I was so afraid that everyone would blame me for what happened. My friends all warned me not to get involved with Dale from the beginning."

When she talks about her friends, her eyes rove over the pictures on the walls and I find myself doing the same. I recognize Sam in a number of them—often with his arm around Agnes, the two of them mugging for the camera—but there's not a single one with Dale Henry. Then I notice that Agnes's hair is shorter in the pictures—chin-length in some, or just grazing her shoulders—and that she's about fifteen pounds heavier. Not fat, certainly, but she has the plumpness of a freshman who's indulged in a few too many late-night pizzas and starchy cafeteria fare. When I look closer I notice that a banner behind one of the huddled groups reads "Sophomore Spring Fling." These pictures are all several years old. Like the Little Mermaid quilt, they seem like relics from a happier, more innocent past.

"When did you meet Dale?" I ask.

"At the beginning of this year," she says. "At first it was really nice to meet someone outside my group, you know? By senior year it's like you've met every boy on campus and he's, like, already dated half your sorority sisters. Dale was older and he thought it was really cool that I'm a classics major. Most of my friends thought it was pretty lame when I declared . . . oh, no offense!"

"No offense taken. It's not the most practical major. What are most of your friends majoring in?"

"Business, communications . . . Sam's in poli sci. Dale was a philosophy major until he dropped out this spring. He seemed, well, I
know this sounds so weird after what he did, but he seemed so
sweet when I met him . . . just kind of lost . . ." Agnes takes a deep
shuddery breath and flutters her fingers in front of her face. I pluck
a box of Kleenex off the desk and sit down next to her on the bed.
"I'm sorry," she says after blowing her nose. "I bet you don't want
to hear that the man who shot you and killed poor Mrs. Renfrew
and Professor Biddle seemed sweet."

"I haven't always been the best judge of people myself." I look
around the room again at all the young faces—all healthy and
glowing with days spent in the sun. What possible preparation had
Agnes Hancock from Sweetwater, Texas, had for assessing someone
like Dale Henry? "You said he seemed lost?"

"Yeah. His father was in the military and so his family moved
around a lot. He wasn't used to having friends. At first he seemed to
like that I did, but then he started finding fault with most of them.
I mean, some of my friends might seem a little silly, especially the
girls from my old sorority, and he thought all the business majors
were too materialistic, which they kind of are . . . I mean, I didn't
grow up with a lot of money, and since my father's a minister I was
taught to give to charity and to help people who are less fortunate.
Most of my friends think I'm really old-fashioned, but Dale
thought it was quite admirable. I think he liked that I had a religious background. At least at first."

"Did something change?"

"Around Christmas he got kind of depressed. I invited him to
come home with me, but he said he was afraid my parents wouldn't
approve of him, which, to tell you the truth, was probably right.
But I should have made him come. When I got back something was
different. Maybe it was being by himself during the break. He
wasn't sleeping much and he'd gone on this weird diet, all raw foods

or something, and he'd gotten real skinny. He was staying up all night reading philosophy books, for the GREs I thought, but when I looked at the books I saw that something was wrong."

"What do you mean?" I ask, my skin prickling.

"He should have been reading a wide range of materials, but he'd gotten stuck on the pre-Socratics. And half the books were some New Age stuff he'd picked up at Book People . . . like crystal healing and astral projection. He kept telling me that my *aura* was the wrong color and I had to stop eating meat. He thought he knew things about people because of what color their aura was—like Professor Lawrence only cared about worldly success and that Sam was really in love with me, which was just so silly because Sam's been like my brother since we were kids." Agnes laughs and for a second she looks like the girl in the pictures, but then a shadow falls over her. "We went away together spring break because I thought it would make things better, but it didn't . . ."

She stops, her chin wobbling, and I guess that whatever happened during spring break is not something she wants to talk about. "And then you moved in here?" I prompt.

"Yes, but now I wonder if I had just tried harder to understand what Dale was going through . . ."

"Your friends were right, Agnes. Dale needed professional help."

"I *did* talk him into seeing a counselor at the clinic, but now they're saying that the pills they gave him just made him worse."

"You couldn't have known that." I squeeze her hand and get up from the bed and go over to the bookshelf above her desk, scanning the titles.

"Gosh, I'm sorry, Professor Chase. Here I am going on about my problems while you came all this way for your books. Here they are—" She hands me the first two volumes of *Athenian Nights.* "Isn't it just so exciting that Professor Lawrence has found a new book by Phineas Aulus!"

I smile, and am about to point out that Elgin didn't exactly *find* the new book, but then, looking down at the books in my hand I notice something.

"Is something wrong?" Agnes asks.

"Oh, it's nothing," I begin, but when she keeps staring at me I reply, "It's just that I thought I gave you all three volumes."

"Oh." Agnes colors deeply, staring at the books in my hand as if she could turn them into three with the force of her mind. "Did you? Gosh, I don't remember. These were the only ones here when I got back and I'm pretty sure I didn't take any Latin books home with me." She starts rooting through her shelves and I'm sorry I said anything. Poor Agnes, if she's this guilty over a lost book, how's she ever going to get over her ex-boyfriend killing two people?

"Don't worry," I say. "It's easily replaceable. I know where I can pick up a secondhand copy cheap."

"Really?" Agnes asks, her face relaxing. "Are you sure? I feel just horrible. Please let me pay for it."

"If you insist," I say, already planning to halve the price for her. I put my arm around her shoulder, only meaning to give her a reassuring pat, but she surprises me by leaning in for a full hug, her arms wrapping around me so tightly that I'm afraid she's going to pull loose my stitches. I squeeze back. I only wish I could replace everything we've lost so easily.

Agnes sees me down the stairs, walking so close to me that her shoulder brushes against mine. She's found some comfort in my presence and would, I think, follow me out the front door and back to my house except that Sam is waiting in the foyer to take my place.

"Chamomile," he says, handing her a steaming mug. I notice that another mug is sitting on the coffee table in the living room next to a stack of books. Sam's obviously been camped out here, waiting for Agnes.

"That's so sweet, Sam, thank you. Hey, do you know if anyone went in my room while I was away? There's a book missing that Dr. Chase needs."

"I made sure your door was locked at all times," Sam says, giving me a suspicious look. "I did go in a few days ago to air it out, but I didn't take any books."

"Of course you didn't," Agnes says, turning to me. "I'm sorry, Dr. Chase, I can't imagine what happened to it."

Sam glares at me and I realize he's angry that I've bothered Agnes about something as trivial as a lost book. He looks as if he might leap on me if I so much as say an unkind word to Agnes. "That's really all right. As I told you, I won't have any trouble replacing it."

Agnes gives me a parting smile but Sam's face is immobile. About halfway down the block, though, I hear the slap of bare feet on pavement and turn to find Sam jogging to catch up with me.

"I need to have a word with you," he says, not in the least out of breath even though he must have sprinted to catch up with me.

"Sure, Sam, but please let me start by saying that I really didn't come over to bother Agnes about that book—"

"It's about the book," Sam says. "I didn't want to go over it in front of Agnes. You see, she was working in the living room the day before her interview, practicing her presentation in front of me and a couple of the guys, and when she went to the campus the next morning she left her books downstairs. Right after she left, Dale Henry came to the house. He stormed in, shouting for Agnes, and when he saw her stuff in the living room he started ransacking through it. Of course, I grabbed him and threw him out—"

"You *physically* ejected him from the house?"

Sam nods grimly. Most young men Sam's age would be gloating, but Sam pales under his tan.

"You realize how lucky you are that he didn't shoot you?"

"Yeah, that's why I didn't tell Agnes about it. I called her that morning to warn her that he came to the house, but I never told her that he forced his way in. Anyway, I remember he had a book in his hands when I threw him out. It fell to the ground when he stumbled on the front lawn and he scooped it up right away. I didn't think anything of it at the time because he was always coming over with a book in his hands to show Agnes something very important, like a fucking Jehovah's Witness or something. But now—"

"You think it might have been one of Agnes's books. Do you remember what color it was?"

"It was red, just like all those Latin books Agnes has. Was that the book you were looking for?"

"It could have been," I say, thinking that there are plenty of red books in the world. "But I can't imagine what Dale Henry would have wanted with a Roman religion historian of the first century AD."

Sam shakes his head, which makes his hair fall over his eyes. He pushes it away angrily. "I've stopped trying to figure out what that sick fuck wanted with anything. I mean, 'That way madness lies,' right?"

I nod, surprised that Sam has a Shakespeare quote ready at hand. "I understand. And if you brought it up in front of Agnes—"

"She'd start thinking about how easy it would have been for Dale Henry to blow the whole house away . . ."

He lets his voice trail off and I finish it for him. "And that way madness lies?"

He looks back at me, his eyes narrowed with suspicion. Does he think I'm making fun of him? "I meant it figuratively, of course," I say.

"Of course," he says, giving me his first smile. It makes the sunburnt skin around his turquoise eyes crinkle. I feel like I've earned a prize.

"Well, thanks for telling me. I promise I won't mention it to Agnes—" I've taken a step backward, but he reaches out his hand, tentatively grazing my elbow with his fingertips to hold me back.

"Can I ask you a favor?"

When I nod he reaches into the pocket of his denim cut-offs and pulls out a slip of paper with a phone number on it. "I'm teaching rock-climbing at this camp in Switzerland this summer, so I can't come to Italy and keep an eye on Agnes and I'm worried about her. Most people think that because she's so pretty everything's easy for her, but I grew up with her and I know, well, she's more fragile than she seems. Anyway, I got one of those cell phones that work over in Europe and this is the number. If she's having a hard time, would you call me?"

"I'm sure Agnes will be fine," I begin, but when I see the stubborn determination in his eyes I take the slip of paper. "But I'll call if I have any concerns. She's lucky to have a friend like you."

A shadow flickers across his blue-green eyes, like a shark moving through shallow water, but then he forces a smile. "I'm the one who's lucky," he says. "Look how close I came to losing her." He turns and walks away. I watch him pad back to the house, the sight of his bare feet on the hot pavement making me cringe for his vulnerability. When I turn around I think that Dale Henry got at least one thing right: I may not be able to see Sam Tyler's aura, but it's clear as daylight that he's in love with Agnes Hancock.

CHAPTER 7

Instead of heading home I turn left on 38th Street and head reluctantly over to Guadalupe. I'd told Agnes the truth when I said I knew where to find a replacement for the lost volume of *Athenian Nights;* it just wasn't a place I wanted to go. Archetype Books, the dusty used-book shop sandwiched between a tattoo parlor and juice bar on Guadalupe, had been the third point on the New Age triangle Ely had sketched out that first night we noticed the Tetraktys house. I hadn't at first realized that it had become a place he frequented as much as Starwoman and the Tetraktys house until a month before he left town, when I noticed the Mandala logo of the store on a bookmark inside one of his books on Pythagoreanism. The same bookmark I saw inside one of the books Agnes had just returned to me.

I had gone there one morning when Ely hadn't come home the night before. The man behind the counter had looked up from the book he was reading when I came in and studied me without saying a word. He had eyes a yellow color I'd only ever seen in cats before. And just as a cat sometimes stares at empty space, so he seemed to be staring not *at* me but *through* me, as if he had X-ray vision. Indeed, he had the high cavernous forehead and oblong face of a mad scientist in some horror movie. I'd taken a step backward, mumbling some excuse that I'd gotten the wrong store, and stepped on something that screeched and then whirled around my feet like a furry dust devil.

"That's just Gus," the book clerk said as if explaining a meteorological phenomenon. The maelstrom of black and white fur surged up onto the counter and bunched itself into the shape of a fat black and white cat who glared at me with eyes the same color as his master's.

"I didn't mean to step on his tail," I said, holding out my hand to the cat as a propitiatory offering. I wouldn't have been surprised if he'd gobbled it like a hungry idol, but he merely sniffed at my fingertips, the white triangle over his nose twitching, and then rubbed his face down the length of my arm. I had to step closer to the desk or the cat would have fallen on the floor. I noticed then that the clerk had a tattoo at the base of his throat: a triangle made out of ten dots.

"Are you looking for something?" he asked.

I had the feeling he wasn't talking about a book.

"Um . . . I think my boyfriend comes in here sometimes . . . Ely?"

"*I* know Ely," the clerk said with such an emphasis on *I* that I expected him to follow with, "Do *you*?"

"I'm looking for him," I said, swallowing my embarrassment. I felt like a fishwife tracking down her errant husband. "He didn't come home last night."

"A teacher came to speak last night at meeting and afterward some of the followers went to one of the member houses to hear about the community in New Mexico. I think Ely might have been one of the ones who was interested." The man paused. He must have seen the tears rising to my eyes. At the mention of New Mexico, my throat had gone as dry as the desert. My worst fear was that Ely would leave me to join a Tetraktys community far away from Austin. I was surprised to see that the clerk looked sorry for me. "I imagine he would have called to say where he was, but the teacher asked that anybody who came to listen observe a vow of silence for the night. We believe initiates should be silent while learning."

"According to Pythagoras," I said, desperate to seem like I wasn't a total idiot, like I was in on at least some of the secret rites and rituals. The name Pythagoras made the cat look up and meow. "Don't tell me," I said, "the cat's a Pythagorean, too."

The clerk smiled and chucked the cat under the chin. "He just recognizes his name. Gus is short for Pythagoras."

I didn't learn the clerk's name on that first visit, but in the coming weeks I stopped by the bookstore often and learned that his name was Charles. In addition to New Age stuff, Charles carried a remarkable selection of Greek and Latin texts, some of which were hard to find anywhere else. "I specialize in myth," he explained, "so of course I carry the classics." I made his classics selections an excuse for my increasingly frequent visits, but we both knew I was using him as a link to Ely. Charles was the only member of the Tetraktys I ever spoke with or knew by name—and I didn't even know his last name or where he lived.

I am afraid as I reach the store today that I'll find it closed—or Charles and Gus gone. When I open the door, though, and step into the store, I might be stepping back in time to my first visit. Charles is in the same spot at the counter, his head bowed over a book until my entrance draws his amber eyes up to mine. I feel something furry brush against my calf and look down to find Gus twining himself around my legs.

"I wondered how long it would be before you came in," Charles says, reaching under the counter. "I've been saving this for you." I step forward, nearly tripping over Gus, and reach for the book. An index card with my name hand-printed on it is paper clipped to the cover, obscuring the title, but when I move the card and read the gilt-pressed lettering I see that it's the third volume of Phineas Aulus's *Athenian Nights.*

I open my mouth to ask a question and then shut it. Experience has taught me that a direct question usually yields unsatisfying results with Charles. If I asked how he knew I needed this particular book he could very well tell me that the knowledge had come to him in a dream. So instead I ask which translation it is.

"The Reverend F. P. Long, MA, Sometime Exhibitioner of Worchester College. Published by the Clarendon Press in 1911," Charles replies without looking at the title page. "Not as good as the LaFleur translation, of course, but those are getting pretty scarce these days."

I lay my fingers on the smooth leather cover and flip through the gilt-edged pages to the marbled end papers at the back. "The end pages look new," I comment. "Did you do the rebinding yourself?"

"No, I farm that work out now to New Mexico. The dry climate is better for old books."

Gus abandons my ankles and leaps onto the counter. He pushes the white triangle of his nose against my limp hand, demanding attention.

"So, you've been out there recently?" I ask, petting the cat.

"Last month," Charles says. "I took a truckload of damaged books I got at the Albuquerque Book Fair and picked up these."

Gus has managed to snake under my arm and push his face against my chest. When he reaches my left ribs, where my bandages are, I'm afraid he's going to dislodge my stitches, but he only sniffs and looks up at me, his yellow eyes solemn.

"You're going to heal well," Charles says. "I can tell."

I stifle the urge to ask "How? By my aura?"

"For a while you're going to feel like something's missing there," he goes on, touching the spot below his own ribs.

"So what else is new?" I ask. "At least Dale Henry left me with my life. Others were not so lucky."

Charles shakes his head sorrowfully. "The emptiness inside him was bigger than the hole he put in you. It was a like a black hole, dragging everyone into it."

"So you knew Dale Henry?" I ask, trying to sound casual.

"He came in here sometimes. A lot of lost souls come looking for something to fill their empty places." Charles holds up his large hands, bracketing the empty air between us to demonstrate the idea of emptiness. I wonder if that's how he saw Ely when he started coming here. As a lost soul. Had he offered him the Tetraktys as something to fill that empty place? I've always wondered if Charles was the one who introduced Ely into the Tetraktys, but as much as I'd like to ask about Ely I have a more important question to ask.

"What did Dale Henry use to fill his emptiness?"

"He used a big gun," Charles says, dropping his hands.

"So he wasn't a member . . . ?"

"Of the Tetraktys?" Charles's eyes slide away from me and his fingers splay over the counter like spiders ready to pounce. He'd looked exactly like this when Ely left town for good and I asked him where he'd gone. "You know we don't advocate violence. Pythagoras wouldn't even allow the slaughter of animals." I notice that Charles hasn't said that Dale Henry *wasn't* a member. Pythagoreans aren't supposed to lie, either, but they can avoid telling an inconvenient truth to outsiders like me.

"But he attended some meetings?" I ask. "He was interested."

"A lot of people are *interested,*" he says, making it clear by his intonation what he thinks of the dilettantes who flit from one New Age interest to another.

"So he came to meetings, but wasn't initiated?" I suggest.

"Many are the narthex bearers," Charles quotes, "but few are the Bacchoi."

I know that once Charles starts spouting quotations I'm about to lose him. I don't have to read auras to see he's shutting down. If Dale Henry was a member of the Tetraktys, it's not a fact its members are going to advertise. I'm not going to get any more information about Dale Henry out of Charles, so I change tacks.

I look back down at the marbled end pages and trace the swirling patterns—a mélange of blues and greens. "These are my favorite colors," I say to Charles. "Ely used to say it was because I'm an Aquarian and these are the colors of water."

Charles's face softens. "Yes, I'm sure that's why he chose them. He wanted you to have this. He said he took your copy of the last volume when he left."

I look up, startled. "He *said* I would want this?"

"Yes, it's been five years. Ely's vow of silence has ended. I was there on the day it ended so those were practically his first words." I look up at Charles to see if he's having a joke at my expense, but his eyes are as solemn as Gus's had been a moment ago. I struggle not to laugh. Five years of silence and Ely's first message to me is "Hey, here's the book I borrowed from you."

"Okay," I say, "so how much do I owe you?"

"Nothing. It's a gift."

"Thanks, Charles, and thank—"

"I won't be able to thank Ely because he's already left the community. Once the five-year period of silence is over, the initiate is sent out on a mission."

"Do you—"

"I have no idea where he's gone. No one is told another initiate's mission."

"And this was last month?"

He checks the ledger he keeps beside the cash register. "I was in New Mexico the second week of May. I saw Ely on the fifteenth."

More than three weeks ago. He could be anywhere by now. "Okay, thanks, Charles." I pick up my book and turn. Gus stands by the door as if he were Janus, the ancient doorkeeper of the Romans, waiting for a tip. I bend to rub his head before going out, like patting a Buddha's belly for good luck. I figure I could use it.

I walk back to my house trying to sort through all the disparate threads I've followed today. "It's a small town," I'd told Ely when he started seeing coincidences everywhere. It didn't necessarily mean anything that a crazy like Dale Henry had wandered into Archetype Books—after all, he was a philosophy major—or a few Tetraktys meetings. Or that the book he stole from Agnes happened to be the replacement of the book that Ely took from me five years ago. A book which Ely happened to be handing over as a gift to me around the same time as the shooting . . . was it only *around* the same time, though? When I open my front door—swiping at the coral vine that has made another tactical assault on the screen—I go straight to the calendar on my desk and, still standing, flip back to May.

The words *Papyrus Project Internship Interviews* are printed in the box for May 14. Charles said that he saw Ely on May 15, which had been the day his vow of silence ended. So if Ely had wanted to warn me about Dale Henry . . .

It's absurd. Even if Ely had known that a crazed gunman was targeting one of my students, which required him to know more about my present life than an initiate of a cloistered community would have any obvious way of knowing, would he really be satisfied with as cryptic a warning as coded telephone rings?

"No," I think, touching the cover of Phineas Aulus's *Athenian Nights*. No doubt the gift was part of some twelve-step program for completion of the initiation process. *Return all worldly goods wrongly borrowed,* or some such ridiculous dictum. Ely was probably just trying to purge himself of any reminder of me. The good thing, I tell myself, is that if Ely felt the necessity of sending the book back with Charles, then chances are he's not planning on coming back to Austin.

Unless the book was some kind of advance calling card announcing his imminent arrival.

I'm startled out of this alarming train of thought by the sound of a loud thump that comes from the back of the house. I get up and walk quickly through the kitchen and my bedroom looking for the source of the noise but find nothing. It must have come from the study. I stand in front of the closed door, chiding myself for the ridiculous idea that has popped into my head: Ely is in there. Released from his five-year vow of silence, he's come back to me. I'm his mission.

And even though I should be frightened, especially if Dale Henry was involved with the Tetraktys, the electric charge surging up through my core is more excitement than fear.

I open the door onto an empty room. My books are as I left them, the pile of typescript beside my laptop undisturbed. The laptop is glowing the tranquil blue of the screensaver. The only addition to the scene is a faint rust-colored smear across the glass window above my desk.

I take a step closer to examine the pale red tint. It looks like blood. I look down and see, on the ground just beneath my window, a melee of black feathers over the crumpled corpse of an enormous black crow. Clearly the sound I heard was its death crash into

my study window. Even after I've donned a pair of leather garden-
ing gloves and bagged the bird's broken body, I keep remembering
what crows stand for in Greek mythology. They're psychopomps—
messengers sent to lead the soul into the underworld. I find it hard
to dismiss the totally irrational thought that the crow, along with
the book, is another calling card from Ely.

That night I dream of Ely again, but it's hardly like a dream at all;
it's more like an appointment Ely's been waiting to keep with me.
The place he's chosen is his childhood bedroom in the split-level
Cape Cod where his parents live in HoHoKus, New Jersey—a
room I slept in for three nights five and a half years ago, but which
apparently I've remembered down to its last detail. It's been waiting
here inside my head, a time bubble, exact down to the burnt umber
shade of the carpet and the Styrofoam model of the solar system
hanging from the light fixture in the ceiling.

We'd gone for Rosh Hashanah, which fell a week before the fall
semester began. It was my last-ditch effort to talk Ely out of going
to the Tetraktys community in New Mexico. I'd thought that if we
went back to his parents' house in New Jersey they'd be able to talk
some sense into him. Instead, by the end of those three nights—
three nights I spent lying awake on a narrow bed staring up at the
pitted Styrofoam surface of Neptune—I knew why he was going.

Ely had lost his brother when he was ten. It was one of the links
that Ely believed held us together, that we had both lost someone
important to us when we were the same age. I had often resented
how my grandparents had tried to erase my mother's memory, but
looking at this room I realized it might have been even harder
growing up beside the lost person's remains. It didn't look as though
Ely's parents had changed a single thing from the day Paul had died,
not one soccer trophy or math decathlon blue ribbon.

It didn't predispose me to think kindly of them, nor did the fact that they weren't home when we got to the house. Ely explained that they often worked late at the high school where his dad, Howard, taught math, and his mother, Ruth, was a guidance counselor. It seemed strange to me that they couldn't get out a little early to welcome their only son home. I'd already painted a picture of them as neglectful monsters, the kind of self-absorbed parents who would raise a kid who'd feel so inadequate he'd have to join a cult to gain any sense of belonging, but when they came home there were tears in Ruth's eyes as she hugged Ely. Howard endeared himself to me by kissing Ely on the cheek (a bit of male intimacy you didn't see often in Texas).

"Call me Howie," he told me as he crushed me in a bear hug.

Ruth had chatted nonstop while pulling a casserole from the freezer and handing dishes to me to put on the table as if I'd been in the family forever. "I thought we'd have something simple tonight since we're having a big dinner tomorrow," she said. "Hope you don't mind noodle kugel."

"Bet that's not something you get much of out in Texas," Howie had said. "Bet you eat a lot of chicken-fried steak and grits—"

"Dad!"

"Howie!"

Ely and his mother spoke at the same time. Their exasperation was good-humored, though, and that good humor lasted through dinner while Howie slung out every Texas stereotype he could think of and Ruth asked me gently corrective questions. "Not everybody in Texas lives on a ranch, Howie. I'm sure Sophie grew up in a regular house, didn't you, dear?"

"Well, actually, I did grow up on my grandparents' ranch in Pflugerville."

Ruth looked at me as if I might have made up the name to tease her.

"See, what did I tell you, Ruth? Not everyone grew up in a fifth-floor walk-up on the Lower East Side eating borscht and bagels. I bet you ate plenty of steak, Sophie."

"Actually, Sophie cooks great Mexican food," Ely said.

I was so happy that Ely was talking about something as ordinary as food that I didn't say that I'd learned how to cook Mexican food from one of M'Lou's boyfriends, or mention that my grandfather had slaughtered a couple of steer and pigs for our private use each year and that we had a smokehouse filled with pork on the ranch, or mention that Ely hadn't eaten a thing I'd cooked for months. He'd been on a raw fruit and vegetable diet since I'd gotten back from the hospital, most of which he pulverized and drank in juice form. The Hyde Park bungalow smelled like carrots and wheatgrass and Ely's skin had begun to take on an orange tint, but at his mother's table he was wolfing down noodle kugel slathered in sour cream and washing it down with Manischewitz wine. He seemed to want to do nothing more than make his parents happy, and although I didn't think that would extend to eating any of the brisket I saw thawing in the bottom of the refrigerator, I was hoping he might listen to them if they asked him not to go to New Mexico.

After dinner Howie dragged Ely out to the garage to see his new carpentry tools and I offered to help Ruth clean up in the kitchen. She donned rubber gloves and an apron and washed the dishes with lemon-scented soap while I dried with a red-and-white-checked dish towel.

"That was a great dinner, Ruth," I told her for the third time. "Ely said you were a great cook." That last part was a lie—Ely had told me next to nothing about his parents or his dead brother—but I wanted to get off on a good footing with Ely's mother and get her on my side on the New Mexico question.

"Did he, now?" she asked, sounding skeptical, but pleased. "Well, Ely was always an easy child. Sometimes I thought too easy."

"What do you mean?" *Easy* is not a word I would have used to describe Ely, and I wondered if his mother was seriously out of touch with what her son was really like.

"He's always wanted to please us. Especially after his brother, Paul, died." Ruth's face tightened at the mention of her dead son's name, but she went on washing the dishes, moving the sponge in counterclockwise circles along the rim of the plates.

"You mean he wanted to live up to who Paul was?" I asked, making my own circles on the plates Ruth handed me. "All those ribbons and trophies in Ely's room—"

"We wanted to take those down." Ruth squirted more liquid soap onto her sponge. "Of course we did, only Ely had a fit. He wanted it all to stay the same. The family counselor we saw said to leave the room as it was as long as Ely wanted it that way. We didn't realize that would be until he went away to college! And even then he made me promise to keep it all the same when he left. I didn't want to do anything to upset him. I know it looks bad— believe me, we've never done a thing or said a word to Ely to make him think we valued him one smidgen less than Paul. Never compared them or tried to make Ely follow in Paul's footsteps. Doing math was all Ely's idea and, truth be told"—Ruth lowers her voice and whispers—"Ely's better at math than Paul ever was."

Ruth handed me a dish and I noticed that there were still suds clinging to the back rim. I swiped them away surreptitiously and stole a look at Ruth. She'd set her mouth in a hard line, trying not to cry, I realized, that little betrayal of her dead son having cost her dearly.

"Ely's never said what Paul died of," I said, at a loss for any way to console a mother for the loss of a child. Where would I have learned? I remembered when the state trooper came to our door to tell my grandparents that my mother had drowned in the San Marcos River. My grandmother had told me to leave off playing jacks on the kitchen floor and go get the man some iced tea. Then she'd told me to sit down on the couch and sit up straight to listen to what the man had to say. The trooper, looking embarrassed to be retelling this news to a ten-year-old girl, explained to me that my mother must not have realized how high the river was. *Drunk, more like it,* my grandfather had said. When the state trooper left we sat down to our usual three-course meal of heavy food—the slightly burned taste of the pork roast the only sign that something had gone wrong.

"Cystic fibrosis," Ruth said, handing me another plate—this one well-rinsed—to dry. "We found out Paul had it when I was pregnant with Ely. I've often wondered if I had known earlier . . ." She let the sentence go unfinished and I heard Ely's voice saying that some of the greatest discoveries had been made through error. Ely, who would have known exactly what the odds were of Howard and Ruth Markowitz having a second son with cystic fibrosis and what his life expectancy would have been if he had been born with the disease. He must have felt the arbitrariness of his having been spared and wondered what he'd been spared *for*.

"So if you're thinking of having children," she said, lowering her voice to a whisper again even though Ely and Howie were still out in the garage, "you ought to be tested. Ely's a carrier. Of course we were heartbroken when we heard you'd lost the baby, but now you can be tested to see if you have the gene and then you'll know for sure when you're ready to try again."

"Ruth," I said, "has Ely told you about his plans? That he's talking about moving to New Mexico?"

"Oh, that won't last." Ruth took the dish towel from my hand, neatly folding it lengthwise and hanging it over the stove handle to dry. "Not if he knows he has you to come home to."

Howie and Ely came back from the garage then, and Ruth busied herself putting the coffee on. (The Markowitz family drank caffeinated coffee after dinner every night, which was one of the reasons I didn't sleep the three nights I was there.) I didn't get a chance to speak with her alone for the rest of the evening, and I knew by the time that Ely and I retired to "our room" that Ruth and Howie viewed the Tetraktys community in New Mexico as a sort of summer camp, like the United Synogague Youth bus tour they had sent Ely on in high school and the Birthright trip to Israel he took two years ago. The fact that the group was named for a Pythagorean symbol seemed to make the Markowitzes think of it as a sort of math club. And if they had any reservations, they were counting on me to be a big enough draw to get Ely back to Austin and grad school by the spring semester.

"Starting her second year already!" Howie had said to Ely, winking sideways at me. "You'll have a lotta catching up to do. Maybe you'll want to stop at the master's and get a teaching certificate. There's always work for a good math teacher and the salary's not half bad around here."

"Sh, Howie," Ruth said. "I'm sure Sophie's got family of her own in Texas she wants to stay near."

"Just the aunt, though, right Sophie?" Howie said. "Really, the two of you should think of moving back East. I'm sure we could find Sophie a job teaching Latin—"

Ruth had halted him with a roll of the eyes and Howie shrugged. "I'm just saying!" he pleaded.

There was never any question of me taking the other bed—*Paul's* bed. I lay awake all that night, clinging to the edge of Ely's narrow bed, staring up at the multicolored planets spinning in the breeze from the open window, and trying to believe in Ruth and Howie Markowitz's vision of our future. I would have been willing, then, to give up the Ph.D., M'Lou's proximity, good Mexican food, and mild winters if it meant I could keep Ely, but I knew that the vision of that life was as far from reality as those Styrofoam balls were from being real planets. I'd felt some hope when I saw that Ely really seemed to like his parents, to want to please them, but then I remembered the way Ruth's face had looked when she'd forced herself to say her dead son's name. Ely would have seen that look every day of his life. He would have heard, too, the muffled weeping I heard that night coming from his parents' bedroom next door. He'd have tried to do everything he could to make them happy—been an A+ student in the subject his father taught and that Paul had been good at, eaten everything on his plate—but he also would have known that he would always fall short. They would never be purely happy. Always the shadow of that lost child would have fallen over any chance of that. No matter what Ely ever achieved, it was not in his power to make them happy. It was a failing I knew something about, having realized myself at age ten that I hadn't been enough to keep my mother home—or to keep her alive.

When I turned on my side, I was looking at the other bed: Paul's bed. There was a shallow depression in the center the shape and size a thirteen-year-old boy would have made scrunched up into a fetal position. I stared at that spot all night until I thought I had its shape and size memorized.

When I wake up in the middle of the night, I'm surprised to find myself in my own room and not Ely's childhood bedroom. I can still see, though, the shape of the depression in Paul's bed hovering in the air and I hear Charles's voice saying: *A lot of lost souls come here looking for something to fill their empty places.* I thought I knew the shape and size of the emptiness inside of Ely.

I get up to dispel the impression that there's a ghost hovering in the room and walk into the study. I'd forgotten to close the shade earlier, but I leave it open for the feel of the night air wafting through the window, smelling like mimosa and jasmine—a scent that reminds me of the evening walks Ely and I used to take in the neighborhood.

Since Charles told me this afternoon that Ely has left the Tetraktys community in New Mexico I can't shake off the feeling that he's coming for me and that these signs—the dreams, the dead crow,

Dale Henry taking the same book Ely had—are all presages of his arrival. What I can't decide is whether it's something I want or dread.

I click open my e-mail and see that John Lyros has sent a reply.

June 5, 2008
Salve!
I can't tell you how pleased I am personally that you are considering joining the Papyrus Project. I've read your articles on Petronia Iusta and thought of you as soon as we learned that Gaius Petronius Stephanus was the owner of the villa and saw Iusta's name mentioned in the text. I'm sure you are as anxious as we are to see what he has to say about her. I've directed the excavation team to concentrate on the room where this scroll was found in the hope that we'll turn up Phineas's waterproof trunk. Who knows? Perhaps we'll find the scrolls Phineas was rumored to have stolen from Greece and Egypt.

So please do come! The villa on Capri has been built as a replica of the Villa della Notte and so, along with state-of-the-art multispectral imaging technology, is the perfect place to study the scrolls discovered there. The foundation's boat, the *Parthenope,* can easily take you to the excavation site more quickly than the train will get you there from Naples, but if you do decide to take a room in Naples I would recommend the Hotel Convento on the Vomero—a fourteenth-century convent recently converted into an elegant hotel. I haven't stayed there myself, so I can't vouch for the rooms, but it has a lovely rooftop restaurant with a spectacular view of the bay and the atmosphere is quite interesting. I've included a link to their website below.

Vale,
John Lyros

I read this missive over twice, parsing each line as though it were written in ancient Greek or Latin, and study the pictures of the Hotel Convento, with its pretty whitewashed, majolica-tiled rooms, spectacular bay view, and rooftop pool. What I can't figure out is why I am still hesitating. Everything is beckoning me to go—the research opportunity of a lifetime, a beautiful villa on Capri, and a handsome billionaire personally inviting me! What else could I require?

Or is it that I am waiting for something here?

As if summoned by the thought, I hear a footstep outside on the far side of the lawn where a tangle of coral vine has spread over the dilapidated garage. For a second I think I see a figure there in the shadow of the vine, silhouetted against the peeling paint on the old clapboard.

Then something beeps on my computer. I look down and see Agnes's IM icon flashing next to the message: "You couldn't sleep, either?"

When I look up a wind blows the coral vine aside and I see that the figure is gone. It probably wasn't there to begin with.

I look back down to the computer screen and see that Agnes has added another line. "Have you decided whether you're going yet?"

I click the reply box and type in, "Yes. I've decided, yes."

CHAPTER 8

Although I've never enjoyed flying, the flight to Naples is worse than any I've ever experienced. Perhaps it's because of my damaged lung. All through the long overnight flight I feel as if I can't get enough air. I keep expecting the oxygen masks to drop. When I finally step out onto the tarmac in Naples and try to take in a deep breath I get instead a lungful of cotton wool.

A taxi strike has descended on Naples so I take a bus to the hotel. The bus is equally vacant of ventilation. I look around at the other passengers, wondering how they all stand it. The bus drops me two blocks from the hotel, which hadn't seemed too far when I'd looked at the map, but when I get off I realize the blocks on the Vomero—the steep hill that overlooks the city and bay of Naples—are nearly vertical. Dragging my rolling suitcase, I feel like I'm scaling a wall. Then I pass the entrance to the Hotel Convento twice before I recognize it: the tall shallow building is hewn out of the same rough stone as the hill and clings to it like a mussel attached to a seawall. Inside, though, the walls are pearly white and trimmed with majolica tiles painted in the yellows and coral reds of tropical fish and the bright blues and greens of the Mediterranean sea. *Like a jewel box,* I think, wondering if the whole hotel is fashioned on such a small, precious scale. Even the reception desk is fitted into a shallow niche, which I imagine was once inhabited by the convent's doorkeeper—the one employed to keep the nuns from escaping. It seems barely large enough to contain the small, neat man with carefully manicured nails and just the hint of a five o'clock shadow who introduces himself as Silvio, the concierge. When he's checked me in he apologizes that the elevator is broken and offers to carry up my bag himself, and so I follow him up four steep flights of stairs. I keep trying to focus on how pretty and clean everything is—the stone floors, the white walls, the majolica tiles, and the perfect framed view of the bay from each landing. When Silvio unlocks the heavy oak door to my room I try not to show my disappointment that my room is the size of my study back in Austin. Well, what had I thought, I chide myself as I tip Silvio and dutifully exclaim *"Che bella!,"* that fourteenth-century nuns lived in Texas-sized ranch houses? At least it has air-conditioning—a small unit beneath the room's one window.

When I lay my hand over the air conditioner, though, I feel only the slightest stirring. It could be the last breath of the last nun to die in this cell. "Is that the highest it goes?" I ask, my accent, which seems to gain strength the farther I get from Texas, twanging the still air between us like an out-of-tune violin string.

Silvio clucks his tongue and shakes his head. "Yes," he says. "You Americans, you are always disappointed in the air-conditioning."

"It's not the air-conditioning," I try to explain. "It's the air. I need some and there isn't any."

Silvio smiles a sibylline smile and points to the window. "You can always open the window," he says. "Ecco! You can see all the way to Capri." Then he bows himself out of my little cell and closes the massive door behind him with the finality of a jail keeper.

I open the window but all that does is let in the noise and fumes of traffic from the busy street below. I sit down on the edge of the bed and sink about a foot into the mattress. Picking up a brochure from the night table I read: "The Hotel Convento originally belonged to an order, founded by a Roman martyr of the late first century AD, of the Sepolte Vive." It takes me only a minute to translate Sepolte Vive: buried alive. I seem to remember some Henry James heroine fleeing to a convent of that order after being betrayed by her lover. The Convent of the Awful Name, James had referred to it in that way he had of making the unnamed sound so much worse than the named. The order had practiced a fervid renunciation of the world, never going out or seeing anyone from the outside world, even sleeping in coffins. No wonder I couldn't breathe in here; those nuns probably thought air was a worldly luxury.

I try to console myself by remembering that I'll only be here for three nights. In the end I'd realized that it was foolish not to stay at Lyros's villa in Capri. Still, I'd wanted a few days on my own in Italy before giving myself over to a summer of forced proximity with Elgin Lawrence. Tomorrow I'll go to Herculaneum and visit the Villa della Notte—John Lyros had sent me a letter to gain admission to the closed site. The best thing I can do now is try to get a good night's sleep.

Sleep, though, proves as elusive a commodity as oxygen in this cell of the buried alive. Every time I begin to drift off, I feel myself sinking into the too-soft mattress and I imagine myself entombed in its coils and padding. I leave the window open, but sometime around three a.m. all the cats of Naples begin a high-pitched keening. At least I hope it's cats. If I were home in Texas I'd say that that chattering squeal could only come out of a possum, but are there possums in southern Italy? I don't think so. And if it's not possums and it's not cats, then it might actually be humans making that sound.

When the cats (or whatever) leave off, I hear a sound like muffled weeping. It reminds me of the sound I heard in Ely's childhood bedroom: his mother's crying coming through the thin plasterboard. Only here the walls aren't plasterboard, they're stone several feet thick. If someone's weeping, they're not in the next room but buried in the walls. It must be the plumbing, I decide.

I finally get a few hours' sleep before dawn and then the light creeping in through the window and the morning rush-hour traffic wake me. Surely a shower will revive me, I think, but the trickle of water in the Plexiglas-enclosed tube is barely strong enough to rinse the shampoo out of my hair, and the water leaves a sulfuric smell on my skin.

Breakfast is on the rooftop. I pick a table in the sun, which, even though it's only eight, turns out to be already uncomfortably strong, and stare at the swallows careening over the bay. The curve of the coast is dotted with industrial buildings and tenement apartment houses stacked on top of each other like LEGOs. The cone-shaped silhouette of Vesuvius is insubstantial against the sky—a painted backdrop, a travel agency poster. Even after two strong cappuccinos and a plateful of sugary pastries, I can't quite believe in it. Maybe when I get to Herculaneum, I'll really feel like I'm in Italy.

Downstairs Silvio informs me that the cab strike is still on. He marks out a route to the train station on a map for me. It's just a short funicular ride down the Vomero to the port and then a short bus ride to the train station where I can catch the Circumvesuviana train to Herculaneum. No problem, he tells me. And I believe him. The funicular can't be bad, I reason. After all, there's a song about it. I hum it—*Funiculì-funiculà*—down the hill to the funicular station. The sidewalk is littered with broken glass and a number of cars parked on the side of the road have cardboard taped over the places where their windows have been punched out. When I had checked the location of the hotel on a map, it had looked like it was on a street in central Naples, just a few blocks from the Spaccanapoli neighborhood and the Archaeological Museum and just up the hill from the port where the cruise ships docked and the ferry boats left for Capri and Ischia. But the curving road is carved into the steep cliff of the Vomero, high above and cut off from the rest of the city. It's clearly not in the best of neighborhoods. I had envisioned myself walking to outdoor cafés in the evening, but now I realize that, without taxis, I'll be pretty much stranded in the hotel after nightfall—the only lifeline to the rest of Naples the funicular.

I'm expecting, I think, something like the cable cars of San Francisco, but instead the funicular turns out to be a sort of vertical subway. The station is underground in a windy, steeply sloping tunnel where a crowd of bored commuters—schoolgirls and laborers, office workers and shopgirls—talk a fast, slurry Italian and cheerfully ignore the nonsmoking signs. A sudden gust of wind roars up from the depths of the tunnel and the metal cable that runs along the middle of the tracks leaps to life like a subterranean serpent awakened out of the bowels of the earth. My eyes are fastened downhill, but the funicular descends from above in a series of glass boxes that look way too small to accommodate the waiting crowd. I'm damned if I'm going to wait underground any longer for the next one, though, so I push on with the rest of them—these Italians apparently having no boundary issues with private space when it comes to public transportation. I end up wedged into the armpit of a man wearing a soccer jersey, behind a man in a business suit whose copy of *La Repubblica* flutters against my head, and an old woman who comes up to my navel.

The car—the *cell,* I can't help thinking, the cell of the dying nun set in motion—plunges downward, its lights flickering off just as we hit the tunnel. We spend most of the descent in impermeable blackness. I close my eyes and try to ignore the squeezing sensation in the left side of my chest, like a hand that's reached in between my ribs and yanked out what remains of my injured lung. I swivel to get my face out of the soccer fan's armpit, but as I turn my hip rubs up against something hard. I realize that the man behind me, the one in the nice business suit, has an erection.

I open my eyes at the same instant that the lights go on and the businessman smiles at me, as if I'd just said something clever to him. He makes no attempt to move. I can feel the acid of two cappuccinos bubbling in my stomach, threatening to erupt, and then, mercifully, the train lurches to a stop, the glass doors slide open, and the crowd spills out.

It takes me a half hour to find the bus stop—the map Silvio gave me having only a tangential relationship with the layout of the streets around the port. The Castel d'Ovo squats between the port and the funicular station cutting off through streets. The streets that do run around it are a maze of construction barriers and deep pits. I turn down one street that's blocked by a mob of angry men shouting *"Sciopero! Sciopero!"* The striking taxi drivers, I realize.

Finally, I find the right bus to the train station and then, what feels like hours later, the train to Herculaneum. The Circumvesuviana is blessedly uncrowded compared to the funicular and the bus, but still un-air-conditioned. Once it moves, though, a breeze blows in through the open windows. When we've cleared Naples I can even smell a hint of salt air coming off the bay. The teenage girls who get on in Portici—once a favored resort of the Bourbons and now part of the urban sprawl clustered at the foot of Mount Vesuvius—are clearly headed for the beach. Neon-colored bathing suit straps slip down their tanned shoulders. They fish in their net bags for suntan lotion and rub each other's backs, chattering a bright stream of Italian out of which I catch stray phrases that flash in the air like tropical birds. *"Pensi che Gianni venga stasera alla festa?"* which I translate to "Do you think Gianni will be at the party?" and *"Mannaccia, mi sono venute le mestruazione!"* which I think means that she's mad she's got her period. Things teenaged girls might say anywhere. I find myself wishing I were on my way to the beach, too.

When I get off at Herculaneum, I smell the salt wind blowing up the street that slopes down to the bay. As I walk down the street, following signs for *Gli scavi,* I see the blue bay in the distance. I can even make out a misty shape on the horizon that might be Capri, and I imagine Phineas Aulus sailing through the straits between Capri and the tip of the Sorrentine peninsula, his ship tossed by a fierce sirocco—a wind that locals claim has sometimes brought rains of blood. Did he make a libation to the Minerva Tyrrhena, whose temple stood above the straits as a protection to sailors? Did he think this shore would be his last sight? Had he deliberately planned to set down near the Villa della Notte with his waterproof trunk? And where was that waterproof trunk now? Still buried in the tufa that entombs much of the villa? Was Petronia Iusta buried there, too?

Since seeing Iusta's name in Phineas's journal I've wondered what I hope to find at the villa. Of course I want to know what Phineas has to say about Iusta and whether she's at the villa as Calatoria's slave. The repetition of her name suggests that she made some kind of impression on him. For now, though, I'll be satisfied to see where she spent her last days.

At the main gate to ancient Herculaneum, I tell the guard that I have an appointment with the archaeological office to see the Villa della Notte. The guard, an old man with lines so deeply engraved into his weathered face that his cheeks look like the droopy folds of a hound dog, waves me in with the back of his hand, a gesture less welcoming than dismissive. He doesn't tell me where to go, but I've studied the map of the excavation and know that I have to keep walking toward the sea and then turn right. The Villa della Notte was just outside the city walls, and outside the gates of the public part of the excavated city, overlooking the sea. I follow the broad elevated road that runs beside the excavations. Below me I can see the ancient town of Herculaneum in a neat grid, many of its rooms open to the sunlight, while some roofs are still intact.

As the road descends and then curves to the right, the view of the sea vanishes. Below me is a row of patrician houses topping the marine wall. Built to catch the sea breeze, they are now sunk below ground level, their sea views blocked by a wall of tufa. I pass the Porta Marina that leads into the town and find the offices of the Scavi Acheologici behind the gift shop and ticket booth. Two gray-haired men—one mustached, the other clean-shaven—are playing a game of cards over a metal desk, their chairs angled toward an ancient rotary fan, frosted bottles of Aranciata sitting in wet rings by their sides. I present my letter of introduction from John Lyros to the man with the mustache and he passes it to the clean-shaven one. He takes out a pair of wire-rimmed eyeglasses, unfolds them, fits them on the bridge of his nose, and squints at the paper like a suspicious border guard. Sweat trickles down my back, my mouth watering for some of the orange soda, as I try to cobble together the Italian to ask where I, too, can buy a cold Aranciata. The dust-engrimed paddles of the fan stir the paper in the man's hand, but I am, maddeningly, just out of its cooling reach.

After examining my paperwork twice, the clean-shaven man looks over the rims of his eyeglasses at his mustached comrade. Lifting his bushy eyebrows, he says something I can't make out. A heated exchange follows that I imagine goes something like this: "You take her." "No, you! I took the last one." "Your ass, you did!" "Go to hell!"

The mustachioed gentleman loses. With barely a glance in my direction he picks up a set of heavy keys from an ashtray on top of the desk and brushes past me uttering the single word *Vieni!* Although his posture is indolent, I have to hurry to catch up to him at the back gate behind the office. He unlocks the gate that marks the boundary of the public excavations and we cross a narrow street where laundry hangs off the balconies of apartment buildings and a group of barefoot children are taking turns crowding onto an ancient Vespa to ride it up and down the street. It throws up a cloud of dust and exhaust fumes that hangs in the still air like a small mushroom cloud—like the cloud Pliny described as crowning the peak of Mount Vesuvius on August 24, AD 79. I check my watch and see it's half-past noon. No wonder the custodians were so disgusted to see me. It's time for the afternoon *riposo*. Only an idiot— or an American—would go out in this noonday sun.

"Mi dispiace," I begin as my escort unlocks a series of padlocks on a high chain-link gate posted with *Ingresso Vietato* signs and topped with concertina wire. But I can't figure out how to finish the sentence. The heat seems to have settled behind my eyes, like a wall between my brain and the rest of my senses, impeding any dialogue between the two. "Perhaps it will be cooler down below," I say aloud in English. My escort laughs, whether from the futility of the hope or the hopelessness of him understanding, I'm not sure.

As we start down the steep path into the pit that holds the Villa della Notte, he seems to take pity on me—or maybe he's given this tour so many times before that the guidebook speech is automatic. *"Ecco,"* he says, pointing to the water dripping down the tufa wall that borders the path, *"Uno dei due fiumi di Ercolano che è stato deviato per consentire gli scavi di questa zona."* He's telling me that the river was diverted to make way for the excavation. He points out where pipes are fitted into the wall. I remember that Herculaneum was built on a promontory between two streams—a situation that made it scenic and cool in the summer, but that ensured its doom when Mount Vesuvius unleashed its final ground surge and volcanic matter flowed down the mountain following the streambeds. At the bottom of the stairs we pass over a metal grate that covers the ill-omened stream. My guide points into the ditch and says, *"Ecco—i rani."*

I look at the green stagnant water, trying to remember what *rani* means, and then the guide kicks a pebble into the ditch and the viscous surface stirs, the green scum writhing like a snake and then breaking into a roiling mass. *"Rani,"* he repeats, chuckling and kicking in some more pebbles. Is *rani* Italian for some mythological creature—a scylla or a medusa—I wonder? And then I remember.

"Frogs," I say out loud. Identifying the slimy inhabitants of this underground river does little to reassure me. Wasn't the River Styx full of frogs? I feel as if I have descended into the underworld and I recall that according to mythology the house of Night is indeed in the underworld. "There also stands the gloomy house of Night," Hesiod wrote, "ghastly clouds shroud it in darkness."

I turn away from the dead river to where the guide is now pointing. *"La Villa della Notte,"* he says. No ghastly clouds shroud it, only stagnant, greenish air through which I squint at the far wall of the ditch. It's hard to make out the lines of the building emerging from the tufa like a body trapped in rock. It reminds me of Michelangelo's "Captives"—those half-finished statues in which Titans struggle against the imprisoning rock—and I recall that in Hesiod's version of the underworld the Titans are indeed chained to the subterranean rock as punishment for rising up against Zeus. I make out a number of gaping holes on the first level, then the diamond-shaped pattern of *opus sectile* on the wall of the second level, and, on the third, a row of columns that would have lined the peristylium that faced the sea, but which now face the blank wall of tufa. And although I know that the villa rests on the same ground it always did—that it's the ground that's risen around it—I have the feeling that the villa has been cast beneath the earth, just as the Titans were, as punishment for some unspeakable transgression.

I'm gasping in the pea-soup air as I follow the guide across the bottom of the pit, my ears ringing so loudly I'm unable to hear what he's saying. He points at the gaping holes near the ground and I assume he's telling me about the tunnels the eighteenth-century excavators dug until they found something worth taking. I nod stupidly at whatever he says, and parrot the stray words I catch: *i tombaroli, i ladri* . . . Presumably he's talking about how the original tunnelers were no better than thieves and tomb raiders. I wish I had thought to bring water. As I follow him up a steep flight of crumbling steps I feel my ears pop, like a diver surfacing too quickly. I close my eyes and try to imagine what this seaside terrace would have felt like on any day before August 24, AD 79. I try to feel the cool sea breeze fanning the terrace and hear the splash of a fountain from the inner courtyard, but all I hear is the croaking of frogs and all I feel is the smothering cloak of fetid air covering my nose and mouth.

"Attenzione, signora!" my guardian cries as I trip over a loose stone and stumble head first onto the peristylium.

My bare knees bang down hard onto the stone floor. What little breath I had flies out of my lungs like a swallow swooping out of my mouth. For a second I don't know if I'll be able to take in the next breath. Everything goes still around me as if suspended in time. I'm facing the far left wall of the courtyard where I see pale and ghostly shapes flitting across its deep red surface. Pompeian red: the color of the Roman underworld. In a flash I take in the struggling form of a girl being pulled into a chariot—Persephone seized by Hades—her mouth open in a soundless scream, and on the far right, her companions, their mouths gaping in horror. The whole scene appears wreathed in black like a mourning tableau, but then I realize it's my vision that's dimming from lack of oxygen. I put my hand on my chest and gingerly, slowly, take a shallow sip of air. It's like trying to drink tea that's too hot. I feel as though the air might burn up what's left of my lungs. It occurs to me that *this* is how many of the residents of Herculaneum died, choking on the poisonous gas let loose in the eruption.

My guide whacks me on the back and the air gusts into my lungs and out and in and out again. I cough and splutter until my throat is raw and my chest feels hollow. The guide offers me a sip of water from a metal canteen, which I take gratefully. He sits on a toppled column like he has all day, as if all visitors to the Villa della Notte came to it this way: on their knees and gasping for breath.

When my breathing has returned to something like normal, I get up and approach the wall painting. I feel light-headed and feverish, but no longer care. Although I've seen digital images of the Persephone frieze, they didn't capture the shock on Persephone's face, the lust in Hades's eyes, or the horror of her companions. There's also a feature to the story I've never seen depicted before. Grieving Demeter, leaving in her wake a trail of dead vegetation and scorched earth, strides toward her daughter's three companions, who cower in fear before her. In the next frieze the three women rise into the air, transformed into shrieking bird-women. Demeter has turned them into sirens as punishment for their negligence.

It's a rather unconventional telling of the myth, but not nearly as unconventional as the subjects on the back wall of the courtyard. I'm sure I've never seen pictures of this wall painting.

"*E stato reinvenuto. . . . recentemente?*" I ask, pointing toward the back wall. This must be the part of the villa only recently excavated.

"*Sì, l'estate scorsa.*" Last summer. "*Non si possono fare foto, signora. Capisce?*" he adds, "Signore Lyros says no photos."

So Lyros hasn't made the find public yet. I recall that for her paper Agnes had to write to him for the barest descriptions of the wall because he said he didn't want any pictures published before the entire wall was excavated. I notice that portions of the wall are still covered with tufa. From what I can see of it, I can imagine why he's keeping it under wraps.

In the first frame, a young girl kneels before a trunk—the trunk itself is painted with another rendition of the Rape of Persephone. Above the kneeling girl are the three winged sirens. One carries a *liknon* and one carries a *thyrsus*—the traditional basket and wand of

Dionysian revels that Agnes had mentioned in her report—but I don't recall her mentioning the object held by the third siren. She brandishes a phallus-handled whip that is arched in the air like an angry cat's back, about to descend on the girl's naked shoulders. In the next two scenes the girl is helped to disrobe by the three sirens and then bathed. The bath she is helped into is shaped like a sarcophagus and adorned with scenes of maenads—female worshippers of Dionysus—dancing and running through the woods in pursuit of some horned animal. Or perhaps, I think, leaning closer, it's a man, wearing a horned mask. It could be a rendition of the scene in *The Bacchae* in which Agave chases and dismembers her own son. Waiting in the next frieze is a naked man with pointed ears sprawled on a couch and holding a lyre, a wreath of grape leaves around his head. From his pointy ears and lascivious grin I would guess he's supposed to be Dionysus.

When I get to the next scene my face goes hot. I suddenly become aware of the warm fetid air, the croak of the frogs, and my mustachioed escort standing quietly behind me. It's not that I haven't seen Roman erotica before. There's a whole room of it in the Naples Archaeological Museum (Gabinetto Segreto, as it's referred to: the Secret Cabinet). But I've never seen an example so brutal.

The girl from the previous scenes lies spread-eagled on a couch. Her arms are held by one of the winged sirens while the other two each hold one of her ankles. Dionysus is climbing onto the edge of the couch, his penis curved like a saber, aimed at the girl's exposed vagina. The girl's eyes are rolled up in their sockets, her mouth open in a scream, but the sirens only smile down at her, their wings beating the air into a lather of white down. For a moment I hear the sound of their wings, but then I realize it's the sound of blood rushing in my ears.

"Il resto è nascosto." The guide gestures toward the right end of

the wall, still covered with the putty-colored tufa. The rest remains hidden.

"Bene," I say, meaning *Okay, I've seen enough,* but when the guide laughs I realize he thinks I mean that I'm glad the rest of the story is still covered. Am I? Then why is it so hard to look away? Why is it that the longer I look at the girl's face the harder it is to tell what I read there: pain, pleasure, fear, knowledge? Or some stranger mixture of them all?

"I Misteri," I say primly, trying to regain a bit of scholarly distance and save face in front of the guide. After all, I know all about mystery rites, from the veneration of the phallus in the Dionysian rites to the ritual whipping in the Lupercalia and the castration of the Galli in the rites of Cybele. By AD 79, most of those rites would probably be more symbolic than actual. The presence of this mural doesn't necessarily mean that such scenes were reenacted here at the Villa della Notte.

Still, I suddenly want to be far away from the villa—out of this tufa pit—and back at my hotel in time for a dip in that rooftop pool, to wash away the heat I feel rising off my skin.

"I've seen enough," I try to explain to my guide. *"A me questo basta."* But he either doesn't understand or he feels obliged to do the whole tour. He proceeds to show me around the courtyard, pointing to the circle that marked the center fountain and the plinth where the statue of the goddess Nyx would have stood.

"A Napoli," he says, by which he means that the statue of Night is now in the National Archaeological Museum of Naples. I'm almost glad. I'd rather not have that gloomy goddess's eyes watching as the guard continues the obligatory tour, pointing out wherever a fragment of painted fresco still clings to a wall. Most of the images seem innocent enough at first—playful cupids riding horses and pulling carts—but when I look closer they're strangely suggestive. In one the tiny cupids are riding sea horses. Charming enough until

you notice one is actually copulating with his mount. In another a winged woman offers a bunch of grapes to a cupid, but if you look closely the grapes appear to be shaped like miniature breasts and one of the cupids is reaching out to pinch the woman's breast.

By the time we've completed the tour and begun the climb up to the modern street level, I feel as though the whole villa is infused with a spirit of corruption that I want to escape. No wonder Vitalis wanted to get her daughter out of here! I shudder, recalling that Iusta had ended up back in Calatoria's clutches, and wonder if she were forced to partake in the villa's depraved rites. Unless, I think as I fish in my purse for a few euros to give my guide, Vesuvius erupted before the rites could take place. I almost hope it did.

When I hold out a five-euro bill the guide shakes his head. *"Non è necessario, signora,"* he says. *"E stato una grande piacere fare conoscere questi misteri a una carissima amica del Signor Lyros."*

My face turns hot again. I remind myself that *carissima amica* may mean any dear female friend, not a girlfriend. I start to explain that I've never even met John Lyros, but the guide has turned to unlock the gates to the main excavations and is shouting a greeting to his colleague, who appears to be awakening from a nap. So I say my thousand thank-yous—*grazie mille*—and wave as I start the walk back to the train station. At the gate I turn back in the direction of the villa and glimpse the bay above the high tufa wall that nearly two thousand years ago sealed this town in its rock tomb. It occurs to me that Phineas Aulus might have come here expressly to witness the rites practiced at the Villa della Notte. He was, after all, a connoisseur of the exotic and the depraved. And now, I think as I turn my back to the sea, those mysteries lie curled tightly in on themselves within a charred papyrus roll, like a butterfly asleep in its chrysalis, awaiting the light of modern science to set them free.

1 buy a cold Aranciata at the station and sit by an open window on the train ride back, but I still feel as though I'm wearing the day's heat like a winding cloth made out of the same green scum that coats the frog river. When the train stops at Portici, a voice comes over the loudspeaker announcing a delay. I can't make out the reasons given—if any—or how long we're supposed to be stuck here. Without the breeze generated by movement, the car simmers in the heat. I look around to see if any of my fellow passengers are bothered by the delay and to see if I can gather from their conversations any more details about its cause and duration, but no one seems the least bit surprised to be sitting here in a stalled train baking in the midday sun.

An old man takes out a salami and pares a thin circle off with his penknife. The smell of the garlicky meat makes my stomach rumble and I remember I haven't eaten since breakfast. Two girls returning from the beach sleepily braid each other's damp hair and the tropical scent of their suntan oil mixes with the garlic. Everyone else on the train—a pair of nuns, three elderly women who look enough alike to be sisters, and a half-dozen workmen—appears to be dozing. I close my eyes, hoping to pass the time in sleep as well, but the moment I start to drowse off a loud plaintive bleat startles me awake. I open my eyes and see that an accordion player has entered the car. As he pumps air in and out of the instrument, a small girl walks up and down the aisle holding out a grimy paper cup for money. Most of the occupants of the train ignore her; one man gives the girl a push and shouts *"Vai!"* The girl's dark eyes narrow and she spits out a curse that, while I can't understand it, sounds way beyond her years.

Not that I can really tell how old she is. She has the height of a seven-year-old, the walk of a preteen, and, when she curses, the face of an old woman. When she approaches me I see how her ribs emboss the thin, stained cotton of the T-shirt she wears as her sole garment. I reach into my purse to extract the five-euro note I was going to give to my guide when I hear a high-pitched keening coming from outside the train. A woman in a long dress, wrapped like a sari, is striding back and forth on the station platform, emitting short, sharp shrieks. I can't identify the nationality of her garb, but I notice she has the same olive skin, lank black hair, and dark eyes as the accordion player and the little girl. Nor can I make out her language. She sounds like a seagull or, I can't help but think, like what I imagine the sirens might have sounded like when they saw themselves turning into birds.

Her cries don't draw the accordion player toward her, though. He folds up his instrument and swoops down on the girl, who's still standing by my side waiting for her five-euro note. As the accordion player picks her up she shoots out her hand and I feel her little fingers clasp onto my wrist with a pincerlike grip.

"Wait!" I say as the accordion player starts to carry her away. I find the five-euro note and press it into the girl's other hand—the one not clamped onto my wrist. *"Per lei,"* I say, meaning, I suppose, keep this for yourself, but as I watch her carried off I realize how futile my gesture was. Of course any money she gets will go to the accordion player, and now I wonder, as the long-skirted woman sweeps into the car, whether the accordion player is even the girl's father. The way the woman is chasing after them he might have snatched the child to use as a lure for begging, and now the girl's mother is trying to get her back. Certainly the way she sweeps through the car, her skirts and long hair flying, her dark eyes flashing, makes her look like a mother whose child has been stolen from her. When I look down I almost expect to see her footprints seared into the train floor—Demeter's feet scorching the earth—but instead I see something almost more surprising: she's barefoot. And yet she's striding through the car as surefooted as a general in riding boots, her gaze swiveling up and down to locate her lost daughter. When her gaze lights on me it's like being swept by a searchlight.

"They went that way." I point to the door the man left by. She turns and sees the accordion player and the little girl at the far end of the platform, begging from a group of tourists, and starts toward the door just as the train jerks to life and the doors begin to shut. She stumbles and nearly falls in my lap. For a second I feel the heat of her and smell some exotic oil in her hair, and then she's gone in a flourish of printed cotton that beats the air like wings. She escapes through the door just before it closes, alighting on the platform with the grace of a dancer. As the train moves away I watch her turn toward the accordion player and the girl, but instead of approaching them she turns in the opposite direction and walks away.

What in the world? I think, staring out the window until her figure disappears in the distance. *What was all that about?* Was she the girl's mother, or was she another beggar protecting her turf? I play the scene over again in my head, searching for clues, but the events remain as elusive as the murals in the Villa della Notte. A modern-day mystery rite. I try to dismiss the whole thing from my head, but I can't forget the woman's cries or the look in the girl's eyes or the way she clutched my wrist. At the memory of her touch I look down at my wrist and find the clue that unlocks at least part of the mystery: my watch is gone.

The trip back seems endless—perhaps because I no longer know what time it is, perhaps because each vehicle I board is a little hotter and a little more crowded than the last. By the time I get out of the funicular station, the street back to the hotel looks as steep as the slope of Mount Vesuvius. I trudge up the hill, listening to my lungs wheeze at every step. I'm almost there—I can see the hotel's awning—when the edges of my vision begin to turn black. I put a hand on the wall and lean up against it, so if I faint I won't fall into the street. The surface I'm leaning against is fluted marble, smooth and cool to the touch, one of two Corinthian columns that frame the entrance to a church, the interior of which looks cool and dim. I'll just go inside for a minute, I reason, and sit in a pew until I feel better.

The church is tiny. Fewer than a dozen pews are on either side of a center nave lined with Corinthian columns. A shallow apse holds a small statue of the Madonna and child set in a niche and surrounded by candles. The floor is marble, too, so old and worn that there are grooves from where worshippers have knelt over the centuries. I imagine that it was built on the site of a Roman temple, as many early churches were, and I wonder if it belonged to the convent that's now my hotel. The faded frescoes lining the deeply shadowed aisles no doubt tell the story of some saint's life, but I'm too tired to look at them. Besides, I'd feel a little guilty acting like a tourist in a Catholic church, even though I haven't gone to church since I was twelve. I had started complaining about going after my mother died. Around that time my grandmother told me I ought to thank God every day that we were Catholics because "your mother wanted to have an abortion but Grandfather and I forbade it." That unwelcome piece of knowledge did not have its desired effect. I stopped going to church altogether. Maybe because I suspected that my grandparents' religion might have saved my life at the expense of my mother's.

I'm surprised at how restful it is here. I light a candle for Odette and one for Barry Biddle in front of the worn figure of the Madonna, and head back to the hotel, holding in my mind a picture of its rooftop pool—its circle of turquoise water beckoning to me like water in the Sahara.

When I ask for my key at the front desk, though, Silvio informs me that not only the pool but the rooftop restaurant as well are closed tonight for a private party.

"What do you mean 'closed'?" I ask, my voice sounding dangerously close to tears. "The website promised a pool!" I sound like a spoiled child who's been denied some treat, but I don't care. "And where am I supposed to eat?"

"There are many excellent restaurants just a short funicular ride away."

"Fuck the funicular," I say, shocking both myself and Silvio. "I am never, ever getting on that glassed-in cattle car again. And look!" I hold up my bare wrist meaning to tell Silvio about my stolen watch, but he flinches as though I had been about to slap him. My hand drops of its own accord, all the fight sapped out of me, shame flushing hot through my face. "I'm sorry. I'm just really hot and tired."

"Of course, signora, you Americans are often unprepared for the heat. Why don't you take a nice cool shower and then have something to eat?"

I bite back the temptation to tell him I'm not an American, I'm a Texan, and I know from heat. Let him come to Austin in August and see how he does! Instead I nod meekly and say, "Yes, that sounds lovely. Something light. I'm sure I'll feel better once I've taken a shower and gotten some sleep."

I go upstairs to my airless cell, strip off my soaked clothes and take a long, cool shower. The water's chill doesn't penetrate the layer of heat under my skin, though. By the time I've brushed out my wet hair, I'm sweating again. I put on my lightest cotton T-shirt and lie on the bed. I'll just take a nap before dinner, I think, and then maybe I will brave the funicular. The thought of being stuck in this cell all night is almost more unbearable than the thought of going out again.

When I open my eyes again I see by the window that it's completely dark out, which means that it must be past nine o'clock. I can't tell exactly what time because there's no clock in the room and my watch is gone. It's probably too late to get room service, which is okay, because I'm not hungry, only very, very thirsty. I get out an aqua minerale from the mini fridge and gulp half of it down in one long swallow and then lie back down in the fleshy embrace of the overstuffed mattress and feel myself being sucked into a tunnel of flesh-colored tufa. It's as if the rock that covered ancient Herculaneum had turned liquid again and swallowed me whole.

I fall into a deep sleep and land in a room painted red as a beating heart, its walls covered with figures from the Villa della Notte: Demeter, Persephone, Hades, Dionysus playing his lyre, and the three winged sirens. Hades wears a suit and tie, his face speckled with unshaved stubble. With flaming footsteps, Demeter walks toward Dionysus and seizes the instrument in his hand. It's not a lyre; it's an accordion. When she squeezes the accordion it makes a sound like an animal being slaughtered, a keening of wild cats . . .

I open my eyes to the room at the Hotel Convento and hear the sound coming from outside my window. I get up to close it, lingering for a moment in the faint stir of air playing over my soaked T-shirt. Had I gone swimming after all? I wonder. I can't remember. My whole body aches as if I had swum the length of the Bay of Naples. My lungs feel as if I've inhaled dirty seawater, and the air in the room ripples as if even now I'm underwater.

I start back to the bed, but find myself on the floor. It seems like too much trouble to get up and, besides, I notice that the majolica tiles around the base of the wall are decorated with little figures: a miniature version of the murals of the Villa della Notte. No wonder John Lyros recommended this hotel, I think, lying flat on the stone floor so that I can see the tiles better. And of course I see now why the air-conditioning wasn't necessary—the floor is deliciously cool! I lay my cheek on it and feel waves of cold emanating up from the stone. Why, it's like a Roman bath! There must be cold water running underneath to cool off the room. I can hear it, flowing like a river beneath me, carrying me along. The figures in the tiles fly by now, like dioramas in a Disney ride: Hades steals Persephone; Demeter ravages the earth, demanding vengeance in sacrifice; her daughter's companions turn into winged sirens; and they in turn sacrifice a young girl. They hold her down as the god approaches. I feel their wings beating the air above me, pressing the air out of my chest like a giant bellows, their bony hands sharp as birds' beaks pecking at my wrists.

Later in the night someone changes the temperature of the water beneath the floor. It's hot now and the water seeps through the tiles. It soaks my T-shirt and my hair. If I don't move soon I'll drown. When I open my eyes, though, I'm distracted by the pictures on the tiles. They, too, have changed. They tell the same story only with different actors playing the main roles. Hades, I see with little surprise, is now played by Elgin Lawrence. I'd always thought that with his high cheekbones, slanted eyes, and pointed ears he looked like a blond Satan.

The next time I open my eyes it's light. Hovering above me is a woman with the same dark eyes as the beggar on the train, only now she's dressed in a maid's uniform. Then beside her appears Elgin Lawrence who tells the dark-eyed woman something and she leaves, shouting someone's name as she goes, the sound of her voice getting smaller and smaller as she runs down the hall. I close my eyes again and press my cheek against the floor. I feel Elgin's arms around me and although I realize that he may take me to Hades, I don't fight. I'm cold again and his arms feel marvelously warm.

When I open my eyes again, I'm in the bed. Elgin is there and another man who, I think, must be the god come to ravage me because his hands are under my T-shirt. Then I feel something cool and metallic on my chest and realize that he's only trying to listen to my lungs. He's a doctor, the small still rational part of my brain tells me. He'll want my medical history—the shooting, the damage to my lung—but does my "history" start there? Don't I have to go farther back? Because, really, my *history* begins with the story of how my mother drowned in the San Marcos River.

"Yes, I know," I say when Elgin looks at me doubtfully, "of all places! Home of Ralph the Diving Pig and the Aquarena Springs Mermaid show! My mother picked me up one day from school and without even stopping to tell my grandparents where we were going we drove all the way to San Marcos to Aquarena Springs. Ralph was a bit of a disappointment. In the postcards he looks like he's soaring through the air, but in real life he kind of skitters up to the bank, herded by a workman in green overalls, and just *falls in*. But the mermaids were the most beautiful thing I'd ever seen. There were three of them—a blonde, a redhead, and a brunette—their long hair streaming around them like floating clouds, and they wore seashells over their breasts and had shiny silver-green tails. I loved them so much I cried when the show was over and then my mother did the most amazing thing! She went right outside and bought us tickets to the next show so we could see it again—and when *that* show was over she turned to me, her eyes shining in the murky light of the Undersea Theater, and asked *Do you want to see it again?*

"She looked as pretty as any of those mermaids at that moment, her skin sparkling as if it had been dipped in the same silver as the mermaids' tails, her long dark hair as light and bouncy as if she were floating in water, her eyes as green as river water. If I said yes, she would be happy for us to sit there all day and watch the Mermaid Show until nightfall. It was an exhilarating idea, like eating as much candy as you wanted, but also somehow frightening, like that part in Pinocchio where the bad boys all go to Boytown. So I said no, I'd had enough, and afterward we sat on the edge of the river, dangling our feet in water so clear you could see all the way down to the bottom, where long strands of river grass waved in the current. A gentle current. How could anyone ever drown in water that gentle?"

Elgin squeezes my hand and nods his agreement. Of course, he's been to San Marcos. He knows.

"So when they told me she drowned in the San Marcos I thought at first it was a lie, but then later . . ." I hesitate, because this is the part I feel worst about, but Elgin squeezes my hand again so I go on. "Later I thought about how my mother had looked that day at the Mermaid Show and I wondered if she just got lost at the bottom of the river—hypnotized by the sway of the river grass—and forgotten to come up for air. And I couldn't help wondering, since my grandmother was always telling me how alike we were, if the same thing mightn't happen to me."

The only person I ever told this story to was Ely and when I did he said it was funny because when his brother, Paul, died he heard his parents say that his lungs had filled with water and so Ely had always thought that Paul had drowned, and so it was like we'd both lost the people we loved the most to drowning, and it meant we were meant to be together. That we were the same.

The two men looked at each other and nodded. The one who'd

examined me took out a needle and gave me a shot in the arm. I tried to explain why I couldn't go to sleep. That I had a hereditary risk of forgetting to breathe and drowning on dry land.

I fell asleep while trying to explain this theory, but I could feel myself falling, drifting away on the current. They must have understood because Elgin lifted me out of the bed. He lifted me up and carried me out of the room and out of the Hotel Convento. When I woke up next I saw blue sky over me and smelled the sea. Elgin was leaning over me.

"We're taking you to the island," he said. "We can take care of you better there."

"As long as you promise not to let me forget to breathe or sink to the bottom of the river," I say.

This makes him laugh. He leans down close to me and I see his eyes are the same blue as the sky. He takes my hand and squeezes it. "I promise I'll remind you to breathe. And I won't let you sink. I'm going to hold on to you the whole way."

And he does. It's a long boat trip, but he holds my hand the whole way and every time I feel like I'm falling he squeezes my hand and says, "Hold on." So I do. When I open my eyes I see an immense tower of rock above me climbing from the sea to the sky. Swallows are looping through the bright air. Houses so white they look like they've been carved out of sugar cling to the steep slopes. The air is so sweet that no one could ever forget to breathe here. We've come, I think, to the island of the sirens.

CHAPTER 10

1 wake up in a white room that smells like the sea, surrounded by the sound of falling water. I've been here some time. Days, I think, but it might just as well be weeks. And I've been sick. There had been an IV, but it's gone now. There had been a wheezing that in my delirium I had thought was the accordion player from the train, but that I realize now was my own breathing. Now, though, the only sound is from falling water that is somewhere beyond an open doorway. There's a glass of water on a wooden table by my bed.

When I sit up, the room moves a little, like a boat rocking on the sea. Then it steadies. I drink some water and listen. The sound of water is real. I get up and find that I can stand. I can walk if I take very small, very slow steps, but it seems like an age before I reach the doorway. I lean on the door frame and look out into the courtyard.

In the center of a circular fountain stands the bronze statue of a veiled woman. I recognize the goddess Night by her star-studded veil, the poppies in her hair, and the owl that sits upon her shoulder. She's less foreboding than I would have thought, standing in the sunlight that turns the sprays from the fountain into streamers of jewels that glisten in the woman's hair and in the profusion of flowers growing around the fountain. It's so bright and colorful that it hurts my eyes and I focus on the shaded walkway that rims the courtyard. What I see there only makes my head spin more. The figures from my dream have followed me here. Beneath the colonnade across from me I see black-cloaked Hades seizing Persephone, fiery-footed Demeter turning the girl's companions into shrieking sirens. When I turn to the long wall along the back of the courtyard I see the outlines of figures, insubstantial as ghosts. The only two figures that have bulk and color are a man with a shaved head and a plump, bearded satyr. It's only a painting, I tell myself, but then one of the figures detaches itself from the wall and turns toward me. As he walks into the sunlight I see his eyes are the light purple of dusk. He moves quickly toward me, as if afraid I'll escape, but I could tell him it's not necessary. The only place I'm going is down.

When I wake up again I'm back in bed and the man with the lilac eyes is sitting in a chair reading a newspaper.

"I thought you were Hades," I say, "but then I guess Hades wouldn't be reading a newspaper."

"Oh, I don't know," he says, lowering the paper and smiling at me. "I think it would please him to see the current state of the world. I can't claim such an impressive lineage, though. I'm John Lyros." He puts out his hand for a formal shake.

"My new boss," I say, putting my hand in his. "How'm I doing so far?"

He laughs. "Well, you're going to live, which is more than we were sure of a few days ago when Dr. Lawrence found you at the hotel."

"So it *was* Elgin," I say. "I thought I might have dreamt him." I wince at a painfully vivid image of myself lying on the floor of my room in the Hotel Convento in my T-shirt and panties, and Lyros's eyes narrow with concern. He takes a bottle of pills out of his pocket and shakes one out. "What was he doing at my hotel? I mean, how did he know I was sick?"

"I told him where you were staying and he went to see if you wanted to go to Sorrento with him. The concierge said you hadn't left your room since the afternoon before and that you hadn't seemed well." I wince again, remembering cursing at Silvio, and wonder what else he might have told Elgin. Lyros helps me sit up and gives me the pill. He holds the water glass to my lips and waits for me to swallow before continuing. "Dr. Lawrence insisted the maid open your door and check on you and they found you feverish and delirious. He called me and I sent for a private doctor who diagnosed pneumonia."

"Why wasn't I taken to a hospital in Naples?"

"My dear, have you ever been to a hospital in Naples? I knew we could take much better care of you here. I sent the *Parthenope*—the institute's boat—and Elgin and the doctor brought you back."

"Yes, I remember that." Unfortunately I also vaguely recall blathering to Elgin about my mother and the Aquarena Springs Mermaid Show. "What happened to Elgin? Is he still here?"

"He had that appointment to keep in Sorrento." Of course, I think, a new flirtation. Trust Elgin to find a new girl in every port. "But he only left when I assured him you'd be taken care of. He's still there, although truthfully I'm not exactly sure what he's up to. There are no archaeological sites or museums in Sorrento."

"Knowing Elgin, it's a girl he met on the plane over. . . . I'm afraid the UT arm of the Papyrus Project has been a disappointment to you, Mr. Lyros. Do I still have a job?"

He laughs and it's the best sound I've heard in a while. "You'd better have. I've got several pages of Phineas Aulus's book scanned and ready for you to read. I can't wait to see what you make of it. But first, let's get you something to eat. We've got to build you up. I don't want you getting pneumonia again."

For the next few days John Lyros personally oversees the project of "building me up." He starts by bringing me tea in delicate china cups and ordering me light lunches of pasta in brodo and hard-boiled eggs, brought to me by a unsmiling matronly housekeeper in crisp white blouse and black skirt. On the second day I graduate to crusty rolls spread with fresh mozzarella and thinly sliced tomatoes and the housekeeper rewards me with a smile and her name— Guilia. I smile back. The tomatoes are amazing. I can't get enough of them. Every time I eat one I can feel my poor dehydrated cells plumping up.

Good for the blood, she says to me in Italian, shaking her fist at me. Then she strikes her own chest. Does she mean that it's good for the heart, I wonder, or is she offering herself as a example of the healing properties of tomatoes? Certainly she is the picture of good health herself, from her plump oval face to her sleekly coiled black hair. Even her coral earrings and the gold cross around her neck seem to gleam with some special power.

By the third day I'm eating the tomatoes with eggs in the morning, with mozzarella and olive oil for lunch, and heaped on pasta at night. (At night the housekeeper looks tired and doesn't return my smile.) It's like getting a blood transfusion, only this red liquid tastes like a mixture of Mediterranean sun and sea air, like it's got oxygen in it. Everything looks brighter, even the housekeeper, who smiles at me again in the morning and who, I notice, has added a string of coral beads around her neck.

After three days on the Caprese tomato diet I'm strong enough to take a stroll around the courtyard. John Lyros insists I hold on to his arm in case I have another fainting spell. We do a slow circle around the fountain, the cool sprays making prisms in the bright air. Then he takes me out onto the peristylium, which faces the sea. At the balustrade he releases my arm, letting me lean on the marble ledge, and points out the landmarks of the bay: the long arm of the Sorrentine peninsula to our right, the cape of Misenum to our left. In the middle Mount Vesuvius stands placidly against a calm blue sky. The whole setting is so serene—even crowded, boisterous Naples looks tranquil from here—that it's hard to imagine the violence of a volcanic eruption disrupting the calm. So it must have seemed to the residents of Herculaneum and Pompeii on the morning of August 24, AD 79.

"There's Herculaneum," he says, pointing straight ahead. "If it weren't below sixty-five feet of tufa, we could see the Villa della Notte. That's why I chose this spot for my restored villa, because it has such a good view of the original. I like to think of the inhabitants of the villa standing on their peristylium looking out across the bay and seeing this spot."

"It's eerie," I say, looking back at the courtyard with its fountain and wall paintings. "It looks so much like what I imagine the original must have that I forgot we weren't in Herculaneum. Is the rest of the villa designed to look like the original?"

"The lower level is laid out according to the plan of the villa we found in one of the papyri, but it's not decorated like the original because we won't know what those rooms looked like until they're excavated. Besides, we need more modern amenities for the labs. Come, I'll show you."

He takes my arm again and we cross the courtyard to the west side and descend a flight of stairs that begin next to my bedroom.

At the bottom of the stairs we enter a small enclosed courtyard, a swimming pool at its center. An orange inflatable raft bobs on the surface of the turquoise water and brightly colored lawn chairs and umbrellas are drawn up around one side of the pool.

"I decided that until we know what kind of fountain the lower courtyard had we might as well have the comfort of a pool. If you prefer to bathe in the ocean, though, there's a staircase down to our own little grotto. Just be careful on the steps—they're quite steep. The kitchens are through there." Lyros points through a doorway on the south side of the courtyard. "And the labs are through here." He leads me to a door opposite the stairs. "We usually have our breakfast around the pool because it's close to the lab. Perhaps to-morrow you'll want to join the others." We walk through a corridor lined with white boards with grids marked out in black erasable ink—like a hospital surgery roster, only the "patients" on these boards are papyrus scrolls waiting to be scanned.

Lyros opens a door to a gleaming lab fitted out with stainless-steel cabinets, glass tables, and several machines that look like a cross between a camera and a microscope, each one perched on long spidery legs above a glass table. The room is a curious mixture of museum, hospital lab, and darkroom. On the walls, held be-tween sheets of glass like laboratory specimens, hang fragments of papyrus scrolls that are the color and texture of dead skin. For a moment the medicinal atmosphere of the room, and perhaps my recent illness, makes me think they *are* pieces of skin and I shiver at the idea.

"I'm sorry," Lyros says, "we keep this room cool to protect the scrolls and the equipment."

"It's probably the best air-conditioned room in the Campania." The voice comes from behind one of the hulking machines, star-tling me because I'd thought we were alone in the room. The man tilts himself sideways and I see why I had missed him: he's so skinny that he'd been totally eclipsed by the scanning machine. In fact, when he stands up I'm struck by how much, with his large wobbly head, dangling arms, and pencil-thin legs, he looks like one of the scanning machines.

"George Petherbridge," he says in a British accent, extending his hand to me. His grip is bony and cool. "Glad to see you up and about, Dr. Chase."

"George is on loan to us from Oxford," Lyros explains. "He worked on the Oxyrhynchus Project."

"The scrolls discovered in an Egyptian garbage dump? I've read about them. Didn't you recover part of a lost tragedy by Sophocles?"

"That's right," George says, grinning. "And we had a lot worse to deal with than a little burning around the edges. The Oxyrhynchus scrolls had been damaged by water and mud. The papyri we're dealing with here are remarkably unharmed inside their charred shells—the trick is separating the layers of writing and finding the right spectrum for the ink used on each individual papyrus. Take the Phineas Aulus scroll—"

"Is that what you're working on there?" I point at the machine George still has one hand on.

"Yes," he says, patting the metal scanner as though it were a pet dog. "As per your instructions, John, I've been concentrating on this scroll. We've been able to scan about half of it. Miss Hancock has been transcribing the results into a computer document."

"Agnes Hancock? Is she here today?"

"She's gone to make us some tea. I know she'll be happy to see you; she's been worried about how sick you were. Would you like a peek at the Phineas scroll while you wait?"

"Yeah, absolutely." Truthfully, I'm more anxious to see Agnes— I guiltily remember that I'd promised Sam Tyler I'd keep an eye on her, and I've been in Italy for over a week without giving her one thought—but once I bend down to the machine to look through the lens and see Phineas's beautifully inscribed letters I feel a tingle of recognition.

"Our friend Phineas used an ink high in iron-gall, which means it shows up best under an ultraviolet spectrum. Here—" Petherbridge adjusts a dial and the outlines of the letters sharpen. I make out the words *whip* and *flagellate* and *flesh* in Latin and suddenly, even though the room is cold, I feel as if I'm back in the hot tufa pit looking at the painted figure of the siren raising her whip over the bare flesh of the suppliant girl. Was Phineas describing the wall painting at the Villa della Notte? But then I notice that the verb is in the first person and I put the sentence together: *I whipped the girl until the blood rose to her skin . . .* I lift my head up so quickly that I make myself dizzy. Lyros grabs my elbow to steady me.

"I think you've been on your feet long enough," he says, helping me to a chair. "Ah, here's Agnes with that tea. Perhaps you can get a cup for Dr. Chase. . . ."

"I already have." Agnes puts down a china teacup at my side. "The intercom was on, so I knew you were here, Dr. Chase."

I look up from the steaming cup to Agnes's face and I am amazed by the transformation that a few weeks in Italy has worked. Agnes's skin has turned golden; her hair is shiny and sun-streaked. She's put on just enough weight to take the gauntness out of her. Clearly there's no need for me to feel guilty about neglecting Sam's charge to watch over her: she's thriving on a Mediterranean diet of sun and olive oil.

"Thanks, Agnes," I say, sipping the hot, sweet tea. "It's good to see you. Capri obviously agrees with you."

"Isn't it just the most beautiful place on earth? Wait till you see the Blue Grotto!" Agnes's eyes shine with the same unearthly blue that the Capri landmark is famous for. "We even have our own grotto. Professor Lawrence and I went swimming there last week. I don't ever want to leave!"

George Petherbridge and John Lyros share a smile at Agnes's enthusiasm, but I take another hurried sip of tea, scalding my mouth, to hide the flicker of worry that darts through my mind. Agnes sounds like someone bewitched, and I'm hardly thrilled to hear she's been spending time with Elgin.

"To tell you the truth, I haven't gotten to see much of the island yet," I say.

"Well, when Dr. Lawrence gets back—" Agnes begins, but John Lyros interrupts her.

"We'll have to rectify that as soon as you've got your strength back. For now, though, I think we'd better get you out of this cold room and back upstairs."

"Yes," I concede, feeling like an ancient invalid, "but I wish I could start doing something for the project. I'd love to have a look at whatever you've got transcribed of Phineas's scroll."

"I can make a copy of the file and send it to your laptop," Agnes offers. "I haven't translated it yet, but the bits I was able to sight-read sounded fascinating. The Petronii really got up to some wild goings-on here . . . I mean . . . there." She giggles. "Sometimes I forget that this isn't the original villa."

"Why don't you do that?" Lyros says to Agnes. Then, putting a hand on my elbow as I get up, he says to me, "Why don't you take a nap and then when you wake up it will be ready for you."

"I'll get right on it," Agnes says eagerly. "It will be the perfect thing to keep your mind occupied while you're recuperating."

I return Agnes's smile, but as John Lyros steers me from the room I can't help but think that from what I've just seen of Phineas's book, it won't be restful reading.

I go back to my room and find the housekeeper setting up a tray for me.

"I'll be eating with the rest of the staff from now on," I tell her in Italian, "so you won't have to keep bringing me my meals. You've been very, very kind," I add, hoping to earn one of her rare smiles. But the face she turns to me is dour and I notice that she's not wearing the coral necklace. Is it that wearing the necklace makes her smile, I wonder, or that she wears the necklace on days when she's feeling happy? It's a mystery.

When I finish my lunch—a delicious pasta dish with a sauce made from eggplants, sardines, and raisins, bread, and, of course, a plate of tomatoes and mozzarella—I try to read some of the Phineas volumes I brought with me, but the heavy lunch has left me too sleepy. I curl up on my bed, planning to take a short nap, but when I wake up it's dark already. I had slept so soundly I hadn't heard anyone come into my room, but there's a tray on a chair by my bed with a covered dish and a note from Agnes that says, "Look in your e-mail—I've sent you the Phineas!"

Not trusting myself to eat another meal without yielding to its soporific effect, or to read in bed, I transfer the tray to my bed, drag the chair to the doorway, use it to prop open the door so that I've got plenty of air from the courtyard to keep me awake, and sit down on it with my laptop in my lap. I check to make sure the courtyard is empty. It is; the only light comes from a full moon that has just risen above the eastern edge of the villa. I open my laptop, download the document Agnes has sent me, and open up the file labeled PHINEAS. Two columns appear: the Latin text transcribed from the scroll, and a "rough" translation she's prepared. I start out by reading back and forth between the two, but after noting how good her Latin translation is I read the English, only glancing occasionally back at the Latin to check a word or two.

I knew it was a lucky day that delivered me from shipwreck and brought me to this safe harbor, he wrote, dating his entry DIES SAT- URNI AD XII KAL. SEP DCCCXXXIII A.U.C., which Agnes has translated as August 21, AD 79, *but I did not know how lucky until last night when the mistress of the house told me its secret.*

I smile at Phineas's teasing introduction and look out the doorway to the courtyard where the bronze statue of the goddess Night gleams in the moonlight. The patter of the fountain and the more distant sound of the sea fade away as I enter Phineas's world.

My hostess Calatoria Vimidis began the evening by apologizing for the fare. "Since my husband's death, and with the children in Rome, I live here quite simply."

"I am most sorry to learn that Gaius Petronius Stephanus is no longer with us. He had a reputation as a man of great learning and discrimination and I would have liked to have seen what he thought of some of the works I have brought back with me. . . . But you mustn't apologize for your more than generous hospitality. Everything is delicious," I told her with perfect veracity. "I have never tasted oysters so fresh! And you would have needed an excellent soothsayer to predict my arrival as I did not know myself that the gods would drive my ship here."

She looked away toward the sea and I was afraid I'd offended her, but before I could apologize she said, "You see, that's the oddity of your arrival. I believe there were signs that told of your coming, but I stupidly misread them. Seven days ago I went to the sibyl."

"At Cumae? How exciting! I am most anxious to pay a visit there myself."

"Well, I wish you better luck reading her meaning than I had," she said, taking a sip of wine.

"What did she say?"

"She said nothing. She scribbled on a leaf three sentences: Poseidon will enact his wrath. The sea will take back what belongs to it. The maiden shall be returned to her mother."

"Ah, so you think Poseidon's wrath might have referred to the storm that caused my ship to founder?"

"Perhaps, although really it wasn't much of a storm. I'm surprised your crew was destroyed by it."

"Perhaps from the safety of this beautiful villa it didn't seem like much of a storm, but from where I stood on the deck of the ship as we passed between the point of Surrentum and the isle of Capreae it felt like all the winds of Aeolus had been let loose and that the whirlpool of Charybdis was trying to drag me down to my death. I even glimpsed the white bones that litter the rocks of the sirens that Homer spoke of. Believing that I must have done something to anger the gods, perhaps by taking from their native shrines the records of their mysteries, I poured a libation into the sea to Minerva whose temple crowns the Surrentum heights. Then I had myself and my trunk put in a small rowboat, hoping that my contagion wouldn't doom the whole ship. I fully expected to perish, but then my little boat found its way to this shore. I can only assume that the gods smile on my endeavors, especially since I was brought here." I toasted my hostess and she inclined her head modestly, showing off as she did an exquisite pearl diadem fastened in her dark hair.

"But the sea did claim the rest of your crew," she pointed out, signaling to a slave girl to refill my wineglass. "Perhaps you had trespassed against some native God. . . . You say you've brought back records of the mysteries?"

"Yes, my own impressions recorded in a journal I have kept over the years and some other texts . . . old books sold to me by priests to increase the wealth of their shrines, sacred texts that I found moldering in bookshops, philosophical treatises copied over by temple slaves and sold on the black market of Alexandria. You'd be amazed at the traffic in magical secrets practiced in the bazaars of the East—it's enough to tarnish one's belief in these religions when so often there's a price attached to their mysteries." I noticed that the slave girl, who was filling my glass, had paused to listen to what I was saying, a becoming blush on her face, and that Calatoria was watching her carefully. A favorite being trained to serve at table? I wondered. "I see by your fine paintings that you honor Demeter and Persephone. You are a follower of the Eleusinian Mysteries, perhaps?"

At the mention of the two goddesses, the slave girl, who was just returning my glass to the table beside my couch, flinched. The glass fell to the marble floor and shattered in as many pieces as the mosaic pattern that decorated the floor. My hostess's face became like stone and in the flickering lamplight I observed that her features, which had seemed lovely only a moment ago, hardened and turned quite ugly. So a passing cloud may transform a peaceful and beautiful landscape into a gloomy scene of violence and destruction. Calatoria leapt from her couch and slapped the girl's face.

"Iusta! Do you have any idea how expensive those glasses were? What a stupid girl—"

The girl—Iusta, what an unusual name!—fell to her knees and hurriedly began collecting the broken pieces, as if she could put the glass back together again if she moved quickly enough, but her only reward for her haste was a cut hand.

"And now you'll drip blood over everything!" With a disgusted sigh, Calatoria sank back down onto her couch and, realizing that I was observing her, tried to resume a placid countenance. "Slaves! This one has received all the training of a patrician, a whimsy of my late husband's, and yet she can't even serve a glass of wine without breaking something."

"Iusta is a rather unusual name. Another whimsy of your husband's?"

"Of the girl's mother. She bought her freedom soon after the girl's birth and she celebrated by giving her daughter that preposterous name. I would not have allowed it, but my husband had a weak spot for the slaves and the girl's mother had belonged to his mother."

Throughout this conversation its object kept her head bent steadily to her task, giving no sign that she heard us except for the rising color in her cheeks, which I detected because of the reflection of the torchlight on her face.

"The mother bought her own freedom, but the girl is still a slave?"

"Yes, well, she was born while her mother was still a slave, so she remains a slave, although her mother tried to claim otherwise and retain the girl, but I eventually prevailed in court and Iusta came back to me—along with some oyster farms her mother had bought. In fact, the oysters we dined upon tonight are from them. Vitalis's oysters have proved a better bargain than her daughter, clumsy as she is. Still, I find she has uses. . . . That's quite enough, Iusta. Go have the cook bandage your hand before you bleed to death and cheat me of your value once again."

The girl rose and with her eyes still on the ground bowed to her mistress. I watched her as she walked across the courtyard and descended the steps to the lower level of the villa. "Yes, I can see what you mean," I said, turning back to my hostess whose eyes, I noted, were glittering as though she had a fever. "She has a certain charm."

"I'm glad you approve. Doesn't she remind you of the Persephone?"

I followed my hostess's gaze to the painting on the west wall of the courtyard, to the figure of Persephone as she was seized by the god of the underworld and saw immediately that she was right. The slave girl did bear an uncanny resemblance to the maiden in the painting.

Calatoria was clearly pleased by my reaction. "Take a closer look," she suggested and I did. I rose from my couch—a little unsteadily, I admit, from my hostess's excellent wine—and approached the painting on the west wall of the peristylium. Calatoria followed me, an oil lamp in her hand, which she held up to the painting. The girl's expression of horror as she is seized by the god leapt out of the shadows—her open mouth and flashing eyes—and I saw that she could be the twin of the clumsy slave girl.

Calatoria lowered the lamp slightly and, following the orb of light, my eyes fell on the girl's breast bared as Hades ripped her stola from her shoulder, his dark hand sinking into the tender white flesh of her shoulder. "A marvel!" I pronounced. "The girl must have modeled for the painter."

"It was her mother, actually. See, she modeled for the initiate as well." *Calatoria led me to the north wall where the figures depicted a series of mystery rites. Calatoria held her lamp up to the face of a young girl kneeling beside a trunk upon which the rape of Persephone was depicted. The girl's posture exactly matched the slave girl's when she had knelt to retrieve the broken glass. I could have sworn that even the color in the painted supplicant's cheeks matched the blush of the slave girl Iusta.*

"Remarkable," I said.

"Yes, so you can see why I insist upon keeping her. Her mother—and her mother's mother and her mother before her—have all participated in the rites of the maiden which we honor here. In exchange for their service they have each in turn been granted the opportunity to buy their freedom, but only after they have provided their replacement. The rite can only take place when the girl attains the age of seventeen, which she just has. And so, you see how remarkable it is that you have arrived at just this time."

"You mean the rites of the maiden will be conducted here—and soon?"

"Yes, this household has hosted the rites for many years, twice since I became its mistress. It is an honor."

"And when do the rites take place?"

"In three days' time, on the evening of Dies Martis, nine days before the Kalends of September."

I didn't have to translate the Roman date into our calendar. I knew full well that nine days before the Kalends of September was August 24, the day Vesuvius erupted.

"I am truly blessed by the gods, then!"

"And we, too. It must be a good sign that only days before the rites Poseidon has delivered you—a man who has been initiated into the mysteries of Eleusis! Of course our rites don't pretend to that grandeur. Rather they are modeled on the Little Mysteries of Agrai, which prepare the initiate for the Greater Mysteries of Eleusis."

"Ah, yes, I attended the Little Mysteries at Agrai. They are most interesting as they combine the worship of Dionysus with the veneration of Demeter and Persephone."

"As do ours, although in a somewhat unique form. You would honor our house by participating in our own rites to the maiden." My hostess bowed to me formally and I noticed this time that the pearl diadem in her hair was shaped like a squid with long tentacles that wrapped around her head.

"The honor will be all mine," I told her.

She smiled. Youth and beauty were restored to her face in the glow of the lamp. Did her own participation in the rites of the maiden endow her with youth? I wondered. But I could see it was not the right time for more questions. Calatoria turned and led me to the door of my chamber, just off the courtyard. "I would love to hear more of your experiences in the East and see the books you've carried with you, but for now you must rest and regain your strength," she said as my eyes followed the path of light her lamp made on the walls. "Participation in the mysteries requires a clean soul and a great deal of stamina." As she spoke these last words, the light from her lamp fell on the god as he approached the maiden and I couldn't help but wonder what part I would play in the mysteries to come.

Later that night, as I was lying in bed writing this account I heard a noise at the door. I called for whoever was there to enter and the door opened. When I looked up I thought that the winged siren of the rites had come to life, but when the figure on the threshold stepped forward I saw the source of my delusion. Diagonally across from my doorway was the painted figure of the winged siren and Iusta, standing directly in front of her, had so perfectly fit the painted figure's outline that she seemed to have sprouted wings. So convincing was the illusion that even when I had uncovered the trick I checked to see if she held the whip that the painted figure brandished in her hand. She did not. But the thought that she might made me shiver and for a moment I saw an image of us—a presentiment of the rites to come?—in which I *whipped the girl until blood rose to her skin. I shook the vile image from my mind, sure that it had been placed there by the strange influence of the house.*

"Well," I asked the girl, "what is it? Has your mistress sent you with a message? You're not a mute, are you? What a shame it would be if Justice was mute as well as blind!" I laughed at my own joke, but it must have been above the girl's comprehension because she didn't even smile.

"No," she answered, "I am not mute. But my mistress's message requires no words or package to deliver. I was told to deliver . . . myself."

It took me a moment to understand what she meant and when I did I confess that I blushed. I am not ignorant of the custom of offering an honored guest the company of a slave girl, but I'd never been offered the gift by the mistress of the house. I considered refusing Calatoria's kind offer, but then looking at the girl—in the lamplight her gauzy stola had become quite transparent—I realized that not only might my refusal offend Calatoria, but it might appear that I had found the girl inadequate and result in the girl's punishment. Always in such situations I try to respect the customs of my hosts. And so I accepted Calatoria's gift and bade Iusta enter.

Although I try to scroll down to the next line my cursor blinks stubbornly on empty space. I've come to the end of the scanned section transcribed by Agnes. I can't help wondering if Agnes stopped here because she balked at describing what would have come next—Iusta's forced submission to her mistress's guest. It's just as I had feared on the day I went to the excavated villa; the house was a corrupt place. Without the tempering influence of her husband, Calatoria abused the girl, no doubt punishing her for the lawsuit she had finally lost. And I had to wonder if the abuse ended with a night spent with Phineas. What part would Iusta play in the rites? Would she be literally raped by the God as played by Phineas? Would she be held down by Calatoria and her attendants and whipped?

What makes me feel sickest of all is my own desire to read

more—a desire that I tell myself is scholarly, but then that sounds as weak an excuse as Phineas blaming his flagellation fantasy on the *influence* of the house. I look back at the transcript and see that the Latin word Agnes translated as influence is *potestas*. Power. That's what I had felt in Herculaneum, the villa's *power*, still potent after its centuries-long sleep under hardened lava.

I close the laptop and stand up in the doorway to get a fresh breath of air. The moon, which had barely cleared the eastern wall of the villa when I began reading, is now directly overhead, its light streaming in through my open door so brightly it feels like a presence. It makes me think of Phineas opening his door to find the slave girl Iusta, the lamplight turning her gauze dress transparent, a pair of painted wings springing from her shoulders. Something about that image strikes me. I put the laptop down on the chair and walk out into the courtyard, following a diagonal path to the back wall. I walk straight to the figure of the winged siren holding aloft the phallus-handled whip. It's the image Phineas was referring to, which means that the room I'm in corresponds to the room Phineas stayed in at the real Villa della Notte.

In the morning I meet the other two members of the Papyrus Project: Simon Bowles, a British art restorer who's working to re-create the wall paintings from Herculaneum here on Capri, and Maria Prezziotti, an Italian archaeologist from the Pontificia Instituto Sacra Archeologia—PISA. If I'd been expecting a dour old nun as the Catholic Church's representative I couldn't have been more mistaken. Maria Prezziotti is no older than thirty. She's dressed impeccably in a dark skirt and crisp cotton blouse; pearls gleam on her earlobes and a gold cross nestles between her ample breasts. It occurs to me that her outfit is nearly identical to the one the housekeeper wears, only on Maria it looks chic and sexy.

I realize right away that I've seen Simon before. He'd been working on the wall painting when I wandered into the courtyard yesterday morning. I'd mistaken him for a satyr and now I see why—he has the fleshy, sensuous lips and full belly of that mythological creature and the fringe of curly red hair crowns his brow like a satyr's wreath. When I enter the lower courtyard where the morning buffet is laid out he's tucking into a full English breakfast of fried eggs, sausage, toast, and jam.

"Ah, she arises like the dawn," he says, patting a splash of egg yolk from his chin. "I was afraid I caused you to faint yesterday morning, Dr. Chase. I'm glad you weren't damaged by the fall."

"It was the verisimilitude of your paintings that startled me," I explain, taking a seat across from the painter. "I thought I'd died and woken up in Hades."

"My paintings have been pilloried by the press before, but never once have I been told they sent their viewers to Hell."

"I can assure you I mean it as a compliment. I looked at them again this morning. The Rape of Persephone looks exactly like the one at the Villa della Notte and the new mural, the one of the mystery rites, it's . . ." I hesitate, recalling the more lascivious details of the painting. I notice that Maria Prezziotti is looking at me as if I'd dribbled egg down my front. Maybe it's just my clothes—a Waterloo Ice House T-shirt and khaki shorts—she disdains.

"Yes," she says before I can finish my sentence, "the mystery rite paintings will no doubt be the images that the press choose to exemplify the villa once they're released. A rutting goat-man and a winged dominatrix. By next summer they'll be on every American tourist's T-shirt." At the word *T-shirt* she curls her upper lip at mine.

Agnes, coming out onto the terrace with a pot of coffee, comes to my rescue. "I'd buy one of that winged siren," she says. "I just love her face, and now we know from Phineas that it's a portrait of that slave girl who lived at the Villa della Notte—Iusta."

"Of her mother actually," I say. "Calatoria tells Phineas that the painter used Iusta's mother as a model, but the daughter must have looked just like her since Phineas mistakes the girl later that night for the winged siren. . . ."

I've been too busy pouring my coffee to notice the silence that's settled around the table, but when I look up I see that Maria and Simon are staring at me while George and Agnes are exchanging guilty looks.

"And where did you read this, Dr. Chase?" Maria directs the question to me, but her gaze is firmly rooted on Agnes. "I thought the scroll wasn't ready to be distributed yet. Did you give Dr. Chase a copy of the scanned material?"

Agnes blanches at the note of accusation in Maria's voice. "Well, yes—" she begins, but Maria interrupts her.

"I see, you Americans really do stick together."

The color returns to Agnes's face as though she had been slapped. "I gave Dr. Chase the transcript because Mr. Lyros, the American who's paying your salary and preserving your country's heritage, asked me to. If you have a problem with that, I suggest you talk to Mr. Lyros." Agnes's voice wobbles at the end of this shockingly, for Agnes, brazen retort, but she holds her ground under Maria's stare. I'm staring at her, too, wondering why usually meek Agnes would talk back to her elders like this. Had Maria done or said something before I got here to make her this angry?

"I certainly will talk to John—"

"Talk to me about what?" The question comes from the doorway that leads from the kitchen to the courtyard where John Lyros, in slim faded jeans and a soft white shirt, stands sipping a cup of coffee. "Is there a problem?"

Maria turns from Agnes to her boss, her expression smoothly morphing from disdain to polite inquiry. "I just wondered why we haven't all gotten to see the scanned portions of the Phineas scroll. It's my job to look for any Christian references in the material recovered. It is why my organization agreed to fund this project," she finishes with a pointed look at Agnes, no doubt to remind her that John Lyros isn't the only benefactor of the Papyrus Project.

"Actually I forwarded the file to everyone this morning; you should find it in your e-mail. I'm looking forward to hearing what you all think of it at dinner tonight when perhaps we'll get the next installment. What do you think, George? Can you and Agnes get the next bit scanned and transcribed by this evening? I'm afraid that once you get started reading it, it's hard to put down. Right, Dr. Chase?"

"Yes," I say, "especially knowing that in three days—"

"Enh, enh." Lyros holds up a hand to stop me. "No spoilers! Why don't we let Simon and Maria catch up with their reading while George and Agnes get to work in the lab. As for you, I bet you'd like to stretch your legs and see a little bit of the island. We wouldn't want you thinking you're in Hades when you're actually on one of the most beautiful places on earth."

"No," I say, wondering just how long Lyros had been listening to our conversation. "I'm sure a walk would do me good."

It is true, I soon see, that Capri is indeed one of the most beautiful places on earth, but it's not true that the walk Lyros has planned for us is little.

"There are really only two choices," he says when we step outside the villa's wrought-iron gate onto a narrow path. "Up or down. Down leads to the town of Capri—La Piazzetta, the Gran'Caffe, shops, droves of tourists—and up leads to the Villa Jovis."

"The palace of Tiberius," I say. "I'd like to see that. But won't it be too crowded?"

He shakes his head. "Most of the tourists are content to stay in the town and shop for duty-free Gucci or take the boat excursion to the Blue Grotto. It's a bit of a hike, though, are you sure you're up to it?"

I look up the path, which slopes gently but steadily uphill between bougainvillea-covered walls and oleander bushes. Taking an experimental breath, I find the air sweet and light and oddly intoxicating. "Absolutely," I say.

We walk slowly and Lyros stops often at water fountains to drink and at benches to retie his sneakers, or at tempting vistas to point out the Marina Grande below us and Monte Solaro towering behind us, or to point past a gate at some villa that lies drowsing in a lemon grove behind mounds of fuschia and azalea, geraniums and jasmine. He always picks a spot well shaded by an umbrella pine or cypress to regale me with a piece of Caprese history and give me a chance to catch my breath. "And this," he says at one gate, "is the Villa Lysis, once home to Count Jacques d'Adelsward Fersen, who so scandalized the Caprese that he had to leave the island. He did return eventually and lived here until he died of an opium overdose at forty-five."

"What was the scandal about?"

"Oh, just another one of those old Caprese stories of degenerate foreigners made up of gossip and lies," he says, turning back up the path.

"You sound like you don't approve of the locals."

"I guess I'm afraid of what they say about me—that I'm just another in a long line of eccentric foreigners come to live out his fantasies—or to escape the demands of Empire like our friend Tiberius." He points upward and I see that the ruins of Tiberius's villa have come into view—a mass of sun-struck brick and limestone crowning a high peak above us.

"Why did you decide to build a replica of the Villa della Notte?" I ask.

Lyros shakes his head. "Well, the funny thing is that I came upon the property here on Capri the same summer that I became interested in the ruins of the Villa della Notte. Except for some eighteenth-century looting of the site, most of the villa was unexcavated. I knew that left to the government the villa would remain underground for decades more, so I decided to fund the excavation. On the same day that I was shown this piece of property here on Capri the excavators found the map of the old villa and I saw that I could create a mirror image of the villa just across the bay. It just seemed like it was . . . fate. I suppose that sounds silly."

"People make decisions for smaller coincidences," I say. "They just don't usually have the means to take advantage of those coincidences on such a grand scale. At least your villa was built to advance the cause of knowledge. If I hadn't been reading Phineas in the villa last night I wouldn't have realized that his room corresponds to the one I'm staying in."

"Yes, you noticed that, too! You realize what it means, right? The trunk might still be there. I've asked the excavators to step up work on that room. If we're lucky, we'll find his trunk and the scrolls he brought with him. I've been thinking about what 'philosophical treatises' and 'magical secrets' Phineas might have brought back from the East. . . . Just think, he might have had an Orphic poem, an unknown dialogue of Plato, the lost writings of Pythagoras. . . ."

"That's great . . ." I stop, feeling suddenly as if the breath had been knocked out of my chest.

"Are you all right?" Lyros touches my elbow. "We can turn back. Tiberius's villa's been there for two thousand years. It's not going anywhere."

"No, I'm fine, and I want to see it." It's just a coincidence, I tell myself, that Lyros has mentioned Pythagoras. It has nothing to do with Dale Henry or Ely. "This is where Tiberius lived out the last years of his reign as emperor, right?"

"Yes, avoiding the intrigues and poisonings of the court at Rome."

"He certainly found an unapproachable fortress," I say. "No one could sneak up on him here."

"That was the idea. There's a story about a local fisherman who thought he'd gain the emperor's favor by scrambling up the cliffs to present him with a fresh mullet. Tiberius was so alarmed that his sanctuary could be so easily breached that he had the man's face slapped by the fish. Like most proud Caprese, the man responded with a joke. He said he was glad he hadn't brought a lobster."

"Don't tell me—"

"Yeah—Tiberius ordered the man's face to be lacerated with a lobster's claw."

"Ugh." I wince, remembering the passage from Phineas that I read last night. Calatoria had only slapped Iusta's face with her hand, but no doubt she could have inflicted harsher punishments on her household slaves. We've reached the ticket booth to the site of the ruins, but John merely exchanges a wave with the man sitting in the shade of the little building.

"Here." Lyros leads me to the edge of the cliff beyond the booth. "Before we see the ruins—this is the Salto di Tiberio—the cliff from which Tiberius was supposed to have thrown his favorites once he had grown tired of them."

"According to Suetonius. Some scholars think Tiberius got a bad rap." I'm trying to reassure myself as I look over the crumbling limestone ledge at the vertiginous drop into the blue sea. It's not nice to think of anyone falling into that void. Yet it exerts a strange pull. I find myself taking a step closer to the edge, and am startled when Lyros grabs my arm.

"Sorry," he says. "I thought you were getting a little too close. Are you ready to see the villa?"

I nod and we start up the stairs that lead to the ruins, climbing past the vaulted cisterns that make up the middle of the villa and up toward the semicircular *ambulatio,* the columned walkway that crowns the peak. The climb is steep enough that we don't talk, giving me time to get over my embarrassment at jumping when he had grabbed my arm.

When I reach the top I'm panting. Even Lyros with his Himalayan hiking experience is breathing heavily. We stand looking out at the view of the strait that runs between the eastern point of Capri and the Sorrentine peninsula. Lyros waves his arm in the air, gesturing toward the water. "This view always reminds me of the view from the Temple of Poseidon at Cape Sounion; it holds such a commanding presence over the sea, and while there's no temple to Poseidon here, there was a temple over there on the Sorrentine coast—" he begins.

"Sacred to Tyrrhena Minerva," I finish for him. "The Athena of the Tyrrhenian sea, patron of navigators. According to Statius, sailors poured libations into the sea as they passed the temple to ensure safe passage through the strait."

"Ah, you know your Statius."

"Well, I boned up when I knew I was coming here. I thought of the passage when I read last night that Phineas lost his crew in this strait. He says he saw the whitened bones on the sirens' rocks and poured a libation. Funny that he survived in a rowboat when his crew was lost."

"Which he calls a sacrifice to Poseidon, thus fulfilling the prophecy Calatoria received from the Sibyl the week before Phineas's arrival, that 'Poseidon will take back what is his.' "

"Pretty convenient," I say. "Do you think Calatoria made up the prophecy to make Phineas feel as though he had been fated to come to the villa?"

John turns away from the view to look at me. His dark sunglasses hide his oddly colored eyes, but I can see by the little lines around his eyes that he's narrowed them. "That's an interesting idea. Why do you think she'd want Phineas to think he was fated to come to the Villa della Notte?"

I have to think a moment. I'd thought at first that Phineas was the one who was trying to create the appearance that he was fated to come to the villa—Phineas who had staged his shipwreck so he could gain access to the villa's library and secret rites—but something about what I had read last night had made me think that Calatoria had her own plans for Phineas.

"It's what she said about the rites requiring stamina and the way she let her lamp light up the sexiest parts of the painting. She needed a male participant for her mystery rites . . . *and* it's the way she brought up the books Phineas had with him at the same time. Like she was offering him some kind of trade: the rare books he was carrying for a night of debauchery."

Lyros nods. "That's an interesting theory. Calatoria did seem interested in those books. We'll have to see what happens to them. One thing, though," he says, looking away across the strait toward the Sorrentine peninsula. "Whoever planned his arrival at the villa, it's kind of sad."

"What do you mean?" I ask.

"If the shipwreck was intentional, it means Phineas's crew were sacrificed on purpose."

The walk leaves me more exhausted than I'd counted on. When we get back to the villa, I take a short swim in the pool in the lower courtyard and then go back to my room for a nap. I only mean to sleep an hour, but when I wake up I see by a small majolica clock on the dresser that I've slept for two. I shower, put on the one dress I brought with me—a Mexican sundress I bought last year in San Antonio—and go out into the courtyard. In honor of my first post-rehab evening appearance, John Lyros has decided to have cocktails in the courtyard and dinner served on the peristylium overlooking the bay. A buffet has been set up along the back wall and heaped with trays of oysters and other fresh seafood. Candles in seashells rim the edge of the fountain and oil lamps hang in between the columns, illuminating the wall painting Simon has been working on. It's these half-finished figures that have drawn the attention of the party. The artist is in the middle of the group, flanked by Maria and Agnes, apparently enjoying pointing out each lascivious detail to the women, while George stands to one side helping himself to the oysters.

"You've made it look like some depraved party," Maria complains as I approach the group. "This innocent young girl looks almost as if she were enjoying what is happening to her. I'm sure that is not how it looks in the original."

"I've studied the original," Agnes says. "And that is *exactly* how she looks . . . not that she's enjoying herself, I mean . . ." Agnes stumbles, looking flustered, "but there's this otherworldly look in her eyes . . . like she's gone beyond the experience. . . ."

"The look you're talking about is the result of the opium her masters would have given her. After all, she was a slave being forced to participate—"

"But not all initiates were slaves. What about the paintings at the Villa of the Mysteries in Pompeii? Scholars think she was the daughter of the household and the paintings are celebrating her marriage."

"Brava," Simon rewards Agnes with a smile, "I can see you've studied the genre carefully. Didn't I see you the other day at the Villa of the Mysteries in Pompeii looking at the frescoes there—"

"What do you think, Dr. Chase?" George Petherbridge hands me a glass of chilled white wine as I enter the group. Agnes is blushing. I have the feeling George is trying to break up Agnes and Maria, and again I wonder what it is about Maria, aside from her general rudeness, that's pushing Agnes's buttons. "Do you think the girl chosen to play the role of the maiden in these rites was scared or honored?" George asks me.

"It wouldn't have mattered much," I answer. "Apparently, Iusta lost her court case and became Calatoria's slave, so she had no choice either way. I doubt, though, that she saw it as an honor."

"But you forget that she had been brought up in the house 'like a daughter.' Perhaps she was raised to consider it an honor to take part in the rites of the household," a male voice from behind me says. I turn and see that it's Elgin, in white slacks and a blue-and-white-striped tunic. The sun has turned his normally blond hair red at the tips, making him look even more devilish than usual. He holds up his glass of wine to me. "Sophie, so glad to see you've recovered. You gave me quite a scare."

My face goes hot remembering all I had told him in my delirium, and wondering what else I might have said that I don't remember. I raise my wineglass to my lips to give me a moment to think. The wine is deliciously cool with a hint of sulfur—a local wine, then, from grapes grown in volcanic soil.

"Thanks to you, Elgin," I say. "It's a good thing you came looking for me. Did you have a good time in Sorrento?"

"Ah, Sorrento." Simon Bowles nearly sings the word. "I adore the Hotel Excelsior Vittoria. One can still imagine Oscar Wilde trading quips in the salon and Caruso singing under the lemon trees. I myself spied Luciano Pavarotti there when I was staying with friends a few summers ago. Who were you staying with?"

"No one you'd know." Elgin turns to the buffet table to sample a piece of fried calamari. "An old acquaintance who has a house there. I stopped in Herculaneum this morning on the way back to see the villa. After reading the section of Phineas that Agnes was kind enough to send me last night"—he salutes Agnes with a fried sardine—"I wanted to have another look at the actual paintings." Elgin moves toward the figure of the girl held down by the two sirens and peers at her face. The figures of the sirens are merely outlines, as is the figure of the god who approaches her, but the face of the supine girl and the face of the siren who holds the whip above her have been painted in. Following Elgin's gaze back and forth between the two faces I see what Phineas saw his first night at the villa: the faces are identical.

"Bravo!" Elgin says, turning to Simon. "You've captured it. They're the same girl: one horrified at her part in the ritual, one reveling in it. What a brilliant way to suggest the dual nature of pain and pleasure. The dual nature of the feminine, one might say, where pleasure and pain—sex and childbirth—are so irrevocably entwined. So you see, ladies," he turns to Maria and Agnes, "you're both right. The girl Iusta was both honored and horrified to play her role in the rite."

Neither Agnes nor Maria seems to be paying attention to what Elgin is saying, though. Simon is whispering something into Agnes's ear that is making her blush even more. Maria watches them with a prim, disapproving look. It must be hard, I think, to be the representative of the Church. I imagine she feels like a Christian martyr thrown to the lions.

Elgin looks none too pleased that his efforts to play peacemaker have failed. In fact, he's glaring at Simon and Agnes—jealous, I imagine, that the older man is flirting with Agnes. He drains his glass of wine in one swallow and then gestures toward the terrace. "And speaking of honors, I believe our generous host has prepared a lavish feast to celebrate Dr. Chase's recovery. May I have the honor of escorting you in to dinner, Sophie?" He holds out his arm to me and there's no way I can refuse it without seeming petty— and without Elgin thinking I'm avoiding him because of our past. And besides, I do owe him thanks for rescuing me from the Hotel Convento. As I take his arm I glimpse a smile from Agnes, who's disengaged herself from Simon, and a frown from Maria. Another example, I wonder, of the dual nature of woman?

As Elgin leads me from the courtyard out onto the terrace, I glance back to the painting on the wall. The problem with Elgin's analysis, though, is that the girl Iusta could only play one role at a time. I can't help but wonder which one she played with Phineas.

CHAPTER 12

*1*t is that time of evening when the sky shifts from indigo to violet. In sympathy, the sea has darkened to purple—a color that could earn the Homeric epithet "wine-dark." Lights are just beginning to come on around the shoreline, like beads being strung, one by one, on a curved diadem crowning the amethyst brow of the bay.

John Lyros is leaning against a column looking out at the view. He turns and I'm startled again by his eyes, which have absorbed all the purples in the landscape. They seem to darken for a moment when they fall on my arm linked to Elgin's, but then he smiles broadly and opens his arms wide, welcoming us all to dinner but also, it seems to me, welcoming us all into the capacious embrace of the bay. Sinus Cumanus, the Romans called it. The Sibyl's Bay. But *sinus* also means bosom or lap and tonight it feels like this landscape is a living being, a siren luring us with her beauty.

John moves to the head of the table set up lengthwise along the balustrade and holds out the chair to his right. "Dr. Chase must have a seat with a view for her first night dining al fresco," he says.

Maria, who had been heading for that seat, shrugs her bare shoulders. "*Va bene.* I've seen the view a million times. I don't mind sitting with my back to it." She skirts around Lyros and takes the seat on his left.

"I don't think I'll ever get tired of looking at this view," Agnes says, sitting one seat away from me—leaving Elgin to take the place between us. Simon Bowles takes the chair at the end of the table, opposite Lyros, shaking out his napkin with a flourish, and George Petherbridge sits down next to him leaving an empty seat between him and Maria, positioning himself directly across from Agnes.

"Is someone else coming?" Maria asks, eyeing the empty chair as though it were an open sore.

"No," Lyros says, his brow creasing with annoyance, "they've gotten the number wrong." He rings a bell and the housekeeper, without coral necklace, I note, appears and scowls at the empty seat and then at each one of us as if clearly we must have murdered one of our own in order to explain the discrepancy between the number of people and chairs. Then she does something truly odd; she shouts her own name: Guilia. Just when I'm beginning to wonder if the housekeeper's alternating moods can be explained by a split personality, Guilia's duplicate appears. As she clears the extra place setting, I notice that she's wearing the coral beads and when she catches me staring at her she smiles.

"Twins!" I say when both women are gone. "I thought they were the same person, only sometimes she smiled and sometimes she didn't."

John Lyros laughs. "Guilia's the one who smiles and Theresa is the one who doesn't. You see, one lost her fiancé in a diving accident—"

"The one who doesn't smile?"

"No, Guilia, the one who smiles, is the one who lost her fiancé. Theresa never had a fiancé. Interesting, isn't it?"

" 'Tis better to have loved and lost than never to have loved at all," Simon Bowles quotes, tilting his wineglass toward Agnes. "Eh, Miss Hancock? I'm sure you've left a trail of broken hearts back in Texas."

"You think Theresa is jealous that she never even had a fiancé?" Agnes asks, pointedly ignoring Simon's remark and looking around the table.

George nods eagerly. "Maybe she was secretly in love with Giulia's fiancé. . . ."

"Maybe she killed the fiancé. . . ." Elgin suggests.

Maria tosses her hair over her shoulder. "Perhaps Theresa is bad-tempered because she works harder. She's always cleaning up after Guila's mistakes—like missetting the table tonight."

I'm about to ask how she knows who set the table when John laughs. "Well, I only hope that you all train your keen investigative eyes on the behavior of Phineas, Calatoria, and Iusta with the same fervor. You've all had time to read the first installment by now. What do you make of it?"

A silence descends over the table while Guilia and Theresa serve the Caprese salads. I imagine we're all trying to think of something insightful to say, or that we're embarrassed by Iusta's nighttime visit to Phineas's room, or maybe we're all just enjoying our tomatoes, which seem to glow an even deeper red than usual in the purplish evening light.

Agnes breaks the silence. "Well, I think it was awful that Calatoria sent Iusta as a present to Phineas . . . as if she were nothing but a . . . a . . ."

"Piece of property?" Maria suggests. "That's what she was to her, after all. You weren't shocked that the girl would participate in a sexual rite, why are you so shocked that she was offered to the guests? At least she probably was tipped by the guests."

"You make her sound like a prostitute!" Agnes exclaims, her voice shaking. "Did you notice she was only seventeen years old!"

"Seventeen would have been considered mature in Roman times," Simon says, tearing off a hunk of bread from a loaf and using it to sop up the olive oil left on his plate. "We can't judge the ancients by our own mores. And you needn't turn it into a feminist thing. Calatoria could just as easily have sent Phineas a young male slave."

"You must have been disappointed that she hadn't," Maria says, smiling, but in John's direction, not Simon's.

I look nervously toward the painter wondering how he'll react, but he only smiles and licks the olive oil off his fingers. "And you, Maria, must have been disappointed that Iusta wasn't really carrying a whip."

"I know I was," Elgin says, winking at me.

"So clearly it's the sex part that everybody's interested in," Lyros interrupts.

There's an embarrassed silence while Guilia clears our salad plates and Theresa serves the pasta course—a thin spaghetti prepared with the delicious anchovy and eggplant sauce that I had for lunch yesterday.

"You know," I say, "I think this sauce is probably a lot like the Roman *garum* that Phineas says he ate his first night here—I mean his first night at the Villa della Notte."

John laughs. "There you go: a Phineas observation that's not about sex. Brava, Sophie! Sophie and I were also discussing today the location of Phineas's bedroom. She noticed from his view of the wall painting that Phineas must have occupied the same room, or rather the corresponding room, as hers."

"Yes, I noticed that, too," George says. "Interesting that he was given a room off the main courtyard instead of on the lower levels where the rest of the household would have slept."

"It was probably cooler on the top level," Maria observes. "I'm sure Dr. Chase's room, for instance, is much cooler than ours are."

"Or maybe," Simon says, ignoring Maria's obvious resentment of the room allocations in the present, "Calatoria didn't want Phineas to see what was happening on the lower levels."

"Yes, they were probably getting ready for the rites." Elgin picks up a long skinny baguette and waves it in the air. "There would have been lots of naked slave girls running around in the halls."

"Well," Lyros says, "whatever reason Calatoria had for assigning her guest a room on the top level, it has important repercussions for us."

"What's that?" Elgin asks, breaking the baguette in half.

"The scroll we possess, that we're now reading from, was found in the middle of the courtyard, as though it had been dropped by someone fleeing the villa during the eruption. We haven't known where to look for the rest of Phineas's scrolls. Assuming that he didn't leave the villa before the eruption, we now know where Phineas's trunk should be—a trunk that apparently contained scrolls Phineas bought in Greece and Egypt—"

"Bought?" Maria scoffs. "It sounds like he *bribed* temple slaves or priests to steal them!"

"Well, however he came by them, they must have been pretty valuable for him to secure them in a wax-lined trunk and then worry about saving them in the middle of a storm," Lyros replies. "I, for one, would dearly love to know what Phineas Aulus thought was so valuable. Tomorrow I'm going to direct the excavation crew to tunnel into the bedroom off the courtyard. I'm curious to see what Phineas had in his waterproofed trunk."

"I'm curious to find out what was on the lower levels that Calatoria didn't want Phineas to see," Simon says. "Perhaps there are more paintings."

"Do you think," Agnes asks, accepting another glass of the deceptively mild Caprese wine from George, "that the mystery ritual actually included everything that's in that painting? I mean, the sex and whipping and all?"

"Oh, I certainly hope so," Simon says. "This setting just screams out for a little old-fashioned S and M. You should read what the foreigners got up to on this very island."

"I don't think that's what Miss Hancock was talking about," Lyros says, glaring at Simon.

"Oh, but I'm sure Miss Hancock would find it interesting to know that the practices of the ancients she studies are not dead and gone."

"You mean like cults and sacrifices?" Agnes asks, her cheeks pinking in the glow of the sunset.

"Exactly!" Simon crows, ignoring the increasingly angry glare of his host. It almost seems as if Simon is deliberately trying to tease Lyros. "You see, my dear, Capri has drawn to it many who sought to reexperience the golden age of antiquity—Axel Munthe, Norman Douglas, Friedrich Krupp . . . but Baron Fersen is my favorite. He came to the island at the turn of the century with his lover, Nino Cesarini, the son of a Roman newspaper vendor."

"Wasn't the boy only fourteen?" Maria asks.

"Fifteen," Simon replies. "And believe me, I'm sure he was happy to trade his working-class life in Rome for the pleasure palace Fersen built for them."

"The Villa Lysis?" I ask, remembering that this was the story which Lyros hadn't wanted to tell me on the walk up to Tiberius's villa.

"Yes, named for the boy to whom Plato explained friendship. Fersen had the villa built just below Tiberius's villa because he had the idea of re-creating the atmosphere of the emperor's sojourn on Capri."

"An odd role model," Agnes points out. "Wasn't Tiberius known for tossing people off cliffs? And didn't you tell me, Professor

Lawrence, when you took me to the Blue Grotto, that there were rumors that he molested boys there?"

"Rumors," Simon Bowles answers before Elgin, who looks embarrassed at Agnes's mentioning of their excursion to the Blue Grotto, can. "But the part about the boys being sacrificed, well, Fersen *did* find that romantic. In fact, he heard a story about a favorite of Tiberius, a boy named Hypatus, whom Tiberius sacrificed to the sun god Mithras—"

"There's a gravestone at the Naples Museum with an inscription describing the sacrifice," Elgin adds.

"Yes, that's how Fersen first heard about it. Somehow he conceived the idea that if Nino were truly faithful to him he'd be willing to sacrifice himself. Or perhaps the boy himself suggested the rite as a proof of his devotion."

"This baron sacrificed a young boy here?" Agnes asks, looking suddenly pale. Lyros's instincts were right, I think; this is no story for a girl who's so recently witnessed another sort of blood sacrifice.

"No, no, no! It was only meant to be a *symbolic* sacrifice. A bit of harmless dress-up, really. Fersen was decked out as the Emperor Tiberius and Nino as the boy Hypatus—although I imagine that his outfit was rather scanty—and all their friends were dressed in Roman costumes as well. After a night of opium smoking, they paraded down to the Grotto Matermania, which Fersen believed was the site of an ancient Mithras cult. They lit incense and sang hymns and then at sunrise Fersen, brandishing a fruit knife"—Simon lifts his own arm, wielding a butter knife—"delivered the tiniest, symbolic cut." He demonstrates by piercing one of the ripe plums that have been laid out for dessert.

"Was the blood symbolic, too?" Maria asks drily. "Or did he bleed real blood?"

"Oh, I imagine there was a little blood," Simon says, biting into the punctured plum, "but nothing more than what would occur while two schoolmates became 'blood brothers.' Unfortunately, a local girl spied on the whole thing and ran to tell the village—no doubt exaggerating what she saw. Rumors flew about the island, as they are wont to do, and before long the incident, referred to as 'the deed in the grotto,' had acquired so much prurient embroidery that Fersen and Nino had to flee the island—and all for a bit of playacting no more sinister than what you Americans get up to at your universities in your fraternities and sororities."

"We never sacrificed anyone at Tri Delt," Agnes exclaims. "Not even in fun! And we certainly never smoked any opium."

"You're saying your American fraternity brothers never wear togas or ingest illegal substances?" Simon asks.

"Well, maybe the boys over in Sigma Alpha Epsilon. There was that horrible hazing incident last year," Agnes admits.

"There you go." Simon slaps his hand against the table so hard that he upsets the demitasse that Guilia has just put in front of him. "We're all hungry for ritual, to experience something beyond the banality of everyday life, to stand outside of ourselves—isn't that what you saw in the initiate's face, Miss Hancock?—to experience, literally, *ecstasy*. That's what all these crazies that you read about in your American newspapers are looking for. Come now, your own native Texas has been full of such incidents—that chap Whitman who shot all those people from some tower, those deluded children in Waco, and just recently—"

"I think you've strayed far from Phineas," Lyros says, interrupting Simon before he can get to the Dale Henry shooting. Thank goodness, I think, looking over at Agnes who's looking down at the untouched fruit on her plate.

"What I think is interesting," Lyros continues, "is the mixture of Dionysian elements and the rites of Demeter and Persephone with this added native southern Italian touch of the sirens legend. According to Livy, the Dionysian rites, or bacchanalias, practiced in Rome during the second century BC were little more than nocturnal orgies in which young men and women were initiated into sexual rituals and, if they refused, sacrificed. They only accepted initiates under twenty because, as Livy puts it, 'They were looking for young people of an age open to corruption of mind and body.' "

"You see," Simon says, "you prove my point. That's what the cults of today do: they recruit the young and the innocent."

"You make it sound as if it was just about sex," Agnes breaks in, her voice trembling with emotion, "and that Iusta was just being used. The rites were supposed to bring enlightenment to the initiate—"

"My dear," Simon says, his calm voice breaking into Agnes's agitation, "what makes you think Iusta was the initiate? And as for who is using whom . . ."

"I think that's enough, Simon," Lyros says. And then turning to Agnes, "I'm afraid the material you're transcribing is upsetting, Agnes, but think of it this way: you're giving voice to Iusta after two thousand years of silence. The picture of her that is emerging in Phineas's narrative is remarkable. I think you'll all agree after you read the section that Agnes has so sensitively transcribed today that Iusta is the real heroine of the piece."

Agnes attempts a small smile to thank John Lyros, but she still looks distraught. "Yes, she's really interesting, but so sad, too. I just can't help wondering what's going to happen to her . . . I mean, it's only three days to the eruption."

The anxiety in Agnes's voice is so palpable that I find myself glancing toward Vesuvius on the horizon, as though we were living in the time of Phineas and Iusta and the volcano was about to erupt. The sky has grown so dark, though, while we've dined that all I can see past the dark sea are the lights that ring the bay and above them a denser cone of black that's the quiet volcano. No trail of steam or glow of fire mars the peaceful scene. But then, nothing about the volcano's appearance would have warned Phineas or Iusta back then, either. Did they both die in the eruption?

"Maybe she gets out," George says hopefully, trying, I think, to cheer Agnes up. "The Herculaneans had a whole day to escape while Pompeii was being covered by ash. True, the ones who tried to escape by sea ended up dying in the boathouses by the marina because the water was too rough to launch a boat, but maybe Iusta was able to get on the road to Naples. We'll just have to keep scanning the scroll to find out. . . ."

George's voice drifts off as he realizes what most of us must have already figured out: since Phineas was never heard from again after AD 79, he must have perished in the eruption, so even if the girl Iusta escaped, it's unlikely that he recorded it.

The first thing I do when I get back to my room is open my laptop and connect to my e-mail. I stand, waiting for the file to download. When I open it I read the first line and sink onto the bed. Then, without changing out of my dress or even moving an inch, I read the second installment from beginning to end.

Many and varied were the pleasures I received from the girl Iusta on my first night at the Villa of Gaius Stephanus Petronius. I have always believed in Solon's dictum "Nothing in excess" and so have ever endeavored to balance the delights of the flesh with the pleasures of the mind. I had not expected, though, to find the latter with a seventeen-year-old slave girl. So after we had taken our physical pleasures I asked her to light a lamp so that I might write. She complied and offered as well to retrieve writing materials from my trunk. It was when she was sorting through the scrolls contained therein that I realized that not only was she able to read both the Latin and Greek tags appended to each scroll, but she was also familiar with the authors of some of the works. She exclaimed over my collection of Pliny's Natural History, explaining that the author himself had many times visited the villa from nearby Cape Misenum where he held command over the naval fleet. She was also most interested in my volumes of Strabo's Geography and asked if I had traveled to all the places recorded by him.

"Not all," I replied, but when I saw the disappointment in her eyes, I added, "but many. My interest is in recording the religious rites in each land I visit. I have spent long months traveling to remote temples and sanctuaries only to find that the rite I wished to observe was some time away and so have been forced to wait."

"It is fortunate then that you arrived here when you did . . ." she began, but then, blushing deeply, she looked away.

"It's all right," I reassured her. "Your mistress has told me about the rites practiced here and invited me to be a part of them, which I accepted as an honor. You also, I believe, have a role in the rites?"

She nodded and answered with lowered eyes. "It is what I have been raised for."

"Ah, it is indeed a rare honor." She lifted her eyes, which I noticed then were the color of amber, and looked at me strangely. "Is that why your master has taught you to read?" I asked.

"I believe that is one reason. My master was most generous. He believed that if I were to take part in the rites I should understand them. And so I have read the story of Demeter and Persephone in Homer and Ovid and of the Eleusinian Mysteries in Strabo and Pausanias. But of course not much is written about the rites performed there as they are kept in secret. Have you been initiated?"

"I have. It was the most sublime experience I have ever had. I cannot, of course, divulge what happened in the inner sanctum, but you are familiar, perhaps, with the little mysteries that occur outside the sanctuary?"

"I have read in Plato that the priestess Diotima compares the lesser—or little—mysteries to the physical experience of love and the greater mysteries to spiritual love, from which I believe is meant that the lesser mysteries are the physical manifestation of the rites: a reenactment of what happened to Persephone when she was seized by Hades and brought to the underworld and then how her mother rescued her and how by the maiden's own carelessness she yoked herself to the underworld by eating six pomegranate seeds. And I understand that by re-

creating these physical rites we seek entry into the deeper spiritual mystery of death and rebirth, just as the physical act of love leads to new life."

She looked up when she spoke of the physical act of love and I confess it was I, an old man who has traveled the world and seen its many marvels, who blushed. It was then that I became afraid that affection for this girl might cloud my objectivity during the ceremony to come.

"You can hand me the ink cake," I told her, "and that untagged scroll there—not the ones at the bottom, they must not be disturbed." I saw her fingering the tags on one of the scrolls that I had recently obtained on my travels, but then her attention was drawn to a little terra-cotta statue I had purchased in Alexandria. "But I see you are interested in the statuette. You may take it out and look at it before you go."

She removed the small statue and held it up to the light, turning it around in her hands so that the light fell on the rounded curves of the goddess and her child. "It's Isis, isn't it?"

"Yes, Queen of the Nile and the Heavens, suckling the infant Horus. Why don't you keep it. Perhaps the contemplation of it will help you to feel less afraid of the coming rites."

She seemed genuinely startled by my offer. "No . . ." she stammered, "you are much too generous. . . . I . . ."

"Please, as a token of my appreciation for tonight." She colored deeply then and I was afraid that my clumsy words had made her feel like a prostitute. "It is not often I have the opportunity to converse with a goddess," I said, trying to put her at ease with a little joke.

She looked from me to the statue and then bowed her head. "I will treasure it," she told me. Then, rising to her feet, she bowed again and left the room.

I wrote this account then as I knew I would not be able to sleep until I had recorded my impressions of the remarkable Iusta. I noted her somewhat naive interpretation of the little mysteries. Plato did not mean, I am sure, to equate the rites with something as banal as the physical act of love—he was simply making an analogy. That said, as unformed as her thinking might be, it was still remarkable for one of her age and sex, and that it might be the first time that the actor *in a mystery rite has voiced her opinion of it!*

When I finished transcribing our conversation, I still felt unsettled. Had I been rash in giving her the statue? Would she boast of the gift to her fellows and perhaps sell it in the marketplace for some worthless trinkets? The thought of the sacred object being so defiled disturbed me. I decided to take a stroll around the courtyard to clear my head.

Even in the courtyard, the air was hot and stale. I walked out onto the peristylium in the hope of catching a sea breeze, but the night was so still that the sea stretched like a sheet of polished silver all the way from the shoreline to the island of Capraea, where even the straits beneath the Temple of Tyrrhena Minerva were becalmed. No sailor would need to pour a libation to the goddess there tonight. The only sign that the bay was not transfixed was the faint sound of water lapping onto the shore just below me. I leaned over the railing and listened to the sound until I thought I could hear voices in it. I thought of my drowned crew and shuddered. Then, as I listened, I realized that the voices were female and that they echoed as though they came from some enclosed space. The sirens, then, I thought, singing their song of seduction in their caves beneath the sea. I remembered what they sang to Odysseus as he listened, tied to the mast of his ship to resist their temptation: No life on earth can be hid from our dreaming, *they sang, promising him all knowledge. How often have I listened to their song, tied to the stiff mast of my unbelieving to keep me from being lured too deep into the mysteries I sought to record and illuminate. I felt now that I stood on the brink—as I had before the gates of Eleusis or before the oracle of Delphi—of some great* knowing. *I felt the pull of that song like a whirlpool waiting to suck me in and for once I was tempted to untie myself from the mast, to let myself follow the song. . . .*

I leaned so far over the railing that had the night not been still, had the faintest wind pushed at my back, I would have fallen from the peri-

stylium and no doubt followed the sirens' voices to the bottom of the sea, but just as I felt myself losing my balance I saw something that startled me upright. Below me something moved through the dark water, a long white sinuous shape that left in its wake a trail of sparks, as if it burned a path through the water like a star falling to earth. I saw that it was shaped like a woman and that its long, loose hair swayed in the current like seaweed. Had I really come face-to-face with a siren? Were the stories true? And if they were, was I truly ready to answer their call?

Before I could decide the creature turned and began to swim back to the shore and when she stood in the shallows and shook the water from her hair I saw that she was no siren: she was the girl, Iusta. There must be an entrance to the sea at the bottom of the villa and she had slipped out for a late-night swim to seek relief from the hot night. As I watched, she turned back to the sea, and loosening something from her robes, which clung so closely to her form that I could see every line of her body, and singing a snatch of the song I had heard before, the words of which I still couldn't understand, she tossed something into the sea. I couldn't see what. Then she waded back to the villa and I lost sight of her as she disappeared under the peristylium.

Now that I had identified the source of the singing and the identity of the siren I was no longer bewitched. Always it is the way: knowledge banishes superstition. But the emotions raised by the experience had left me worn out. I turned from the sea and made my way back into the courtyard. As I was crossing to my room I tread on something soft and, kneeling, found that the path had been strewn with flowers. I picked one up and held it in the moonlight to identify it. It was a poppy, the flower sacred to Demeter. I understood then that the rites had already begun.

I close my laptop and put it on the chair by my bed. As soon as I move I realize that I have been sitting motionless for so long that my legs have fallen asleep. I stand up and feel a painful tingling coursing through my calves. I pace twice across the short length of my room, then open the door and walk barefoot out into the courtyard, trying to revive the circulation in the lower part of my body and, I realize, to shake the spell of Phineas's words from my head. Why, I wonder as I complete my second circuit around the fountain, do I feel so *entranced* by this section? Is it because I was reading it in a place that resembles the setting of the original rites? Or is it because Phineas himself, usually the model of objectivity, seemed to be falling under the spell of the Villa della Notte?

And who wouldn't have, if the original was anything like this modern restoration? The courtyard is full of the scent of the night-blooming jasmine that circle the fountain like a ring of stars. Inside this circle, the goddess Night seems to brood under her starry veil, her arms half raised, palms turned up to the moon, as if she were about to perfom a rite to raise the spirits of the underworld. Uneasy under her gaze, I walk out onto the peristylium and stand at the railing looking down at the sea. It's quite a lot farther down than it would have been from the villa in Herculaneum, but John Lyros told me that there are steps leading down from the lower courtyard to the sea, just as there apparently were in the original villa. I wonder what he made of this section, and if anyone else feels so . . . disturbed by it. I turn back to the villa, thinking about the six other people who have read the same passage that I have. It's almost as if we are all engaged in the preparation for some rites, as if we are all partaking of the "little mysteries," the ritual that prepared initiates for the greater mysteries.

I shake the idea off and decide that it's a lingering effect of the pneumonia, not some kind of mass hysteria, that's gotten to me. Before I leave the terrace, a sound from below draws me back to the railing. I half expect to see a midnight swimmer, as Phineas had, but instead I see two dark shapes silhouetted against a white outcropping about one third down the steep slope. The sound I'd heard was pebbles falling into the sea—one of the figures is pitching them one by one over the cliff into the water below. When he turns sideways I can see by the round slope of his belly that it's Simon. The other figure is tall and slim—Elgin, I think at first, but then I hear his voice raised and I realize it's John Lyros.

"That's absurd," Lyros says in an irritated pitch that carries up to the terrace. I hear the low bass rumble of Simon's reply, but I can't make out the words. But again I can hear Lyros's reply.

"You've filled your head with these Caprese stories of cults and sacrifices. This isn't the Villa Lysis and I can't allow that kind of talk to get around."

Of course, I think, Lyros was angry at Simon for telling those stories at dinnertime in front of Agnes. I lean over farther to see if I can catch what Simon says next . . . and remember what Phineas had written about almost losing his balance and falling over the parapet. I have a strong sensation that someone is behind me, someone who would only have to place a hand on my back in order to push me over.

I spin around and for a moment catch the flash of movement in the courtyard. Then I realize it's only the moonlight reflecting off the bronze statue of Night.

I look back down over the railing. Simon and Lyros have vanished.

Serves me right for eavesdropping, I think, taking a deep breath to calm myself. I should be in bed instead of imagining cultish conspiracies.

As I make my way back to my room, though, I see that I may not have imagined that someone was in the courtyard. In Night's outstretched right hand, which only a moment ago was empty, there is now a bright red flower. I lean over the water to take it and see that it is, indeed, a live poppy. The flower of Night and the underworld. I suddenly have the same sensation that Phineas describes: the rites have begun.

CHAPTER 13

The next morning I carry the poppy—kept fresh overnight in a half-filled bottle of mineral water—downstairs to the lower court-yard and casually lay it down next to my plate at the breakfast table where Simon, George, Agnes and Maria are gathered.

"Ah," Simon exclaims, looking up from his eggs and sausages, "*Papaver Somniferum.* The flower of sleep and forgetfulness. Where did you find it? I haven't seen any growing at the villa."

"I found it in the courtyard last night . . . after I finished read-ing the Phineas section."

"Of course," George says, "just where Phineas finds it. Someone was playing a little joke on you."

I look around the table. Agnes is engrossed in reading a letter and Maria is stirring her coffee and staring into space. After a minute, she notices me looking at her. "Perhaps Dr. Lawrence left it for you," Maria suggests. "He is your admirer, no?"

"No!" I say a bit too vehemently. Agnes glances up from her letter looking puzzled. Maria smiles and taps a manicured fingernail beneath her right eye.

"Ah, I've found you out," she says. "I suspected there was something between you two when he went running off to find you in Naples."

"Who?" Agnes asks. "Something between who?"

Maria sips her coffee and shrugs.

"That's ridiculous," I say. "Elgin and I are colleagues." *I don't even like him very much,* I'm tempted to add, but that would only add fuel to Maria's flame and seem petty after Elgin rescued me from the Hotel Convento. "Besides, I don't see Elgin going out flower picking late at night. It must have been someone who had read the Phineas earlier than the rest of us though—" I look at George and he shakes his head.

"It wasn't me! I drank so much wine at dinner I was asleep by ten. Nor would I have any idea where to find a poppy. They certainly don't grow in the garden here."

"I bet it was Mr. Lyros." Agnes puts her letter down and furrows her brow. "He read the section as soon as I finished transcribing it before dinner and he'd know where to find a poppy. And he's so into re-creating the atmosphere of the original Villa della Notte. He wanted you to feel like the events in Phineas's book are happening here, now." Agnes picks up the flower and holds it to her nose, inhaling its spicy scent.

"Careful," Simon warns. "You know what happened to Dorothy when she ran through the poppy field."

Agnes looks up at Simon and I fear that she's going to get upset again as she had last night when Simon recounted the story of

Baron Fersen and started talking about American cults. Instead, she smiles sweetly at him. "That's my favorite part of the *Wizard of Oz*," she says. "When they all fall asleep until the snow wakes them up. I never thought of it being about drugs, though. I mean, it's a children's story."

"So's *Alice in Wonderland*," George points out, "and there's all that hookah smoking and tablets that say 'Eat me.' Drugs have been a source of religious and artistic inspiration for millennia."

"Like the oracle of Delphi," Simon adds. "They think the fumes that came up through the cracks under the temple brought on hallucinations. And there are poppies carved into the gates of Eleusis. The initiates no doubt ingested opium to prepare themselves for the rites."

"I bet opium was part of the rite performed at the Villa della Notte," George says.

"Of course," Simon says, "the girl playing the part of the maiden would have been given opium as well. So you see, Miss Hancock, you needn't have worried so much about Iusta's role in the ceremonies. She would have been so insensible from the drug that she wouldn't have felt a thing."

"You think that makes it all right?" Agnes drops the poppy as though she'd suddenly noticed an insect on it. "That she was drugged? I suppose you think roofies and date rape are okay, too?"

George and I exchange looks, both of us surprised, I think, at Agnes's irritable tone, but Maria looks up from her breakfast genuinely confused. "Roofies? Date rape? I don't know these terms. Do rapists make a date with their victims in your country? On a roof?"

Agnes's eyes widen and I'm afraid she's going to throw something at Maria or Simon, but instead she bursts into tears and runs from the courtyard. Simon turns to watch her go.

"What?" Maria asks in response to a glare from George. "What did I say wrong? The girl is a bit hysterical, no?"

"Yes," Simon says, turning back to the table and helping himself to a cornetto. "She seems quite overwrought. She seems to take this whole business personally."

"You might want to remember that a month ago Agnes's ex-boyfriend shot and killed two people and then himself right in front of her," I tell Simon. "You'd take it personally, too."

"Perhaps the Phineas material isn't helping," George says. "She does seem to identify with Iusta, and that's bound to get more disturbing the way things are going. I think I should give her the morning off and transcribe the next section myself. Maybe you could talk to her, Dr. Chase, take her to the beach or into town for some shopping or something." George's long thin fingers flutter in the air as he conjures up these feminine diversions. I can see he's genuinely concerned about Agnes but that he feels out of his depth.

"I'd be happy to talk to Agnes," I say, "but I ought to check with Mr. Lyros before I leave the villa—"

"Oh, that's not necessary," Maria says. "He and Dr. Lawrence left for Herculaneum early this morning to oversee the excavation of Phineas's room. I imagine they won't be back until dinner and I don't think there's much work here for you. Perhaps you should look at the shops in town," she says, eyeing my madras skirt and tank top as though they came from the Salvation Army. (The skirt, in fact, was from a thrift shop on South Congress Avenue.) "Or go to the beach. You could use some color."

I smile, hoping to hide my chagrin at Maria's critique of my wardrobe and complexion. "You know," I say, "I think I'll do both. Thanks, Maria. Have a good day in the lab."

It takes me a while to find Agnes's room in the maze of what would have been the slave quarters in the original Villa della Notte and now houses the staff of the Papyrus Project. It's a tiny room with whitewashed walls that Agnes has decorated with postcards from tourist sites around the Bay of Naples: the lovely yellow-robed Flora from Stabia, the portrait of a young Pompeian matron holding a stylus to her lips that's in the Naples Museum, a dancing maenad from Pompeii's Villa of the Mysteries. Interspersed with these images of graceful Roman women are views of the Swiss Alps. Agnes is lying on her bed, still clutching the letter she'd had at breakfast. *Of course,* I realize, *it's from Sam.* I'm about to ask her if that's what had upset her when my attention is drawn to a small plaster statue on her nightstand.

"I've seen this before," I say, picking up the statue of a mother holding a child.

"Isn't it sweet," Agnes says, sitting up and smiling at the statue. "It's called the Madonna della Mare. The Madonna of the Sea. I bought it at a little shop near the ferry in Naples. The old woman who sold it to me said it was a copy of a statue in a church in Naples and that people prayed to it when they or their loved ones were taking a sea journey. Look, she's wearing a crown shaped like waves. I don't usually like Catholic things, but she doesn't look like any other Catholic saint I've ever seen. She has the sweetest smile."

I look into the face of the little figure and see what Agnes means. The face is simply carved, almost primitive, and her smile is enigmatic, as if she held the secret to all of life's mysteries. "I think I saw the original in a little church near my hotel in Naples," I say, looking down at Agnes. Although she's trying to smile, I can see from her red eyes that she's been crying hard. "Speaking of the sea," I say, putting the statue carefully down on the nightstand, "get your bathing suit. I'm dying to get in the water."

After I've changed into my bathing suit, terry-cloth cover-up, and sandals I meet Agnes back in the lower courtyard. The stairs to the beach start on the north end of the courtyard and descend several stories belowground. It feels like we're going into a catacomb.

"Mr. Lyros says that the stairs are part of the original plan of the Herculanean villa, only it's not clear where they went. When I read the section of Phineas yesterday I thought that maybe they led to an underground grotto, or nymphaeum, with access to the sea. That would explain how Iusta appeared in the water beneath the peristylium. I bet that's where the rites took place."

"An underground sanctuary to represent Hades," I say, "perfect for reenacting the abduction of Persephone into the underworld." Concentrating on the scholarly puzzle keeps my growing anxiety at bay as we descend deeper underground. I'd never been troubled by claustrophobia before, but since the shooting and losing part of my lung, I'm finding it hard to breathe in enclosed places. The stairwell is amply lit by shell-shaped sconces set into niches, the walls are newly plastered and dry, the steps carved from cool, white marble, but still, I feel uneasy. I focus on the top of Agnes's head below me—on her blond ponytail that bobs up and down as she trips lightly down the stairs. With the yellow bow of her halter bathing suit top at the nape of her neck, her orange UT T-shirt, and rubber flip-flops she certainly doesn't look anything like a girl descending into Hell.

"And if the underground grotto had access to the sea," I continue in my professorial mode, "then the women playing the sirens could have come and gone through the water. I bet that would have made for a dramatic effect."

"Kind of like the old mermaid show at Aquarena Springs in San Marcos," Agnes says, glancing back over her shoulder at me. "Did you ever go to it before they turned the theme park into a nature center?"

"Yes," I say. An image of my mother, her eyes sparking green in the murky underwater light, appears in my head. "But I'm surprised you're old enough to remember it. It closed down in the early nineties."

"Oh, I've heard people talk about it. You know how Austinites are always going on about the good old days."

"Yeah," I say, "it can get kind of annoying, like you've missed out on something." Something about Agnes's answer strikes me as evasive and I wonder if it was Elgin who told her about the Mermaid show, and whether he told her the story I told him about my mother and the mermaids on the boat ride to Capri. The idea of him sharing that intimate bit of my history with Agnes makes me flush with shame. I'm glad that Agnes isn't looking at me—and that she drops the subject when we reach the bottom of the steps.

"In the original villa, these steps would have ended here," she says, opening the door, "wherever it was they led, but we're quite a bit farther above the sea here so . . ."

Beyond the door is wide open blue sky and a limestone ledge a hundred feet above the sea. The steps continue down in the open, hugging the limestone cliff. There's a low wall, about four feet high, on the sea side, but beyond that it's a sheer drop to the rocks below.

"Keep close to the cliff wall," Agnes instructs as she starts down. "The stairs are steep and the rock is uneven in places. Mr. Lyros says the stairs were here when he built the property and were probably built by fishermen who used this cove."

Or by mountain goats, I think, clinging to the limestone wall. It's hard to imagine any other creature scaling this vertical rise. But when I feel something skitter over my hand I discover the other inhabitant of the island capable of navigating this terrain: the blue lizard.

"Aren't they darling?" Agnes asks when she sees me staring at the creature. "I wish I could take one home with me. C'mon, we'd better get going or we won't have much time before the tide comes in."

Agnes starts back down the stairs as the blue lizard disappears behind a veil of yellow broom and sea fennel. Something else is in the little niche. I push the greenery aside, releasing the sharp scent of licorice, and see that it's a satyr with an enormous phallus and that the phallus itself has two eyes and a leering grin. I'm so startled by the unexpected lewdness that I step back, trip over a loose stone and land on the edge of the sea wall. For a moment the sea and sky spin around me, the steep cliffs looming over me like leering giants ready to brush me loose like a fleck of dust from their shoulders. I squeeze my eyes shut and clutch my nails into the crumbing limestone until the vertigo passes.

When I open my eyes, the world has righted itself and the obscene little statue is once again hidden in its green shrine. I release my hold on the wall and find I'm gripping loose pebbles. A pile of them are neatly stacked on the wall. This must be where Simon and John Lyros were standing last night when I saw them from the terrace. Lyros had said something about Simon imagining cult practices all around them. I'd thought he was just reprimanding Simon for teasing Agnes at dinner, but now I wonder if instead they had been arguing about this statue. Had Simon found the statue in the niche and suggested that Lyros was practicing some kind of modern cult ritual? The idea that Lyros might be re-creating some kind of ritual here in his re-creation of the Villa della Notte is alarming. It's the last place Agnes should be after what she's been through.

I look down the steps to reassure myself that she's okay, but Agnes is nowhere to be seen. The vacant stone steps plunge into the rough tide—too rough to swim in, I'm sure. I scan the cliff face, but there's no place where anything bigger than a lizard could perch. Could she have fallen without me hearing her while I was transfixed by the little priapic devil? Should I try to search the rocks at the base of the steps where the surf churns, or go back to the villa to get help? And how in the world will I ever be able to face Sam Tyler and tell him I lost Agnes on a trip to the beach?

I hear someone call my name. The sound is hollow and echoing and reminds me of Phineas's description of the siren song he heard from the peristylium, only I can't imagine the sirens would address me with my full title.

"Dr. Chase?" the voice calls again. Then Agnes's blond ponytail pops out from a crevice in the rock. "Hey, what are you still doing up there? The grotto's right here—" I follow Agnes's voice to a cleft in the rock—so narrow it had been invisible from above—and slip in between the limestone walls.

"Careful, there's a ledge right here. It takes a second to adjust to the light." Agnes takes my hand and guides me into the grotto. After the brightness of the sun outside, it's dark as night, only it's a night unlike any I've ever seen: a shimmering azure night. At first I can't tell where the water begins and the light ends. It's like being inside a glass bowl filled with blue light. Slowly, as my eyes adjust, I make out the roof of the grotto about fifteen feet above me and the rock ledge that rims the pool of sparkling blue water. The light seems to be pulsing up from the water and casting reflections on the stone walls.

"The tide's higher than I thought it would be," Agnes says, "but we can swim here for a little bit and then, if you don't mind diving, we can go through the opening underwater. There's a rock just outside where we can lie in the sun."

I nod, not sure I like the idea of diving, but embarrassed to look fearful in front of Agnes. All my worries about her seem silly now; she seems perfectly at ease and confident in this environment. I take off my cover-up and sandals and lower myself into the water. It's warm as bathwater and tingly, so salty I feel buoyant. I breast-stroke across the grotto and then flip over onto my back to bathe the back of my head. Wavy bands of light ripple on the stone dome above me. As I follow them they turn into undulating shapes: the curve of a woman's hip, the flick of a tail, the roll of a shoulder, a sinuous curl of hair. Light mermaids, I think, delighting in the spectacle.

The source of the light is a triangular cleft in the rock on the north side of the grotto. I follow Agnes toward it and then watch as she dives and disappears into a fissure of light beneath the water. I have the uneasy feeling that she's been transformed into one of the light mermaids racing across the domed ceiling, but take a deep breath and follow her. The saltwater stings my eyes, but I force them open to steer myself into the narrow cleft. Am I as slim as Agnes? I suddenly wonder. What if I get stuck underwater between the rock walls? I feel the pressure on my lungs as I squeeze through the split, and the scrape of rock on my right shoulder and then my left hip, then I'm surfacing into bright light. When I break the surface of the water, the sound of the surf crashing is all around me but the water is calm. I'm in a little cove at the entrance to the grotto, protected by a circle of rocks that absorb the force of the waves. Agnes is treading water, waiting for me.

"Isn't it great!" she says, her smile beaming in the sunlight. "Every time I do it I feel like I'm being born all over again."

I nod, my breath still too ragged to speak.

"Let me show you the sunbathing rock," she says, turning and swimming about ten feet away from the grotto's entrance. We pull ourselves up on a flat, smooth rock that's just big enough for two of us to stretch out. The contours of the rock seem to fit the shape of my body perfectly and the stone is warm and dry. I'm on the side facing the open sea and when I turn my head I'm looking out on an expanse of water that seems to stretch into infinity and contain every shade of blue and green ever dreamed of by every painter in the world. The only object in view is a blue-and-white sailboat, about forty or fifty feet away, bobbing on the water, its sails down and its deck empty.

"Oh, gosh, I feel so much better now," Agnes says, sighing. "I'm so glad you thought of coming down here. Being someplace so beautiful makes all my problems seem so . . . so unimportant."

"I hope Simon Bowles hasn't upset you with all his talk of cults and sacrifices—" I stop, unsure if it's a good idea to bring up the subject, but Agnes seems unperturbed by my reference to last night's dinner conversation.

"Oh no, Simon's just a bit of a dirty old man. He likes to tease me just to see if he can get a rise out of me. I think the whole thing upset Mr. Lyros more than it upset me. He's sensitive about his reasons for building this place, and Simon seemed to be suggesting he built this villa as a sort of playground instead of for scholarly research. Anyway, it wasn't Simon who upset me, it was the letter I got today. It was from Sam . . . you remember Sam, right?"

"The cute boy who's obviously head over heels in love with you? Yeah, I remember him."

"He *is* cute," Agnes says, giggling, and then, her voice grows abruptly serious, "but he's not in love with me. At least not anymore. We went out in high school for a while but then . . . when he went off to college the year before me I broke up with him. I didn't want him to feel hemmed in by having a girlfriend back home. I'd seen how that had worked out for some of the older girls in school. They'd start out the year with the guy's pictures all over their lockers and wearing his college ring on a chain, and then at homecoming the guys would come back and follow the girls around to parties looking like a bunch of sad-eyed dogs on too short a lead. I didn't want that. I told him if he still wanted to date we could when I got to college the next year."

"That sounds pretty generous of you," I say.

She doesn't answer for a few minutes and then she says, "No. I wasn't being generous at all. I didn't want to hang around waiting for him to come home. I didn't realize, though, how much it would upset him. He had a pretty wild freshman year as a result."

"That's not your fault," I reassure her, thinking of all the wild antics that UT freshmen get up to with or without their girlfriends from back home breaking up with them. "What happened when you got to UT?"

"Oh, you know how it is," she says. "People change, find different interests. He was living with a bunch of guys and I moved into a sorority. We still hung out, but it just wasn't the same. When I had to leave the sorority, though, he was really nice, inviting me to move into his house, but sometimes I think it was a mistake. He started acting like he was my big brother—criticizing me, making fun of the stuff I was into, which was pretty hypocritical considering all the stuff he experimented with *his* freshman year. I should have realized that he was just looking out for me, but I thought he was trying to control me and, well, I didn't act very nice to him."

"But you stayed in the house. . . ."

"He insisted. Said if I didn't he'd call home and tell my father that I had to leave school because Dale was dangerous."

We're both quiet for a while contemplating just how right Sam had been. I turn my head and look toward the sea. The sailboat has drifted at its anchorage so that the stern of the boat faces me. Its name, I'm surprised to see, is *Persephone.* Its port of call, Samos, Greece. "What does he say in the letter?" I ask.

"He says he needs to know if I still have any feelings for him and that he can't wait any longer for me. He has to know now. I think it's because he's met someone else."

"It sounds to me that you do still have feelings for him, Agnes. Why else would the letter upset you?"

She doesn't say anything and when I turn and look at her I see that she's crying. I look away again, toward the sailboat, not wanting to embarrass her.

"I guess you're right," she says after a few minutes, her voice tight with the effort of not sobbing. "But I just think it's probably too late. I mean, do you think you can ever get back together with someone after you've broken up and so much time has gone by? Would *you* go back with an old boyfriend if he had made a stupid mistake?"

Agnes asks this last question so earnestly, as if I were an oracle that possessed the secrets of the universe, that I'm afraid to answer.

Considering the bad choices I've made with men, how can I possibly advise her? But then I remember how Sam had looked when he asked me to keep an eye on Agnes and I figure that the least I can do is do him a good turn. But how can I describe what it feels like to love someone so much that their absence marks you?

"Do you remember when I talked in class about Wilhelmina Jashemski?"

Agnes looks at me as if I might be losing my mind. She's asked for advice about love and I'm talking to her about an archaeologist. "Uh, didn't she do something with gardens in Pompeii and Herculaneum?" Agnes asks.

"Yes," I say, pleased that she's remembered the detail from a class she took sophomore year. "She discovered that the roots of the trees and shrubs that had been growing when Vesuvius erupted had decayed beneath the hardened lava, leaving breaks in it, which then filled up with little pebbles. When Jashemski cleared the pebbles she poured plaster in the empty spaces and made casts of their roots—"

"Like the plaster casts of the people who died in Pompeii?"

"Exactly. I've always thought of them as ghost roots."

"That's really fascinating, Dr. Chase, but I don't see how—"

"Don't you see? When you lose someone you love you carry around that empty place they once filled, in just that same shape. No one can ever fill it but them," I finish lamely, feeling like I've utterly failed at trying to convey this idea to Agnes, but when I look at her I see that she's staring at me, widening her eyes as if she's trying to hold back tears.

"So what kind of 'ghost roots' are inside you, Dr. Chase?" she asks.

The question and how she's phrased it, echoing my own words, takes me by surprise. I'm saved from answering by a motion from the boat that draws Agnes's attention.

A dark head has appeared above the railing; someone coming up onto the deck. I watch the slim man in red T-shirt and white jeans lift a pair of binoculars to his face and point them in our direction. I have an irrational urge to wave.

Agnes is still waiting for me to answer her question, but I can't take my eyes off the man in the red T-shirt. He's taken the binoculars away from his face but he's still looking at me. Although we're more than a hundred feet apart I feel like the space has contracted to inches. Maybe it's what we've been talking about—the particular size and shape of the ghost roots inside myself—that creates the illusion, but I could swear that the man on the boat looks an awful lot like Ely.

CHAPTER 14

"Is that boat back again?"

I turn to Agnes. She's sitting up now, shading her eyes with one hand, looking out toward the bay.

"You've seen it before?"

"Yeah. The *Persephone*—who could forget that name considering what we're doing here? And besides, the guy on it is awfully cute, don't you think?"

I turn back to look at the lone figure on the deck. Tall, slim, dark hair and eyes, a high forehead, he looks a lot like Ely, but then, how many times in the last five years have I glimpsed Ely—in the checkout line at Wheatsville, on the hike-and-bike trail by Town Lake—and been wrong. Still . . .

I raise my right hand tentatively, less in greeting than as a question, and the figure on the boat does the same. I feel ridiculously as if we are trading semaphore signals across a battlefield, but then, for one moment, I feel as if we're only inches apart, eyes locked.

Then he disappears below deck.

"Wow, you've made contact," Agnes says, her voice giddy at the prospect of meeting the mysterious stranger. "Good for you, Dr. Chase."

I feel something lift in my chest, a swelling lightness that could be happiness or fear, but then the still air is rent by the whine of an engine and the boat begins to motor away from us.

"Actually it looks like I scared him away," I say, trying not to sound as let down as I feel.

"Maybe he just went to get a friend," Agnes says, patting me on the shoulder. "After all, there are two of us. Unfortunately, we can't wait around to find out. The tide is coming in and it's a little tricky getting through the grotto when the water's high."

Agnes dives into the water, but I keep my eyes on the *Persephone* until she disappears around the rocky headland to the east.

It turns out to be more than a little tricky getting through the grotto at high tide. The sea entrance is completely below water level and whereas the cleft had been outlined in light on the way out, it's barely visible going back into the grotto. I follow Agnes through the now churning surf, under the water, and through a dark tunnel. I can't help but wonder if there's more than one opening in the limestone cliff. What if she's chosen the wrong one? What if she's leading us into an underwater tunnel with no way out? I recall reading somewhere in a book on southern Italian folklore that in primitive fishing villages women were left bound in narrow sea caves to drown when the tide came in as a punishment for infidelity. As I grope my way through the narrow cleft I imagine what it would feel like to be trapped in a limestone coffin slowly filling with seawater.

When I surface, gasping for air, I nearly bump my head on the rock. This grotto looks nothing like the one we came through and for a moment I'm sure we are trapped underground in a rapidly filling tomb. But then I see Agnes at the far end of the grotto, silhouetted against a jagged seam of light. She waves for me to swim toward her and when I reach her she shows me where to put my feet to climb out of the grotto. We emerge into bright sunlight on the steps, next to where we left our clothes.

"I'm sorry," Agnes says as she hands me a towel to wrap around my shoulders. Even in the sun, I am shivering, unable to shrug off the chill of the underwater cavern. "I should have kept better track of the time. I didn't realize the tide was so high."

"Does the grotto fill completely with water?" I ask, my teeth chattering.

"Well, I've seen water spilling out of that opening," Agnes says, pointing to the seam we've just climbed out of. "So, yeah, I guess it does. You could still get through the grotto, only you'd have to make it from one opening to the other without surfacing for air. It's the kind of daredevil stunt Sam would love," she says with a little smile, "but I don't think I'd want to try it."

"Me neither," I concur, remembering my diminished lung capacity. "I guess we wouldn't have been good candidates for the Aquarena Springs Mermaid Show."

When we get back to the courtyard Agnes says she's going to go straight to the lab to see how George is getting on with the day's scanning. I volunteer to go with her, thinking that I might be able to get a head start on the next Phineas section.

"You're hooked, aren't you?" Agnes asks.

"I guess so," I admit. The truth is that my head is filled with the image of the man from the *Persephone,* with trying to line up his face with my memories of Ely, and the only thing I can imagine that will take my mind off the identity of the mysterious stranger is the next installment of Phineas's journal. If I had any doubt that the next installment was worth getting hold of, it's erased when we enter the lab and George looks up from the scanner, his bloodshot eyes gleaming.

"You're going to love this next part," he tells me and Agnes. "It's like getting a guided walking tour through Herculaneum two days before it was destroyed."

"Cool," Agnes says, "I was afraid the whole thing was going to be Phineas wandering around the villa chasing after poor Iusta."

"Well, here we've got him going to the baths, and *then* we get him chasing Iusta around town. Here are the photocopies of what I've scanned today," George says, handing Agnes a thin stack of papers. "And my transcription of the Latin awaiting your exceptional translating skills."

Agnes blushes at George's compliment, confirming my suspicion that there's a flirtation going on between these two. *What about Sam?* I want to ask.

"I'll get right to work on it," Agnes says. "I'll have it ready by dinnertime."

I look over Agnes's shoulder at the pages of Latin and decide that unless I want to spend the afternoon pining for failed love affairs (mine, Agnes's, Sam's), I'd better get myself something to do. "Why don't you give me a copy?" I ask.

Agnes looks up, a flicker of wariness in her eyes, and I realize she thinks I don't trust her translating ability. "That way we'll both have time for lunch and a siesta before dinner," I add, hoping she'll see that I'm treating her as an equal.

"Okay," she replies, yawning a little as she takes the sheets to the copying machine. "I didn't get much sleep last night. You look tired, too, Dr. Chase. I think our swim took a lot out of you."

I decide, though, that instead of lunch and a siesta I need to get out of the villa for a bit. I change back into my skirt, tank top, and sandals and, tossing my wallet, a Latin dictionary, and the Phineas transcript in a canvas bag, head out the gates and down toward town. I pass iron gates covered with bougainvillea affording glimpses of majolica-tiled walkways and grape-covered pergolas. Each one looks more secretive than the last—a hidden bower where just about anything could be going on, a private Eden for those eccentric foreigners Lyros spoke of before, come to live out their fantasies.

As I approach the town, the private villas are interspersed with small hotels and shops until I'm walking in a narrow cobbled street between high whitewashed walls. It could be a medieval city except that here the ancient walls are pierced with shop windows full of gaudy resortwear and jewelry carved from coral and shell. I stop at one of the windows to look at the cameos, which are my favorites. There among the Victorian profiles and half-nude goddesses I find one that depicts two women in profile—Day and Night—a common motif in nineteenth-century cameos. The woman who represents Day has her head lifted, her hair is adorned with wheat and roses, and a dove spreads its wings across her bodice. Her sister, Night, is behind her, her star-veiled head bowed, her hair bound with poppies, an owl nestled between her breasts. No wonder this motif was so popular with the Victorians: it represented what Elgin had called last night "the dual nature of the feminine."

The merchandise becomes pricier near the Piazzetta—designer shoes and handbags and Cartier—to go with the seven-euro lemonades served in the Gran'Caffe. It'll cost me a fortune to drink enough lemonades to last through a reading of the Phineas, but I sit down anyway, determined to enjoy a restful hour away from the intrigues at the villa.

I order a *pizza all'Acqua* and a lemonade. The waiter brings me a tall glass with fresh-squeezed lemon juice, a pitcher of water, and a smaller pitcher of sugar syrup. The pizza is covered in the fresh mozzarella I've become addicted to and studded with local *peperoncino* chilis. It's like eating a meal of dichotomies: the hot peppers pillowed in bland, creamy mozzarella, the tart lemon juice tempered by the sugar. At first I'm so seduced by the food that I can't focus on the Latin words in front of me, but slowly, between bites and sips, I unravel Phineas's day in Herculaneum.

When I awoke the next morning the villa was so silent that I almost believed it had fallen under a spell, or at least that the revelries of the previous evening had left all the inhabitants so drained that they still slept. But then the grizzled old servant—I could tell by his pilleus that he had recently been granted his freedom—who brought me my morning bread and drink told me that far from being asleep, his mistress and her handmaids had arisen at dawn to travel to Surrentum to pay homage there at the temple of the sirens. "As they always do before the rites," he told me. "It's part of the preparation."

"And the girl Iusta," I asked, "has she gone, too?"

"She had errands in town to perform for the mistress this morning," he told me. I thought I saw an impudent smile creeping over his face and so I cut short our colloquy by demanding hot water.

"I'm afraid there's none to be had as the slaves are all busy with preparations for the rites," he told me, again with a smile that suggested he was secretly pleased at my inconvenience. I made a note to myself to speak to Calatoria about her servant's impudence and asked if there was a decent bath in town.

"We have two," the old man said, "a large one in the forum and a smaller, but more refined establishment on the walls of the marina. You

would no doubt prefer the Suburban Baths. It is only a short walk along the marina wall."

"Good," I told the servant, not wanting him to think I was in any way inconvenienced by this turn of events. "I wanted to look at the marina to see if there are any boats I might commission for the rest of my journey. And I am always glad for the opportunity to see new sights."

"Then you've come to the right place," the old slave told me. "You will see things here that you have never seen before."

The old man departed and, if I'm not mistaken, I heard him chuckling to himself as he went. No doubt he was alluding to the rites that I would be taking part in soon and trying to alarm me, I conjectured as I dressed and left the villa. Little did he know what marvels I had witnessed in my travels. I have seen in Egypt the embalmed bodies of centaurs and mermaids and in Sicily and Rhodes I have been shown the bones of giants that, according to the natives, were spewn forth from the earth during times of earthquake. I have taken part in the mysteries of Eleusis and Agrai and inhaled the vapors that rise up from the bowels of the earth at the oracle of Delphi. I doubted that anything dreamed up in this little provincial town could rival the things I've seen.

I did notice, though, as I made my way through the gate to the marina and down a long ramp to the baths that it is a town quite preoccupied with the pleasures of the flesh. Numerous inscriptions and drawings on the walls indicated that sexual liaisons of many kinds were practiced here on Herculaneum's waterfront. One named Sturnus had written, "And willingly we perform the act to which the permissive Longinus consented with pleasure: quick carnal union," and another had drawn a picture illustrating a similar union.

In contrast to these lewd decorations, I found a terrace of shrines dedicated to the gods, local and imported. In one reposed a statue of Isis suckling her son, the god Horus, which reminded me of the little statue I had given Iusta. I wondered if she had already taken it to the market *and sold it, but then I reproved myself for the base thought and looked around for the baths. I found them on the last level before the beach, built right into the marina wall. Its roof formed a terrace for a private house, from which I could hear voices and laughter. I passed through a courtyard, where a statue of Marcus Nonius Balbus commemorated the proconsul's restoration of the town after the last earthquake and then through an arched portal that had been partially and inelegantly bricked up—a result, I deduced, of damage from the same earthquake. I had observed similar signs of damage in my hostess's villa and it now occurred to me that the dissolute nature of the town might be a result of living on unstable ground.*

I descended into an elegant vestibule supported by four enormous red columns and washed my hands at a small basin with water that flowed from the head of Apollo. I had to admit that the old freedman had been right about the elegance of these baths. The cloakroom where a slave took my clothing was quite beautifully paneled in polished woods, the linen I was given to wrap myself in was of the finest weave. As I took my place on the marble bench of the apodyterium, I admired the panels of warriors locked in combat and cupids engaged in their own sports. A group of men sat across from me, too engrossed in their conversation to notice a stranger in their midst, and I settled down, patient to wait my turn in the tepidarium if it afforded me a chance to listen to the locals' conversation.

It soon became apparent that the three men were discussing a lawsuit in the local courts and that the case concerned the disputed manumission of a slave.

"It all came down to the birthdate," one man with a weak chin and prominent nose said to his companions. "On whether she was born before her mother was freed or after."

"I thought there was a witness who said she was born after," his companion said.

"Yes, but the same man changed his testimony," the first man said. "They say he gained his freedom by lying in court."

"I say they shouldn't have taken the word of a slave," contended the youngest of the three, a handsome youth with a feminine face and ringleted hair. "Of course he'd say what his mistress bid him to say."

"If the word of a slave is so suspect, my dear Dexter, then why should we listen to you?" the third man said, draping his arm around the shoulder of the youth and twining his fingers through his curls. "And why should anyone believe the word of this girl who could not be expected to remember the day of her own birth?"

"An excellent point, Apelles. I could have told you the outcome of the case before its conclusion. Why would the family have allowed a pregnant slave to buy her freedom before the birth of the child when they could just as easily wait and retain a replacement for the lost slave? It makes no sense at all."

"Ah, but I've heard that the master of the house was fond of this slave and so granted her the right to buy back her freedom before the child was born. How else could she have set herself up in such a lucrative business if not with her former master's backing?"

"Hm, I did wonder about that," the long-nosed man said. "I've tasted her oysters—they're the best in the Cup."

"Yes," the boy Dexter said eagerly, "and now all those oyster beds have become the property of—"

"Her mistress," Apelles concluded, clapping Dexter on the back. "And none too soon. The word in the marketplace is that since her husband's death Calatoria's household has been severely depleted of finances. They say Gaius Petronius made a number of unwise investments and gambled away his wife's fortune. No wonder it is said that Calatoria despises all men and practices rites only to female gods in her household. They say—"

I had perhaps unwisely shown my interest in the conversation since hearing the name of my hostess and the man called Apelles now stopped, seeming to take notice of my presence for the first time. At the same moment, a slave appeared, telling the three men that their guest had arrived and was awaiting them in a private room. Then, turning to me, the slave indicated that I could now enter the tepidarium. I was sorry that we were separated before I could learn more. Even the pleasures of the warm bath, followed by a good sweat in the sudatorium and then a plunge in the frigidarium, did little to distract me from pondering the conversation I had overheard. Clearly they were talking about Iusta—the daughter of the oyster vendor who gained her freedom either just before or after giving birth to her. I found I agreed with the long-nosed man when he said it didn't make sense for Gaius Petronius to grant Vitalis her freedom before she gave birth . . . unless she was a particular favorite. As I was toweled off and rubbed by a most efficient masseuse I thought about the pictures of Iusta's mother on the wall in the courtyard, depicting her as the young frightened initiate. Who, I wondered, had played the role of the god Dionysus in that rite? Had it been Gaius Petronius himself? And if he had played the role of Dionysus with Vitalis, might he have been Iusta's father? That might explain why he would give Vitalis her freedom before her child was born. It would also explain the superior education he had given Iusta. I determined that the next time I saw Iusta I would ask her if Gaius Petronius ever gave her reason to believe he was her father. The old man had said Iusta was doing errands in town; perhaps I might find her in the forum.

So anxious was I to leave the baths in order to pursue this goal that I became lost in the back rooms. I opened one door and found the furnace, then hearing voices and thinking that it must be the exit I opened another.

It was not the exit. It was the private room to which the men whose conversation I had overheard had repaired, along with their guest. The guest was a lady whose age it was difficult to judge both because of the great quantity of powder on her face and the unusual position she had assumed—a position I am reluctant to describe, suffice it to say that she was doing her best to entertain the gentleman with the long nose while the other two men, Dexter and Apelles, did their best to entertain each other.

I hastily closed the door, muttering apologies, and went in search of the exit. By the time I found it, I was sweating—the effects of the cold plunge already negated by the heat of the day and my exertion. The door I came out of let onto a narrow alley leading away from the sea and toward a steep flight of steps back up onto the level of the town. At the top of the steps I found myself at the crossroads of three streets marked, fittingly, by a shrine to Hecate, goddess of crossroads.

"And which way now?" I asked the three-bodied goddess. I noticed that one of the figures carried a torch, the other a pomegranate, and the third a poppy. Because I had been given a poppy last night I decided to take the street the last figure faced. "After all," I said to myself, "it is a small town organized along a grid. How lost could I get?"

It seemed though that no matter how many turns I made none led to the forum, nor did I see anyone of whom I could ask directions. The entire town seemed to be deserted. Had they all gone to Surrentum to worship at the Temple of the Sirens? Or were they all inside, engaging in recreations like those that occupied my friends from the baths?

Laughter and voices came from deep inside the houses I passed, but I was reluctant to venture inside any more private rooms. Then, as I turned down yet another long deserted street I saw a woman in a saffron-yellow stola and green palla framed in an archway, her back to me. Her head turned as she looked over her shoulder. Our eyes met and I recognized Iusta. I lifted my hand to summon her, but she must not have seen me because she disappeared around the corner. I ran up the street, determined to catch up with her, but when I reached the street she had gone down and turned in the direction she had gone, I found myself facing a blind and empty alley. It was as if she had been swallowed up by the earth. I ran to the end of the alley and pressed my hands up against the stone wall, as if I could melt through it and join her, and then I noticed that there was a small doorway in the wall to my right that was so covered with trailing flowers that I had at first missed it. Above the doorway, scratched in the stone, were three signs: a boat, a woman holding a child, and a crudely drawn fish. Was the girl here being prepared for Calatoria's rites? If that were the case, and I blundered into a secret rite only for women, mightn't I be subject to some awful punishment? I recalled what the men at the baths said about Calatoria's hatred toward men. Did I want to earn her wrath? I was on the verge of turning away, but then I heard a sound come from inside the house: a low moaning as of someone who had been gravely injured. Without further considering the consequences, I pushed aside the vines and entered . . .

"You've got to be kidding me," I say aloud to the blank page. "Damn it, George! That's where you break off?"

I've spoken louder than I meant to and as I look up I notice several tourists staring at me. Including one man at a table at the edge of the square in a red T-shirt and white jeans and dark sunglasses. He smiles at me and holds up his hand in the same gesture he'd made from the boat. As my hand moves to mirror it, I knock the pitcher of water into my lap. I look away—for only a moment, concerned mostly for the transcripts, forgetting for the moment that they're not originals. When I look up, the man is gone.

I stand up and take off after him. He can't have gone far, I figure, passing under a tiled arch. I see a flash of red in a crowd of tourists outside a gelateria halfway down the street, but by the time I struggle through the crowd he's gone. I turn up a winding street lined with souvenir and postcard shops and get stuck in the crowds spilling out of the funicular station. Past the station is a terrace overlooking the steep streets descending toward the Marina Grande. I scan the whole terrace and the streets I can see from there, but there's no sign of him. It's then that I realize I left my purse at my table in the Piazzetta. I run back, sure that my bag with my wallet will be gone, but when I reach the square I find that my bag's still hanging from my chair and my books and papers are still on the table.

A miracle, I think, gathering up my things. I get my watch stolen off my wrist, but when I leave my bag for anyone to take it's spared. I check my wallet and see that the cash is all there and then, as I'm counting out change for a tip I notice that, far from anything having been taken from the table, something's been added. Three small cards, each about an inch square, are lying in the plastic tip tray. Each one has a small, cartoonish figure on it: a man sweeping with a broom, a frying pan, and a sun. Signs as enigmatic as the one's Phineas found over the door in the alley. Unlike Phineas, though, I have no way of tracking down the meaning of the signs, so I pick up the little cards, slip them in my skirt pocket, and head back to the villa.

$\mathcal{A}$t the villa, I find everyone gathered at the table on the peristylium.

"Did you read it?" Agnes asks me. "I ended up translating the whole thing and distributing it because it wasn't very long."

I nod as I collapse into one of the chairs. Looking around the table, I see that everyone has a slim sheaf of papers in front of them. Elgin and Lyros are still reading theirs—presumably because they've just gotten back from Herculaneum. Simon is using his to fan himself. Maria has rolled hers into a tube and is tapping it on the arm of George's chair. "How could you stop just as he was going to the girl's house?" she asks. "Were you trying to tease us?"

George, the only one of the group who's not holding his manuscript, drags his long bony fingers through his hair as though he were trying to pull it out by the roots, but from the way he's looking at Maria I guess that it's her hair he'd like to pull out. "As I told you, that part of the papyrus is badly damaged. I'm not sure we'll be able to decipher it at all."

"You mean we may never know what happened in the house?" Agnes asks, her eyes wide. "Or who was screaming or why Iusta went in there?"

"I imagine Phineas was right: she was engaged in some purification rite," Elgin says. "The symbols sound like they could be associated with Isis."

"Then it really is a shame we don't have this section," Simon says. "The only details we know of the Rites of Isis are from Apulius and those are quite . . . tantalizing. It almost seems as if Phineas deliberately damaged the scroll at this point in the narrative to keep us in suspense."

"Or someone else did," Elgin says, looking up from his copy, "in order to keep the rites secret."

"Where does the papyrus become legible again?" Lyros asks.

George closes his eyes and recites from memory. "At the line: 'As I walked back to the villa, I pondered over all I had learned of Iusta and her unusual situation and wondered what would come of the pact we had entered into together.' "

A groan rises from the whole group.

"Maybe he tells us later," Agnes suggests. "I say we go on scanning and see if we can figure out what happened in the house from the rest of the papyrus."

Maria shakes her head. "It's like reading a mystery with half the clues torn out—"

"Or like coming into a Buñuel film half an hour late," Simon adds.

"Really?" Elgin asks, tilting his head toward Simon. "I can't make head or tails of Buñuel even if I'm there from the beginning."

"We'll just have to hope the rest of the journal explains the lapse," Lyros says. "In the meantime, the good news is that we think we've located Phineas's trunk. We should be able to open it by tomorrow. I thought perhaps some of you might want to be there."

"Well, I have to be there," Maria announces.

As the rest of the group wrangles out the details of tomorrow's excursion I turn back to the bay and reach into my skirt pocket to touch the three cards left for me at the cafe. There was no scroll to scan or trunk to excavate that might throw light on their meaning. I wondered if I'd ever figure it out.

At breakfast the next morning, Agnes offers to stay behind and work on scanning the next passage, but George insists she go to Herculaneum with the rest of us. "You really shouldn't miss seeing the villa," George says. "After all, you did your paper on the paintings there and you haven't even had a chance to see them in person yet."

"I'll be happy to show them to you," Simon offers. "I have to make some sketches for the reproductions. There are some details I think you will find especially interesting."

Agnes blanches, no doubt envisioning that she'll have to endure Simon Bowles pointing out the more lascivious features of the paintings. I'm expecting another outburst like those of yesterday, but to her credit Agnes composes herself and answers calmly. "Since I've studied the paintings, perhaps I could show *you* a thing or two about them. Why don't I bring my paper on the murals with us? You can start by reading it on the boat."

"I think you've met your match, Simon," Elgin says. Simon laughs, but when I look at Elgin I notice he's not smiling, and I wonder if he's worried that he's got a competitor for Agnes's attentions.

On the boat trip across the bay Agnes seems to have completely forgiven Simon's teasing from last night. She spends the whole trip down below in the cabin showing Simon her paper on the paintings of the Villa della Notte and discussing her theories. With Lyros at the helm, and Maria sunbathing on the prow of the boat, that leaves me with Elgin Lawrence for company, the last person I want to spend time with.

"I'm rereading the description of Isis in Apulius," I tell him when he settles down next to me.

Elgin ignores the hint and instead leans close and whispers in my ear. "There's something I have to talk to you about alone."

I pull back to look at him, to see whether he's flirting with me, but his expression is masked by dark sunglasses. I look back to the helm and meet John Lyros's gaze. I return his smile and say to Elgin in a low voice, "Why did you wait until today when we're on a field trip? You've had plenty of opportunity to talk to me alone."

"No, I haven't. You've been avoiding me."

"Me? You're the one who took off to Sorrento when I was bedridden."

Elgin's head moves back abruptly and his nostrils flare, looking a bit like the angry cobra on Isis's headdress that I've just read about in Apulius. "Is that what you're angry about? I couldn't help that, Sophie, honest. I left only after I was sure you were safely on the island"—he looks over his shoulder at John, who, I notice, is watching us—"and then I had to go. I had an appointment."

"Well, I hope she was worth it." As soon as the words are out, I'm ashamed of myself. Where did all this spite come from? Surely I'm long over my little fling with Elgin. It's been five years, after all, and it isn't like I'd ever really been in love with him. I'd turned to him out of anger at Ely, as a distraction—a distraction I'd paid heavily for.

Elgin must think my reaction is strange, too, because he's studying me with the same intent look he uses to examine difficult

Latin inscriptions. "It wasn't a woman," he says at last. "I have to explain—"

I'm spared Elgin's explanation by a summons from our captain. "Professor Lawrence," Lyros calls, pitching his voice to be heard above the roar of the engine and the slap of the waves. "Why don't you take a hand at steering. You mentioned you were a yachtsman."

Elgin winces. True, he keeps a sailboat on Lake Travis, but even he wouldn't refer to himself as a yachtsman. He clearly doesn't want to disappoint our rich benefactor, though. As he rises to go he whispers in my ear, "Let's talk when we get to Herculaneum. I'll figure out a way for us to be alone."

Elgin's rather transparent method of ensuring us privacy is to turn to me as we approach the excavation site and loudly ask, "Didn't you say you wanted to take a walk through the town, Sophie?"

Lyros, who's unlocking the gate, looks back at us, puzzled, but Maria says, "That's a good idea. We can't all crowd around the workmen." She glares at Agnes, but Simon comes to her rescue. "Don't worry about Agnes and me. We'll be busy looking at those paintings."

"Okay, then," Lyros says, checking his watch. "We should be done by noon, so if you want to be there at the unveiling—"

"Wouldn't miss it," Elgin says, winking at Lyros. Then he turns to the gate that leads back to the public excavations.

"Sophie," Lyros says before I can turn away, "I'll make sure we don't open it before you get back."

"Okay," I say, unsure how I'm supposed to respond to this. "Thanks. I won't be late." Then I turn to catch up to Elgin who, unlike the gentlemanly Lyros, hasn't waited for me at all. Finally, at the Porta Marina, the old entrance to the city, I catch up with him. He's striding down the cobbled streets of the ancient town as if down an avenue in a modern city, only here the streets are paved with giant blocks of stone worn smooth by pedestrians of two thousand years ago and rutted by cartwheels. At each intersection there are square-shaped blocks in the center of the street to make crossing easier, but which now impede our progress. Although it's only nine it's already brutally hot, and I remember that after my last visit here I collapsed with pneumonia.

"Slow down," I say.

"I will as soon as we're far enough away from the others," he says. "I don't want to risk being followed." We go three city blocks before Elgin slows down his pace to a manageable clip. I make him stop so I can catch my breath at the open doorway to a house. Looking inside, I can see that its atrium is still perfectly preserved from the open skylight to the mosaic floor of its impluvium—a shallow basin for collecting rainwater. The simple plan of the entrance hall, common to most traditional Roman houses, evokes a sense of order and peace, perhaps because the house seems to be welcoming rain and sunlight into it along with its guests.

"I'd forgotten how amazing this place is," I say. "It really feels as if you're in an ancient city."

Elgin sees me looking longingly into the house and after taking a quick look up and down the street steers me into the atrium. "This is probably as good a place as any," he says. "I think there's a garden inside this house that's pretty private."

As soon as we're inside the house it's cooler. The marble mosaic floor is buckled from the eruption, but it's still beautiful and the proportions of the house are so perfect that I immediately feel peaceful inside its walls. I feel as welcomed as the long bars of mote-filled sunlight that slant across the walls. The Romans had a god dedicated just to thresholds, and I can still feel its presence in this entrance.

"Do you know what this house is called?" I ask Elgin. But he's busy peering into the side rooms to make sure we're alone. I follow him into a small room off the atrium and gasp at the sight of the household shrine: it's a green and blue mosaic, perfectly preserved, and glittering in the morning sunlight. It depicts a goddess rising from the sea surrounded by dolphins. Venus perhaps? Or Neptune's wife, Amphitrite? Or even Isis, whom Apulius describes at the end of *The Golden Ass* as emerging from the sea, "shaking off the brine" before his eyes? But this figure has none of the other features Apulius described—no moon disk on her forehead or viper by her side or wreath of corn on her head. She could be one of many sea-born goddesses. It hardly seems to matter. The residents of this town wedged between sea and volcano no doubt prayed to every god of sea and underworld just to keep the ground beneath their feet steady.

In among the shiny glass tesserae are seashells and tiny pearls. A small marble statue of the goddess stands in the little niche, her features so worn that her face is little more than a smooth stone. And yet some spirit still radiates from her. I'm surprised to feel my eyes stinging, moved by the ancient shrine in some inexplicable way. Is it the thought of generations kneeling before the pretty little goddess, praying for the daily blessings of food and children and another day, all to no avail? For the first time I feel acutely aware of this as a place where many people died, suddenly and unexpectedly, their daily routines interrupted in medias res and frozen for all time for us to gawk at.

"There you are," Elgin says, poking his head in. "Come on, you'll love the garden. It's been restored according to the research done by your beloved Dr. Jashemski."

I follow him to an open courtyard rimmed by slim marble columns. In the center is a small fountain with a bronze statue of a leaping faun. The partitioned beds have been planted with oleander and box hedges to replicate the plan of the original garden. "She's not my *beloved* Dr. Jashemski . . ." I begin.

"Ha! You wrote a poem about her. I think it was the first time a student of mine ever wrote an archaeological sonnet. Let's see, how did it go?" He looks up at the sky, puts his hand over his heart in what his students always called his Cicero pose, and much to my embarrassment recites the poem I wrote for him.

> "When Wilhelmina F. Jashemski found
> Vesuvius had captured the ghost-roots
> of trees beneath the lava-sheeted ground—
> empty spaces traced with pebbles—long-lost truths
> of leaf and bark, species, were brought to light.
> Her plaster casts could resurrect the dead,
> at least as sculpture, art. And now the flight
> of sea hawks hints at pterodactyl blood
> while ancient sunlight shimmers on the Bay,
> and our thoughts turn to love, which if it lasts
> a year will flirt with immortality . . ."

He stops before the final lines, recalling, I imagine, the way the poem ends and the occasion for which I had written it. "So look," he says, sitting down on the edge of the fountain. "The reason I went to Sorrento—"

"Oh, for God's sake, Elgin, I don't care!" I say much too loudly and with an embarrassing wobble in my voice. "I really am over you."

"Nice to hear, Dr. Chase," he says, one side of his mouth quirking into a grin. "As I was saying, the reason I went to Sorrento is that I was meeting an FBI agent there."

"Why? What did they want with you? Are you in some kind of trouble?"

Elgin laughs. "Your faith in me is touching, Sophie. No, I haven't done anything wrong. I've been working with the FBI for some time to keep track of a certain cult operating in Austin."

"You mean you've been spying on the Tetraktys," I say, unable to keep the emotion out of my voice. We both remember the last time we talked about the Tetraktys and what that conversation led to.

"I suppose you could call it that. I'm not sorry about doing it; I'm only sorry I didn't do it better. If I had, Odette Renfrew and Barry Biddle might still be alive."

I feel suddenly cold. "Because Dale Henry was a Tetraktys member?"

"You knew about that?"

"I knew he'd gone to a few meetings, but I didn't know he was a card-carrying member. But even if he was, how do you know they had anything to do with the shooting?"

"Because the gun he used has been traced to a dealer in New Mexico ten miles from the Tetraktys compound. Also, there's a former member of the group who's working with the FBI who says that Dale Henry was at the compound this spring."

"That's when he and Agnes broke up and he disappeared from campus," I say. "This former member—"

"I can't divulge his identity," Elgin says quickly and without looking at me. "They've got him in a safehouse in Sorrento at great personal risk to him so that he can advise us on any new developments at the dig. I can't risk anyone finding out who he is."

"Okay," I say. "And has this informant . . . has he given you any useful information? Like why the Tetraktys would be interested in the Papyrus Project and the Villa della Notte?"

"We think they're interested in one of the scrolls that's turned up at the villa . . . possibly by Pythagoras himself."

"Pythagoras never wrote anything," I say.

"Not that anyone has ever found." Elgin shrugs and looks at me for the first time since he's mentioned the Tetraktys. "I can't vouch for these crazies' scholarship, but I think they believe that Pythagoras's *Golden Verses* were real and that Phineas had a copy with him when Vesuvius erupted."

"But how would they even know that Phineas was at the villa? You didn't even know until recently . . ." I stop as Elgin looks away again. "There's someone from the Tetraktys working on the project," I say. "Do you know who?"

"No, not yet. But I wanted you to know that someone is, so you'd be careful."

"How can I be careful if you don't even know who it is? And how could you have invited me here knowing there was a Tetraktys member on the project after what they cost me? And what about Agnes? How could you endanger her?" My voice has been steadily rising in pitch as my anger escalates. Elgin only nods glumly at each accusation, but suddenly he cocks his head and then holds up a finger to his lips to silence me. There are voices coming from the atrium heading in our direction. I see flashes of bright clothing and hear a child's voice ask as he is shown the household shrine, "What did the pagans pray to if they didn't believe in God?"

Instead of waiting for the tourists to leave, I get up to go. Elgin tries to follow me but the father of the group waylays him to ask directions to the Villa of the Mysteries. If I weren't so angry at Elgin I'd have to laugh. It's not the first time that Elgin's khakis and tanned good looks have gotten him mistaken for the resident tour guide. By the time Elgin explains that the Villa of the Mysteries is in Pompeii, I've gotten a substantial head start. He doesn't catch up with me until the Porta Marina.

"Sophie, please," he calls, grabbing my arm, "don't be angry. If I thought you were in danger I'd never have asked you here. I knew I'd be here to keep an eye on things."

"Oh, great. My protector. A lot of good you did when Dale Henry burst into that conference room. If I remember correctly, you dived under the table with me."

He looks so stunned that I instantly regret what I've said. After all, I was under that table, too. It's not fair to have expected more from Elgin. Before I can apologize, though, he lets go of my arm and draws himself up to his full six feet two of dignified pique. "I'm sorry I was such a disappointment to you," he says coldly. And then he turns and walks away, through the Porta Marina and past the bookstore and gift shop, turning left to follow the old sea wall to the Villa della Notte. I'm too angry to call him back, too proud to run after him. For a moment, standing here between the town and the old sea wall, I feel as trapped as the Herculaneans must have felt with their backs up against a wall of approaching ash and their only retreat a violent and impassable sea.

CHAPTER 16

1 catch up to Elgin at the entrance to the Villa della Notte. The gate to the site is locked, but Elgin surprises me by producing a key.

"Lyros gave it to me," Elgin says, noting my surprise. "We *are* partners on the Papyrus Project after all." He still sounds a little touchy.

"Listen—" I begin.

"It's okay, Sophie, you're completely right. I shouldn't have asked you here. It was selfish. I suppose I hoped that being here together, well, I see how silly *that* idea was. I promise not to bother you anymore. And I promise to keep an eye on Agnes."

It's on the tip of my tongue to ask what his silly idea was, but Elgin's already through the gate and then the noise is too loud to say anything without shouting. While the pit had been silent save for the croak of frogs on my last visit, now the air is full of the dull whine of a drill and a fine gray dust. We pass the boarded-up tunnels bored into the lower levels of the villa by eighteenth-century "excavators" (little better than tomb raiders). I notice that some of the boards have come loose. When I step onto the stairs I think I see why: the whole structure is vibrating.

"Is this drilling good for the rest of the excavation?" I shout at Elgin as we climb the stairs.

"It's not ideal. Usually they'd use chisels and go slower to minimize damage to the rest of the villa, especially with a structure like this that's been undermined by tunneling by eighteenth-century looters. Lyros must be pretty anxious to get to that trunk."

When we step into the ancient courtyard, I experience a moment of vertigo—the result, I imagine, of all the time I've now spent at the restored villa on Capri. The space and proportions have become so familiar to me that for a moment an image of that villa is superimposed over the ruin, a veil of bright sunlight reflecting off the fountain's spray and the burnished bronze of the statue of Nyx, and then all that brightness is eclipsed by the gray shroud of tufa dust, a pall of sadness that settles over me as if Vesuvius had just now erupted and I was watching the villa fill with ash and volcanic rock as it had on that August night so long ago.

"Here, you'd better put this on." Elgin hands me a face mask and we dive into the thickest dust that's coming from what I can't help but think of as *my* room. A narrow tunnel has been bored into the room, at the entrance of which Lyros and Maria are crouching. Maria has a camera strapped around her neck, presumably to record the trunk in situ, but right now she's not using it. The noise of the drill makes it impossible to get their attention. A workman crawls out, so covered in dust that he looks like a piece of living rock. He says something to Lyros in Italian, but before Lyros can respond, Maria answers in a stream of fast, angry Italian I can't begin to decipher. A fountain of invective that reminds me of the woman on the Circumvesuviana. The man turns away from Maria, slips his mask from his face and spits in the dust.

"What's going on?" Elgin asks.

Lyros turns to us and says, "They're ready for their lunch break, but we're within an hour's work of freeing the lid to the trunk." He turns back to the workman and in a less fluent, but politer Italian that I can understand, offers the man a bonus to continue work.

Maria rolls her eyes, but she doesn't interfere. What is she hoping is in Phineas's trunk, I wonder, that makes her so anxious to get to it?

The workman haggles with Lyros over the amount of the bonus for several minutes and then a deal is struck. I lean over Maria and ask where Simon and Agnes are.

Maria shrugs. "I think he offered to show Agnes some dirty pictures in the tunnels below."

"Really?" Lyros asks. "I didn't know that. Those tunnels aren't safe. I'm going to go down and tell them to get out of them. Elgin, why don't you take my place here?"

Elgin squeezes into the narrow opening beside Maria. I see right away that there isn't room for me and Maria doesn't look as if she's willing to give up her place. "I guess I'll go down with you," I tell Lyros.

"Sure . . . or if you'd like you could log on to my laptop and see how George is getting on with today's section of Phineas. It's behind the west wall of the courtyard."

Maria's mouth twitches when she realizes I might get a head start on the Phineas, but she puts her mask back on and turns toward the tunnel with all the resolution of Cerberus guarding the mouth of Hades. Lyros is already heading down the stairs for the lower level.

I turn away and cross the courtyard and go behind the west wall, where I find a small field office in what might once have been a storage room. Plastic tarps hang around a couple of chairs and a folding table upon which is a silver laptop—a Lyrik, of course—a thermos and a stack of books, notebooks, and a packet of envelopes tied together with string: mail for the villa, which Lyros must have picked up at the dock before setting off this morning. The screen-saver on the computer is a model of the solar system, the planets moving in elliptical orbits shown by dotted lines. When I touch the space bar the image fades and I see I'm already hooked up to the Internet. An Instant Message displayed from GPetherbrid reads, "You might want to see this."

I click on the reply box and type in: "Hey, it's Sophie. Lyros is busy with the excavation, but he said to check in and see how the Phineas is going." I hit Send and turn to the stack of books, looking for something to distract me while I'm waiting for a response, but the laptop chimes and George's reply pops up.

"Have they opened the trunk yet?"

"No," I type, "but Lyros says we should be able to in the next hour."

I hit Send and stare at the blank screen long enough for the screensaver to kick in again. What, I wonder, could the problem be? Had George found something in the next section about what was in the trunk? Whatever it is, how much difference could it make? There weren't explosives back in AD 79—except for the volcanic kind. Still, I have a sense of foreboding as I wait for George's reply, heightened by the tremors underfoot and the stultifying heat in my plastic lair. To distract myself, I untie the string holding the villa's mail and leaf through it even though I don't really expect anything for myself. M'Lou's not much of a letter writer and she's the only one I've given my summer address. I'm surprised, then, to find an envelope with my name typed across it. There's no address or post-mark, so it must have been hand-delivered. When I pick it up, I notice that it's lumpy. For a second, I entertain the paranoid thought that it could be a letter bomb. I open it quickly, like tearing off a Band-Aid. Inside is a blank piece of white paper with three cardboard tiles taped across the page. A smiling crescent moon, a man falling down a flight of stairs, and a masked man. I turn the paper over. The reverse side is blank.

The computer's chime startles me and I quickly fold the sheet, put it back in its envelope, and stuff it into my bag. Then I look back and find George's reply.

"Read this," it says, as succinctly as the command "Eat me" in *Alice's Adventures in Wonderland*. And so I do. The section starts out with the line that George recited to us last night.

As I walked back I pondered over all I had learned of Iusta and her unusual situation. I wondered what would come of the pact we had entered together. I had, of course, heard of the cultus *to which Iusta belonged, but I had to admit that I knew little about it and, in truth, I didn't care if I learned more. Iusta's secret, however, had been useful in extracting from her a promise to show me the mysteries practiced by her mistress.*

As I approached the villa, I scanned its walls for any openings into the sea. I saw none, but I did see that part of the wall was under the level of the sea. There could be, as I had surmised last night and Iusta had confirmed today, an underwater entrance to the sea that led to the grotto where the rites were held. This part of the rites was limited to the women, and normally I would not have been allowed to witness them, but Iusta had promised to show me a way that I might spy on them from a secret room behind the grotto. As I entered the villa, I felt confident that I would soon be master of its secrets.

I can't help but smile at Phineas's swaggering arrogance, and at the fact that I had guessed what kind of arrangement he had made with Iusta. We really haven't lost much in the missing section of the papyrus, except for the name of the cult to which Iusta belonged and in which Phineas had so little interest that he couldn't even be bothered to name it. I am beginning to think that the section has little in it to surprise me when I read the next paragraph. My assumption, I see, was as arrogant as Phineas's. I quickly jot down the lines in shorthand on a page torn out of the notebook on the table and take it with me across the courtyard.

Outside the plastic tarps the air in the courtyard is so thick with dust that I can barely make out the figures crouched around the entrance to my—to Phineas's—room. When I come closer, I see that Elgin is working with a chisel to clear the remaining scraps of tufa from the edges of a small trunk. Maria is sitting on her heels, her hands held in her lap grasping each other so tightly her knuckles are white under the gray dust. I gather from her rapt expression that she's restraining herself from grabbing the chisel away from Elgin and hacking her way into the trunk. She also looks, curiously, as though she were praying.

"You guys," I say, "I think you'd better hear this before you open that."

Maria swings her head in my direction, her eyes gleaming white in her begrimed face. *"Aspetta,"* she hisses. "We're almost there."

"But listen, this is how the section George just scanned ends: *My confidence in my mastery of the situation dissolved, however, when I entered my room. My trunk lay open . . ."*

As if the words were a spell to release it, the lid of the trunk swings open. Maria and Elgin lean forward, batting the dust plumes out of the air to see better. But I don't have to see or hear Maria's anguished cry to know what they see. I read the last line. *"My trunk lay open and empty. Someone had stolen my scrolls."*

"No!" Maria cries. "Who could have taken them?"

She sounds so despondent that I feel sorry for her. I move forward to put my hand on her shoulder, but as I do I feel the ground shift under my feet and hear an echoing thud from below me. It feels as if the foundations of the villa have been yanked out from beneath us and, for a moment, the only explanation I can come up with is that there's been an earthquake. Another volcanic eruption that this time will split the floor of the villa and suck us all down into the underworld.

The motion stops. In the eerie silence that follows, Maria crosses herself and Elgin gets shakily to his feet.

"What was that?" I ask.

Instead of answering, Elgin gets up and rushes across the courtyard to the peristylium and looks over the edge of the railing. There's so much dust in the air that it's as if a premature dusk had descended over the pit. It's hard to see anything at all. Then a dust-covered figure emerges from one of the tunnels. It takes me a moment to recognize John Lyros.

"Are you okay?" Elgin calls.

Lyros is coughing too hard to answer. He points at the tunnel and gasps something. I run back to where I've left my knapsack, grab the water bottle in it, and run down the stairs. Elgin is already down there examining the rubble outside the collapsed tunnel. I hand Lyros the water bottle. After he's taken a long swallow, he manages to make himself understood. "Simon and Agnes," he croaks. "I was trying to tell them to get out of there. They're still in there."

CHAPTER 17

Elgin is the first to run to the tunnel. Lyros is leaning heavily on me, limping, so I'm unable to keep up with him. I watch helplessly as Elgin is swallowed up in a cloud of dust at the mouth of the tunnel. When I try to follow, Lyros pulls me back.

"There's no sense risking your life, too," he says. Lyros calls to the workmen, who have come down to the pit but are hovering far from the building as if they are afraid the whole villa is about to come down. He tells them to bring shovels and lights.

"What the hell were they doing in there?" I ask, still trying to get close enough to the tunnel to see what's going on.

"You heard what Maria said, Simon was showing Agnes some paintings. The man's a fool! He somehow got the idea that there were more paintings in there that could be copied for the restorations, but I've told him the tunnels aren't safe. . . ." A coughing spasm compels Lyros to stop talking. While I'm waiting for him to recover I wonder if this is what Lyros and Simon were arguing about the night before last on the sea-steps. I also wonder if the paintings were all Simon was looking for in the tunnels. Could it be that Simon is the Tetraktys member on the project? "When I got down here, I heard their voices coming from this tunnel so I followed them in. I got about three yards in when the ceiling started to collapse. I could see them, about another fifteen yards in, I would say. I saw the support beam over their heads come down and then the one just in front of me came down as well and tore out a piece of the wall. There was too much dirt for me to dig through so I came back out, but with shovels . . ."

Lyros turns to two workers who have arrived at the scene with shovels and shouts for them to start digging for the *signorina Americana*. They spring to attention to save the pretty American girl, moving far faster, I imagine, than if it were only old, fat Simon trapped in there. Simon's lucky he's got Agnes with him, but what about poor Agnes?

"Shouldn't we contact the archaeological office?" I ask. "They must have more experience with this kind of situation."

"They do," Lyros says, "but it's a holiday. By the time they assemble a crew Simon and Agnes could be dead. We should notify them, though, and tell them to call an ambulance. You and Maria should go. . . . Where is Maria anyway?"

"I don't think she ever came downstairs," I say. "I'll get her."

I leave Lyros crouched in front of the tunnel and run up the stairs to the third level of the villa. The courtyard is empty, though, save for the painted figures on the wall, still moving through their rituals as if nothing had happened. Hades ravages Persephone, Demeter in her grief scorches the earth and transforms her daughter's companions into shrieking sirens who then lead a young girl through the steps of initiation. Even the brutal assault of the young initiate seems like a staged scene, both actors a little bored. They have, after all, been at it for nearly two thousand years; not even a volcanic eruption had fazed them. The only sound in the courtyard is a faint patter, like raindrops, coming from behind the west wall.

When I walk around the wall I see Maria seated at the field desk, typing on the laptop. Behind the plastic tarp she appears spectral and blurred, less substantial than the painted figures on the other side of the wall. When I lift the tarp, she startles and slams shut the laptop.

"*Dio!* You scared me! I was just letting George know what happened. Have they gotten them out?"

"No," I say, wondering why she'd think alerting George, across the bay on Capri, would be a top priority, "but they're going to go in. John wants us to go to the archaeological office to notify them of the accident and call an ambulance." When she fails to get up, I add: "I need you to go with me to give the directions in Italian."

She sighs and gets up, casting a reluctant parting glance at the laptop.

"How did George respond when you e-mailed him about Agnes?" I ask as we go down the stairs. "He's so protective of her."

"What?" Maria looks distracted by the scene at the bottom of the pit. The workers have returned with high-powered floodlights that they've trained on the opening of the tunnel. Elgin and Lyros must be inside already.

"George," I repeat. "You said you e-mailed George to tell him what happened to Agnes and Simon."

"Ah, I didn't actually reach him," she says. "*Andiamo.* We ought to hurry."

She quickens her pace so that I have to jog to keep up with her. Clearly she's trying to avoid my questions—probably because she hadn't been e-mailing George at all. What *could* she have been doing on the computer? Checking her e-mail? Online shopping?

Whatever she was doing, she's clearly not going to tell me. The one good thing about her running from me is that it gets us to the archaeological office fast. By the time I catch up with her, she's gotten them to call an ambulance and deputized two young men to go back to the site to help with the rescue mission.

"You lead the way," Maria tells me.

"Where are you going?" I ask when I realize she's not coming back to the site.

"Family emergency," she says, gathering her thick dark hair and coiling it into a knot at the back of her head. Beads of sweat dampen her forehead and the collar of her gauze blouse. There's a streak of gray tufa dust on her cheekbone, but after a few minutes of patting and smoothing she manages to look more put-together than I generally do after an hour's primping. She takes out of her bag a lipstick and a pair of heels that she exchanges for the flat sandals she wore at the site. *"Mia zia,"* she says when she sees me eyeing the heels and lipstick. "If I'm not dressed properly, I'll never hear the end of it from my aunt. Now go! Tell John I'll meet you back on the island tonight."

The two young men, who have decided to bring a portable stretcher even though it seems to me that the ambulance will have one, follow as I head back to the villa, and I feel as if I am leading some sacrificial procession. Every time I glance back at them I half expect to see them carrying a slaughtered lamb between them instead of the stretcher. Instead of chanting, though, I hear a low sibilant exchange that seems to concern various parts of my anatomy. By the time we reach the site, I feel as though I'm to be the sacrificial lamb, but when I hold the gate for them they return my glare with such open smiles that I find myself smiling, too. All our smiles vanish when we see what's waiting for us at the bottom of the pit.

Simon lies gray and motionless just outside the entrance to the tunnel. Elgin is thumping on his chest and then breathing into his mouth. I rush on ahead of my litter-bearers and kneel down next to Elgin just as Simon's chest spasms, his ample belly rippling as he begins to cough.

"Thank God," Elgin says, his voice shaking, and then, noticing me, "If I lost one more person on this project, I might not get any more grants."

I lift my hand to slap Elgin in the arm, but then I notice that his face is as white as Simon's under the grime and I squeeze his arm instead.

"Agnes?" I ask, afraid to hear his response.

"She's okay," Elgin answers, pointing with his chin toward the villa. "She's right over there."

I look over his shoulder. Agnes, dusty but apparently unhurt, stands at the mouth of the tunnel. I rush to her, certain she must be in shock, but when I get to her she seems calm and collected. She's holding a flashlight with a steady hand, shining its beam through a broken gap in the wall about three yards from the entrance.

"Agnes, thank God you're all right," I say, grabbing her arm, which I see now is scratched and bleeding under the layer of grime. "But you have to get out of here and go with us to the hospital—" I stop when I see what's beyond the hole. A painted swan hovers on the opposite wall. When I move closer I see that the walls are covered with paintings and that the space isn't another tunnel, it's a stairway leading down into the ground. "Wow," I say. "It must have led under the villa and it seems to be completely intact."

"It's carved out of rock," she says, in a girlish wispy voice that sounds strange coming from her soot-covered face—like the voice of an angel emanating from the mask of a gorgon. "These walls must be three feet thick." She stops because we hear Simon moaning behind us. "Simon's coming to?" she asks.

"Yes, but he's still badly injured and you—" I scan her up and down, looking for injuries, but except for a few scratches and a torn shirt sleeve, she looks fine. "You still should go to the hospital to make sure you don't have a concussion. Did you get hit on the head?"

Agnes reaches the hand that's not holding the flashlight and rubs the top of her head, more like a sleepy toddler trying to wake up than someone who's been hurt, but then, I think, her baffling affect might be the result of a blow to the head. "Um, maybe, it all happened so quickly, but yeah, I think something did graze my head. But Simon's the one who really got hit hard by a big rock. Are you sure he's okay?"

"I'm not sure at all. We'd better get both of you to the hospital."

She nods slowly, like a person in a dream. "Yeah, I think that's a good idea." Then she turns and walks out of the tunnel. I follow, giving one backward glance to the painted swan, which seems to be hovering in the space above the hole, feeling irrationally that it will escape before I get a chance to see it again. I remind myself it's been waiting there behind that wall for centuries. It will wait one more day. I turn and join Elgin and Agnes, who are both kneeling next to Simon. He appears to be breathing, although raggedly. His eyes flicker open for a moment, but he groans and closes them again.

"Don't worry, old man," Elgin says. "There's an ambulance on the way, right?" Elgin turns to me, his face imploring.

"Yes, it should be here any minute," and then I mouth, "Where's Lyros?"

"He ran upstairs—leaving me to do mouth to mouth with Simon here when he stopped breathing. I guess that's what being a billionaire's all about: getting other people to do your dirty work."

Simon opens his mouth as if to say something, but all that comes out is a hoarse rasp that sounds as if he's drawing breath through a cheese grater. Agnes winces at the sound and pats Simon on the shoulder. "Don't try to talk, Mr. Bowles. Here's Mr. Lyros now."

I turn and see John Lyros, his laptop case strapped across his chest, coming down the stairs. At the same moment I hear the sirens approaching.

"Where's Maria?" Lyros asks.

"She said she had a family emergency and had to go," I answer.

"Damn, I was going to suggest she go to the hospital with Simon and Agnes and that you go back on the boat with Elgin. But you can probably handle the *Parthenope* yourself, right, Elgin?"

"Well, yes, but . . ." Normally I would expect Elgin to leap at the chance to take control of such a luxurious boat, but he seems oddly reluctant.

"Good. Sophie, why don't you go in the ambulance with Simon and Agnes? I'll meet you at the hospital with my car."

"Dr. Chase doesn't have to go with us," Agnes pipes up. "I can look after Simon."

"And who will look after you?" Lyros asks.

"Really, I'm fine—" Agnes begins, but Lyros is already walking away to let the paramedics into the site and lead them down the ramp.

"Really, Dr. Chase, you should go back to the island with Dr. Lawrence. I'll be fine."

"I wouldn't think of leaving you alone," I say. "I'm sure Dr. Lawrence agrees."

Elgin looks at me and then at Agnes. "Dr. Chase is right, Agnes," he says, then switches his gaze back to me. "Someone needs to keep an eye on you. Perhaps Dr. Chase can do a better job of it than I have."

He's still angry with me for blaming him for bringing Agnes here. Well, too bad, I feel like saying, look at what's happened.

The paramedics strap Simon to a stretcher and carry him up the ramp toward the street where the ambulance is waiting. They try to make Agnes lie down on a stretcher, but she insists she's well enough to walk. Still *I* insist on walking by her side with my arm around her in case she feels faint. When we're all in the ambulance,

John Lyros sticks his head in to confirm with the driver that we're going to the Ospedale Santa Maria del Popolo degli Incurabili.

"Doesn't that mean the hospital for the incurables?" Agnes whispers in my ear. "Is Simon really that bad?"

I start to explain the origin of the hospital's name, but a noise from Simon distracts me. He's struggling with the oxygen mask that's strapped over his mouth, his eyes darting from me to Agnes. I squeeze his hand, pretty sure what he's trying to ask. "It's okay," I tell him, "Agnes is okay and you'll be fine, too. We're getting you to a hospital."

He squeezes my hand again, this time so hard that I inadvertently pull back. Abruptly, he wrenches his hand from mine and bats the oxygen mask away from his face. When he opens his mouth, though, the only thing that comes out is a sibilant hiss— the sound a tire makes when it's been punctured. I snap my head up and yell at the paramedics.

"His lung!" I say, pointing to Simon's chest while I try to remember the word in Italian. But it's not necessary. It's obvious right away to the paramedics that one of Simon's lungs has collapsed. I move back as they converge on him with needles and tubes. I can see by the color returning to his face that they're able to keep him breathing, but he rides the rest of the way with the oxygen mask over his face and eyes tightly closed. Agnes takes my place by his side, holding his hand and telling him over and over again that he's going to be okay. I spend the rest of the trip with my hand over my own chest, trying to ease the sympathetic tightening I'd felt there when Simon's lung collapsed.

The Ospedale Santa Maria del Popolo degli Incurabili is an old cavernous building near the Piazza Cavour, built originally in the sixteenth century for those suffering from the then incurable disease of syphilis, which the Neapolitans had christened "the French disease." (The French returned the favor by calling it the Neapolitan disease.) Not a particularly cheerful history, I think, as Agnes and I follow the paramedics carrying Simon past doleful plaster madonnas and black-robed nuns. He looks frightened as he's whisked through doors where we're not allowed to go. I try to explain to a passing nun that we want to stay with our friend, but she takes one look at Agnes, who has turned as white as the plaster saints on the walls, and reaches out a black-robed arm to steady her as she begins to sink to the floor. Agnes responds by screeching and clutching at me.

"Please don't leave me alone," she hisses in my ear. "I hate hospitals . . . and *nuns*."

"Don't worry," I say, a little shocked at Agnes's outburst, "I'll stay with you." I smile at the sweet-faced elderly nun and tell her in Italian that we'll follow her. I hope she doesn't know enough English to have understood what Agnes just said. She turns around without a word, her long black habit dusting the floor, and leads us to a private room. Above the door is another one of the ubiquitous saints—this one, I notice, has the same crown of waves as Agnes's little statue. I'm about to point it out to her, but Agnes balks when she sees the narrow whitewashed room with its narrow metal cot.

"Why is she taking me to a room? I'm not going to have to stay here, am I?"

"I think she just wants to make sure you don't fall down and hurt yourself," I tell Agnes. The nun returns with a bowl of water, cotton gauze, and antiseptic. "Just try to relax. I'll stay right here."

I sit next to Agnes on the cot as the nun swabs her cuts gently and efficiently. Through the whole procedure Agnes shakes like a leaf. Why in the world, I wonder, is she so afraid of nuns? I went to parochial school myself until eighth grade, when M'Lou finally convinced my grandparents to let me go to public school, and I've encountered my share of unpleasant nuns. I've also known some remarkable ones, including my eighth-grade Latin teacher, Sister Francis Genevieve, who inspired me to study the classics. But Agnes was raised in a Baptist family. It's unlikely she had any experience of nuns growing up. Has her Baptist minister father filled her with horror stories about the Catholic Church? I've experienced a fair amount of prejudice against Catholics in East Texas, so I suppose it isn't impossible.

Still, Agnes's reaction seems extreme. Her shaking gets so bad at one point that the struts of the metal bed clang like bells. The nun steps back, looking critically at Agnes, and then says in perfect English, "She seems to be going into shock. I'm going to get the doctor."

When they return the nun stays in the doorway and lets the young—and handsome—doctor examine Agnes's head. He can't find any sign that she suffered a blow, but he says that her behavior is alarming enough to warrant an MRI and overnight observation in the hospital.

Since I'm not allowed to accompany Agnes to the MRI lab, I tell the nun that I'd like to check up on Simon. She shows me to a waiting room and tells me someone will come tell me when Simon gets out of surgery.

I sit there for over an hour feeling totally useless and wishing that I at least had the Phineas transcripts to read while I'm waiting. Anything to make me feel like I'm doing something. The only "reading material" I have is the peculiar cards I was sent in the mail. I take them out and examine them: a moon, a man falling off a ladder, and a masked man. Could the man falling off the ladder represent some kind of accident? Could it have something to do with Simon getting injured in the tunnel? But then, how would the person who sent them know Simon was going to get hurt today?

"Do you play the lotto?" a voice asks me in accented, but carefully formal English.

I look up at a young man sitting in the row of chairs across from me. He's wearing a navy suit and tie, his hair neatly combed, as if he'd been on his way to the office and made this detour to the hospital of the incurables unexpectedly.

"*Scusa?*" I say, even though he's addressed me in English. I'm not even sure he was talking to me. "Lotto?"

"Yes," he answers, stubbornly sticking to English. "You call it the lottery in America. My cousin lives in New York and I visit him in summer last year. I see the lottery there. Long lines"—he spreads open his arms—"many people hoping to win the . . . the jackpot?"

"Uh, yeah, I mean, no, I don't play it," I say. Ely had, though, I remember. Although I always thought he was more interested in picking number combinations than in winning money. "Why did you think I did?"

"Those are *smorfia* pictures," he says, pointing to the cardboard tiles. "They are used to, um, how do you say? . . . to read the dreams. Each one means a number." He picks up the card with the moon on it and turns it over. "Ah, someone has taken the number off the back." He shows me the back of the tile, and I see that the paper backing is rough, as if one layer had been peeled away. I look at the other two and see they both are missing their backings.

"The moon is six. I remember because my aunt Angelina once dreamed she looked up at the moon and saw her brother Tito's face in it, so she played a six and a thirty-seven—for brother—and fifty-nine for La Casa because the dream was in the house where she grew up. And she won! But then my uncle Dominic took all the money and bought a fishing boat and the boat sank! My aunt said it was because her brother Tito could never keep a lira in his pocket and so the boat had as many holes in it as her brother's pocket."

I nod at this long story of the inevitability of fate. How could you avoid it? It was Oedipus all over again: fleeing his hometown because the oracle tells him he'll murder his father and marry his mother but neglects to mention that his parents aren't the people he grew up with but the ones he'll meet out on the road. Or like me:

coming all the way to Italy to get away from Ely and finding him here. I'm sure now that this is Ely's handiwork. A system that attaches numbers to dreams is right up his alley.

"So each one of these cards has a number?"

"*Sì,* from one to ninety-nine," he tells me. "And also a name. This one"—he points to the middle card—"is called La Disgrazia. It stands for seventeen, which is always an unlucky number. These cards are from a game, like your American bingo, called Tombola della Smorfia. I bought one for my niece last Christmas."

"Where can I get one?" I ask.

The young man—Gianni, I soon learn—gives me directions to a nearby *farmacia* that usually carries the game. He then confides to me that he's in the hospital because his fiancée is having her appendix removed. When I wish her a quick recovery, he responds, "I am sure we will both have good luck now." He taps the card with the moon on it. "Six is my lucky number. And then this last card, the masked man, it means a stranger. You see: it's lucky that I met you!"

I tell him I'm sure it's lucky I met him, too. When I see John Lyros enter the waiting room I get up and shake Gianni's hand. I want to avoid him mentioning the Smorfia tiles to John and, given Gianni's volubility, I realize he's likely to recount our whole conversation. Mistaking my eagerness to be gone, Gianni winks at me. "Don't worry, I don't want to make your husband jealous! Or my fiancée. *Ciao,* signora. Don't forget to play your numbers."

As I approach John Lyros, I can't help but smile, picturing the couple we make in Gianni's eyes. Although he's still wearing his khakis and dusty shirt from the dig, something about Lyros exudes wealth and confidence. I notice that women look at him and then at me when I join him.

"I've been waiting here to find out how Simon's doing—" I begin, but he cuts me off.

"Simon's out of surgery," he says. "He's still in critical condition, but he's expected to recover."

"Thank God," I say. "I should go back and check on Agnes then—"

"I just came from her room. She's sedated and resting comfortably. There's really nothing we can do for either of them right now. I thought we could go get a bite to eat and then check in on them later before catching the ferry back to Capri. I bet you're starving."

As soon as he says it I realize I haven't had anything to eat since breakfast. I *am* starving. "Okay," I say, "but would you mind waiting while I run into a local *farmacia* for a few things?" I say *things* in a way I hope Lyros will take to mean private *female* things so he doesn't offer to accompany me, which he doesn't. Instead he tells me he'll be waiting outside the main entrance of the hospital.

I buy the Tombola della Smorfia game in the pharmacy. The cover shows a game board divided into little squares with pictures like the ones on the tiles I've found. I'd like to look at it right away, but I don't want to keep Lyros waiting.

When I get back to the hospital entrance, I find John Lyros standing outside. He's holding open the passenger door of a bright red Alfa Romeo.

"Wow," I say, sliding into the leather seat, "this isn't a rental, is it?"

"No." He shifts gears and steers around the crowd of teenage boys that have assembled to admire the car. "I bought it last month, but it's really no use to me on the island so I'm keeping it in a garage here. It seems a shame, though. I haven't been able to take it out on the open road." He turns to me, those lavender eyes glinting. "Would you like to take a drive?"

And of all the questions I've been asked today this one seems the simplest, and least mysterious, to answer. "Sure," I say, adjusting the seat to a more comfortable position. "Why not?"

CHAPTER 18

*I*nstead of heading south toward the more glamorous destinations of Sorrento and Amalfi we drive north toward the Phlegraeon Fields.

"I know a great little seafood place near Baia," John tells me, "and the area's less touristy than the Sorrentine Peninsula."

"Maybe because of the name. I've always thought 'Phlegraeon' sounded like a skin rash. The translation—the burning fields—isn't much more appealing."

Lyros laughs. "You're right, but let's not suggest an alternative to the tourist board or the place will be swamped. The ground *is* geologically unstable. Although there hasn't been a major eruption in the area since 1538, the ground level of the port of Pozzuoli moves up and down when the magma beneath the sea level surges. You can still see sulfurous vapors coming out of craters and cracks in the ground. That's why the Greek settlers thought it was the entrance to the underworld."

"Basically, you're taking me to Hell for dinner."

He half turns to me, smiling. "Yes, but I promise to bring you back."

"Hm, easier said than done. As Virgil says, *Facilis descensus Averno.*"

"The way to Hell is easy," John translates, his eyes darting between me and the sharply curving road.

"But the way back isn't. Look at poor Euridice—thrown back into the pit because her husband, Orpheus, couldn't resist a backward glance."

John steals another look at me. "True. I might have a hard time keeping my eyes off you during the trip."

I blush at the compliment, surprised at how quickly he's taken the conversation from geology to mythology to flirtation. I'm not sure where he means to take it next—or how far I want him to go. Now that his eyes are back on the twists of the road, I study his profile, noticing the bump in his nose where it looks like it was broken and the faint scar near his jawline. It's not a pretty face, but it's a strong one—like a Roman general who's been in the field. And those eyes. When he turns those lavender eyes on me, I find myself not wanting him to stop . . . at least not yet.

"Well, I'll just have to lead the way," I say.

He keeps his eyes on the road, but I see his lips curve into a smile. Then we go into a tunnel and I can't see anything.

When we emerge from the tunnel, the Gulf of Pozzuoli is before us, its calm blue expanse, cradled protectively by Cape Misenum, belying the surging magma beneath. "That's where Pliny the Elder watched the eruption from," I say, pointing to the cape, glad to be back in the safer realm of ancient history and geography for the moment. I turn my head back to look in the direction of Naples and Vesuvius, trying to imagine what the view would have been like on that fateful morning. A cloud like an umbrella pine was how Pliny the Younger described the emissions that issued out of Vesuvius in his letter to Tacitus describing his uncle's death, but I can't see the volcano from this angle.

"We'll have an excellent view where we're going," he says. "And hopefully a more tranquil one than Pliny's."

"Good," I say as we follow the coast road to Baia. "After all the excitement today, I could do with a little tranquillity. I have to say I'm really surprised—and a little embarrassed, considering I recommended her for this project—that Agnes would be foolish enough to go into those tunnels."

"What makes you think it was Agnes's idea?" he asks, his eyes flicking off the road for a moment to look at me.

"Oh, I didn't . . . I mean, I thought it was probably Simon's idea, but I'm surprised she would go along with it." I glance at him and see that his eyes are back on the road. "Why do you think Simon was willing to risk his life and Agnes's in those tunnels?" I ask.

"I'm afraid it's my fault," he says, "I'm the one who should be embarrassed. Ah, here's where we turn off. . . ." He turns the car at a sign for Lake Lucrino—famous in ancient times for its oyster beds—and we climb into low hummocky hills on a narrow twisting road that demands all John's attention. He turns in at an entrance that is nearly hidden behind oleander bushes, driving down a lane bordered by tall hedges alive with small brightly colored birds and tiny white flowers. I smell jasmine and salt and hear birdsong and breaking surf. The lane opens up to a promontory overlooking the sea and a low stucco building with a green clay tile roof. Next to the building is a patio set with wrought-iron tables.

"Is it open?" I ask, noticing that the patio is empty. There's only one car in the driveway.

"Oh yes, I know the owner," John says, parking the car. "But it's a little early for dinner. We could take a walk first—there are some ruins along the ridge here—if you're not too tired."

"Not at all," I tell him. It's true; although I should be exhausted from everything that's happened today, when I open the car door and smell the sea and the sharp tang of rosemary and pine in the air, I don't feel tired at all.

We walk up a narrow dirt trail behind the low building. The path is steep for a bit, and rocky—John offers his arm over the rougher parts—but then it flattens out on the top of the ridge. I see the remains of a tile floor beneath the grass and a few low stone walls.

"A Republican villa," John says, "probably built around Cicero's day when this area became popular as a retreat for wealthy Romans. Not as fancy as the ones closer to Baia"—he points down toward the fishing village below us—"but it had a pretty view."

I nod, speechless at just how perfect the view is. To the east, I see all the way across the Gulf of Pozzuoli to Naples and the cone of Vesuvius. To the south is Cape Misenum and the deep blue of the Tyrrhenian Sea. Below us lies Lake Lucrino and a little farther west another lake, which I guess is Lake Averno and which the ancients believed was the entrance to the underworld.

"You were going to tell me why you thought it was your fault that Simon went into the tunnels," I say, sitting down on the stone wall.

John sighs and sits next to me. "Yes, I think I may have given him the idea to look for something there. You see, I've wondered whether the eighteenth-century tunnels might lead us to the stairway that went down to the underground passages and the sea grotto. In the plan of the villa we found there's an entrance to the stairs from the lower courtyard. But then the rest of the plan is blank. It doesn't show what was on the level beneath the lower courtyard. When I read Phineas's description of seeing Iusta swimming below the terrace and his conjecture that there must be a sea grotto on the lowest level, I felt sure that there must be a way to find those stairs."

"And you mentioned that to Simon?"

"I'm afraid so. He came to me the night before last concerned there might not be much more work for him because he's almost finished the paintings in the courtyard. I told him that it depended on what we found next, that I'd like to reproduce the murals in the lower levels, but obviously we couldn't do that until we uncovered those levels."

I think about the little bit of the conversation I overheard between the two men. It didn't sound like they were talking about their business arrangement, but then, I only overhead a small part of the conversation. Still, I'm sure Lyros is leaving something out of his account of the conversation: certainly the part where he admonished Simon for indulging rumors about cults and sacrifices.

"So you think Simon was looking for a way into the stairs?"

"Why else would there have been a collapse? Those tunnels have been there for centuries. He must have been doing a little tunneling himself—boring holes into the walls hoping to find the stairs to the underground passages—and he managed to undermine one of the supports. It's ironic, really."

"Ironic?"

"Yes. The cave-in he inadvertently caused *did* uncover the stairs. And from the glimpse I had of that painted swan, I think we'll find some spectacular murals. But it doesn't look as if Simon will be in any shape to reproduce them any time soon."

"That is unlucky," I agree. "For Simon, at least."

"I'm afraid this isn't the first stroke of bad luck the project's had."

"You mean the shooting in Texas?" I ask.

"Actually I'd call *that* a tragedy, not bad luck. I was thinking of smaller bits of bad luck: tools have gone missing from the site, a strange stain appeared on the north courtyard wall, and right after that noxious fumes started emanating from the tunnels. On July 10, a workman fell off a ladder—" I think again of the cardboard tile of the man falling off a ladder. Is that what the cards are about? A warning that the Villa della Notte is cursed?

I'm distracted from this thought by something else John is saying. ". . . and then there are the triangles showing up on everything."

"What triangles?" I ask, my skin prickling.

"Since May we've been finding triangles on everything. One was spray-painted on the site gate in Herculaneum and one on the door to the villa on Capri the next day. I've found three stamped on our mail and one punched into the tires of the institute's truck, and just two days ago there was even one scratched into the side of the *Parthenope*."

"What kind of triangles?" I ask, cutting short his list.

"Oh," he says, reaching into his pocket. "Here's one I found today. It came with the mail." He removes a postcard—the kind that's blank on one side—and hands it to me.

The triangle is formed of ten dots, each one printed in red ink. A tetraktys.

"Do you know what this is?" I ask.

"No," he says, "but I think you do. Do you want to tell me about it?"

"It's a long story."

"Well, then, we'd better eat while you talk. You look a little pale. Shall we?" He offers his arm for the walk down to the restaurant and I take it. Suddenly I'm feeling unsteady on my feet.

"I've always thought that if I had been paying more attention it wouldn't have happened," I tell John Lyros on the patio of the restaurant. The waiter has brought us a ceramic pitcher filled with crisp white wine and scattered a handful of tiny fried fish and calamari over the brown butcher-paper-covered table, sprinkling them with coarse sea salt and lemon juice before discreetly retreating at a look from John. I can see that it will be a leisurely dinner, giving me lots of time to tell my story. Even the sun seems to be hesitating in its descent over Cumae, the sky melting in slow degrees from bright blue to lavender to indigo. "But I got pregnant and that's all I was really thinking about. By the time I realized that Ely had joined the Tetraktys, he was already deeply involved."

"What happened to the baby?" John asks.

"I went into premature labor on the day I found out about the Tetraktys. We lost her, Cory, three days later."

"I'm sorry," John says, grimacing.

I nod and look out over the water. For a moment I smell sulfur and I can feel the prickle of cottonwood spores on my skin. I remember Ely's face when he came out of the Tetraktys house, how I saw myself transformed by his look into a monster. A siren, I think now, one of Persephone's companions punished for her carelessness. If I'd been paying closer attention Ely wouldn't have drifted into the Tetraktys. If I'd been enough for him, he wouldn't have needed it.

"Surely that must have been sufficient reason for him to leave the cult."

"No," I say. "He felt more than ever that he had to figure out why we'd lost Cory and that the explanation somehow lay in numbers. He thought the day of her birth—June 17—was unlucky . . ." I falter, remembering suddenly that Gianni had said the same thing. He said that the middle card—La Disgrazia—stood for the number seventeen, which was considered unlucky.

"Huh," John says, "that's interesting. The Romans thought seventeen was unlucky, too." He takes out a pen from his shirt pocket and writes a Roman numeral on the butcher paper: XVII. "See, if you rearrange the letters you get the Latin word *VIXI.*"

"I lived," I translate. "The perfect tense of the verb to live. What's wrong with that?"

"Well, as you know, the perfect tense always refers to an action *completed* in the past. . . ."

"Oh, so it means 'I'm dead now.' I see." I wonder why John Lyros knows such a thing. Is he, like Ely, obsessed with numbers? It seems an odd coincidence, but I push it away. After all, in addition to studying classics, Lyros also studied mathematics and founded a computer software company. It makes sense that he'd be interested in numbers. "Well, Ely didn't mention that, but I wouldn't be surprised if he knew it. He was obsessed with numbers and had an uncanny memory for them. He remembered the exact date of every important event in his life, and if you gave him any date, in the past or the future, he could tell you what day of the week it fell on."

"He might have been a talented mathematician—" he begins.

"Or suffering from obsessive compulsive disorder," I finish for him. "I wanted him to see a psychiatrist. He did just once. When the doctor suggested taking an antidepressant, he balked and refused to go back. He wouldn't medicate away 'his gift,' as he called his ability to see number patterns. He thought it was the only way to see the world clearly. He thought Pythagoras had had the same gift: an ability to see mathematical patterns in the natural world and so make sense of the world, to discover its laws, in a way no one else could have."

"He may have been right," Lyros says, "but he couldn't have been easy to live with. How much longer after you lost your baby did he stay?"

"Six months," I answer. "Nearly to the day. He left just before Christmas. Actually, he left on the solstice—" I try to smile, but find that my lips, coated with the salt from the fried seafood, feel stiff.

"Another numerically significant day," John says, nodding.

"Yes," I say, wondering how John knows that the Tetraktys assigned special significance to the solstices and equinoxes. But then, so do a lot of New Age groups. Another coincidence? I take a long gulp of the crisp white wine and stare hard at the line on the horizon where the dark blue of the sky meets the lavender sea, then at the lemon wedges on the table and the bloodred oleander blossoms edging the terrace. I'm trying to concentrate on these details rather than relive the day when Ely left our house in Hyde Park for the Tetraktys community in New Mexico. Telling this story has taken more out of me than I thought it would.

"You were probably better off that he left," John says, a little brutally I think, but it feels good, like the bracing wind coming off the sea now that the sun has almost set. "A man on a religious mission is not good company, not even to himself."

"And you know this because . . ."

He smiles wryly. The waiter's appearance with a bowl of steaming mussels allows him to delay answering, but when he's gone, John cracks open a shell and, spearing a dark purple mussel, carries on as if there had been no interruption. "I know from personal experience. I was on a quest once myself."

"That trek in the Himalayas to find yourself?" I ask.

He laughs so hard he spills the broth from a mussel shell on the cuff of his white shirt. "I see I'm not the only one who's done a bit of cyber-stalking! It's hard to believe I was ever young enough to use a phrase like that. Finding myself!"

"Well, did you?" I pop a mussel in my mouth. I have to stop myself from sighing at the explosion of flavor, like the whole sea contained in the silky morsel.

"Find myself?" he repeats, still laughing. But when I continue to hold his gaze, he purses his lips and nods, serious. "I found, I suppose, the *limits* of myself, the borders. How far I could go on how little food or how little sleep—even how little oxygen on the top of those mountains. I think that's why men—and women," he adds at a lifted eyebrow from me, "pit themselves against the elements. And it *is* useful information. I won't deny that. But after a couple of years I felt as if I knew my outlines—" He lifts his hands and holds them a foot apart, giving the space in between them a little shake so that I can almost feel the weight of the air cupped between his large sturdy hands. "As though I were a cartoon figure the artist hadn't filled in. I was no closer to really understanding what was inside." He lowers his hands and lets one rest on the center of his chest. "So I came back and went to work—"

"You founded Lyrik," I fill in, "and then sold it ten years later."

"You *have* done your homework," he says, holding up his glass of wine to me.

"But I couldn't find anything else about you for the next few years, the time in between selling the company and founding the Lyrik Institute. Is that when you went on your spiritual quest?"

He turns his head away, toward the sea, so I'm looking at his profile. "Yes, like your ex-boyfriend I thought the answers might lie in ancient cultures. I'd always been interested in the classics because, I suppose, I thought that if you could go back to the beginnings of civilization, to that moment when primitive man becomes rational man, you could glimpse the essence of what man is. So I founded the institute to pursue archaeological digs—in Samos, Delphi, Eleusis, Cape Sounion. And then I came here"—he sweeps his arm in a wide arc, taking in the panoramic view—"to this amazing land. There's Lake Avernus—the entrance to the underworld according to Virgil. And beyond that, along the western coast, is Cumae, the oldest Greek colony in the western world, where the Sibyl foretold the history of Rome and, according to some revisionist church historians, the birth of Christ from her cave." John turns around and points east across the gulf toward Pozzuoli. "And there's ancient Puteoli where St. Paul first stepped on Italian soil in AD 61 and San Gennaro was martyred in AD 305. It's like we're at the epicenter of some great spiritual center here."

He swerves his head back to me suddenly—his pupils contracted from staring at the sky to tiny purple dots in a sea of lilac—and I remember the impression I had, when I looked at his picture, that his eyes had absorbed the colors of all the seas and mountains and skies he had looked upon. In real life, with those eyes trained on me, the impression is even more startling, as if he could absorb my very essence.

"Funny," I say. "That's what Ely used to say about our neighborhood in Hyde Park."

John starts to say something but pauses while the waiter serves our main course from a platter of whole grilled fish, octopus, and small Mediterranean lobsters—nearly as small as the crayfish I used to catch in the creek behind my grandparents' ranch. When the waiter leaves John asks, "Do you think your boyfriend—"

"Ex," I correct.

He smiles and I realize belatedly that I sound like I'm flirting. It must be the wine, I think, taking another sip of the nearly colorless liquid. It's so light and crisp it's like drinking water, but clearly it's a little more potent.

"You think your *ex*-boyfriend Ely and this group, the . . . what did you call it?"

"The Tetraktys," I say, wondering if John's a little drunk himself that he's forgetting the name of a cult I told him not half an hour ago.

"You think the Tetraktys might be interested in the Papyrus Project?"

"I'm beginning to think so," I say. "I found out in Austin that Dale Henry attended some Tetraktys meetings, but I thought the reason he chose the project interviews as his target was that he was angry that Agnes was going away for the summer . . . and that he was jealous of Elgin Lawrence."

"Did he have any reason to be jealous of Dr. Lawrence? Was he involved with the girl?" The look of distaste on his face tells me what he thinks of such student/professor liaisons.

I shrug. "I don't know. I thought it was possible. It wouldn't be the first time Elgin had an affair with a student." I busy myself dismantling a lobster, hoping John doesn't see me blush. Although I've already confessed to more dire mistakes, I find I don't want to tell Lyros about my affair with Elgin, not after that disapproving look on his face. "But now I wonder if it didn't have something to do with the project itself. Maybe it was the Tetraktys that didn't want the project to happen."

"Or maybe," John suggests, "they wanted to change the personnel."

"What do you mean?" I ask.

"Well, if not for the shooting and Barry Biddle's death, you wouldn't be here. Perhaps this group thought that if you were here, Ely could use you to infiltrate the project." John pauses, studying me, but I'm too stunned to say anything. It's a dreadful idea: that Barry Biddle was killed so that I could take his place.

"But it can't be," I finally say. "I haven't been contacted—" As I say it I realize that it's not entirely true. The boat in the cove, the man who looked like Ely in the Piazzetta, the Smorfia cards . . . perhaps these were all overtures.

John takes my hand in his. "I'm glad. I want you to stay on this project." He looks straight into my eyes and squeezes my hand. "And I can promise you that my wanting you on this project has nothing to do with ancient cults and transmigration of the souls and lucky numbers." He holds my gaze for a long moment before taking his hand away. I'm waiting for him to say something about my academic expertise or classical training, something to dispel the electric charge in the air between us, but he doesn't.

CHAPTER 19

All the way back to Naples I feel that charge sparking the air between us, even as we talk of other things: the dig, Simon's condition, the fate of Phineas's scrolls, and the interest the Tetraktys could possibly have in them. I sense that John is giving me time to decide how I'll want to respond to his still-unvoiced proposition. We lapse into silence as we reenter the city and wind through the darkened streets toward the hospital. Perhaps, I think, the proposition was only in my imagination.

But as he pulls up in front of the hospital he says, casually, as if he only just thought of it, "You know, we're not far from the Hotel Convento. Perhaps we should spend the night in town so that we can check on Simon and Agnes in the morning. The concierge felt so bad about you getting sick there he told me we could always use the manager's suite."

I smile remembering Silvio, and because I'm wondering how big a *suite* at the Hotel Convento could be. John smiles back. I realize that he's taken my smile as encouragement. The space in the car suddenly feels small, the leather upholstery too snug and the seat belt across my chest like a hand squeezing my lungs. I have the feeling that when I try to draw in my next breath I won't be able to, and for the life of me I can't tell whether this is attraction or fear. Whatever it is, I need to get out of the car.

"Let's see how they are first," I say, opening the door.

He catches up with me on the steps to the hospital. "I'll go check on Simon while you see how Agnes is doing," he says, opening the door for me. "She may have woken up from her sedation and be upset that she's in a Catholic hospital."

"I had no idea she had this peculiar fear of nuns," I say, relieved to be talking about something other than our arrangements for the night.

"It might be that she was in a Catholic orphanage for the first couple of years of her life." He stops when he sees me staring at him blankly. "You didn't know she was adopted?"

I shake my head, amazed that he's acquired a piece of information that I've missed after knowing Agnes for over three years. He really is amazingly thorough. "No, I didn't know that," I say. "Poor Agnes. Yes, you're right, I'll check in on her right away. Maybe I'd better spend the night with her—" I'm just elaborating on this plan, which suddenly seems like the perfect solution, when we turn a corner and run into Elgin Lawrence.

"There you are!" Elgin exclaims. "I've been trying to call your cell all night!"

"What are you talking about?" I ask, annoyed at Elgin's transparent attempt to keep tabs on me. "I didn't bring a cell phone with me." Too late I realize Elgin was talking to John, who's now pulling out his cell phone and looking at it with a puzzled expression on his face.

"I think Elgin means my phone, which, I'm embarrassed to say, I apparently switched off." He smiles ingenuously. Elgin narrows his eyes suspiciously and I can't say I blame him. A man who's made his fortune in communication technology can't even remember to keep his cell phone on?

"What's wrong?" I ask. "I thought you'd taken the *Parthenope* back to Capri."

"I decided to take it to Naples instead to check in on Agnes and Simon and when I got here I found out that Simon had taken a turn for the worse," he answers. "A reaction to one of the medications he was given. He went into respiratory failure, and then cardiac arrest. I'm afraid they couldn't resuscitate him. He died an hour ago."

"But he was expected to recover." John's tone is angry, as if a subordinate had failed to meet an expected deadline.

"There were complications," Elgin responds. "You'd better talk to the administration. They wanted to talk to Simon's employer . . . something about his insurance. Sophie and I will go check on Agnes. She'll take the news about Simon better coming from her." Without waiting for a reply, Elgin steers me around by the elbow and leads me down a long corridor. As soon as we turn a corner, though, he pulls me into an alcove, a sort of niche with a plaster saint. "Did you know Simon was diabetic?" he asks.

"No," I say. "Why should I have? Do you mean to say *that's* why he died? But that's awful—"

"Yes, it's awful *and* strange. Lyros must have known about Simon's medical history. He did such a thorough background check on me that he knew the real story behind how I got my name."

Elgin always tells his students and colleagues that he was named after Lord Elgin, the British earl who brought back the Parthenon frieze from Athens, known thereafter as the Elgin Marbles. But the truth, as he admitted to me after a night drinking Coronas and tequila shooters on his boat on Lake Travis, was that he was named after the town of Elgin, where he was born—nineteen miles east of Austin, famous as the sausage capital of Texas. I'd told him on that night that I thought it was better to be named for the sausage capital than an antiquities looter.

"Lyros also knew that Agnes had been in a Catholic orphanage," I tell Elgin. "That's why she's so freaked out about the nuns here."

"Really? That explains a few things."

"She could be in danger." I start down the hall and Elgin follows me. "If anything's happened to her I'll never forgive myself." We turn into another corridor and I recognize the plaster saint with the crown of waves. Miraculously, we've found Agnes's room. When I enter it, though, I'm afraid we're too late. The bed is empty and stripped of its bedding. The room smells forbiddingly of antiseptic and ammonia.

I feel a light touch on my shoulder. Turning, I see Agnes, looking not only very much alive but the picture of health. Her cheeks are pink and her eyes glowing as if she'd just finished a morning jog.

"Thank goodness you came back for me! That shrew of a nun wouldn't let me check myself out without someone to take me back to the villa and I'm going nuts here. I know it sounds crazy, but nuns always make me think of the Grim Reaper. I was afraid I wouldn't last the night here!"

Elgin and I tacitly agree not to tell Agnes about Simon until we're on the *Parthenope*. Perhaps we're both afraid she'll start accusing the nuns of the Hospital for the Incurables of committing murder. When we do tell her, she doesn't blame the nuns; she blames herself.

"If he hadn't wanted to show me those pictures he wouldn't have gotten hurt," she says, weeping into my shoulder. I had volunteered to stay below deck with her on the voyage back even though the smell of the engine makes me feel nauseous. I'd much prefer to be up in the fresh air where Elgin and Lyros are, but Agnes is acting so distraught I don't want her near any railings.

"Agnes, you couldn't have known there'd be a cave-in," I tell her.

"But people keep dying around me. It's like I'm jinxed. It's not just Simon. What about Professor Biddle and Mrs. Renfrew? And even poor Dale. My own mother died giving birth to me."

"I didn't know that," I say, remembering what John had told me.

"I don't tell people that I'm adopted because usually it makes them act funny. My birth mother died having me and I wound up in one of those Catholic charity places. I was there for two years before my parents adopted me. So you see, it's like I'm cursed."

"Of course you're not cursed, Agnes. You were adopted by loving parents and you grew up strong and beautiful and smart." I stroke Agnes's shiny blond hair as I list her assets and her good fortunes. Slowly her sobbing eases and she falls asleep on my shoulder, lulled by the movement of the boat and my assurances. Asleep, she looks even more angelic. I can't help thinking, though, that all Agnes's good looks have brought her has been the wrong kind of attention: Dale Henry's obsession, Simon Bowles's attempt to impress her with some lascivious wall paintings. Like Iusta Petronia's, her beauty is more of a curse than a blessing.

Agnes wakes up just enough to be loaded sleepily into a taxi at the waterfront, but by the time we get back to the villa she's fully awake and seemingly over her hysterics. We find George and Maria on the terrace, a bottle of grappa between them. Maria's changed into white slacks and a cotton sweater and her hair is damp. Whatever family emergency called her away this afternoon doesn't seem to have required too much of her time.

"Ah, finally!" she says as we come onto the terrace. "George refuses to let me see this next installment until we are all gathered and have had a drink in Simon's honor. It's really too bad, but I don't see how waiting to read what Phineas had to say will bring Simon back from the dead."

"It's just the right thing to do," Agnes says. "I think it's very sweet of George to think of it." George blushes as he hands Agnes a glass.

"Yes," I say, sitting down at the table and accepting a glass of grappa. "I'm afraid I didn't really know him very well, but I know he was a remarkable artist." I hold up my glass in a toast.

"And he certainly knew how to enjoy the good things in life," Elgin says, holding up his glass.

"Poor old sod," George says by way of benediction.

"To Simon," John says. "May he live on in his paintings." He raises his glass to the mural at the back of the courtyard and we all look in that direction. Perhaps by design the lamp above the portrait of Dionysus has been left on, lighting up the full cheeks and plump lips of the smiling god. I remember how I had thought Simon *was* Dionysus that first morning I woke up here and I see now that he has given the face something of his own features. Perhaps Lyros has been struck by the same resemblance, because he proceeds to recite from Elizabeth Barrett Browning's poem about the death of the pagan gods.

"Gods of Hellas, gods of Hellas,
   Can ye listen in your silence?
   Can your mystic voices tell us
   Where ye hide? In floating islands,
   With a wind that evermore
   Keeps you out of sight of shore?
      Pan, Pan is dead."

In the silence that follows the only sound is the wind buffeting the surf against the rocks below and the fountain splashing against the solemn figure of Night. It's not hard to imagine that we are on that floating island, the last abode of the pagan gods.

John turns to George and says, "I'm sure Simon would have wanted us to go on with our work. You have another portion scanned?"

"I've transcribed it," George says, opening a laptop and palpitating the touch pad to wake up the screen. "And my Latin was adequate enough to get the gist of it, but I was hoping Dr. Chase might be able to translate it aloud."

John looks at me. "What do you think, Sophie, are you up to a little sight-reading?"

I angle George's laptop so that I can see the screen and read the first couple of lines. I've gotten so used to Phineas's style that not only can I translate the lines easily, I can practically hear his voice in my head.

"Sure," I say, taking a swig of grappa. "Here goes."

My trunk lay open and empty. Someone had stolen my scrolls. My first thought was to raise an alarm, alert the house, demand that Calatoria summon all her slaves and have them questioned. But then, as my rage withdrew, like a wave retreating from the shore leaves smooth sand, I found myself oddly calm. I sat on my bed to think through the situation.

Iusta had told me much about my hostess today—enough to form two conclusions. First, that Calatoria wanted one of the scrolls in my possession very badly—the one about the mysteries—

"Hold on," Elgin asks. "The one about the mysteries? What's the Latin?"

"De mysteriis," I read, wondering if Elgin is thinking what I'm thinking—that *On the Mysteries* was another name for Pythagoras's *Golden Verses*. But all Elgin says is "Go on." So I do.

—which, Iusta explained when I asked why her mistress was so avid for this little book, she believed would increase her power as a priestess of the cult she presided over. Second, that she would not hesitate to steal it. She had already stolen a diary belonging to Iusta, which included in it a letter from Gaius Petronius. In it he had stated that he had granted Vitalis her freedom before Iusta's birth precisely so that Iusta would be born a free woman. This letter was of course of vital importance to Iusta, and she also valued the whole diary. She had kept it for her master as a means of advancing her education.

Elgin looks over at me and smiles. He knows what such a find—a diary written by a first-century freedwoman—would be to me. The successful conclusion to her court case could be the conclusion to my book on Petronia Iusta. I can't help feeling that, even coming centuries after her death, it would be a victory for Iusta. I smile back at Elgin and continue reading.

And so if I reported the theft to Calatoria she might torture all her slaves to death and fail to extract a confession, as even a false confession would be impossible to validate by producing the stolen scrolls. How then should I proceed? If I concealed the theft and Calatoria was the thief then she would find my silence suspicious. Of course, I realized, that was exactly how I would proceed! I would act as though nothing had happened. Then if Calatoria acted suspicious of my silence, my suspicions that she was the one who stole the scrolls would be confirmed.

I spent the rest of the afternoon lying in my room. I told the servant—the same disagreeable freedman to whom I had spoken this morning—that I was worn out by the unusual heat and that I did not want to be disturbed until dinner. I was, in reality, far too excited to sleep, but I wanted to keep to myself until Calatoria returned lest some chance slip of the tongue reveal the theft to one of the household and thus spoil the advantage of surprise. I spent the time writing this account, but unfortunately I was so excited about the coming evening that I spilled ink on part of the scroll—on the section in which I recounted my earlier conversation with Iusta—

"Which is why, by the way," George says, interrupting my reading, "we couldn't read it."

I will have to recopy that section later but I am in too much of a hurry to do it right now. I have just heard Calatoria's voice in the courtyard admonishing a slave for breaking a lamp, and so it is time for me to go and play my role.

I stop and look up at George. "There's a break here."

"Yes," George says. "The handwriting was very bad here. It's the worst I've seen in this scroll so far. As he says, it's late and he's had too much to drink, but something else is going on here. I think he was genuinely shaken by some of the things he saw."

CHAPTER 20

*T*he first dish was a plate of oysters served in their natural state with only seawater as garnish.

"I hope you do not mind if we have a cold dinner tonight," my hostess said, handing me the first oyster. "My slaves have been busy preparing for the rites tomorrow night."

"Not at all," I said, taking the shell from her hand and holding it up like a libation. "In this weather, I prefer to eat cold food." I tipped the fleshy morsel into my mouth and swallowed it whole. It tasted like the sea. "But I admit I am curious about your preparations for the rites. You went to Surrentum today?"

"Yes, to the Temple of the Sirens, along with all the women of the bay who also practice the rites of the maiden."

"Ah, so there will be a large group tomorrow night?"

"Yes, twenty-one women, including myself, from the most prominent families in the bay. The number is always kept at twenty-one—"

"Ah, twenty-one—the product of seven and three! I see you are a Pythagorean."

Calatoria merely bowed her head at this compliment and continued. "As I was saying, we keep the number at twenty-one. Many more would like to join, but it is a most select group."

"It must be quite an honor, then, to preside over the rites in your own house."

My hostess smiled and ate an oyster. I could see the muscles of her neck throb as she swallowed it. "Yes, it is. Many contend for the honor, but it has been mine these last seventeen years and I hope to keep the rites here for the next seventeen years. At the end of each rite the head priestess is confirmed for the next time."

"And how is it decided?"

"I'm afraid I can't tell you that. Nothing about the rites can be revealed beforehand to the initiate. Are you having second thoughts about taking part?"

"Not at all," I answered with as much conviction as I could muster. I took another oyster, but this time when I swallowed the muscles of my throat constricted so that for a moment it stuck and I was afraid I might choke. The taste of salt was so overpowering that I felt like I was drowning. Could it be that having saved me from drowning, jealous Poseidon was now claiming my life with an emissary from his realm? But then the oyster slipped the rest of the way down my throat. "You must forgive my curiosity," I managed to say after a sip of wine. "It is the old habit of a chronicler, one that is hard to give up. I won't ask any more questions about tomorrow's rites. Instead, I shall compliment you on these oysters. I've never had better. Do you get them from Lake Lucrinus?"

I thought a shadow passed over her face, but it may have been merely a cloud passing across the sun as it sank into the sea. Indeed, the light suddenly took on a distinctly reddish hue, as though the terrace had been doused in blood. It made me shiver despite the heat.

"We'll have to ask Iusta. She brought them back from town today. Iusta!"

I immediately regretted my comment about the oysters as she summoned the girl. Would she think I had revealed her secret? "It is not necessary to call the girl," I said, perhaps a little too avidly because Calatoria looked at me strangely. "I am sure she needs to rest to preserve her strength," I explained, "for the rites tomorrow."

"Nonsense. I gave her the day off to rest and to visit some relatives of her late mother. . . . Here she is now. See, she looks perfectly rested."

Indeed Iusta, wearing a saffron yellow dress, her hair newly washed and oiled, looked lovely. As she stepped onto the terrace, the light of the setting sun gave her gold skin a ruddy glow that only enhanced her beauty. The light fell in long strips over her bare arms and shoulders, looking like blood rising to the surface of the skin when the flesh is struck. I was reminded of the painting in the peristylium of the siren lashing the initiate with her whip.

"Iusta, our guest has a question for you."

Iusta's black eyes slid nervously in my direction and I realized she was indeed afraid I had betrayed her secrets. Oh, how I wanted to be a conjurer then, to send my thoughts into her thoughts and let her know that I had not betrayed her secret! "I only wanted to know where these delicious oysters came from," I said.

"They are from Lake Lucrino," Iusta answered. "That's where the best oysters come from. Some say it's because of the lake's proximity to the entrance to the underworld. That pleasure sweetened by the approach of death—"

"Ugh, what a morbid thought! Begone, Iusta, before you ruin our guest's appetite."

Iusta lowered her eyes demurely and turned to go, but not before treating me to a secret smile. She knew I hadn't betrayed her and she was promising me just what I had asked for in exchange: a glimpse of *the inner workings of the mysteries of the house. I was glad not only on account of the promised pleasure, but because I needed to see her later to tell her about the stolen scrolls and enlist her help in recovering them. As she left, I realized that I had still not tested my hypothesis that Calatoria was the thief.*

And so I turned to my hostess and said, "When I returned from my trip to the baths today I made an unfortunate discovery. . . ." I allowed my voice to trail off to see if my hostess's face revealed any sign of guilt.

"Oh?" she asked, her face as calm as the flat surface of the sea behind her. "I hope it wasn't any fault of my slaves. I've purchased a few new ones who have given me trouble and I'm afraid that they may act badly when I'm not at home to supervise them."

"Unavoidable, of course."

She nodded and waited for me to say more. I felt sure I had caught her. Why else this long speech about untrustworthy slaves unless she thought I was about to reveal a theft? Still, I wanted to keep her in suspense a little longer to see if she might reveal, by nervousness, her own guilt. "I'm sure it's been difficult managing the slaves since your husband's death," I said. She blushed and sat upright on her couch.

"Whatever my slaves have done amiss you can be sure they will be punished for it. Is something belonging to you missing?"

"Yes, when I came back to my room today I found that something was missing from my trunk," I said. "Something I brought from the east that I thought might interest your husband . . ."

"I will call the slaves at once," she said, jumping up from her couch. "This is unforgivable. I do apologize—"

"No, no, no," I said, holding up my hands. "You misunderstand me. I realized when I looked in my trunk today that the scroll in question was in my other trunk. The one that was lost at sea."

"Scroll? You're missing one scroll?" she asked, looking at me oddly.

"As I just said, I'm not even missing that one," I said smiling. I was sure now that she had stolen the scrolls—why else would she remark on my missing only one?

She sat back down, her expression a mixture of confusion and suspicion. She could say nothing, though, without casting blame on herself. As the next dish was brought out—a plate of pickled sea
urchins—she reclined on her cushions. "Well, if you're absolutely
sure . . . it would be inconvenient to have the slaves tortured on the eve
of the rites. And bad luck, too."

"Exactly," I agreed, eating an urchin. "Don't give it another
thought."

But I could tell that she did continue to think about it. She must
have wondered all through the rest of that dreadful meal—food without the benefit of fire is a dreary thing—whether I had truly forgotten
the contents of my own trunk or I was playing a game with her. She
plied me with barely diluted wine hoping, no doubt, that I would give
myself away, and though I tried to moderate my consumption, I must
admit I was drunk by the end of dinner. I had to excuse myself before
I became too inebriated. I meant to stay awake until she retired, but I
fell asleep as soon as I lay down on my bed.

I would have slept until morning if Iusta hadn't awoken me in the
middle of the night. The moon was already sinking below the western
side of the courtyard when I opened the door to her; it shone through
the folds of her saffron dress, turning it into a shower of gold like the
one in which Zeus came to Danae.

"If you want to see where the mysteries will take place, you must
come now," she said.

"Yes, yes," I whispered. "Only there is something else." I pulled her
into my room and closed the door.

As I pulled her toward the bed I thought I heard her sigh. "There
isn't time . . ." she began, but I quickly corrected her assumption.

"Here, look, my trunk . . ." I was finding it difficult to speak. The
effect the girl had on me was strangely powerful, or perhaps it was the
wine I had drunk at dinner. "It's empty. . . . The scrolls are gone."

"Gone?" Iusta asked. "Do you mean stolen? Did you tell Calatoria *that they were missing?" Iusta asked, her eyes still on the empty trunk as if by looking at it longer she might discover the whereabouts of its missing contents.*

"No. I knew she would blame the slaves and have them tortured. And you told me today that Calatoria especially wanted the book about the mysteries. I wondered if she might have stolen it."

Iusta lifted her gaze from the empty trunk to my face. "Yes, you may be right. She may have decided that she needed it for the rites tomorrow. She'll be sure to secure her role as head priestess if she produces such an illustrious and rare work and reads from it at the rites."

"Why is it so important to her to be head priestess?" I asked. "Is she really that pious?"

Iusta smiled. "Hardly. But the women who follow the Rites of the Maiden pay tribute to the head priestess—gifts, food, clothing, jewelry, even money. Without those tributes, even my mother's oyster beds won't keep Calatoria in the lavish lifestyle she has come to enjoy—and which had brought Gaius Petronius to the edge of penury before his death. I also believe she enjoys the power."

"So she'll never give the scroll back to me? Or pay me for it? But I depended on the sale price to set myself up in Rome in the necessary style. How can I get it back from her?"

"She'll keep it close to her until tomorrow night. The only chance you'll have to get it back will be during the rites themselves. I believe she'll display the scroll and read from it just before she and the other women purify themselves by bathing in the sea. Then she'll replace it in her hiding place in the grotto, which is where I believe she has hidden my diary, and then they will all swim out of the grotto and into the open sea, as though they had become the sirens whose carelessness allowed Persephone to be seized by Hades and carried to the underworld."

"So you think I might take the scroll then?"

"Yes, but there's one problem. Remember that you're to take part in

the rites. Your role is to represent the God and so you'll be kept in an underground cell—the Chamber of the God—until it's time for you to appear."

Iusta blushed as she told me this, no doubt because of the role she was to play in the rites with me. If I were the God, then she could only be Persephone, and it would be my role to ravish her. No wonder the color rose to her cheeks as she spoke of it. I could feel the blood rushing under my own skin.

"And you?" I asked as gently as I could. *"Where will you be?"*

She looked up and I could see that she was struggling to master her fear.

"I am kept in another chamber—the Chamber of the Maiden—and I will be bound. After the women have purified themselves in the sea they come to me and bring me to . . . to you." She had been about to say *"to the god."* I was glad she was able to think of the creature in this drama as me. Perhaps it would enable her to control her fear.

"So we must act before you are brought to me, while the women are still in the sea. Is there any way out of the chamber where I will be kept?"

"Yes, there are secret passageways beneath the grottoes, many of them—like the labyrinth of King Minos—you'd never find your way through them, but perhaps . . ."

"Perhaps what?" I asked anxiously.

"The passageway between the Chamber of the God and the Chamber of the Maiden is short. I could show you the way and then, when you've unchained me, we could both go to the sirens' grotto and retrieve the scroll—and my diary. We could hide them and then recover them after the rites."

"But won't Calatoria know something is wrong when she sees that the scroll is missing?"

"When the women come out of the sea, they drink a potion. It opens them up to the power of the god and makes them quite insensible, mad even." Iusta shivered. *"Calatoria won't be thinking of the scroll. She'll*

be focused on the god: on you. As long as you play your role she won't have the wits to notice a missing scroll."

I nodded, not trusting myself to speak for the moment. My throat felt tight—as it had earlier tonight when the oyster was lodged in it—at the thought of the role I was to play. Iusta was looking at me closely. I had to maintain the appearance of calm to ease her fear.

"Very well. This is what we will do. Can you show me the Chamber of the God and the Chamber of the Maiden tonight? I will have to know how to get from one to another in order for our plan to work."

She nodded. Although her face was solemn, I detected a faint smile. I had gained her confidence. "Come with me," she said.

I followed Iusta down the stairs to the lower courtyard. The moon had set now and I could barely see her as she crossed the courtyard. She seemed to melt into a painted wall, but when I got closer I saw that she had only slipped inside a narrow gap in the wall. I could see nothing but blackness beyond, but I could feel a dank draft rising from the gap and smell the brackish odor of the sea rising from far below. I could also smell Iusta: the perfumed oil she wore on her hair and musk of her skin as she knelt by my feet. When she rose, she was holding a lamp that cast a weak yellow light on her face and arms.

"The passage is narrow," she told me. "You'll have to follow behind me and you must stay close to me or you won't be able to see where I turn. There are many false turns that drop off steeply. If you fall into one I won't be able to get you out."

With that warning, she started down the stairs. The passage was indeed narrow—so narrow that my shoulders brushed against the stone walls and I had to crouch to keep from hitting my head against the ceiling. Iusta kept the lamp close to her body—to keep the flame from blowing out, I supposed. I only caught glimpses of the paintings on the walls as we descended: a flutter of wings, the curled tail of a serpent. Only when we reached level ground did the passage widen enough for me to stand beside her, and then I could clearly see the paintings on the walls.

I almost wished I couldn't.

I'm not a prudish man by any means, but I admit that the scenes that decorated the underground passage shocked me. All the creatures of the sea and land were here and all were breeding with one another. Some of the scenes I recognized from myths: above us a great swan beat his wings between Leda's legs, Pasiphae crouched inside her cow-disguise as she was mounted by the great bull of Crete, Oreithyia was ravished aloft by Boreas, the North Wind. But others came from no myth I recognized. Sea-nymphs writhed with dolphins and serpents sodomized satyrs . . . unspeakable couplings that I am too ashamed to record here. Up to all of this, the girl Iusta held her unwavering lamp. No wonder she was frightened by the coming rites.

I motioned for her to move on. Instead, she crouched on the ground and, passing me the lamp, lifted up a stone lid covering something that looked like a well. She unwrapped a rope from around her waist and secured it to a bolt in the wall.

"I'll go down first," she said, "and then you pass me the lamp and I'll light the way for you."

I did as she said, crouching at the edge of the pit, holding the lamp for her, but the light barely penetrated the darkness. I could feel, too, the darkness at my back—and all those leering figures ready to pounce on me. Then I saw Iusta's upturned face and her hand reaching out for the lamp. What if I dropped it and plunged us into blackness? My hand shook as I passed the lamp to her. Her hand was steady.

"Now you," she said. I did as she said. When I was once again on solid ground, I was amazed to find myself in a perfectly circular room, the walls and floor painted red, with many strange figures on the wall, but these I could not make out so well.

"A chamber fit for the God of the Underworld!" I said, turning around in a circle. "But I don't see any way out except for the grate in the ceiling and that, I presume, will be locked."

"That's what you are meant to think so that when I appear it will

be as if I had materialized out of thin air, but see here—" She removed from her robe a long flat piece of iron—a tool from the kitchen used to lift hot pots from the fire, I believe—and slid it into a crack in the wall. "I will leave this here for you so that you can open the door," she said as the door swung open onto darkness. She held up her lamp and motioned for me to step through, into another tunnel that branched into three directions.

"Three! Like the faces of Hecate!" I exclaimed.

Ignoring my comment Iusta showed me which sign to follow to find her in the Chamber of the Maiden—

"He doesn't tell us what the sign is?" Maria asks.

"No," I answer, "the word he uses is *signum*."

As I followed her I saw the path we took went downward. "Deeper yet!" I remarked. "How far underground does the villa go? We'll be in Hades soon!"

I meant to lighten the mood with a joke, but when she looked over her shoulder at me she wasn't smiling. "If Calatoria catches me showing you this, that's where I will be. You must promise not to tell anyone what I've shown you tonight."

"Of course," I assured her.

"You must not even write it down."

I assured her again, although I already knew I wouldn't be able to resist recording the experience, as I am doing right now. I have never been able to resist recording the wonders I have witnessed, even the secrets I was sworn never to reveal.

We descended through the tunnel to the chamber where she would be kept. As we crept along Iusta pointed out the false turnings I must avoid. She warned me that if I fell into them headfirst I would be trapped, my body wedged in between the stones. "Calatoria has had these caverns so shaped that a man would hang upside down in them for a long time before he died. It's how she punishes slaves if they steal or disobey her."

"How dreadful—to be buried alive!"

"Yes. She believes that she avoids the pollution of murder by letting them starve to death beneath the ground."

"Don't they suffocate first?"

"No, the rock is porous enough to let in air and even a few drops of fresh water from an underground spring so that the captive is kept alive for days, weeks even."

I shuddered. "An ingenious punishment. I'll be careful. When I've found your chamber, are you sure you'll be able to find our way to the Sirens' Grotto?"

"I've explored these caverns since I was a child. My mother showed them to me."

We had come to the Chamber of the Maiden, as Iusta called it, a narrow cell hewn out of the rock, less lavish than the Chamber of the God. Then Iusta made me lead the way back to be sure I had memorized the path. I did so easily—I've always had an excellent memory—and then we climbed back though the grate and into the passageway. We ascended up to the lower courtyard without speaking, Iusta following me so quietly that for a moment on the stairs I grew afraid that I had lost her. When I turned to her she said, "If you were Orpheus and I were Euridice you would have sealed my fate right then."

I started to laugh, but then I felt a tremor beneath my feet. It was only a small tremor, common to these parts, but enough to make me wary of joking about the gods. She, too, looked suddenly serious. "You must promise me that tomorrow night you will do exactly as I have told you to do and that you won't breathe a word of this to anyone. My life is in your hands."

I promised. Then I came back here to my chamber where I wrote down what had transpired.

CHAPTER 21

"*S*o the very first thing he did upon leaving her was to break his word," Maria states after I've closed George's laptop.

"Maybe he didn't think anyone would ever read this," Agnes says. Then, looking flustered, she adds, "I mean, this journal is so . . . intimate. I've never read anything from this period that feels so confessional."

George shakes his head. "That's true, but still, Phineas always wrote for publication. He says himself that if he doesn't retrieve his stolen scroll he'll be penniless. He dealt in secrets. He was planning to sell this mysteries scroll to Gaius Petronius—and *would* have sold it to Calatoria if she hadn't stolen it first. Why should he worry about keeping the secrets of a slave girl?"

"Or of the hostess who had stolen his property?" I add, giving Agnes a sympathetic smile. I, too, am oddly reluctant to admit Phineas's perfidy. I'm not sure why. I've never thought well of his character—and nothing in his journal so far has shown him in any better light—but I realize that I'm growing unaccountably fond of the man. Maybe it has something to do with what Agnes has pointed out: I, too, have never read anything of this period that is so candid. Phineas's voice, rising out of this long-buried, charred scroll, sounds so *alive.* A phoenix rising from the ashes of Vesuvius.

"You realize," Elgin says now, "that we don't know for a fact that Calatoria stole the scroll. I, for one, am not convinced by Phineas's reasoning. It could have been one of the slaves."

Lyros nods. "Yes, but the only slave who sounds like she had enough education to recognize its value was Iusta."

"But what would Iusta want with it?" I ask. "She'd already made some kind of deal with Phineas to get her diary back. I have to confess that's what I'd like to find: Iusta's diary. Imagine a correspondence between a first-century slave and her master, who may actually have been her father. We have nothing like it; what an exciting find!"

"Really?" Maria asks, arching one carefully plucked eyebrow. "It sounds rather banal to me. But this scroll on the mysteries, *that* sounds intriguing. I wonder what it could be."

"It could be about any of the mystery rites—" Agnes begins, but I interrupt her.

"Actually," I say, looking at Lyros, "*On the Mysteries* was another name for Pythagoras's *Golden Verses.*"

"I thought Pythagoras didn't write anything," George says.

"There was debate about that in the ancient world," Elgin responds, "and false manuscripts circulating that people called *The Golden Verses* or *On the Mysteries.* This could be one of the false manuscripts."

"Or it could be the real thing," John says. Glancing at me, he adds, "There's something I should tell the rest of you. Sophie and I already discussed this at dinner—" He takes out of his pocket the postcard printed with the red tetraktys and tells the rest of the group about its odd appearances at the project sites.

I explain the sign's significance to the cult of the same name. I notice that Agnes pales and I wonder if she's remembering Dale's connection with the group and beginning to suspect what role the cult might have played in the shooting.

"Do you think this group—the Tetrads or whatever you call them—is targeting the project because they think their sacred master's book is buried under the Villa della Notte?" George asks. "How would they even know? Only the people in this room have read these Phineas transcripts."

There's a moment of silence during which I become aware of the splash of the fountain in the peristylium and the hiss of the waves hitting the rocky shore far below the terrace, and I sense that everyone is doing what I'm doing: looking around the circle of six assembled people and wondering who might leak information to a fanatic cult.

"This is ridiculous," Maria says. "So what if some crazy American cult is interested in this scroll. We're not even sure it's still there."

"That's true," I say, "we don't even know if they went through with the rites. On the morning after this last journal entry Mount Vesuvius erupted. Wouldn't they have fled?"

"Possibly," Lyros says. "But where to? The prevailing wind on August 24 was toward the southwest. Pompeii received most of the ash and volcanic stone debris—some pumice fell on Herculaneum but it probably didn't look life-threatening right away. The pyroclastic flow that destroyed Herculaneum didn't happen until midnight of the next day. Calatoria's household might have thought they were safer staying where they were than trying to travel."

While John talks I look out at the calm, moonlit bay, trying to imagine the chaos and confusion that struck on that day, the horror of not knowing whether safety lay in fleeing or hiding. What I remember, suddenly, is the moment Dale Henry opened fire, how I'd found myself under the table and not wanted ever to come out from under it again. "Or they would have gone underground to the grotto," I say aloud. "They might have thought that going ahead with the rites would appease the gods of the underworld and protect the household."

"But then they all would have been underground when the blast hit at midnight. They would have been buried under there!" Agnes cries, her voice trembling. "How awful!"

Maria makes a clucking sound with her tongue. "It would have been quick. And if that is what happened it would be a lucky thing for us."

"Lucky!" Agnes echoes, staring at Maria.

"Why yes," Maria says, ignoring Agnes's outraged tone. "It would mean the scroll is still there. Now all we have to do is follow those tunnels to the sirens' grotto and we'll have it."

I leave while the rest of the group make plans to explore the underground passages tomorrow. I suddenly feel too tired to keep my eyes open a minute longer. When I get to my room, though, something on my bed wakes me up: three cardboard tiles like the ones I'd found in the cafe and in the envelope addressed to me, laid out on my pillow like after-dinner mints.

The first one is a picture I haven't seen before: three soldiers in peaked caps carrying bayonets forked like lightning bolts. They look like they might have marched with Napoleon. The next two tiles are familiar: a hand lifting a frying pan and a man wearing a mask. I take the other six tiles out of my pocket and arrange them on the pillow in the order in which I found them: the sweeping man, the frying pan, the sun, the moon, the falling man, the masked man, the three soldiers, the frying pan, and the masked man. Three sets of three. Ely had been obsessed by threes. I feel sure that if Ely is really the one sending these, then I've got a "set," the message is complete. But what is the message? I can imagine that some of the symbols—the moon, the sun, the masked man— would mean something to Ely, but soldiers? And a frying pan?

Then I remember what Gianni had told me about each picture corresponding to a number. I take out the game I bought in the *farmacia* and unwrap it. Inside I find a playing board divided up into ninety boxes, each one containing a picture and a number. The pictures are a little different from the tiles I have, but they're close enough. I take out my notebook and, turning to a blank page, write down a description of each card and then, below it, the number that corresponds to the card. When I'm done I have a chart that looks like this:

Sweeping Man	Frying Pan	Sun
11	22	1
Moon	Falling Man	Masked Man
6	17	2
Soldiers	Frying Pan	Masked Man
12	22	2

I stare at the numbers for a long time, willing myself to see some pattern in them, trying to remember patterns that meant something to Ely. I remember he liked the Fibonacci Sequence, prime numbers, the digits of pi, and palindromic numbers, but none of those seem to fit these numbers, and if it's a more complicated pattern I'm not going to recognize it. Nor would Ely have any reason for thinking I *would* recognize it. When the numbers start to blur together I realize I have to go to sleep. Maybe when I wake up, the numbers will make more sense. Ely said that sometimes if he went to sleep with a problem in his head he would dream about the numbers, then wake up with the problem solved.

I don't dream about the numbers, though. I dream about the figures from the Smorfia board. First I am standing outside my house in Austin. I can feel the sun hot on my back and when I turn I see an enormous sun rising above the house roofs and treetops across the street. I turn back to my house and see that there's a man on my porch sweeping up broken pecan shells. As I walk past him he lifts his head and looks at me with yellow eyes; it's Charles from the Archetypes Bookstore. He's grinning at me as if he'd just told me a joke. Of course! Opening the screen door I realize that's what the symbols on the cards are: *archetypes.*

I walk through the house, aware that with each step I take the sun is tracking my progress, moving so fast through the sky that by the time I reach the kitchen the windows there are dark. Odette Renfrew stands at the stove cooking something in a cast-iron frying pan. An overpowering smell of burned sugar and nuts fills the air. When I look inside the pan, I see it holds a pecan pie.

"Honey," Odette says, "this isn't the right pan and it's not the right day. Go back out and try again."

So I go out the back door just in time to see the moon slip behind the house next door. Ely is at the edge of the yard, his back to me. I start down the back porch stairs to reach him, but the three steps that are usually there stretch out below me into a long stone stairway. I hurry, afraid that I'll miss him, but the steps are wet and slippery, coated with a film of white down. I slip, falling down into the stairwell, and as I reach for Ely he turns and I see he's wearing a mask shaped like the leering face of a satyr.

I turn back to my house, but it's gone. All that's left is rubble, as if leveled by a hurricane or a neutron bomb. Or, I realize as I pick through the debris, a volcanic eruption. A thick coating of ash lies over everything. I suddenly know that Ely and our baby are buried somewhere beneath the debris and ash. I dig, frantically scooping handfuls of dust until my eyes sting and my throat and lungs are coated with the stuff. There is broken glass in the debris as well, shards of glass covered with scraps of white paper with blue letters. Hebrew letters. I try to fit the pieces together to see what they say, even though I can't read Hebrew, and I cut my hand on the glass. Still I keep digging until I feel arms pulling me back and something sharp prodding my back. The soldiers have come. They're dragging me away just as I find, at the bottom of the rubble, the cast-iron frying pan, scorched and rusted and glowing red. I reach for it but the soldiers pull me away. I turn on them, ready to fight their bayonets with nails and teeth if I have to, but find myself facing the masked man. The eyes behind the mask are Ely's. I reach to pull the mask off. My fingers graze the hard plastic surface, warm to the touch. It's only when I hear Ely's screams that I realize my mistake. The heat of the eruption has melted the plastic mask and fused it to Ely's face. Peeling away the mask, I peel away his flesh as well.

I awake, still hearing the echoes of his screams, my skin on fire and the taste of ash in my mouth. I reach for the glass of water on my bedside table and gulp down what's left in it, then stumble to the dresser where a ceramic pitcher holds more. I pour some into my hands and splash my face, letting the water drip down my neck. My T-shirt is soaking. I wonder if I'm sick again, if I've had a relapse of the pneumonia. I haven't had such frightening dreams since my last night in the Hotel Convento. Am I delirious? But when I look down at my notebook, which lies on the dresser open to the chart of symbols and numbers I'd made, my head feels perfectly clear. I know exactly what the numbers mean. They're dates. 11/22/01, 6/17/02, 12/22/02. Anniversaries. The Thanksgiving Day when I brought Ely back to my house for pecan pie and we slept together for the first time. The day Cory was born. The last one is the day Ely found out that I was sleeping with Elgin and left me to go live with the Tetraktys.

The sweat is drying on my skin and my breathing has slowed, but still I feel like I'm suffocating. I slip a terry-cloth robe over my T-shirt and grab my sandals. Outside, the peristylium is still dark, the air still. The only sound is the restless surge of the ocean far below the cliffs. I feel like I have to be closer to the water, to immerse myself in it. It's the only thing that can stop me from burning up while I think about that day.

Clearly that's what I'm supposed to do. Why else would Ely send me those dates? He wants me to remember the history of *us*— from beginning to end.

I fumble through the dark, down to the lower courtyard, passing the pool, which I dismiss as not cold enough to slake the fire in my skin. I find the stairs down to the grotto. When I come out onto the outer steps, the sun is just emerging above the Sorrentine peninsula to the east. But still, there's barely enough light to make my way down the stone stairs to the sea. I don't stop to think how foolish a trip it is. I could fall and break my neck. No one would look for me here for hours. I could drown in the grotto and no one would even know what had happened to me until my body washed ashore somewhere. None of this bothers me. I make my way down to the grotto and slip through the cleft in the rock, leaving my robe just outside. I hesitate when I see that it's completely dark inside, but then a faint glimmer of light makes its way through the jagged opening to the sea—a forked beam like a lightning rod that magically ignites the water, turning it an electric blue. It's enough for me. I dive into the fire-blue water, like a phoenix that needs the fire in order to be born again.

The water isn't a bit like fire, though; it's shockingly cold. I surface—the gasp I take for air echoing off the domed ceiling like the dying cry of a drowning woman. I tread water until I can catch my breath, but it's too cold to stay still, so I dive under again and make my way to the opening out to the sea where, hopefully, the sun has reached the rocks and I'll be able to find someplace to warm myself. Only when I pull myself up on the rock and stretch out in the first rays of the sun do I let myself think again about the message Ely has sent me. Our three anniversaries. I have no need to think about the first two because I've relived them in my head often enough. It's the last, painful one I always try to keep at bay. But now, on this rock surrounded by water, there's nothing else to think about.

CHAPTER 22

After Ely and I came back from visiting his parents, we made a deal. He wouldn't go live at the Tetraktys community in New Mexico, but he'd continue attending the meetings in Austin and I would come along. I would keep an open mind and give the Tetraktys a chance. I would see, Ely assured me, that it wasn't an evil cult, but an enlightened philosophy.

The meetings in the bungalow on Speedway consisted of some chanting and a lot of silent meditation—not so different from the yoga classes I sometimes went to with M'Lou. The study groups I attended in the members' houses were, I thought, surprisingly scholarly. Most members read, or were at least learning, Latin and

Ancient Greek. They'd all read the major sources on Pythagoras, as well as Plato, Aristotle, and a sprinkling of the Neoplatonists—often in the original. The main thing that distinguished these sessions from the seminars I was taking at UT was that here the theories and precepts we read were followed religiously. Because Pythagoras believed that the souls of men could transmigrate into the bodies of animals, the Tetraktyans were vegetarians. This wouldn't have seemed so odd a dietary restriction except that because Pythagoras had also once told a bull not to eat beans, we weren't supposed to eat beans, either.

"That doesn't make a lick of sense," M'Lou told me over dinner at El Azteca, the East Side Mexican restaurant where we'd been eating since I was a kid. "How can you be a vegetarian and not eat beans? What do you do for protein?"

"Cheese," I told her, holding up my cheese quesadilla, "and eggs. But mostly they all seem to subsist on wheatgrass and carrot juice."

"It sounds to me like they're starving you into a suggestible state so they can brainwash you. You make sure you keep up your strength." She slipped me a bean burrito and half of her carne guisada, which I ate with guilty pleasure. "I don't want you kidnapped by any cults and ending up like that gal there." She pointed at the painting above our booth—one of the many paintings-on-velvet that, along with photographs of Pancho Villa and tapestry portraits of John F. Kennedy, adorned the walls of El Azteca. This one depicted a curvaceous Aztec maiden being sacrificed at the foot of a pyramid.

"She doesn't look like she's been starving on any juice diet," I said, laughing. And then, because I felt guilty for laughing, I added, "It's not really fair to call it a cult, you know. I mean, you could say the same for Judaism or Christianity when they started—at least the Romans thought of them as cults and made fun of their dietary laws. Professor Lawrence says the thing about the Jews that really puzzled the Romans was their refusal to eat pork. The Romans loved a good suckling pig."

"Well, I'm with them there," M'Lou had said, and then she'd let the subject drop. I think she was relieved to see that I didn't seem to be taking the Tetraktyans too seriously, and that I'd finished the rest of her carne guisada.

She was glad, too, that I was taking the ancient religions class with Elgin Lawrence because she thought it would give me some perspective on what I was hearing in the Tetraktys meetings, which is why I was taking it in the first place. Dr. Lawrence had a reputation as a keen skeptic who disabused his students of any lingering romanticism about the early Christians, the pagan Romans . . . or, really, just about anyone or anything. It was there that I was introduced to Phineas Aulus, the Roman writer who had traveled the Mediterranean collecting the secrets of mystery rites like so many exotic souvenirs. At first Ely was glad that I was taking the class, too. He was proud of the bits and pieces I could bring up at meetings, until I started also carrying home my professor's attitudes.

In addition to Phineas Aulus, Dr. Lawrence was fond of quoting Juvenal, who railed against the eastern cults that had flooded his Rome, and of drawing analogies between the proliferation of oriental religions in ancient Rome and the popularity of Eastern religions in modern-day America. In addition to classical authors, he brought in newspaper horoscopes, videos of the 1993 standoff between the FBI and David Koresh's Branch Davidians in Waco, and clippings from the *National Enquirer* and *The Star* on modern-day cults. One of the articles he brought in, published in the *National Enquirer* soon after the Waco siege, was called "The Ten Most Dangerous Cults in America." I was more than a little startled to see that the Tetraktys was listed as number seven.

After that class, I went to his office to ask if I could have a copy of the article. When he asked me why I wanted it I admitted my boyfriend belonged to the Tetraktys and then burst into tears. Dr. Lawrence (as I still thought of him then) closed his office door and sat on the edge of his desk handing me tissues until I was done crying. When I started to apologize for my outburst, he cut me off.

"It's okay," he said. "My sister Patricia belonged to the Branch Davidians. My folks went bankrupt paying deprogrammers to get her back. When my mother was dying of cancer in ninety I managed to get a message to her. I got a telegram back pretty much blaming the cancer on our mother's lack of belief. The only good thing about my mother's death from the cancer in ninety-two is that she never knew all that stuff that came out about Koresh— about how he was sleeping with the women and children in the group—or that Patricia was killed when his followers set the compound on fire." I murmured condolences, but he waved them away and kept talking. I could tell he was talking a lot to give me a chance to gain control over myself, for which I was grateful. "I'm afraid I haven't had much patience with cults since then. I suppose the bias shows up in how I teach this class, but I figure, what the hell, maybe it'll save some kid from joining a crackpot group. Show this to your boyfriend," he said, handing me the article. "Maybe he'll see reason."

Of course, showing the article to Ely made things much worse. He tore it apart, first figuratively, discrediting point by point the article's allegations against the Tetraktys, then literally, scattering the newsprint confetti across our bed. From then on not only was any information I carried back from the class suspect, but Ely said he could tell when I was carrying *bad energy* to the meetings. Other members noticed it, too, he told me. At one meeting, when I asked why the initiates at the New Mexico compound weren't allowed contact with their families, a wan red-haired girl stood up and asked if I could please not come anymore because I was polluting the atmosphere.

So instead of attending Tetraktys meetings and study groups I joined the little circle of students who accompanied Elgin Law-rence to Schultz's Beer Garden over on San Jacinto. Elgin (as I then began to call him) held forth about philosophy under the live oaks like Plato on the steps of the Academy—only with a bottle of Shiner Bock instead of wine.

I found during that fall, which like most Austin autumns held the summer heat far into October, that I liked nothing better than to sit under a live oak at Schultz's and tip an ice-cold bottle of Shiner Bock down my throat. I grew more and more reluctant on those afternoons to make the long trek back to the shuttle bus, so I started taking lifts from Elgin.

He'd just bought the yellow Porsche with money he said he earned consulting on a Hollywood gladiator movie. It seemed a shame not to take the car farther than the couple of blocks up to Hyde Park when the house was empty and when the roads climb-ing into the hill country west of town beckoned. Driving with the top down, the sun setting over the mesquite-covered hills, the air smelled like mimosa and smoke. We drove out to The Oasis on Lake Travis, where we'd have frozen margaritas and steak fajitas. (So what if this cow had once been a man, I'd think. If you really be-lieved in transmigration then the butcher had only freed the cow's soul to move on to a better host.) Heading back into town, we'd end up at Elgin's house in West Lake Hills for a nightcap and a swim in his pool. We drank so much and drove over so many dark twisting roads it was a miracle we didn't get killed. I half expected it to end that way. If there was order in the universe (as Ely be-lieved) and what I was doing was wrong, we'd end up wrapped around a pole on 2222—a road that had claimed three of my high school classmates before graduation.

We didn't die. We didn't even get caught. The later I stayed out, lingering at Elgin's practically until dawn, the later Ely stayed at the meetings. In the back of my mind I thought I'd stop when it got cold. It just never did. That year the heat tenaciously held on all the way to Halloween, the time when usually the cold fronts would move in and break the heat. This year there were only a smattering of rainstorms and then more warm weather.

It wasn't until the last week in November, when Elgin went to a conference in Los Angeles, that I started coming home earlier in the afternoons—and so did Ely. We had Thanksgiving at M'Lou's: Ely filling up on sweet potatoes and corn bread, but saying he wanted to save the pecan pie M'Lou had baked for later. When we got home that night he made me wait in the living room while he went into the kitchen. Then he reappeared, holding the pie aloft with a candle burning in its center to celebrate our "anniversary." Blowing it out, I promised myself that I would end the affair.

When I knew Elgin was back, I left him my final paper on Phineas Aulus with a note asking if I could have the rest of the term off to study for my orals. I also gave him a poem I'd been working on all term about the archaeologist Wilhelmina Jashemski. I'd finally thought of the last three lines.

Vesuvius has nothing new to say,
haze-shrouded, calm. This all goes by so fast.
There's more than one kind of catastrophe.

He sent me a note that read, *"Ita vero."* Latin for yes, but also, literally, "So it's true." Code, I surmised, for "So it really is over."

I told myself I was relieved that he hadn't made a fuss.

On the last day of the fall term, though, I found a note in my box from Elgin asking me to come meet him at Les Amis. I took the fact that he'd chosen a coffee place instead of a bar as a sign that he'd accepted the change in our relationship, but I'd forgotten that Les Amis served wine and beer as well as coffee—and I'd underestimated Elgin's vanity. If a relationship was going to end, he'd be the one to end it.

"So how are things with your true believer?" he asked when I sat down. His hands were folded across a manila folder and a bottle of red wine stood on the table between us. There was an empty glass at my place that he filled before I could say no. He'd picked up a tan in Los Angeles—and a new suit. Compared to the bedraggled students and professors around us Elgin positively gleamed. I took a sip of wine and told him that Ely seemed to be spending less time with the Tetraktys.

"But he still belongs?" Elgin asked.

I admitted he did.

"Then I think you ought to see this." He slid the file folder across the table. I opened it, expecting another newspaper article. Instead, I found a copy of a report headed "Investigation into the Tetraktyan Community." Above the title was a round symbol: a shield wreathed by laurel, surrounded by stars and then encircled by sun rays. The symbol itself seemed vaguely cultish, but when I looked closer I saw it was a government seal.

"This is an FBI report," I said, looking up. "How . . . ?"

Elgin held a finger up in front of his lips. He looked so much like a stern librarian that I started to laugh, but then I saw how serious his expression was.

"Are you . . . ?"

Then he laughed. He'd been trying not to, which is why he'd looked so serious. "I've got a friend in the Bureau," he said. "Never mind how I got it, just read it. You're not going to like it, but I think it's best you know."

I started to put the folder in my bag, but he shook his head. "Read it here. I've got a conference with another student I'm meeting here, but I'll be back in half an hour."

He got up and went to the front of the restaurant where a young girl in jeans and pink navel-baring T-shirt stood. Sure, I thought, *a conference.* I suspected he wanted me to know that it wouldn't take long to replace me. I also suspected that he'd dug up this official-looking report as a parting salvo to Ely, who he must see as his competition. Who knew if the report was even genuine? It was a Xeroxed copy so the seal could have been faked. It occurred to me that I should close the folder and walk out, but what if it were real? I read the first line: "The Tetraktyan Community, although outwardly benign in appearance, bears striking similarities to the Branch Davidian Community founded by David Koresh. It could well be another Waco in the making." Then I read the whole thing.

The report described the community in New Mexico as a walled compound with underground bunkers well supplied with water and nonperishable foods. The compound also had its own generator and water tower. The report went on to describe the eerie silence of the site: "Initiates are sworn to a five-year vow of silence that is strictly enforced. This includes written contact with the outside. There is only one telephone in the main office and calls out are taped in order to prevent initiates from trying to make contact with their families. By cutting them off from family and friends, new members are vulnerable to brainwashing. They are also kept on severely limited diets of grain and vegetables, leaving them physically weak and impressionable."

Just what M'Lou had said.

The report recommended increased surveillance of the compound and infiltration by undercover agents to prevent another situation like Waco. I noted that despite its somewhat histrionic tone, the report contained no proof the group was purchasing firearms or that members were being harmed or abused. Still, I couldn't dismiss it. One thing was for sure: if I showed this to Ely's parents, they would no longer think that the Tetraktys was a math club.

I looked up and scanned the room for Elgin. He sat at a table with the pink-T-shirted girl. She twirled her long blond hair and laughed at something Elgin had just said. As if aware of my attention, Elgin turned his head and saw me looking. He rolled his eyes at the next peal of giggles from his companion, no doubt to convince me he was above such amusements. It made me wonder what he'd told people about his time with me. Had I been just another diversion that he made light of with his colleagues? When he looked back at the girl I took the last page of the report with its dire prognostications and official-looking seal and stuck it in my bag. Before Elgin could extricate himself from the giggling co-ed, I got up and left.

I walked home, quickening my pace when I saw that it was growing dark. I'd promised Ely I'd be home before dusk. It was the solstice, which the Tetraktyans celebrated instead of Christmas or Hanukkah. Ely had told me that he had something special planned. When I turned onto Avenue B a block south of our house I saw that our little bungalow's windows were ablaze with flickering light. I had a vision of the Waco Siege, which M'Lou and I had watched on TV, with armed FBI agents in armored vehicles circled around the compound as it burned to the ground. I ran toward the lit house, scenting smoke on the air and hearing the crackle of flames, but when I got to the house I realized the smell came from our neighbor's fireplace. The crackle was just the sound of pecan shells underfoot. My house *was* ablaze with light, but that was because there were lit candles in every window. Dozens of them. Opening the front door, I saw glass votives on every available surface. A double row on the living room floor made a pathway—like the luminarias the Mexicans put out on the East Side.

My breath still coming in short gasps from running, I followed the candled path to the back of the house, to Ely's study where he sat cross-legged on the floor in a circle of candlelight. His closed eyes flicked open as soon as I stepped over the threshold.

"What are you doing?" I asked.

"Fighting back the dark," he answered. "Don't you remember what day it is? You were supposed to be back hours ago. Where were you?"

"I . . . I had a conference with a student . . ." I then remembered that classes were over. Who would I have had a conference with? "Here," I said, taking the last page of the FBI report out of my bag and handing it to him. "You'd better have a look at this. It's about the Tetraktys. It makes them sound dangerous. I don't know if it's true, but . . ." I heard the quiver in my voice, an aftereffect of thinking the house was on fire, and let it swell into a sob. Let Ely see how upset I am, I thought, let him see I'm afraid. If he loved me, he'd want to protect me from being afraid. He'd reassure me or, better yet, quit the Tetraktys altogether.

Ely read the page without speaking, without so much as blinking. He must have read it twice because I saw his eyes go back to the top of the page. When he was finished, he lowered the paper and looked up at me.

"Who gave this to you?"

This was not the question I was expecting. I thought Ely would be shocked at how the Tetraktys was portrayed here, or that he'd attack the writer, not whoever gave it to me. So I was taken by surprise. Still, I should have just told the truth: that *Professor Lawrence* gave it to me. After all, I was taking a religion class with him and Ely knew he devoted class time to modern-day cults. But standing there, in the glow of all those candles and caught in Ely's gaze, I just couldn't bring myself to say Elgin's name. Maybe I thought I was in a grade B horror movie and that the flames would whisk out at the sound of my lover's name.

So I lied. "One of my students came across it when she was researching cults for her Roman Life paper. She showed it to me when I questioned her sources. She's the one I had the conference with."

"Really?" Ely asked, holding the page up by his thumb and forefinger and tapping its top edge with his index finger. "Then why does it have Dr. Elgin Lawrence's fax number here on the top?"

No avenging wind blew out the candles but my guilt must have been clear on my face.

"You're sleeping with him." Ely's voice was curiously flat, as if he were reciting something.

"Not anymore," I said.

It was as if I had kicked the air out of him. His body collapsed in the middle and he bent over at the waist, his forehead nearly touching the floor. A lock of dark hair fell so close to a lit candle that I could smell it singe.

I knelt beside him, upsetting a candle, which poured out hot wax onto my hand. I didn't cry out. Instead, I poured out my confession. I'd felt so empty after losing Cory, I told him; he had the Tetraktys, he'd retreated from me. I knew it was wrong and I'd ended it a month ago when things started getting better between us.

He flinched when I said a month ago. He sat upright, the blood draining out of his face. "It was going on up to a month ago?" he asked.

I could only nod. He got up and left the room, kicking over candles as he went. I sat where he'd left me, listening to glass shattering throughout the house. I almost hoped then that Ely would burn down the house around us. Surely with all those candles being knocked over, that's what would happen. But then I looked at one of the candles at my feet and saw the Hebrew letters. Yarzeit candles. I remembered Ely's mother saying that she kept them for blackouts because they went right out if you knocked one over. When I'd asked her if that wasn't sacrilegious she'd shrugged. *I say a little prayer with each one,* she told me. *After all, every day is the anniversary of someone's death.*

The twenty-second of December became the anniversary of our death: Ely's and mine. He'd packed and left that night and I never heard from him again. Not until . . . unless these cryptic signs could be considered *hearing* from him. Will there be more? Will there ever be more than signs? I close my eyes against the glitter of the sea. The sun has fully risen now and my T-shirt has dried in the warm breeze. I say a little prayer for just one more sign and when I open my eyes I see I've gotten what I prayed for. Coming around the headland to the east is the same boat I saw two days ago: *The Perse-phone.*

CHAPTER 23

When the boat is about twenty feet away it stops. The engine dies and the man who had been steering it, whom I'm unable to identify because of his cap and dark glasses, tosses an anchor off the bow. Without another glance in my direction, he takes off his T-shirt, jeans, cap, and glasses, leaving on navy swim trunks. For a moment I think, no, this can't be Ely. Ely was thin and pale. This man is lithe, muscular, and, in the early-morning sun, golden. Then he dives into a patch of sea so lit by the sun that it looks as though he has leaped into fire and been consumed by it. He reappears beneath the surface, coming toward me like a flaming arrow shot through the water. He surfaces beside the rock, tossing his head to shake his thick black hair off his brow, and smiles a smile as dazzling as the glittering water.

"Hello Sophie," he says, as if it had been five minutes instead of five years since we saw each other last.

"Ely," I say in return, less in greeting than to convince myself that it's true, that it's really him. I hold out my hand to help him up onto the rock, but he scrambles up without my help and sits a foot away from me, cross-legged, grinning.

"Come here often?" he asks. It's not much of a joke, but I'm so relieved that he's willing to attempt any humor that I laugh. The Ely I first knew had a good sense of humor. He'd lost it when he joined the Tetraktys.

"It's only my second time," I say, gazing around us at the bright blue water, "but it's already one of my favorite places on earth."

He looks around, too, and nods approvingly. "Yeah, it's pretty cool. All it's missing is food. Have you had breakfast?"

I shake my head, amazed that otherworldly Ely would bring up something as mundane as food.

"Then you'll be my guest," he says, waving his hand toward the anchored boat. "I think the coffee should be almost done."

We swim to the boat, Ely leading. He scrambles up the stern first and then lowers an aluminum ladder for me. When I'm on deck he gives me not just a towel, but a terry-cloth robe and slippers. I smell fresh-brewed coffee.

"I thought you'd given up coffee." I don't know why of all the peculiarities of our present circumstances I pick on this one to single out. Perhaps because it was one of the first things I missed when he joined the Tetraktys, how we used to drink coffee together on the front porch and watch the sun come up.

"I gave up a lot of things I came to regret later," he says. He's toweling dry his hair, head ducked, so I don't see his expression, but I hear sadness in his voice. "Sit in the sun," he says. "I'll get you a cup."

He disappears belowdeck and I sit down on a padded bench, on lemon-yellow cushions resting on polished teak. The boat must be at least forty feet long—bigger even than Lyros's *Parthenope*. A billionaire's toy; I can't begin to imagine what Ely's doing with it.

Ely comes back with a cup of coffee and fresh-squeezed orange juice in a crystal glass. Then he goes belowdeck again and within minutes there's the unmistakable odor of frying bacon. Clearly he's no longer part of the Tetraktys, but then who is financing this little outing? What *is* Ely a part of?

He comes back with a tray filled with scrambled eggs, crisp bacon, a basket of rolls, and dishes of strawberries—all on Capodimonte china and served with white linen napkins and silverware. I have a thousand questions, but the one that pops out of my mouth is, "Where'd you learn how to cook?"

He laughs. "Yeah, I was a pretty bad cook when we lived together, wasn't I? I couldn't believe it when I pulled kitchen duty on the ranch—"

"The ranch?"

"That's what we called the community, or rather what the *didaskaloi* called it. We didn't *call* it anything because, of course, we weren't supposed to talk."

I'm about to ask him who the *didaskaloi* are, but then I recognize that it's Greek for "teachers." Instead I ask him, "You really didn't say anything for five years?"

"Unless you count talking in my sleep, which I did for the first few months. A lot of new initiates do it. You can hear them in the novice dorm, calling out names mostly—" He stops, looking embarrassed, and I wonder what names he called out. "But then that stops and after a while you don't even speak in your dreams. I wasn't even sure my vocal chords would work after five years."

"Is that why you didn't speak when you called me the morning Dale Henry went on a rampage?" I ask. If I'd had any doubts it had been Ely calling they're banished when I see the grieved expression on his face.

"If you had answered I would have tried, but I couldn't have my first words in five years be to a machine. Besides, I knew the phone line was tapped. I'm ashamed to say that I was afraid of what they might have done to me if they heard me warning you."

"So you *were* trying to warn me. You knew what Dale Henry was going to do? You knew Dale Henry?"

"I didn't really know him. New initiates are kept isolated for their first six months—and he'd only been there for about two months before he left in May." I think back to what Agnes had told me and realize that this meant he'd been in New Mexico since spring break—since he broke up with Agnes, in other words. "I saw him a couple of times working in the garden and I noticed he was wearing a UT T-shirt, but then a lot of initiates come out of UT. I also noticed that during chanting he was very intense. He'd stay at it for hours while most initiates could only last a couple of hours."

"A couple of *hours*? You mean some stay at it longer?"

"Some chant for days on end without stop. It's kind of the endurance test for newbies." Ely grins sheepishly. "Heck, we didn't have a lot else to do besides growing garlic and binding books. Pride manifests itself in every setting. You weren't supposed to use chanting as a competitive sport, but plenty did. So people noticed when Dale Henry lasted eight hours on his first day. The leadership noticed. He was removed from the communal dorm and he took his meals with the *didaskaloi*. He was obviously being groomed for something. I was curious . . . okay, I was jealous. I'd spent almost five years in silence—fasting, praying, studying. After all I had given up"—he looks at me and then quickly looks away—"I thought that if the *didaskaloi* had a special mission they should have sent me, or at least one of the others who had been there as long as me, not a newbie. But then I started listening in on the *didaskaloi*—"

"Wasn't that dangerous?"

"I didn't think so at first. I still had no idea how far the leadership had strayed from the ideals of Pythagoras. One of the chores you could always do was sweeping. There was no end of sand in the halls. I started sweeping near the library where the *didaskaloi* were talking to Dale Henry. I realized why they wanted someone new: they wanted someone who wouldn't be connected to the Tetraktys, and they wanted someone who hated Elgin Lawrence."

"Elgin Lawrence?"

"I was as surprised as you are to hear his name come up. For me it was like the demon I thought I had slain had risen again."

"Ely—"

"It's okay." He lays his hand lightly over mine. "You don't have to say anything."

"No, I do. I never said how sorry I was . . . how sorry I *am* that I betrayed you like that—"

Ely shakes his head and squeezes my hand. "It was my fault. I had pushed you away, retreated so far into the Tetraktys that I wasn't really there anymore. I might as well have transmigrated into another body! I had already left you in spirit. How could I blame you for leaving me in body?"

I shake my head. "It's no excuse for what I did. For hurting you that way. Did you really think of Elgin Lawrence as a demon?"

"For a while, yes. It was easier than blaming myself." Or *me,* I think, amazed at how generous Ely has been to my memory. I'm startled at how relieved I am to know he hasn't spent the last five years hating me. "I thought he'd turned you against me and turned you against any kind of faith with his skepticism. And I admit that when I first heard the *didaskaloi* talking about him as an enemy of the Tetraktys I felt, well, a little vindicated."

"An enemy of the Tetraktys? In what way?" I ask cautiously, not wanting to be the one to give away that Elgin is working with the FBI. It turns out that I don't have to.

"They said that he's been assisting the FBI in their surveillance of the Tetraktys. Didn't you know?"

"Not until recently."

"Well, it didn't come as a big surprise to me. I remembered that he had given you that FBI report on the Tetraktys, and I'm afraid I told them about that when I first came to the ranch." Ely rakes his hand through dark curls dried by the sun. "I swear I never thought they'd do anything to hurt him. For the first time since I'd entered the community I questioned the *didaskaloi*. In a way, it's what the vow of silence is all about. It's supposed to open space in your head so that you can listen and judge what you're hearing without planning what to say in response. It removes your ego from the equation. I listened to what the *didaskaloi* were saying to Dale Henry and I judged. They were using him as a tool in their machinations to get the scroll."

"What scroll?" I ask even though I already suspect what the answer will be.

"You've figured it out, haven't you? Pythagoras's *On the Mysteries*—or as it's also called, *The Golden Verses*."

"Even if such a scroll existed in AD 79, isn't it likely it was a forgery, something falsely attributed to Pythagoras?"

"Maybe, but that's not what our *magos* believes."

"Your *magos*?"

"That's what the Tetraktyans call their leader. It means wise man—"

"I know the Greek word, Ely. It can also mean magician . . . or impostor."

Ely nods, seemingly unoffended by my translation. I can't help but notice, though, that he'd referred to him at first as *our magos*. "The *magos* believes that the poem really did exist and he has been tracking it down for years through all the sacred sites of Greece—

Samos, where Pythagoras was born, Delphi, Eleusis. He'd finally concluded that its last known location was the Temple of Poseidon at Cape Sounion in Greece, but that it was stolen from there sometime around the time of the birth of Christ. He believes that the poem predicts the birth of Christ and that, in fact, Pythagoras believed that he would be reborn in the body of Christ. Yes, I know, it sounds nuts. It probably *is* nuts. I'm just telling you what the *magos* believes. He's convinced the *didaskaloi* that if they can find this poem, it will usher in a new world order. It's been the quest of the Tetraktys for decades. And now the *magos* believes that the poem was stolen from the Temple of Poseidon by Phineas Aulus. He thought at first that meant the scroll had been lost when Phineas died in a shipwreck, but when he discovered that Phineas had survived . . . when Phineas's journal showed up at the Villa della Notte in Herculaneum, he believed that the poem might be there, too."

"How did this *magos* know about the discovery of Phineas's book? The only people who knew were on this project. I only learned about it after the shooting. Do the Tetraktyans have an informer on the project?"

Ely looks at me and then, noticing that my coffee cup is empty, refills it. "You could say that. I'll tell you more when I've finished the story, okay?"

He raises his eyes from my coffee cup to my eyes, his look imploring, and I feel a charge at the contact, which startles me. I nod my compliance, not trusting myself to speak. *Am I still in love with Ely?* I hear the question in my head, but file it away. *Stay quiet,* I tell myself, *listen and judge.* For now.

"The problem, though, as the Tetraktys saw it, was that Elgin Lawrence was heading the project. They didn't want Elgin to be the one to find *The Golden Verses.*"

"But Elgin's a scholar." I've broken my resolve to stay quiet not ten seconds after I made it. I'd never last five years. "No matter

what you might think of him, you can't think he'd suppress a scholarly find like that, even if he didn't believe it was authentic."

"It doesn't matter what you or I think. The *magos* knew Elgin
was working for the FBI and he believed he would suppress *The
Golden Verses* if he was the first one to find it. He could say that it
was being kept back from publication until it could be fully translated and placed in context, until it could be verified and its source
could be discovered—" I open my mouth to object, but then I remember that sometimes it takes years for scholars to publish their
finds. "But the real reason would be that the material is far too in-
cendiary. Imagine finding a sixth-century BC document that accu-
rately predicted the birth of Christ and claimed that Christ was the
reincarnation of a Greek philosopher. Imagine the controversy it
would cause in Christianity, not to mention other religions. And
then imagine the power it could give a group like the Tetraktys,
which claims to represent Pythagoras."

"Well, I can assure you that Elgin Lawrence wouldn't care about
that!" When I see the look on Ely's face, I wish I had taken a vow of
silence. How could I have sprung so eagerly to Elgin's defense in
front of Ely? "I mean, you know what a religious skeptic he is. He'd
like nothing better than to see believers in Christianity embarrassed."

"Well, there are others who might feel differently, who might
try to get the scroll because they wanted to protect their Church. As
for Elgin . . . no, I don't believe that would be his motive, but you're
forgetting what such a document *would* prove: a sixth-century BC
philosopher had the ability to foretell the future."

"Oh, I'm sure he'd dismiss it as a late-third-century AD forgery.
Oh, but it couldn't be, not if it's buried in Herculaneum. . . ."

Ely nods. "Yes, you see the problem. It would have to date prior
to AD 79."

"Well, then, a first-century forgery. There were Christian communities in southern Italy by then. St. Paul landed at Pozzuoli in

AD 61," I say, recalling John Lyros pointing out the spot just yesterday. "So there were bound to be Christian communities in Herculaneum. Or Phineas himself could have been carrying an early Christian document, something that tried to link Pythagoreanism to Christianity. I can well believe that Elgin Lawrence would try to discredit the scroll, though he certainly wouldn't destroy it."

Ely shrugs. "I'm just telling you what the *didaskaloi* believed. They didn't want the scroll falling into Elgin Lawrence's hands and that's what they explained to Dale Henry. The *magos* himself put in an appearance to tell Dale Henry that Elgin Lawrence's Papyrus Project must be stopped."

"By shooting Elgin Lawrence?"

"I didn't hear the *magos* tell Dale Henry that in so many words, but it's clear that's what he meant. I heard him say that Elgin was a danger to the Tetraktys and that he must be stopped. I heard him say that if Elgin was *gone,* the Papyrus Project would fall apart and that Agnes Hancock wouldn't be going to Italy this summer. That Agnes would someday realize that he had saved her from Elgin Lawrence and that she'd be grateful."

Despite the warm sun on my back I feel suddenly cold imagining disturbed, delusional Dale Henry, already obsessed with beautiful Agnes Hancock and half-believing he had some special destiny, listening to an enigmatic cult leader give him a target for his paranoid fantasies. It was like giving whiskey to an alcoholic. "So did this *magos* give Dale Henry the gun?" I ask, remembering what Elgin had said about the gun being traced to a store in New Mexico.

"That I don't know, but Dale would have known where to get a gun on the property and I believe that the room where the firearms were kept would have been left open for him."

"Then your leader might as well have murdered Odette Renfrew and Barry Biddle himself," I say. "Didn't he realize that Dale could kill everybody in that room?"

"I don't think that's what was supposed to happen. The *magos* said that Dale should be careful not to hurt Agnes or Agnes's woman professor."

"Agnes's woman professor . . . are you sure that's what he said?"

"Positive. That's when I thought about you. I knew you were teaching at UT because I'd used the computer in the office and Googled you. . . ." He grins when he notices me staring at him. "Yeah, I know, pretty pathetic, huh? Anyway, I knew you were teaching there and it occurred to me that *you* might be the woman professor the *magos* was talking about. There are only two other female classics professors at UT right now. I didn't like the odds. So even though the *magos* specifically told Dale Henry not to harm you—"

"Why would he do that? I mean, did he say not to harm Barry Biddle? Or Odette Renfrew? Or any of the dozen students in that room?"

Ely shakes his head. "No, he didn't. And to tell you the truth, I wasn't thinking about anyone else. All I knew was that if you were going to be in that room—" He stops because his voice has grown suddenly hoarse. He gulps down air and looks away. "I just knew I had to warn you. The only phone was in the office and I knew it was tapped. I had to steal a key and sneak in there before the secretary arrived, then wait until I knew you had office hours—" I start to ask how he knew that, but then remember my office hours are posted on my faculty profile. "I let the phone ring three times and hung up . . . at first just because I'd chickened out. I was thinking: she won't believe me anyway, why should she listen to me after all this time? And then I called again and I hung up again. That's when I realized I'd let it ring four times and I thought: she'll know it's me if I ring in patterns of 3, 4, 5. I know it sounds crazy, but I hadn't slept all night. I suppose it didn't mean anything to you at all."

"No, I did think of you. But Ely, it didn't make me think I should stay away from the meeting I was going to. How could it?"

"I guess I thought that you would pick up the phone when you thought it was me and that I would warn you even if it meant being overheard. But you didn't pick up." He looks up at me, but I find it hard to meet his gaze, nor can I think of anything to say. Why hadn't I picked up the phone? The truth was that the idea of Ely calling me had frightened me. I look at Ely and see the look of betrayal in his eyes: the same look I'd seen when I had admitted my affair with Elgin.

I look down. We're even again. Ely joined the Tetraktys and I slept with Elgin Lawrence. He was afraid to speak into the phone, I was afraid to pick it up.

"Ely, you have to tell the FBI about this—" As soon as the words are out I remember what Elgin told me: there was a former Tetraktys member working with the FBI.

"You're the FBI informant," I say. "Elgin told me there was one—"

"But he didn't tell you his name, did he?"

"No," I admit.

Ely nods. "I'm not surprised. He's not happy that I'm the one working on this. I don't think he likes me being so close to you. He told me that I had hurt you too much, left scars on you . . . ghost roots, he called them."

I shiver at the phrase I had used in the poem I wrote for Elgin when I broke up with him. I'm sure he'd never have shared it with anyone. Any lingering doubt that Ely is telling me the truth is banished. He really must be working with Elgin and the FBI.

"Where are you staying?" I ask.

"With two agents in Sorrento—a convenient midway point between the dig and Lyros's villa. They're watching the dig so they can see what happens when the scroll is found, because if what I'm telling them is true then the *magos* will steal it. Then they can arrest him for that, bring him back to the States, and also try to make the case that he influenced Dale Henry. Otherwise, they just don't have anything to charge him with. Who's going to believe me against a man as rich and powerful as he is?"

"A man as rich and powerful . . . ?" I turn around and look up the hill toward the villa—the replica of the Villa della Notte on the cliff above us, its colonnaded portico clinging to the edge of the cliff like a face set into stone—and have the uneasy sensation suddenly that we are being watched. But the portico is empty.

"Ely, who is the *magos*?" I ask, even though I already know the answer. What Elgin told me in Herculaneum—that the FBI was working with a former member of the Tetraktys to catch the cult member who was inside the Papyrus Project—now makes perfect sense: Who better than the head of the project?

"You've guessed already, haven't you?" Ely says. "The *magos* is John Lyros."

CHAPTER 24

In the silence that follows Ely's declaration, I find myself staring at the Sorrentine peninsula and remembering what John Lyros said to me the day we climbed up to Tiberius's villa. He said that the view reminded him of the view from the Temple of Poseidon at Cape Sounion, which is exactly where it turns out Phineas found *The Golden Verses.* And where else had Lyros excavated? Samos, Delphi, Eleusis . . . the birthplace of Pythagoras and then the two most important religious shrines in ancient Greece—the same places Phineas had traveled to. Had they both been tracking the lost writing of Pythagoras?

I remember, too, that at our dinner last night Lyros had pretended never to have heard of the Tetraktys, and yet he'd known without me telling him that the cult believed in the transmigration of the soul. I had also noticed Lyros's own obsession with numbers. It made sense, but one thing bothers me.

"If John Lyros is really your *magos,* and he wanted all along to keep Elgin away from *The Golden Verses*—"

"He didn't just want to keep him away," Ely corrects me, "he wanted him dead. But he couldn't try again after Dale killed himself."

"Then why did Lyros invite the Papyrus Project here to use his villa for lab space and living quarters? Elgin told me the invitation came after the shooting, which surprised him because the Lyrik Foundation had turned down the project to begin with. . . ." I pause, remembering that I had thought they turned down the project because Elgin didn't have reliable proof that the MSI technology worked. But if what Ely is saying is true . . . "Lyros turned down the project at first because he wanted the scrolls himself?"

"Exactly. But once Lyros realized he couldn't stop Elgin from coming here he decided that the best he could do was keep him close so he could keep an eye on him." Ely gets up and starts clearing away the breakfast things, plucking up plates and snatching at crumbs like a gull swooping down on moving prey. He's clearly agitated. I wonder if it's because I referred to Elgin by his first name. Is he, I wonder, still jealous? "You see, Lyros needs to see Phineas's journal as it's scanned to find out where the missing scrolls are. Now he knows they're buried in the Sirens' Grotto or one of the underground passages leading from the grotto to the Chamber of the God."

"How do you know that?" I ask. "Agnes and George only just scanned that portion yesterday."

Ely pauses in his cleaning-up and stares into the bottom of a china teacup as though he were looking for the answer to my question in the cup's pattern of blue and white flowers. "The scanned portions of the Phineas scroll are being sent to the FBI agents I'm staying with." He raises his eyes from the teacup and meets my gaze. "I shouldn't really say by whom."

"It must be George," I say. "I'd know if it were Agnes, and Maria wouldn't want to cooperate with the American government. Simon couldn't have sent the last scan. . . . My God, Lyros must have been the one who killed Simon! I saw them arguing the other night about something. Simon must have realized what was going on and threatened to go to the police—"

"Or tried to blackmail Lyros. I knew as soon as I heard about Simon that I had to contact you and warn you about Lyros. I assume that after reading this last installment Lyros will want to explore the passages underneath the Villa della Notte, right?"

"Yes, he wants to do that today."

I look back up at the villa, but there's still no sign of life there. "They plan to get an early start. If I don't get back soon, they'll know I'm missing."

"Were you planning to go to the site?" he asks.

"I hadn't decided. I went to bed before we discussed who would work on the site and who would stay here. I assume George will stay to scan the rest of Phineas's journal. I bet they're working on it now—and Lyros and Lawrence will go to the site. And Maria, of course. After all, she's supposed to keep an eye on the excavation for PISA. Wait. How would Lyros plan to smuggle the scroll away from Maria?"

Ely shrugs. "I presume by bribing her." He's gotten all the breakfast things onto the tray and now turns to carry it down below.

"Hm. I don't like her much, but she doesn't seem like the kind of person who would be influenced by money alone. There must be something else."

"The *magos* is very good at finding people's weaknesses and working on them," Ely says as he comes back up on deck. The way he looks at me makes me wonder how much he knows about my dinner with Lyros and his invitation to stay with him in Naples last night. "I don't know what Maria Prezziotti's weakness is, but I wouldn't count on her to protect *The Golden Verses*. You should go to the site. If a scroll is discovered, someone will have to take it back to the lab to be scanned. Both Lyros and Dr. Lawrence will trust you to take it back to the villa, but Lyros will also make sure that he gets the scroll back from you once it's been scanned. He'll make up some story about why you have to give it to him and he'll think that you'll do it because, well, because he'll think he's charmed you."

"Because he's made love to me, is that what you mean? He hasn't, you know."

"But he's tried, right? He asked you to stay in Naples last night."

"How do you know that? Do you have his car bugged?"

"No. I guessed. It's what I'd have done. You didn't go with him, though."

"No, I didn't." I don't admit that I'd even considered it. The thought that I might have gone with him makes me shudder. Ely steps near to me and puts his arm around me, pulling me close. It's the first time he's touched me since we've come onto the boat, but I instantly feel that it's what he's wanted to do all along.

"I can't tell you how relieved I was that you didn't spend the night with him. I know how persuasive he can be, how seductive . . ." Ely's hand touches the collar of my robe, drawing it across my throat. His fingers graze my skin and linger on my throat. "But believe me, he can be brutal when he's crossed. Did he become angry when you refused to stay with him?"

"I demurred more than refused," I answer, being as truthful as I dare. "And besides, he's the kind of man who always thinks he's got a chance with a woman. I doubt he was that put off by my hesitation."

Ely's hand, which had begun to stray from my throat to my collarbone, grasps one lapel of my robe instead and, taking his other arm off my shoulder, grasps the other, tugging the robe around me tighter. I realize it's because I'm shivering. "Then he'll think he can trust you. Besides, he has another form of leverage: Iusta's diary. He knows how much you want that. I saw that you ended up doing your thesis on her and I remember how excited you were when you first read about her. Don't be surprised if Lyros offers to trade you *The Golden Verses* for the diary of Petronia Iusta. "

"And if I don't agree to let him have *The Golden Verses*?"

"I'll be watching you—and of course Elgin Lawrence will be there."

I'd almost forgotten about Elgin's role in this. "Does Elgin know about this plan?"

"It was his idea. He counted on the fact that you'd want Iusta's diary enough to get the scroll for yourself. That's what he used to lure you here to Italy in the first place, isn't it?"

I nod, remembering the day that Elgin dropped by my house with that first fragment of Phineas's that mentioned Iusta.

"And, of course, when you saw it was *The Golden Verses* you'd hand it over to him. Lawrence just didn't think it was necessary to tell you everything that was going on, but I didn't like that idea. I'm not sure I like the idea of you being involved in this at all. You can leave right now. I'll take you to Naples. I can put you on a plane this afternoon."

"No," I say. "If John Lyros is really responsible for the deaths of Odette Renfrew and Barry Biddle, then I want to help you get him. Just tell me what I have to do."

It doesn't take long for Ely to outline the plan that he and the FBI have worked out. Clearly they were confident that I would agree to help. When we've gone over it twice, Ely says I'd better get back to the villa before the tide blocks the passage through the grotto.

I'd almost forgotten I had to swim back through the grotto. When I look in that direction, I can't see the opening. Ely must notice my apprehension. He offers to swim back with me. I'm glad because when we get past the rock I see that the opening to the grotto is, indeed, completely underwater. I can't even tell where it is. Ely finds it, though.

"I'll go through first," he tells me as we tread water above the entrance to the grotto. "All you have to do is follow. Are you ready?" I'm not really, but the longer we wait, the more tired we'll become and the higher the water level inside will rise. I nod my assent and take as deep a breath as my damaged lungs can manage.

Ely porpoise-dives, jackknifing his body straight down along the rock face. I follow, keeping my eyes open, even though the saltwater stings, and fixed on Ely. The cleft in the rock is visible only as a pale blue seam, like a half-closed blue eye in the yellow face of the rock. It looks narrower than I remember. Ely slips easily through it, vanishing into the rough limestone as if absorbed into it. I hesitate, resisting the urge to surface, and then I force myself down deeper, grasp the edges of the rock on either side of the seam, and pull myself into the blue eye. My head and shoulders clear the cleft, but then, as I start to push myself free, something catches at my hip and holds me back. I twist around to see what it is and the pressure increases, like an arm circling my waist, as if the rock had pulled me into an embrace. Only it's an embrace that will drown me.

I twist further left. The edge of my T-shirt has caught on a sharp outcropping. By turning, the shirt has wrapped itself around my waist. I try to grip the shirt to pull it away, but the cloth is twisted so tight I can't get any purchase on it. It's so tight that I can feel the pressure now on my chest and lungs. *You just have to turn the other way,* I hear a voice inside my head say. The voice sounds far away but I obey it, spinning my torso to my right. My shirt loosens, but doesn't come free of the rock. I try to look for Ely but I'm facing down and Ely, of course, would have swum upward to the surface. I try to look up, but that only tightens the rock's hold on me. Finally, though, I catch a glimpse of strong legs kicking up to the sunlit surface—gold merging with gold while down here in this blue glass crypt I slowly begin to drown.

If only I could call out, I think, and then, as if I had, Ely turns. He dives back and swims toward me, a streak of gold cleaving the blue. When he reaches me he tugs at my shirt, but I've managed to twist it so securely onto the rock it won't come off. He tugs at it, trying to tear me loose, but the fabric holds. Then he looks up, his face level with mine, his black eyes wide and intent as if he were trying to communicate something to me through his look. But I can't think what. Once again I've failed to understand his meaning, I think as even his face begins to blur in front of me. The water seems to be growing darker and colder, his hair and eyes melting into the blackness, retreating from me. I can feel his hands, though, moving down my body, under my shirt, over my breasts and shoulders, pulling me . . . but not up. He's pulling me deeper into the water, his limbs wrapped around mine.

I recall a painting that my freshman college roommate had tacked to our dorm room wall. She liked Pre-Raphaelites—pictures of nymphs with long hair pulling unsuspecting boys into lily-covered ponds. One picture—I think it was by Burne-Jones—showed a nymph or siren wrapped around the body of a handsome youth, dragging him down to the depths of the sea. That's what it was called, I remember now: *The Depths of the Sea.*

We've arrived at the cave at the bottom of the sea. I begin to make out others in the murk, black shapes flitting through starlit blue, all those who have died in the sea. Slaves still bound to the galley oars of their Roman triremes, fishermen tangled in their nets, village girls tossed into the sea as punishment for losing their chastity. I imagine their long hair billowing in the water like the mermaids at Aquarena Springs. One turns to me and it's my mother, her eyes shining with that same excitement she had that day at the Mermaid show. It had scared me that day. I had thought the excitement came from the idea of staying on at the show for as long as we wanted, but now I see that the light in her eyes has nothing to do with the show. The spark in her eyes is her love for me. I feel an answering spark in my own chest, a flame that grows until it cleaves me open and leaves me gasping, drawing in raw, fiery mouthfuls of air, shipwrecked on a rocky shore.

I open my eyes. Instead of my mother, I see Ely's face hovering above me. His hair drips saltwater into my mouth and eyes. He lowers his face and presses his lips against my lips and blows air into my mouth. My lungs fill with his breath, reaching into the empty place in my chest that my damaged lung hasn't filled yet. He pulls back, sees that my eyes are open and lays his hands on my bare chest to feel it rise and fall. I feel the ache of the emptiness under his fingers. He moves away, but I pull him back, unable to bear the feel of that yawning chasm anymore. He hesitates for just a second, searching my eyes for something. What he sees decides him. He lowers his head again and presses his lips to mine. Stretching out beside me on the rock shelf, Ely presses the length of his body against mine. I twine myself around him, drawing warmth out of his skin just as I'd drawn breath from his lungs.

His chest, slim hips, and long legs are crisscrossed with waves of light reflecting off the water. Like a tattoo of scales. As I trace a wavy line from collarbone to pelvis, my hand absorbs the same pattern and the same blue glow. We've been transformed by the same spell—a couple from Ovid whose love turns them into blue-scaled sea serpents. Maybe we've both drowned, I think, tasting the salt of his shoulder as he presses himself on top of me. Maybe this is what happens when Orpheus goes back into the underworld to bring back Euridice, or Demeter sends Mercury for Persephone. *Facilis descensus Averno.* It's easy to go down to Hell, but not so easy to come back. Maybe the price you pay is that you are branded with the mark of death, just as I've been branded by his absence these last five years—the ghost roots Ely left snaking deep inside of me.

Above me, he hesitates, eyes as dark and fathomless as any underworld lake. Do I want to make that journey? they ask. I wrap my legs around him and pull him into me, hanging on to him as if I'd drown were I to let go.

We stay until the tide reaches the edge of the shelf and licks at our naked bodies.

"I have to swim back or I won't make it," Ely says. "If you want to come back with me . . ."

"I'd better go back to the villa. They'll wonder where I've gone and come looking. Besides, you need me at the excavation to watch for the scroll—to find *The Golden Verses*."

"Sophie, I don't want you to think what just happened has anything to do with getting the Pythagorean scroll. I didn't plan for this to happen."

"Of course not," I say, laughing. The sound echoes in the grotto, the blue waves of light dancing like mocking imps. Ely has pulled on his swimsuit and dangles his legs over the edge of the stone shelf. I retrieve my robe from the step right outside the grotto and put it on. When I turn back to Ely, I see that he's watching me. I bend down to kiss him, my damp hair falling between us. He wraps a lock around his finger, giving a little tug.

"Don't take any chances. If they find anything in the tunnels today, try to be the one who takes it back to be scanned. If Lyros objects, don't argue. Don't do anything to make him suspicious. When you come back to the island go to the Gran'Caffe and order a lemonade. I'll know, then, that you found something. Then come here as soon as you can."

He kisses me again. Then he lets my hair go and dives into the water. The light reflections on the domed ceiling sway wildly, like a school of fish wheeling at the approach of a shark. I watch him swim through the crack underneath the water until I'm sure he hasn't gotten stuck in the cleft as I had, and then I hurry outside onto the steps to see if I can get a glimpse of him swimming back to the boat. When I step outside, though, I'm blinded by the sun. I cover my eyes for a moment. When I open them, I see Maria standing two steps above me, hands on her hips, glaring at me through white-framed sunglasses.

"There you are! They sent me down here to see if you'd gone swimming. Everyone was afraid you'd drowned!"

I shrug, moving quickly up the steps to block Maria's view of the water so she doesn't notice Ely swimming back to the boat. "Well, as you can see, I didn't." I put my hand on her elbow and steer her back up the steps. "Let's hurry back to reassure the others."

Maria raises her glasses and gives me a hard look. "Something has happened," she says. "You look different somehow. You are, how do you say? *Ardente.*"

"Glowing," I translate. "It must be the Mediterranean sun and all the olive oil I've been eating." I smile at the word Maria had chosen. *Ardente.* Yes, I feel like I'm on fire.

CHAPTER 25

*E*veryone is gathered in the lower courtyard at the breakfast table when Maria and I return. If I'd been expecting cries of relief that I haven't drowned I'd have been disappointed. Only Elgin looks happy to see me even though his greeting is none too cordial.

"You're late, Chase, and you've missed Phineas's account of the eruption. George and Agnes stayed up all night scanning it."

"She can catch up while we're gone," Lyros says, his lilac eyes rising from his china coffee cup and traveling up my body from my toes to the crown of my head. I'm uncomfortably aware that I'm naked under my robe and that he might wonder why I hadn't worn a suit for my early-morning swim. "You went down to the grotto very early. You must not have gotten a lot of sleep."

"I woke up early, but I feel fine," I say more curtly than I mean to. "I'd like to go to the site. It won't take me a minute to change."

"I'll make you a copy of the latest scan," Agnes offers, getting up from the table. "And then I thought I'd go, too." She looks toward George. "That is, if you don't need me for anything. After reading this"—she holds up the slim sheaf of paper in her hands—"I'm dying to see those tunnels."

"It's fine with me," George says, yawning. "We don't have anything left to scan after this and I'm exhausted after working all night. I plan to sleep all day while you folk toil in the salt mines. I don't know how you're so fresh."

"One of the blessings of youth," Lyros says, smiling at Agnes. "By all means, join us. The more the merrier."

I detect a tightness in his smile, but it might be my imagination. He can't welcome so many extra witnesses if he plans to steal *The Golden Verses*. It's Elgin who makes me realize I'm staring at Lyros. "Well, don't just stand there, Chase," he snaps. "Go get some clothes on."

I shower and dress quickly, but when I get out to the front gate only Agnes is there waiting for me. "Elgin and Mr. Lyros have already gone down to the dock to get the boat ready. They left the cart for us to take. Maria went with them, but she's taking the ferry in because she has business in Naples and will meet us at the site later."

"Thanks for waiting for me," I tell Agnes, opening the wrought-iron gate so she can drive through.

"No problem," Agnes says after I've closed the gate and climbed onto the seat next to her. "To tell you the truth, I'd just as soon avoid being alone with the two of them. You can practically *smell* the testosterone coming off them in waves. I haven't seen two guys hate each other so much since Sam first met Dale Henry—oh, gosh!" Agnes claps a hand over her mouth, almost swerving the cart off the path into an oleander bush. "I shouldn't joke about that after what happened. Maybe if I had taken Dale's jealously more seriously . . ."

"You can't blame yourself for that, Agnes. You couldn't have known that Dale Henry was that crazy or what other influences he might have been exposed to." I'm thinking about what Ely told me, angry that on top of everything else that's happened to her Agnes blames herself for Dale Henry's rampage when it's really John Lyros who's to blame. But Agnes reads the emotion in my voice differently.

"Like *your* ex-boyfriend?" Agnes asks shyly. "Didn't he leave you to join some kind of cult?"

"Who told you that?" I ask more sharply than I mean to.

"I'm sorry. I didn't mean to upset you. Elgin said something about it, to make me feel better about Dale, I think. He said if even a smart, beautiful woman like Dr. Chase could make a mistake like that, it could happen to the best of us."

"Hmph," I snort, trying not to feel pleased at Elgin's description of me. "That's very generous of Dr. Lawrence, considering the mistakes he's made. Yes, my boyfriend, Ely, did join a cult, but that's not why he left. He left because I was seeing another man."

"Oh," Agnes says. "I *am* sorry. I didn't mean—-"

"It's okay, Agnes. Elgin's right about one thing: we all make mistakes. The important thing is what we do after we've messed up. We can give up or we can try again. And we can try not to mess up if we're lucky enough to get a second chance." *If your lover comes back from the underworld,* I want to say, remembering how Ely touched me this morning in the grotto, *you should not second-guess your good luck by looking over your shoulder to see if he's still there—like Orpheus did when he lost Eurydice.*

Agnes gives me a long, searching look, but she says nothing. I imagine she's thinking about Sam and wondering if it's too late for them. "Everyone deserves a second chance," I tell her as we arrive at the dock where the *Parthenope* is anchored. She nods and looks away, but not before I notice her eyes filling with tears.

Clearly Agnes has taken my exhortation to heart. As soon as we're on the boat she asks to borrow Lyros's laptop and then spends the trip e-mailing and IM-ing, her body curled around the screen so that no one can see what she's writing (as if we'd all want to see the romantic dialogue of two twenty-two-year-olds!). Lyros steers the boat and Elgin stands at his side, keeping his eyes on a chart of the bay as if he doesn't trust Lyros not to run us into a sand bank. Although I feel a bit neglected, I'm glad to have the time to read Phineas's account of the morning of August 24, AD 79. Once I've begun, I hardly notice I'm on a boat at all.

Because I had stayed up so late the night before—and anticipated an-other late night to come—I ordered the slaves not to wake me in the morning. I was, however, awoken by a loud clamor, a sound I first thought was a thunderclap. Good, I thought, a thunderstorm will re-lieve this infernal heat. I fell back to sleep and dreamed that I was at sea in the storm that had besieged my ship on the journey from Alexan-dria and left me shipwrecked. In my dream, I couldn't escape into the sea because I was chained to the oarlocks along with the galley slaves. Just as I realized that this terrible trick had been played on me, and that I was to be drowned at the bottom of the sea along with my slaves, the deck of the boat pitched upward, borne aloft by a towering wave, and then slammed down into a wall of water, shattering the bow. I clung to broken boards as I slipped down into the maws of the sea that opened like the jaws of a giant serpent hungry for my flesh.

I awoke to find myself on the floor, pitched from my bed, which was in fact rocking back and forth like a ship upon an angry sea. It took me another moment to realize it was not the bed that was moving, but the floor I lay upon. The whole house shook so hard that I could not get to my feet. I crawled through the door to the courtyard, believing that I would be safer in the open than under a roof.

The courtyard offered little promise of safety. The columns ringing the pool swayed like snakes writhing on a Minoan priestess's arms and clay tiles from the rooftop were flying through the air. Most horrible to say, the painted figures on the wall appeared to be dancing—some dreadful celebration of death and destruction, the sirens cracking their whips to the sound of thunderclaps that rent the still, dry air. Dionysus leered as he bounced up and down atop the virgin suppliant bound beneath him.

Everything stopped.

The stillness that followed was unnaturally silent. The water in the fountain had ceased to run. Even the sea had been silenced and as I crept toward the balcony, I was almost afraid to look, so sure was I that I would come eye to eye with avenging Poseidon, holding back the wrath of the deeps to unleash a last fatal blow upon me.

Instead I found myself eye to eye with a dying gray mullet gasping its last breath on the railing. The sea did appear to have retreated, leaving the stranded bodies of many sea creatures—fish, octopi, sea urchins—on the beach, but no avenging god stood ready to strike. Instead the air was now full of the shrieks and lamentations of the slaves in their quarters below. I turned to see what damage had been done by the tremor.

All was chaos: amphorae and statuary toppled and broken, roof tiles scattered about, slave girls crying hysterically and older slavewomen on their knees praying before the lararium, through which a crack, a hand's-breadth across, had opened, shattering the clay figures of the household gods. And amidst this chaos stood the goddess Night, impassive and regal. Of course, I thought, recalling my Hesiod: Chaos gave birth to Erebos and black Night. *And standing before the statue of Night was another figure, so still in the midst of all the tumult that for a moment I thought that she was Night's sister, Day. Then I realized it was Calatoria standing in front of the fountain, one arm held out, her hand cupped as if offering a libation to the goddess Night. Indeed some liquid dripped through Calatoria's fingers, staining the still water of the fountain red. I stepped closer to see what she held in her hand and saw that a sickle of broken pottery was lodged in the palm of her hand. It was her own blood that dripped into the fountain.*

"Domina, you're injured—"

"Struck by the gods." She turned to me with a ghastly smile on her face. "I was trying to gather the lares for safety when the second tremor hit and it shattered in my hands. I believe the genii of my husband's house are angry with me."

"Nonsense!" I said. "You yourself know how common tremors of the earth are in this region. Let us get your wound bandaged and then discuss where the safest place might be. . . ." I faltered. As much as I wanted to reassure Calatoria I was not sure if the tremors were really over. She did not seem to notice my hesitation. Instead, she extracted the shard of broken pottery from her flesh without so much as a wince, then washed the cut in the water that remained in the fountain basin. She cupped a handful of water in her hands and brought it up to my nose.

"Do you smell it?" she asked. I noticed then that the pupils of her eyes were unnaturally large. She had taken a drug—in preparation for the rites, I guessed. No wonder she spoke so strangely. To humor her, I sniffed the water. It did have an odd smell, familiar, like the fumes I had smelled wafting up from the cracked earth below the tripod that supported the Oracle of Delphi.

"Sulfur," I said.

"Yes," she agreed, nodding. "From Hades. The Queen of the Underworld approaches. We must be ready—" She turned from me and called to her slaves to make haste to clean up the debris. The house had to be readied for tonight's ceremony. I was surprised that she intended to go through with the rites, but realized that there was no point in arguing with her in her current state. I resolved instead to go into the town to see what damage had been done to other buildings and what

plans were being made to ensure the safety of the residents. Before I left, I stopped Calatoria to ask what had become of Iusta.

"One of the other slaves saw her running toward town after the first tremor," she said, sniffing distastefully. "She's always running off to town for some reason or other. Perhaps she has a lover," she added, with a mischievous glint in her eyes. "If you see her, please tell her she must come back right away. She must be prepared for tonight."

I told Calatoria I would give Iusta her message. I had an idea where she had gone.

As I made my way along the seawall toward the Porta Marina I passed small groups of people discussing the earth tremors. Voices were high-pitched with fear, but I also heard laughter among them. The general tone was relief that the worst seemed to have passed without much damage. One old man said that this morning's shaking was nothing compared to the convulsions that had occurred seventeen years ago. Another responded that smaller tremors had, at that time, preceded the larger convulsions and that one shouldn't assume that all danger had passed. Precautions should be taken, but what precautions? As I passed from one group to another, I gathered that there was no consensus as to what course of action would best ensure safety. Where could one flee if the very earth was unstable? Better to stay at home and pay homage to one's household gods than to take one's chances on the open road.

The sea, which had been calm and flat these last few days, was now rough and flecked with white foam. Turning my face away from the city, I saw why. At last a wind was blowing—from the northwest. The breeze felt mild enough on the sunny sea wall, but apparently it must be stronger on the open sea. The fishing boats on the water were encountering rough waves. No, after my last experience at sea I had rather take my chances on land.

I turned my face back toward the town and my eyes traveled quite naturally up the steep slope of Mount Vesuvius, which loomed over it.

The area around the summit was covered with a white substance. If it had been winter, or if this were Germania or Helvetia, I would have thought it was snow. Plumes of the stuff moved in the wind, sifting toward the southeast like a great rainstorm. Whatever it was, it was headed in the opposite direction from Herculaneum.

Once inside the city gates, I found myself caught up in the human traffic that flowed toward the Forum, where larger groups had gathered. A priest of the Collegium of the Augustales was addressing the masses, ordering what sacrifices and prayers should be made to avert the wrath of the gods. I quickly passed by this group, dispirited by the rather lackluster approach to calamity. Although I have no objection to the deification of the emperors, I often find the religious practices surrounding their worship rather colorless. I could sense in the mood of the crowd a certain tension that was not dispelled by the priest's assurances. What was needed was a dramatic flourish: a blood sacrifice—animal, if not human—and a little magic. I passed out of the Forum in search of Iusta, hoping that I could retrace my steps to the house where I had found her before.

I was not at all sure that I could find my way. Here, in the poorer section of town, the streets were more chaotic. More damage had been done to cheaper edifices. Rubble blocked the narrow alleys and the smell of smoke and incense hung in the air, as well as the smell of blood as the inhabitants killed animals to appease the gods. There was chanting amidst the crying of children and the lamentations of women. I stopped outside one house to listen to voices raised in song. Looking up, I saw carved above the lintel waves, a mother and child, and a boat—signs, Iusta had told me, that her religion held sacred because their leader was a fisherman and his birth had been a miracle. The singing was coming from inside the house.

In the garden, I found Iusta, who in only a few hours would play Persephone to my Hades. She was seated in a circle of men and women singing a prayer. A silence descended on the group when they heard me enter. Since Nero punished the Christians for setting Rome on fire some fifteen years ago, the sect had been driven underground, which was why, of course, Iusta had made me promise not to reveal her affiliation with it to her mistress. Her compatriots, though, might not know that I had agreed to keep her secret. As they looked up at me I sensed distrust. What I did not sense, surprisingly, was fear. Unlike the rest of the townspeople I had passed on my way here, this fellowship appeared calm. I couldn't help wondering if their faith gave them this peace, or if perhaps they were too simple to appreciate the danger.

"Your mistress sent me to bring you back to the villa," I said, addressing Iusta, ignoring the glances of the other members of the group. One of them, a young man with dark curly hair who wore the iron neck ring of a slave, was glaring at me most rudely.

"She's not her mistress," he began, but Iusta silenced him with a look.

"It's all right, Tiro. After tonight, I'll be free."

"But at what price?" Tiro asked. "Is this the man who has the temerity to play a god?"

"Enough, Tiro!" Iusta spoke sharply to the youth and he blushed. She laid a hand on his arm and whispered something in his ear. Then she got up and came quickly to my side. "Let's go," she said, steering me away from the angry young man. "The smell of sulfur and fear have no doubt made Calatoria more eager than ever to proceed with the rites. We might as well get them over with."

We made our way through the town, which had grown quieter now that the time of the siesta had come. It must be near the seventh hour. I had been gone longer than I'd thought. Calatoria would be anxious. I hurried us through the Porta Marina, but just as we were coming out onto the seawall, we heard a loud explosion and the ground jolted beneath us. I grabbed Iusta's arm just as a crack opened up in the stone beneath our feet and pulled her to safety—or at least the closest I could find to safety. As we crouched in the shadow of the seawall, I saw that the great stones were rolling like dice thrown by the hand of a giant. I felt fine dust and small pieces of rubble sifting down on our heads, and when I looked up, expecting to see the wall above us toppling over, I saw instead that the dust and rubble were falling from the sky: a gray rain that had dimmed the sun. I looked back toward the town, expecting to see the buildings reduced to rubble, but the town was intact. What had changed was the mountain behind it. At first, I wasn't sure what I was looking at. The summit of the mountain, which had appeared snow-capped earlier, was gone. In its place was a silver crown—a great plume that rose above the peak like the trunk of a tree and then swelled like the branches of an umbrella pine, only this tree was made of clouds and stood taller than any tree I had ever seen.

I put my hand out to feel the patter of dry rain and it quickly filled with ash and small porous rocks that were warm to the touch.

"What is that?" Iusta asked.

I looked down at her. There was a streak of gray ash across her right cheekbone and one on her shoulder where her dress had torn. Her face looked white in the dim gray light and different somehow—younger, more open. It was the first time I had seen her really frightened and I realized then that what I had thought was fear on the first night she came to me had been an act. This is what she looked like when she was really afraid.

I wasn't sure what was happening. I had never seen anything like it. But I didn't want to admit my ignorance to this frightened girl.

"It appears to be a cloud of ash," I replied, "disgorged from a fire burning inside the mountain. I believe Strabo recounts something like it in Sicily. . . . Luckily the wind is blowing most of it away from us. Come, when your mistress sees this she will surely decide to abandon the rites and seek a refuge farther away from the mountain." I looked back at the top of Vesuvius and saw that the cloud was spreading a pall of black over the eastern side of the bay. I could no longer make out the towns of Pompeii or Stabiae or Surrentum. "We should head west along the coast road to Neapolis, perhaps farther to Puteoli or Cumae.

Don't worry," I said, putting my arm around her. "As long as the wind continues in this direction, we should have plenty of time to reach safety."

"And you would leave without recovering the scroll that was stolen from you?" she asked.

"Yes, of course! Do you think I would risk all our lives for a mere book? No matter how ancient or rare?"

She didn't answer at first. I felt her dark eyes holding mine, looking for something in my face. We had no time to waste, though, so I turned us toward the villa and hurried her along, thinking as we went that there should be some way to convince Calatoria to admit she had stolen the scroll and get it back before we departed on the coast road to Neapolis. Maybe she had already retrieved it from its hiding place in preparation for our departure. I had meant what I said to Iusta—that I would choose our lives over an old book—but I hoped I wouldn't have to make that choice. And when we got back to the villa, I found I didn't. Calatoria had already made her choice.

The lower courtyard was full of women, all dressed in black robes, their hair loosened around their shoulders. Calatoria held a torch in one hand and a sheaf of wheat in the other. "Hurry. Hades has sent us a premature dusk to urge us early to the rites. My handmaids will prepare you, Phineas, while Iusta descends below to make the Chamber of the God ready for you."

"But my dear Calatoria," I began, "do you think it wise to stay? If another tremor should strike . . ."

"The underground chambers are carved into the cliffside. They have survived hundreds of years and tremors far worse than this. There is no place safer. It's what the gods demand of us and we won't be safe until we appease the god of the underworld and he has his bride." She looked at Iusta as she said bride and Iusta turned her eyes to me. I saw that same look I'd seen on the seawall—fear, yes, but also something else. She trusted me to make the right decision. I had told her I *wouldn't sacrifice our lives for my lost scroll, and yet, clearly if Calatoria believed the underground caverns were the safest place to be . . .*

"Very well," I said, turning from Iusta to Calatoria. "Let's be quick about it, then. Let the rites begin!" I had tried to make my voice sound calm and cheerful, but instead it rang hollowly in my ears. Had Iusta noticed? When I turned to her, she was already gone. "You must give me half an hour to prepare myself," I told Calatoria. I went back to my chambers where my clothes had been laid out for me: a clean white linen tunic and a robe of purple silk. But before I changed into my garments, I wrote down all that had happened this remarkable morning while my impressions were still fresh. The account took up the rest of this scroll and so I will take a new scroll of papyrus with me to recount what I experience below. And so I prepared myself in less than a half an hour for my journey to the underworld.

So Phineas must have taken both scrolls with him, I reason, but he dropped one in the courtyard where the excavators found it. How frightened he must have been to leave his precious book behind! I lift my eyes from the page and am startled to find that we are close to the shore. The modern coastline is some distance from the ancient city and all that can be seen of it from here is a wall of tufa, but I can see Mount Vesuvius, looming over the bay, and its sudden closeness, after what I've been reading, gives me an uneasy feeling. Agnes, too, has lifted her eyes from the laptop screen and is staring at the apparently peaceful volcano.

"Poor Iusta!" I say. "She must have been afraid that if she refused to go with Phineas, he would expose her as a Christian to her mistress—and expose her friends as well. But if she had left Herculaneum right away, she might have survived. As it is, she probably died under the villa, trapped in those underground tunnels."

Agnes turns to me and I notice that her face is wet. Tears? I wonder, or just salt spray? "Maybe," she says, "but then I wonder about that 'dark-haired youth' at her mother's house. Maybe he came to find her at the last minute and he rescued her."

"Maybe," I say, without really believing it, but not wanting to extinguish Agnes's hopes. She has cast herself in Iusta's role and sees the "dark-haired youth" as Sam. She finishes typing something on the laptop, taps the mousepad with a decisive strike, and snaps the lid closed. I can't help but think that whatever message she's sent is like the papyrus Phineas left aboveground before going down into the tunnels—the same tunnels we'll explore today—another missive to the living by those headed toward the underworld.

CHAPTER 26

When well-diggers in Resina, the modern town that sprung up over Herculaneum's ashes, struck carved marble instead of water in 1709, there were no trained archaeologists, no protocol for excavating ancient ruins. Herculaneum's theater became a quarry for an Austrian prince's Portici villa. Later, after the Austrians were expelled from Naples, Herculaneum was a treasure trove for the Bourbons. Charles III assigned his engineer, Alcubierre, to the excavation of Herculaneum, which meant tunneling into the ground and retrieving whatever they found of value: statues, friezes, wall paintings, vases, bronzes. The Villa della Notte lay undiscovered until the mid-eighteenth century, when tunnelers happened upon the central courtyard's bronze statue of the goddess Nyx, which gave the villa its name. Luckily, the Swiss engineer who was then in charge had the foresight to restrict tunneling to only what was necessary to make a plan of the villa. The bronze statue and charred papyrus scrolls were removed to Naples, but most of the villa was left intact and unexcavated inside its tufa carapace until John Lyros began excavating five years ago.

"If the eighteenth-century *tombaroli* had known about these wall paintings just on the other side of their tunnels they would have taken them, too," Lyros tells us as we stand outside the entrance of the tunnel that Simon went into yesterday. He steps into the tunnel and holds up a battery-operated lantern to illuminate the section of wall that collapsed on Simon. The wings of a swan are visible just above the gaping hole, as though the huge bird has been hovering behind the wall, just waiting for a chance to break out of the crypt that has kept him captive for nearly two thousand years. But when I step beside John and hold my lantern up to the gap I see that this swan is otherwise engaged—his enormous wings beat over the spread legs of a naked girl, his long neck curved sinuously between her breasts. Zeus come as a swan to ravish Leda. Even faded and peeling, the painting has the power to disturb by its erotic power.

"I thought these tunnels were dangerous," Agnes says from behind me, her voice trembling. I wonder if it's the safety of the eighteenth-century tunnels or the subject matter of the painting that has frightened her. Last night she'd sounded so eager to come with us.

"They *are*," Lyros answers. "I'd never agree to going any further into the tunnels dug by those Bourbon looters—death traps, all of them—but remember what Calatoria told Phineas: this stairway and the passages below were carved out of the cliff thousands of years ago. If they didn't collapse during the eruption, I don't think they're going to cave in now."

"I'm not sure I agree with your logic," Elgin says. "It could be that the vibrations of our footsteps are all that's needed to set off a collapse."

"If you're afraid, you needn't come with us, Dr. Lawrence," Lyros tells Elgin. "None of you do. This is a strictly voluntary exploration."

"And an unauthorized one," comes a voice from outside the tunnel. Maria's slim figure, clad in black capris, snug T-shirt and silk head scarf—an excavation outfit as imagined by Gucci—is silhouetted in the lit entrance to the tunnel. "I stopped by the excavation offices and I noticed that you haven't requested a permit for this excavation."

"What excavation?" Lyros asks, holding his hands up, his lantern dangling from his right hand, his left empty and turned up to the tunnel ceiling. "We're merely taking a stroll down a path that has fortuitously opened up for us. Did you lodge a complaint?"

I lift my lantern up so I can see Maria's expression, but the light makes her turn her head away and shield her eyes with the back of her hand. "No," she says. "As you say: it's not technically an excavation."

"And besides," Lyros says, smiling, "aren't you curious about what we'll find, especially now that we know Iusta was a Christian? Who knows? Her diary might contain a debate on the relative merits between Christianity and pagan worship. Wouldn't that be something for Church historians? Perhaps we've found ourselves an early Christian martyr. I know Dr. Chase must be dying to see the diary. I think we're all pretty curious about what we may find down there, aren't we?" He swings his lantern in a slow circle from face to face. No one says anything. "I thought so. The only problem is that one of us should stay up here to call for help in case there is a collapse."

"I'll stay," Agnes offers. "But how will I know if there's a problem, and what should I do if there is one?"

"Here—" Lyros removes three walkie-talkies from the canvas

bag he has slung across his chest and distributes them to Elgin, Maria, and me. He then hands the bag to Agnes after removing a bottle of water and a coil of nylon rope, which he gives to me to put in my bag. "There's another walkie-talkie in there, a cell phone, and my laptop. If you get a distress call from any of us, e-mail George and then call the Scavi office here. The number's programmed into my phone along with the local police and hospital. And then run to the office just in case. But really, don't worry. We'll be back in an hour."

As I step into the stairwell, I smell, faint but unmistakable, the briny breath of the sea. Could it really be? Two thousand years ago this stairwell led down to the sea, but now the shore is five hundred yards away. Growing up on my grandparents' ranch outside Austin, I used to find chunks of fossiliferous limestone imprinted with the ridged fans of ancient seashells from the inland sea that had dried up seventy million years ago. When I pressed their chalky and coolly curved surfaces to my face, I would catch the faintest whiff of that sea-smell. If the scent could last seventy million years in those lumps of stone, why not in this sealed stairwell? Or maybe the smell is suggested by the paintings that leap to life under the light from our lanterns as we make our way down the steps.

"It's like an underwater orgy," Elgin remarks, holding his lantern up to a painted octopus. Its long tentacles are entwined in a sea nymph's hair, its suckers attached to her breasts and, I see as Elgin moves his lantern lower, insinuating themselves between her legs. Most disturbing though is the nymph's expression—a mixture of fear and ecstasy.

"Hmph!" Maria sniffs. "What an abomination! Imagine how morally deficient and jaded these people must have been that they needed to invent such strange couplings to excite themselves."

"And yet," Lyros says from a lower step, "if these images were meant solely as titillation, why have them here, underground, and not in a bedroom? It feels to me more like an explosion of barriers than an exercise in pornography. The initiate as he descended past these images would shed his preconceptions of *categories*—of what went with what. . . ." His voice trails off as his lantern lights on the leering face of a satyr mounting a sea horse.

"In other words: anything goes, eh?" Elgin says. "It certainly sets a mood. Poor old Phineas probably thought he was in for the time of his life—not the end of it."

"We don't know that he died here," I say, turning to Elgin and stopping a few steps above Maria and Lyros. "If they came down here just after the initial eruption, it was only about one o'clock in the afternoon. They had time to perform the rites and still get out."

Elgin shakes his head. "If Phineas survived this, we'd have heard from him again. He'd never be able to resist writing this up. You heard him in the last section. He brought papyrus and pen along to take notes! Besides, I have a feeling that he might not have gotten out of here even if there'd been no eruption."

"What do you mean?"

"I just have the feeling he was being set up by those women—Calatoria and her cronies, Iusta . . ."

"Iusta? But she was a powerless slave, a plaything for Calatoria's amusement."

"You're underestimating her," Elgin says. While we've been arguing, Lyros and Maria have reached the bottom of the stairs. Elgin puts his hand on my arm and whispers in my ear. "I want you to stay close to me when we get down there."

I stare back at him, surprised. Ely had said it was Elgin's decision *not* to tell me that Lyros was the *magos*. Has he changed his mind?

"Why?" I ask. "Have you figured out who the Tetraktys informer is?"

"No," he says. His eyes slide away from me the way they would slide to me when he was spinning some outrageous yarn at Schultz's

Beer Garden. He's keeping something from me. "But until we know who it is, you should be careful around everyone, especially—"

"Let me guess: especially John Lyros?"

Elgin looks as if I've just slapped him, perhaps because I've guessed the identity of the Tetraktys informer or perhaps because he suspects who told me. But I don't get to find out which because we're interrupted by John Lyros's voice calling from below.

"We've found it," Lyros calls. "We've found the Chamber of the God!"

Lyros is crouched at the bottom of the stairs brushing dust off something on the ground while Maria holds the lantern above him. Emerging beneath the layers of dust is a circle carved into the floor—about five feet in diameter—with some kind of raised design in its center.

"It looks like a manhole cover," I say. "How thick is it?"

"I can't tell. The lid is flush to the floor. There seem to be holes in the center that could be used as a grip. If you two could hold your lanterns up . . . there . . ." Lyros sits back on his heels so we can all see the design. It's a face, crudely carved into the stone, wreathed with snakes, the mouth open in a gaping howl.

"Medusa," I say. "I suppose she's there to discourage interlopers." I'd been about to say *grave robbers,* forgetting for a moment that this isn't a tomb.

Lyros slides his index and middle fingers into the Medusa's eyes and his thumb into her mouth, like he's grasping a bowling ball, and pulls up, but the stone doesn't budge. "The weight of this thing alone would discourage all but the most dedicated. I don't see how Calatoria or any of her women could have opened it."

"But Phineas wrote that Iusta opened it herself," I say. I kneel down on the ground and run my fingertips along the perimeter of the circle. I find a small hole, no wider than a pencil, that looks like it was drilled into the stone. Feeling along the rim, I find another hole about six inches away.

"See if you can find any more of these holes," I say. "Maybe there was a pulley attached to them."

Elgin kneels down and begins looking with Lyros and me for the drill holes. Maria remains standing, holding the lantern aloft. "If there was a pulley, then where is it now?" she asks.

"The women might have removed it after they sealed Phineas in here," Elgin says. "I bet they had no intention of letting him out."

"You seem awfully suspicious of the opposite sex," John says, smiling at Elgin—only in the glare of the lantern the smile looks more like a leer. It looks, I suddenly think, like the expression of that satyr we just passed on the stairs. "Bad relationship history, eh?"

"It's not women I mistrust," Elgin replies. "It's cults. It's the surrender of reason to the herd mentality that I distrust. Hey, I've found two more holes."

"Me too," Lyros says.

"Okay," I tell them, glad they've been distracted from their argument. Had it been my imagination, or had Lyros flinched when Elgin mentioned *cults*? "Now look for holes on the stone outside of the circle. I think you'll each find two pairs, one of which will line up with a hole inside the circle—"

"Yeah, here's a pair . . . and here's another," Elgin says.

"I've found two pairs as well," Lyros says. "What do you think they're for?"

"I have an idea." I lean forward and slip my fingers into the eyes and mouth of the Medusa. The stone is cold and smooth, curving inward so that my fingers curl toward my thumb. Instead of lifting, I rotate my hand clockwise as if I were putting a spin on a bowling ball. The rasp of stone grating on stone, like the hoarse gasp of a dying man's last breath, fills the chamber. "Tell me when the interior hole is in the middle of the two exterior ones," I say.

"Now," Lyros and Elgin both say at the same time.

I stop rotating the stone and rest my fingers for a moment. Then I pull straight up. The stone lifts a quarter inch. My fingers feel like they're being yanked out of their sockets, but I keep lifting. The stone lifts another inch and then another—enough so Lyros and Elgin can grasp the sides and help lift it clear of the hole.

"Let go, Sophie. You'll break your hand," Elgin tells me.

I let my fingers slip out of the three holes and step back as the two men lift the stone circle and slide it clear of the hole. A rank odor fills the landing—no longer the smell of the ocean, but a reek of sulfur and decay so putrid it makes my eyes sting and the back of my throat clench.

"Dio Mio!" Maria says, crossing herself. "It smells like the pit of Hell."

"Some*thing* or some*one* sure as hell died in there," Elgin says. He takes out a bandanna and starts to cover his nose with it, but then he offers it to me. I take it gratefully and tie it over my mouth and nose. It smells like the lemony aftershave Elgin uses. A scent that once had the power to make my knees weak, it now steadies me enough so I can hold the lantern over the gaping hole we've uncovered. The hole is too deep for the light to reach the bottom.

"Someone will have to go down there." Lyros leans over and, without asking, takes out the coil of nylon rope he'd put in my bag earlier. "I have quite a bit of experience rock climbing—"

"Doesn't it make more sense for someone lighter to go? A woman, for instance?" Maria suggests.

"Good idea," Elgin says. "A woman *with* rock climbing experience. Don't you climb Enchanted Rock every year with your aunt?"

"Yes, but—" I'm about to explain that Enchanted Rock, a granite batholithic dome in the hill country west of Austin, is a pretty easy climb. M'Lou and a bunch of her old college friends go out there every year on the vernal equinox and climb to the top with backpacks full of wine, cheese, bread, and fruit—an expedition that hardly requires any rock climbing experience, which I'm sure John Lyros, expert rock-climber, knows.

But Lyros is handing me the rope. "Perfect. Do you want to do the honors, then?"

"Sure," I say, taking the coil from him and securing it around my waist. I slide my canvas bag around against my back so it won't get in my way. Lyros takes the other end of the line and starts to wrap it around his own waist, but Elgin takes it from him.

"Why don't I hold on to this end?" he says. "You can fix a line to a lantern to lower down once she gets to the bottom. I'm sure you'll be better at that than me."

Maria clucks her tongue and says something in Italian I can't make out—something about men and rivalry, which makes me blush. They're not fighting over me, I'd like to tell her, this is about the Tetraktys, not jealousy. Elgin smiles at me now, his face lit by the lantern at his side. The effect reminds me of something: of Elgin's face under the boardroom table at UT lit by his cell phone as Dale Henry made his way toward Agnes. He'd been trying to tell me something, but I'd ignored him, sure that I was doing the right thing and that he was the coward, the one hiding from danger. But if I'd listened to him and stayed put, Dale Henry wouldn't have fallen as he shot himself, the bullet wouldn't have gone through the table and through my left lung. I might have wished for a more active sort of heroism, but at least I can count on Elgin to be level-headed.

"Okay, I'd better go now before I lose my nerve. You've got me?" I ask Elgin.

He smiles. "Absolutely."

I lower myself through the manhole, holding on to the edge until I can feel the rope tighten around my waist, and then I let go and grab the rope instead. My legs dangle free while Elgin slowly lowers me. Maria is leaning over the edge, holding a lantern, but I soon pass out of the circle of its light. What if Phineas was describing a different chamber than this one, I wonder, and I'm dropping into a bottomless pit, one of the traps for disobedient slaves that Iusta described? Or what if the chamber has become a home for snakes in the years since it was abandoned? I hardly know whether I want to reach the ground anymore, but then my feet touch smooth cold stone.

"Okay," I shout up. Above me I see only a dimly lit circle with a woman's head silhouetted against the light. That's what Phineas would have seen, I think, before the chamber was sealed. "I'm down. Send the lantern."

The second lantern appears at the edge of the hole and then floats down, swinging on the rope so that its light arcs over the chamber's walls. I catch glimpses of painted figures—satyrs chasing naked women, wild beasts ripping apart men. They seem to move under the swaying light. As soon as I can reach it, I grab the lantern and pull it close to me to still the nauseating motion, but even when I've got it in my hands the light still quivers because my hands are shaking. It skitters over the rock walls as I turn in a circle, making the room pulsate and turning the rock blood red. I move closer to see if I'm imagining the color, but no, the walls are, in fact, painted red. I take another step closer to make out what the painted figures are doing and trip over something on the floor—a stick of some kind. The floor is littered with them and there's a little heap of them against the wall. I move closer, holding the light directly above it, trying to make sense of what I'm looking at. At first I think it's a pyre of firewood, the thickest log lying on top of the smaller sticks and something round perched on top. . . .

"What is it?" I hear Lyros call from above. "What have you found?"

Even though I've guessed, I still don't want to believe it. I turn the round object around and look into two vacant eyes. It's a skull. The thing that looks like a charred log is actually a papyrus roll, but the rest of the heap is made up of bones. And the thing I tripped over is also a bone. The cave is littered with them as if an animal had torn this man apart.

"Sophie, are you okay?" Elgin calls.

"Tell us what you've found!" Maria calls impatiently. "We can't see what you're looking at."

"I think I've found Phineas," I call. Looking closer at the skull I add, "It looks like someone bashed his head in."

CHAPTER 27

*M*aria insists on coming down next. She claims that as a representative of the Catholic Church she has a right to examine any significant finds—and human remains certainly constitute a significant find. I haven't mentioned the papyrus to them yet, but I'm sure she would include that, too, if she knew about it.

When I hear that she's winning her argument, I unclip my harness and send it back up with the rope, watching it twitch its way back into the light like a snake slithering up a hole. It gives me an uneasy feeling to be untethered from the upper world.

I wonder if Phineas felt the same when they left him here. Was he killed right away, I wonder, or did the blow come after he had taken his role in the rites? Had he been sacrificed as part of the ceremony or killed because he tried to steal back the scroll Calatoria had stolen from him? Only if that were the case, why was the scroll still here?

I hold my lantern above the charred scroll and gingerly touch it. Its blackened surface is smooth to the touch, like polished wood. Even here, below yards of rock, the temperature of the volcanic flow that covered Herculaneum had been hot enough to char and carbonize the outside of the scroll. If Phineas had been alive when the surge hit, he would have been killed instantly by the heat and poisonous gases, but judging from the crack in his skull and the condition of his bones I'm guessing he wasn't alive. The question is, why didn't Phineas's killer take the scroll? Surely if it was Pythagoras's *Golden Verses,* the killer would have taken it. The only conclusion I can reach is that this scroll is not *The Golden Verses.* In which case it could be Iusta's diary. It won't matter, though; if Lyros gets hold of it he'll think it's *The Golden Verses* and he'll take it. I might never get a chance to see it, never get to hear Iusta's voice.

I look up. The dimly lit circle is empty. I hear the voices of Elgin and Lyros arguing about who should go after Maria, who is swearing in Italian as she tries to figure out how to secure the climbing harness. They aren't paying any attention to me. I notice that the light from their lanterns only lights the center of the chamber. I've had my back to them since I found the skull and the scroll and, as Maria pointed out, they weren't able to see what I was standing over. No one but me knows the scroll is even here.

I hear Maria beginning her descent into the chamber. I lift the scroll gingerly, afraid that it will fall apart in my hands as some recovered papyrus scrolls have been known to do, but it doesn't. I look up once again and I slip the charred scroll into my canvas bag. I take out the bottles of water and move them to outside pockets. It's bad enough that I've just committed theft, I don't want to add destruction of precious antiquities to my transgressions.

I'm fastening the buckle on my bag just as Maria begins to descend into the chamber. As soon as she gets down, she sends the harness back for Lyros. When he joins us, I step back so he and Maria can examine the pile of bones and skull, dreading every moment that my theft will be revealed. My hands, I notice, are stained black from the charred scroll. Will Lyros or Maria notice traces of the blackened papyrus and realize I've taken it? If they do, neither says anything. In fact, they spend precious little time looking at the bones at all. Instead they're both examining the wall opposite the pile of bones, searching for the secret door that Iusta had shown to Phineas, the one that led to the tunnels and the Chamber of Persephone.

"Here it is!" Maria calls out, holding her lantern up to reveal a long crack in the stone. "But there's no handle on this side of the door and Iusta said it opened into the chamber."

"That's right. Iusta left Phineas an iron rod to pry it open, but I don't see anything like that here," John says, sweeping the lantern over the floor. There are plenty of bones, but no iron rod.

"Of course not," Maria says, slapping ash and dust from her hands. I'm relieved to see that she's black with the stuff; no one will notice or remark on the charcoal stains on my hands. "She would have made sure the rod was gone so Calatoria wouldn't see it."

"She?" I ask.

"Iusta, of course. Who else could it have been? She used Phineas to get the scroll back from her mistress and then either killed him herself or, more likely, left him here to be sacrificed."

"It does seem the most likely scenario," Lyros says. "The question is, did she get out alive with the scroll or did she get trapped somewhere in the tunnels with it?"

"I bet she got trapped." The voice comes from above, like the voice of God condemning Iusta to eternal hellfire. "As punishment for her sins." Elgin delivers his verdict in impressively somber tones. He's leaning over the opening, dangling a lantern below him so that his face is lit up ghoulishly, like a kid telling ghost stories around the campfire. He seems to be staring at me. I wonder if he saw me take the scroll and it's me that he's warning, but then he ruins the solemn effect by laughing and I remind myself that Elgin's an atheist. He doesn't believe in hellfire.

"The only way to find out is to explore these tunnels," Lyros says, trying and failing to pry open the door with his fingers.

"But remember what Iusta told Phineas?" Maria asks. "There are dozens of false passages that lead to drops where a person could be trapped."

"Yes, but we can go in teams, with ropes and flashlights—we can even take oxygen. I've explored caves far more dangerous than this. Of course, I'm happy to be the one who goes."

"I'll go with you," Elgin shouts from above. "But we'll have to come back tomorrow with something to get that door open. Besides, I can't raise Agnes on the walkie-talkie and she's probably worried by now. We've been down here for over an hour. I think we need to go back."

I can see by the way that Lyros is eyeing the sealed door that he wants to go now, but he agrees with uncharacteristic humility. He takes off the harness he's still wearing and hands it to Maria. "Ladies first," he says. Maria narrows her eyes suspiciously but puts the harness on and accepts a boost from Lyros up toward the surface. It's harder going up than coming down, of course, and it suddenly occurs to me that it's going to be difficult for the last person to get out. I point this out to John when the rope descends a second time, but he only winks at me and says, "Don't worry. I've gotten myself out of trickier spots."

I put on the harness, being careful not to crush my pack and the delicate scroll inside. Then I put my foot in Lyros's cupped hands and both hands on his shoulders. For a moment before Elgin gives the signal for me to hoist myself up I feel Lyros's face pressed against my breast and become uncomfortably conscious of his breath tickling the inside of my arm. My eyes fix on one of the leering satyrs on the wall and I feel a queasy mixture of arousal and fear. I realize it's exactly the mixture of emotions on the face of the nymph caught in the octopus's embrace. I can feel its tentacles wrapping around me . . . but it's only the rope. I step hard into Lyros's hands and scramble up the rope, not waiting to be pulled up, but climbing as fast as I can to get out of the underground pit.

When we get back to the island, everybody is hot and tired. Agnes has been IM-ing on the laptop all the way back on the boat and appears agitated. Elgin keeps staring at me as if he knew what was in my bag. Lyros, Maria, and I are covered with black soot from the Chamber of the God—a soot that I have begun to associate with the incinerated flesh of Phineas. I want to shower more than anything, but first I take my canvas bag with the scroll inside it and lock it inside my suitcase. Then I get in the shower and stay in there for a long time to scour every trace of the soot off of me—and also because I'm revolving a conundrum around in my head. How can I find out what's inside the scroll and, once I know, what will I do with it? Should I tell Ely that I've found it? But if it's not *The Golden Verses* he won't care about it, and if it's Iusta's diary I want first crack at it.

When I notice that my skin is pink and puckered, I get out of the shower. I still haven't decided what to do, but I have decided to enlist a confidante. I towel myself dry, rubbing my skin hard. When I look at my hands I see specks of black under my fingernails. I scrape at them with my toothbrush—and then throw away the brush. I dress quickly in light slacks and a loose gauze top and then go downstairs to find Agnes.

She's in her room staring at her laptop and crying. Things must not be going well with Sam.

"Let's get out of here," I suggest, "and go into town for a drink. I need to stop at a *farmacia* for a new toothbrush anyway."

The *farmacia* is closed by the time we get to town, but Agnes tells me I can have one of her spare toothbrushes. "My dad packed three. Like he didn't think they sold toothbrushes in Italy."

We go to the Gran'Caffe. Ely had told me to order a lemonade if I'd found *The Golden Verses*. Instead I order a Campari and soda with a lemon twist. Let him figure out what *that* means, I think; he's the one who's so good with symbols.

Agnes orders a coffee gelato and a cappuccino.

"Won't that keep you up all night?" I ask.

Agnes shrugs. "I don't expect to sleep much anyway," she says gloomily. "I might as well be alert."

"Boy trouble?" I ask.

She widens her glassy eyes, holding back tears, and flutters her hands in front of her as if her emotions were a flock of unruly geese she was trying to shoo away. "I think maybe I'm too late. I think he's fallen for someone else."

She looks at me with those wet eyes and pink nose and I can't help but feel I've just adopted a puppy at the pound—a puppy who's going to grow too big and have housebreaking issues. Who am I to give this girl relationship advice?

"Maybe he's just trying to make you jealous," I suggest, remembering how worried Sam had looked when he talked about Agnes coming to Italy, "perhaps because he's jealous himself. I think he might be jealous of Dr. Lawrence."

Agnes lets out an exasperated gasp. "Well, that's just nuts," she says, "when it's clear as day that it's you Dr. Lawrence likes."

I brush this remark aside. "We're just colleagues, Agnes. But I *am* glad to hear you're not involved with him. He can be . . . a tad unconventional with his students."

Agnes tilts her head to one side and furrows her brow. "I know he has that reputation, but honest, he's never been anything but professional and generous with me. And although I've seen a couple of grad students flirting with him I've never heard that they got anywhere. The rumor around the department is that he had an affair with a grad student a few years ago and she broke his heart and he's never gotten over it."

I nearly spit out my drink at this fanciful theory. Instead I make a snorting sound that makes the waiter lift his eyebrow at me. *"Un'altra, signora?"* he asks.

"No," I say, *"uno espresso, per favore."* After all, I plan to stay up late. *"Con limone,"* I add, making a gesture with my fingertips to indicate a twist.

"I sincerely doubt that Elgin Lawrence has ever had his heart broken," I tell Agnes when the waiter has gone.

"Really?" Agnes asks. "So you weren't the grad student who broke his heart?"

"Where did you hear that?" I ask, twisting the lemon peel from my drink into a knot.

Agnes tilts her head and smiles: the first smile I've seen from her all evening. "I didn't. I guessed from the way Dr. Lawrence looks at you, and I can tell from how you're blushing that it's true. Is that why you broke up with your ex-boyfriend? Because you fell in love with Dr. Lawrence?"

"I didn't fall in love with Dr. Lawrence," I snap, a bit too shrilly, I'm afraid. Agnes is staring at me as if I've come unhinged. "But yes," I admit, "I did have an affair with him. It was a huge mistake, which is why I've been worried about you getting involved with him."

"You don't have to worry about *that*," Agnes assures me. "Dr. Lawrence isn't interested in me. Maybe you should give him another chance. Like you said, everyone deserves a second chance."

As uncomfortable as I was giving advice to Agnes, I like her turning it back on me even less. It's time to turn back the tables.

"Don't worry about me, Agnes. You should just tell Sam how you feel and let him know that if he wants you, he has to let go of that other girl."

"Yeah, that's what I told him. I even called him. I'm afraid I used Mr. Lyros's cell phone; I hope he won't be mad about it. I left a message on Sam's voice mail and texted him twice. Then . . . nothing. Nada. Zip. I haven't heard from him now in"—she looks at her watch—"five hours. I think he's really mad."

"Maybe he lost his Internet connection," I say, patting Agnes's hand, "and is out of cell phone range." It strikes me that this is the curse of Agnes's generation; they're so *wired* that there's never a good excuse for not calling back and no down time to cool off.

Agnes nods, looking absurdly hopeful, and I decide it's as good a time as any to change the topic. "The thing to do with boy trouble," I say, "is take your mind off the boy. I've got just the project for you, if you don't mind doing something a little"—I search for the right word: illegal, unethical, dangerous, and stupid all come to mind, but instead I finish with something that sounds a little more romantic—"clandestine."

When I tell Agnes I have a scroll I want to scan that no one else knows about, her eyes get so wide I'm afraid she may call a carabiniere over to the table right away and turn me in to the authorities. But instead she leans across the table and whispers, "It could be that book by Pythagoras that Phineas took. We'd be the first people to see it in almost two thousand years."

"It could be that. Or Iusta's diaries."

"Yeah, either way it would be cool to be the ones to see it first. Besides, I'm tired of George hogging all the glory. He never lets me see the scans until he's done with them. And if this is really Iusta's diary, well, then who better to see it first than two women?"

"Are you sure you can operate the spectrograph yourself?"

"Absolutely. I've watched him do it a dozen times. We'll have to wait until everyone else is asleep, though."

"I was thinking we'd start around two. Can you stay up until then?"

Agnes downs the rest of her cappuccino and holds the empty cup up to the waiter to indicate she wants another. I do the same with my espresso cup. Before I put it down, Agnes clinks her cup against mine. "I can't wait to see Maria's face when she hears there was a scroll in the Chamber. She looked like she was going to cry when you guys came back empty-handed."

I hadn't noticed Maria's disappointment, and I wonder what she had hoped to find in the chamber: Iusta's diary or Pythagoras's *Golden Verses*? I don't admit to Agnes that I have no idea how I'm going to explain to Lyros and the rest of the project how I came by the scroll. Downing another shot of espresso, I decide to worry about that once I know what's in it.

Agnes and I agree to meet in the lab at two a.m. Luckily, she's got a set of keys and the lab's separated from the sleeping quarters by the lower courtyard. Passing the splashing fountain I hope that the sound of falling water's enough to disguise the noise of the spectrograph.

"You don't have to worry about that," Agnes tells me when I confess my worries while we're positioning the scroll in the spectrograph. "The labs are soundproofed. Mr. Lyros didn't want modern noises ruining the illusion of being in an ancient villa."

"Lovely what money can buy," I say. "I wonder if he pays to reroute air traffic over this part of the island."

Agnes looks up from the viewer with a furrowed brow. "I thought you liked Mr. Lyros."

"Oh," I say, sorry I've let on that I no longer do. "He's okay, I mean, he's been tremendously generous putting us all up here and helping the project. It's just, um . . ."

"That he seems a little creepy?" Agnes suggests, looking back down and adjusting the settings on the machine.

"I was going to say *otherworldly*."

Agnes nods. "It's his eyes. They're so pale it's like there's nothing there behind them. Anyway, I'm glad."

"Glad about what?"

"Glad that you don't *like* him. I'm still rooting for you and Dr. Lawrence."

"Agnes—" I'm about to correct her misassumptions about me and Elgin but stop when an image of the charred scroll appears on the screen. As the spectrograph scans the layers of tightly rolled papyrus the image of the scroll appears to swell, the layers gently separating like a wet newspaper swelling in the rain. "Wow," I say instead. "How can it differentiate between the different layers?"

"George wrote a program that recognizes the blank side of the papyrus and the space between columns of writing. Look, once it separates the layers it begins to *digitally unfurl* the scroll."

I watch as on the screen the scroll appears to unroll from left to right as though invisible hands were opening it. Agnes shows me how moving the cursor unrolls the scroll on the right and rolls it up on the left, just as it would have if an ancient Roman were reading it.

"A totally unnecessary effect," Agnes says, "but George says it makes him feel like he's browsing through the library of Alexandria with an invisible slave holding the scrolls open."

"It's amazing," I say, peering closer at the screen, "but I can't make out the writing."

"I have to adjust the contrast. This ink isn't the same as what Phineas was using—" As Agnes adjusts a knob on the machine, the letters on the screen sharpen and darken while the background of charred papyrus grows dimmer. The first thing I notice is that the letters aren't Greek, they're Latin—so it's not the *Golden Verses*. The second thing I notice is that the handwriting is familiar.

"He's using a different kind of ink and he's not writing as neatly, but it's definitely Phineas. Sorry, I know you were hoping it would be Iusta." Agnes sounds as disappointed as I feel.

"Well," I say, "at least maybe we'll hear more about what happened to Iusta. This must be the scroll Phineas took with him underground and that he wrote while he was in the chamber. That's why the handwriting is different—he probably didn't have much light or a good writing surface—"

"And he was rushing to finish before they came back for him. Doesn't this line say, *I must write in haste?*"

"Yes," I say, sight-reading the next few lines. "*. . . so that I might record the marvelous things I've witnessed today before it is too late. Even now the ground trembles and I smell the reek of sulfur. I fear this chamber might indeed become my tomb, my Hades, and this might be my eulogy.*

"Leave it to Phineas to write his own eulogy," I say, irritated that we haven't found Iusta's diary. Still, there's always the chance that he'll tell us what became of the diary—and of Iusta herself. "We might as well see what he has to say for himself."

CHAPTER 28

I must write in haste so that I might record the marvelous things I've witnessed today before it is too late. Even now the ground trembles and I smell the reek of sulfur. I fear this chamber might indeed become my tomb, my Hades, and this might be my eulogy.

Everything was done so as to make me believe I was descending into the underworld. Calatoria and her attendants stood in a circle around the statue of the goddess Night. Like the goddess, they were arrayed in veils embroidered with stars, their loose hair wreathed with poppies, the flower of sleep and forgetting. Twelve guardians of Night: a fitting escort to the land of the dead. The effect would have been more pleasing, though, if the women had been younger. They were all matrons of Calatoria's age, and none nearly as attractive as Calatoria herself, a club *of bored magistrates' wives who whiled away their time at the seaside by playing at sacred rites. I couldn't help feeling a bit disappointed.*

Still, I could tell I was being infected with the spirit of the mystery rites. Each attendant held a little basket—not unlike the liknon *carried in Dionysian rites, only these were made of metal and held burning incense. They filled the passage with a sweet heady smoke that made me feel light-headed. Opium, I imagine. Calatoria led the way down the stairs, holding a torch high above her head so that as we descended I caught fleeting images of the paintings on the wall. I was glad I had seen them before with Iusta because I am sure that if I had encountered them for the first time in this atmosphere, intoxicated by the opium smoke and the peculiar keening of the attendants, I would have been even more unnerved than I was. Even forewarned, the quivering intertangled limbs of human and beast seemed to come alive in the flash of Calatoria's torch. I could almost believe that at any moment the tentacle of an octopus or the hand of one of these sea nymphs would reach out and grab me from behind. The world above seemed suddenly far away, its rules and strictures more illusory than the laws that governed these strange aqueous couplings. Every step downward was taking me closer to the core, not just of the earth where Hades and his queen rule the shades, but into the core of my very being. This, I said to myself, is the secret of the mystery rites: they reveal what it means to be human. They show us where we've come from and where we all end up: Chaos, as Ovid has described it, a rough and undigested mass clotted with the warring seeds of things not yet yoked together. This is what we come from and, perhaps, what we return to at the end.*

When we came to the bottom of the steps, the attendants circled round the stone lid of the chamber. I tried not to give away by glance or gesture that I recognized the place. Instead, I stood with respectfully lowered eyes, looking into the face of the carved Medusa, as still as if I had indeed been turned into stone by her.

"Are you ready to assume the role of the god?" Calatoria asked.

"Yes. I am ready."

"First, then, you must cleanse yourself of all earthly stain. I will ask you three questions. You are not to answer them now, but must think on them in your chamber while we cleanse ourselves for the sacrifice. Have your answers ready when we come for you."

I nodded my assent without speaking and waited for my questions, wondering if this is how Oedipus felt before the Sphinx.

At an invisible sign from their mistress, the attendants began to chant together, their voices all as one. The words were in Greek.

Where did I go wrong today?

What did I accomplish?

What obligation did I not perform?

I'm ashamed to say that I nearly laughed at hearing the three questions posed by Pythagoras in his Golden Verses. *Was Calatoria taunting me with her theft? Or was this the clue to why she had stolen the scroll? Were these women Pythagoreans? True, the philosopher had dwelled in a part of Italy not far from here. Perhaps this little group was a remnant of his followers. The idea was so intriguing that I missed whatever Calatoria said next. Some more nonsense about preparing myself and cleansing my soul. Then the attendants knelt around the stone circle and, intoning a series of random words and numbers, turned the lid. I noticed, as I had not when Iusta turned the stone, that when the lid was in the right position a series of triangles were formed by the dots on the interior circle and the exterior rim. I saw then that beneath their veils the women wore painted dots shaped like triangles upon their foreheads. I felt sure then that I had penetrated at least one secret of Calatoria's little mysteries: they combined some primitive worship of Pythagoras with the rites of Demeter and Persephone with perhaps some elements of Dionysian worship thrown in. I was so busy pondering this that I was startled to notice that the attendants had moved closer and were encircling me with ropes. I jerked away, merely a natural reaction to the sensation of being bound, and two women wrenched my arms behind my back with surprising strength and quickness while the others tightened their hold on me.*

"*Must they be so tight?*" *I asked, surprised at the fear in my own voice.*

"*We wouldn't want you to slip while you're being lowered to your chamber,*" *Calatoria answered, nodding to one of the attendants who stepped in front of me and, without any warning, dropped a hood over my head.*

The instant I was plunged into blackness the women began to moan and wail, letting loose a torrent of such wild unbridled lamentation that my hair stood on end and my skin tingled as if a million pins were pricking its surface. Pins were *pricking my skin and hands were moving all over me, pinching, tickling, prying . . . so many sensations I could no longer tell what was happening to me. I felt myself lifted off my feet and laid flat—only I was lying on nothing. I was held up by a dozen hands as if carried on a bier, and all the while the women keened their loss, mourning the death of a god. Of course, I thought, this is the Dionysian element of the rites. I am Zagreus, devoured by the Titans, later to be reborn as the god Dionysus. I could feel the women plucking at my arms and legs as if to tear me limb from limb. I could even feel their mouths on my flesh—sucking, nipping—symbolizing the ritual eating of the god. Indeed, some of the women, carried away with ecstasy, actually bit me. I tried not to scream out, but if I did I'm sure the sound was covered up by their ululations. Just when the sensations were becoming unbearable, I felt myself plummeting through space and I dropped onto hard cold stone.*

I lay there, stunned, while above me I could hear the grating of stone against stone as the lid was replaced. I waited until I could tell by the muted wails of the women that the chamber was sealed. Then I struggled against the ropes. Iusta had not prepared me for this! What if I couldn't untie myself? But the ropes, while tightly wrapped around my body, did not secure my hands and I was soon able to free myself. The first thing I did was to take the hood off my head. It did no good; I was immersed in total darkness.

This, too, I guessed, was part of the ritual. I was the god who has been killed and eaten awaiting my rebirth in the stomach of great Zeus. I heard rumblings in the earth not unlike the growlings of a great stomach—sounds made, I imagined, by Calatoria and her attendants as they moved through the tunnels that were hewn through the rock around my chamber. They would go now to the grotto and bathe in the sea, then return to celebrate my rebirth, bringing me the goddess Persephone, but at that point I admit that I grew confused. According to the legend, if I were Zagreus, then actually Persephone was my mother. So she wouldn't be offered to me as a bride. But if I were Hades, Persephone's ravisher and husband, then why had I been subjected to the ritual dismemberment and eating? I could only assume that Calatoria and her women had gotten their myths mixed up. I would have to ask Iusta about it later.

Now, though, I had to collect my wits and find my way to the Chamber of the Maiden. I found the iron rod Iusta had left and used it to open the door into the tunnels. Following the tunnels marked with the sign of the pomegranate, I found the chamber of Persephone with Iusta bound in it. She, however, had been left with a torch stuck into a crack in the rock, which she grabbed as soon as I untied her. She led me into another series of tunnels, following the path marked with the double-tailed siren that led to the grotto.

"Even without these signs, I think I would be able to find my way to the grotto by following the sound of the sea," I told Iusta.

"I wouldn't count on that," Iusta replied. "The sea enters a number of caves inside this cliff and produces confusing echoes in the many caverns and tunnels. Listen."

She made me stop and I heard what she meant. The sound of the sea was all around us, as if we had traveled beneath the bottom of the ocean into the lair of Poseidon. Threaded inside the music of the ocean was the sound of women's voices; Calatoria and her attendants had given over their keening for singing now, but their song had something wild and savage in it. I felt sure this was how the sirens sounded when they lured men to their doom. It almost made me afraid to follow their voices to their lair, but I could also feel the pull of the secret knowledge their song promised.

"Here," Iusta said as we reached the end of a long tunnel. "If we climb onto this ledge we will see into the Sirens' Grotto. Be careful to keep your head down so that they can't see you."

Iusta climbed up onto the ledge first and then offered me her hand to help me up. There was hardly enough room for both of us even though Iusta is slight and I have always observed the stoic's diet and so remain slim at an age when other men have grown stout. I could feel her flesh pressed against mine and her breath on my neck as she leaned forward to look over the ledge into the grotto. She smelled like lemons and rosewater, I noticed, a refreshingly sweet smell in this dank, incense-laden cavern.

"They've almost reached the part where Calatoria will read from The Golden Verses. We must be sure to see where she's hidden the scroll."

I tore myself away from the contemplation of Iusta's charms and looked into the grotto. It looked like a natural sea cave, hewn out of limestone and filled with water of an ethereal blue. Around its edges was a shallow ledge and on this Calatoria and her attendants positioned themselves, each one holding a torch so that the light of the flames reflected in the water and danced on the ceiling, like phosphorescent sea creatures swimming in a moonlit ocean. With their loose hair and wild eyes, I could well believe they were actually sirens. One by one they lowered their torches and doused them in the water where the flames seemed to glow blue before dying and then, marvelous to say, the flames leaped back to life as the torches were lifted back up.

"Ah," I whispered to Iusta, "it's a trick played by the Bacchantes in Rome—I read about it in Livy. The torches are coated with a mixture of chalk and sulfur. I can smell the sulfur from here."

Iusta looked at me and smiled, impressed, I imagined, with my learning. "It must be wonderful to possess such a store of wisdom."

"*I find it especially useful in these situations. Once you understand the mechanics of such exhibitions, they cease to have the power to frighten.*"

"*And does your knowledge also insulate you from amazement and wonder?*" she asked.

I stared at her. Did I detect a note of mockery in her voice? But she seemed quite serious. She looked, oddly enough, as though she pitied me. "*Perhaps it does,*" I answered. "*I never thought of it that way. I suppose it's the price one pays for plumbing the mysteries of the world that they cease to amaze one, but what is the alternative? To be tossed to and fro on a sea of superstition and emotion? I will try, though, to suspend my reason for the duration of the rites so that I might experience them to the full.*"

At that, she looked troubled and was about to say something, but a sound from the grotto distracted her. "*Listen,*" she said, "*Calatoria is reading.*"

Calatoria was holding a scroll open in her hands while an attendant held a torch above her head. We had missed the moment when she retrieved the scroll from its hiding place. Still, we would see where she hid it when it came time for the women to cleanse themselves in the sea. I strained to hear what she read. It sounded like it was written in Greek hexameters.

A fish whose bright scales shimmer in shallows
never weeps for her mortality,
but when we do for ours we quite forget
our many other lives, past and to be:
as fish whose glimmer makes love to the sun,
or sea birds whose white feathers blur to streaks of foam,
who glide and skim above seas vast as all eternity;
even the squid deep in green water once
was a swallow whose life could come to you or me,
soft wings swooping through dusk's pinkest glow.

Mother of life's the sea—
by it we must gather now, to sacrifice, exult
and praise blue mother waves and father sky
until the time comes when we have to flee,
casting off the Night for Day!
We are a shining circle. We!

When she finished reading the poem, Calatoria carefully replaced the scroll in a hole in the wall. Turning back to the circle of her attendants, she sang in a loud ringing voice:

Until the time comes when we have to flee,
casting off the Night for Day!
We are a shining circle. We!

She drew the fibula from her robe, releasing the black cloth so that it fell from her shoulders, slid down her body, and puddled around her ankles. Thus she cast off the mantle of night and stood naked in the torchlight, her skin as whitely iridescent as a freshly shucked oyster. Each of her attendants in turn, after first placing their torches in brackets on the wall, removed the pins holding their robes and stepped out of them as though discarding a shell they had outgrown as certain mollusks are said to do. When they were all naked, they each repeated the line: *We are a shining circle. We! And* then one by one they dived into the sea and disappeared.

"Where have they gone? It's as if they have vanished into the sea," I observed.

"There's an underwater passage that leads to the open sea. They'll be back soon, so we must hurry." Iusta was already climbing over the ledge into the grotto and feeling along the wall for the place where Calatoria had replaced the scroll.

"That poem Calatoria read," I said, following her, "was definitely from Pythagoras' *Golden Verses, but I don't understand why she chose* that one. I thought these little mysteries were more about Persephone and Demeter and yet the rites as I've seen them so far seem to be markedly Dionysian. . . ."

"It's a combination of the two," Iusta said, cutting me off quite brusquely. I suppose she was merely anxious to retrieve the scroll and be gone before Calatoria and the women resurfaced. "I thought you understood that. Here. I think this is your precious Golden Verses." She withdrew a rolled scroll from the wall and handed it to me. I opened it to the first column of writing and saw that it was indeed the scroll I had brought with me from the Temple of Poseidon—the only extant copy of Pythagoras's famed Golden Verses, a work that some have even doubted existed, believing that the great philosopher never wrote down his teachings. I had counted on selling it to Gaius Petronius Stephanus for a large sum of money, but instead I would take it to Rome and it would be the making of not only my fortune, but of my fame.

I looked up to tell Iusta that it was indeed the right scroll and to share with her my joy at rediscovering it, but she was still looking for something in the hole, her arm submerged in the crack in the wall up to the shoulder. Finally she retrieved another scroll: her diary, no doubt. She unfurled it to check that it was what she sought—it was only a short length of papyrus, loosely wrapped in a leather cover—and then, satisfied, she rolled it back up and slipped it into a soft leather pouch that was slung across her chest. I was touched to see that she had also brought with her the little terra-cotta statue I'd given her.

"We have to hurry," she said. "Look how rough the water is. Calatoria and her women won't stay out long in this."

I saw what she meant as we made our way back to the ledge. The surface of the water was choppy as if stirred by a strong wind, but there was no wind in the grotto. Iusta had already climbed up onto the ledge, but I knelt by the water, stirred by curiosity, and scooped up a handful of tiny stones that floated on the surface, each light as air, like petrified sea foam.

"Hurry!" Iusta called.

I followed her, still holding a handful of the frothy stones, over the ledge and then through the tunnel, only catching up with her at the entrance to the Chamber of the God. She was kneeling in the open doorway, looking for something on the ground.

"I think this is discharge from the mountain," I said, showing her the little stones. "I'm afraid that if this material is falling into the sea this far west that it might be wise to remove ourselves farther west, perhaps to Neapolis or even Misenum."

"Yes," Iusta said, getting to her feet. I caught a glimpse of the iron bar she had left for me before. Of course, I thought, if she left it behind, Calatoria would know she had helped me. "I think you're right. There's a way to the surface that would take us up outside of the villa not far from the road to Neapolis." She hesitated while she caught her breath, and stared hard at me as if she were trying to solve some problem or decide a question. "We could both go now."

"Oh, but then I'd miss the rest of the rites and I have to admit I'm intrigued by this mixture of Eleusinian and Dionysian elements. And of course my absence would alert your mistress to the theft. . . ."

"Yes, I suppose you're right," Iusta said, the look of uncertainty fading from her face. She added: "As usual, your logic is infallible. Calatoria would certainly be disappointed to find you gone. You are the main event. You stay and I'll go ahead with the Golden Verses. I'll wait for you at the end of the tunnel and we can go on to Neapolis together."

"Oh," I said, disappointed. "Aren't you to be included in my part of the rites? I thought you were to be Persephone to my Hades."

Iusta looked away, embarrassed no doubt by the role she would have played in that scenario. "No," she said, looking back up to me. Her look was almost one of pity. "I really don't play that important a role in Calatoria's scheme. My part is over and you . . . you do get to play a god, but not that one."

"Oh," I said, striving for a light tone, "as long as I get to play one of the gods. I'm not picky." I'd meant it as a joke, but she didn't laugh. Instead she lifted a hand as though to touch my cheek, but instead she took the scroll from my hands and began turning away. She opened her pouch and took out her diary. "Here," she said, "I'll protect your precious scroll with my own life, so to speak." She wrapped the layer of papyrus and leather around the Golden Verses and then placed the whole back in her pouch.

"Aren't you forgetting something?" I asked teasingly.

She turned to me and for a moment her face looked ghastly. Poor girl, the theft of the scroll must be weighing on her. "What?" she asked.

"You have to tell me the signs to follow to find my way out," I said.

"Of course. The way up is not as simple. First you choose the tunnel marked with a lyre—"

"For Orpheus, no doubt, who made the trip back to the surface."

"Yes, but then you will come across several forks, each path marked with a different symbol. I have not seen the paths myself, but I have heard Calatoria say that you must chant as you go, 'The evil I flee, the better I find.' "

"Ah, that is a quote from Demosthenes's account of a Dionysian ritual! So to escape the underworld you must always shun the evil way and choose the better one."

"Yes, I can only hope the choices will be clear when I see them. You, I have no doubt, will have no problem choosing as you are so learned in signs and portents."

I bowed my gratitude at her compliment and once again she turned to leave, but once more I detained her. "I wish I had a light to write by." She stopped and felt inside her pouch then and withdrew a small shell filled with wax and lit its wick from her torch.

"Here," she said. "I wouldn't want you left in the dark. I'm sure you have a lot to write down."

"Indeed I do. What a marvelous story I'll have to tell. I don't doubt but that my story will make me as popular a figure in Rome as will my possession of the Golden Verses. Especially when I add to my account the experiences that I'm about to have."

"Yes," Iusta said, "that would be something to read. Well, then, until we see each other again," she concluded, "in the other world."

I laughed, realizing she meant the upper world as opposed to the underworld we now inhabited. She left through the secret door, closing it behind her, and I made myself comfortable with my back against a wall to write this account.

Now that I have come to the end I look around me and see in the light of Iusta's candle that the walls are painted with the story of Dionysus Zagreus. Here is his birth by Persephone and Zeus. (Of course, I realize now, that is why Iusta's role was done. She was the mother of the god in this rite, not his wife!) And here is jealous Hera tricking the titans into devouring the baby. The picture of the Titans tearing the child limb from limb and eating him is quite vivid. So, too, is the picture of Athena carrying the child's dripping heart to Zeus and Zeus eating the heart so that his son may be reborn as Dionysus—or Dionysus Zagreus, as he is sometimes called. Now I understood why Calatoria had wanted the Golden Verses so badly. It's all about re-birth—dying and transformation—the road to perfection that comes through transmigration.

I hold my candle up and see the story repeated on the walls, only in some versions it's a band of women who hunt down a man who stands in for the god. Here they are ripping him apart and here they are stuffing their mouths with his torn and bleeding limbs. . . . Ah, I hear them now. Calatoria and her women risen from the sea. They are singing. The ground shakes with their dance. I hear the rasp of stone as the secret door opens. They have come for me. I must blow my candle out and lie down so that they don't know I am unbound. I must put down my pen now and prepare myself to become a god.

CHAPTER 29

"Oh my God," Agnes says when we've both come to the end of the scroll. "Those women are going to eat him, aren't they, Dr. Chase?"

I think of the scattered bones in the chamber and the shattered skull and the paintings on the wall. Zeus swallowing his son's heart, raving women taking down a running man as though he were a deer.

"I guess it's possible." I stare at the characters on the screen as if they might rearrange themselves and tell a different story.

"Iusta knew and she still left him there. She could have saved him."

I glance back over Iusta's parting lines to Phineas. "She gave him a chance. She offered to lead him back to the surface, but Phineas refused. He was too enamored of the part he was going to play in the rites."

"Still, she could have told him—" Agnes breaks off. I realize that she's crying. When I put my arm around her, she crumples against me, her body racked with sobs. Is she really crying for a betrayal that occurred almost two thousand years ago? Or is it the more recent tragedy that's caught up with her?

"We shouldn't judge Iusta too harshly," I say, aware that I, too, am disappointed in the girl. She'd been my "lost voice" speaking for enslaved ancient women, and now I find she was a thief and a betrayer. Sure, Phineas was a bit of an ass, but he didn't deserve to be torn apart and eaten by a bunch of crazy maenads. I suppress these thoughts, though, because I realize that Agnes has been identifying with Iusta all along—just as I had—and now she's transferred her own guilt over the Dale Henry shooting onto Iusta. "After all," I say, "she was a slave. She had no freedom to make her own choices. Maybe she saw this as her only shot at liberty. We can't blame her for trying to save herself." I pause and then add, "Just like you can't blame yourself for what Dale Henry did or feel guilty for surviving when Odette and Barry didn't."

She goes still, caught in mid-sob, then she glances up at me, a tentative smile on her lips. "How'd you know I felt that way?"

"Because it's also how I feel," I say. "Don't you think I go over and over in my head what I could have done differently that morning? I should have paid more attention to how worried and scared you were when you came to my office. If I'd encouraged you to talk about Dale we could have alerted campus security. And then, when he burst into the room, well, I could have done something other than hiding under the table! Someone could have had the courage to tackle him—"

"Dr. Lawrence did."

I laugh before I can stop myself—a mean-spirited bark that surprises me as much as it does Agnes, who stares at me with her wide open china blue eyes. "What are you talking about? Elgin was under the table with me."

Agnes shakes her head, her long blond hair whisking over her shoulders. "He was at first, but when Dale started toward me, Dr. Lawrence got back up. He was grabbing for Dale when he put the gun in his mouth and killed himself. I was screaming 'No' because I didn't want Dr. Lawrence to get himself killed."

I distractedly pat her shoulder. In my head, I'm replaying those moments under the table. I had tried to let Elgin know that I was going to grab Dale's feet to stop him from shooting Agnes, but I'd thought that he didn't understand me. Then I had looked away, concentrating on those bloodstained high tops as they made their way toward Agnes's navy pumps with those red and white bows that had somehow infuriated me with their innocence. I hadn't seen what was happening above the table: Elgin had gotten up when he saw me crawling toward Dale. I say, "I'm surprised . . . I mean . . . none of the newspaper accounts mentioned that Elgin tried to stop Dale."

"I think I was the only one who saw what he did. Everyone else was down on the floor trying not to get shot, and Dr. Lawrence told me afterward that it wasn't necessary to tell anyone, that he hadn't made a difference anyway."

"Huh," I say. "I guess if he couldn't be a hero—" I stop myself. Agnes doesn't need to listen to another bitter tirade against her beloved professor from me. No wonder she idolizes him! Besides, I'm beginning to sound mean-spirited even to myself. At least Elgin tried to do something. "Think of it this way," I say instead, "we hardly understand what happened less than two months ago. How can we judge what happened nearly two thousand years ago? Maybe Iusta changed her mind and went back for Phineas." I don't really believe it, but Agnes is ready to grasp at any straw.

"She could have . . . and then gotten trapped on her way back. The tunnels could have collapsed. She may be there still, and then she'd have the scroll, both scrolls together! Her diary and *The Golden Verses*."

"My thought exactly. So if we take the tunnel marked with the lyre, and then follow the signs Iusta told Phineas about, we could be the ones to find Iusta and the scroll. We might also find her diary."

Agnes rewards me with a smile. "We'll be partners," she says, holding out her hand to seal our pact with a handshake. "We'll find her together."

I take her hand. What I don't say is that I suspect that if Iusta is somewhere in the tunnels it's more likely she was trapped on her way out than on her way back to rescue Phineas.

It's after four a.m. when I leave Agnes. I tell her we'd both better get some sleep, but instead of going back to my room I cross the lower courtyard and take the stairs down to the grotto. When I step inside, I think for a moment that I've crossed the bay, and the centuries, and that I'm in the Sirens' Grotto as Phineas described it in his last account. A dozen flickering flames ring the blue pool of water, their reflections dancing over the water's surface and rock ceiling like a swarm of crazed fireflies.

"Pretty, isn't it?" Ely is sitting cross-legged on the ledge between two of the votive candles. "I remembered how you lit candles in the house when we came back from our walks."

"It's beautiful," I say. I don't say how it reminds me of Calatoria's attendants' torches. "I'm sorry I couldn't get here sooner. We had to scan the scroll—"

"We?"

"Agnes and I."

He nods. "She was the only one you told about the scroll?"

"Yes. I'm sure we can trust her. But I'm afraid it's not *The*

Golden Verses. I'm sorry." I see a flicker of disappointment cross his face.

He pats the rock by his side and I crouch down beside him. "Did you at least find Iusta's diary?"

"No, it was just another of Phineas's accounts—his last, I'm afraid. It looks like Iusta took *The Golden Verses* and left Phineas in the Chamber, left him to be sacrificed in some horrible rite practiced by Calatoria and her women. Anyway, there's a chance that Iusta didn't make it out of the tunnels. Phineas said he felt the ground shaking as the women approached. He was so wrapped up in the ritual he thought it was their dancing that caused it, but clearly it was an earthquake. Iusta might have gotten trapped underground."

"In which case *The Golden Verses* and her diary might still be with her."

"Yes. Fortunately, she tells Phineas that the path to the surface is marked with signs. At each turning you're supposed to choose the 'better' sign over an evil sign."

"The evil I flee, the better I find."

"Exactly," I say, startled that Ely knows the words to the Dionysian chant that Iusta quoted. "Hopefully, we'll be able to figure out which symbol is for evil and which one is for the better."

"You shouldn't go alone," he says, taking my hand. "Perhaps you shouldn't go at all. I've already exposed you to enough danger."

I'm about to disagree, but then, because I've been reliving that morning, I think about Ely making those silent phone calls, about him not leaving a message. I now have the uncharitable thought about Ely that at least Elgin tried to do something.

As if he can read my mind Ely hangs his head. "I want to be with you tomorrow," he says.

"But you can't. The site is gated and Lyros would never let you into the excavation—"

Ely, smiling, holds a key up.

"Where did you get that?"

"From Elgin, but he doesn't know I plan to be there. Just make sure that he and Lyros don't go in the same direction as you once you're down in the tunnels."

"I'll suggest we go in pairs and make sure Agnes and I are teamed up."

Ely smiles. He slides his arm around my shoulders and pulls me toward him. I feel stiff, unable to let myself relax. Maybe it's because this place reminds me of the scene in Phineas's account, or because I'm nervous about tomorrow. Ely senses my tension and lets me go. "You should probably get some rest." He kisses me lightly on the forehead. "You have a long journey tomorrow, all the way to the underworld and back again."

I go back to my room and try to sleep, but I don't get any real rest because my dreams are visited by Odette. She's wearing the orange dress and head scarf she wore on the last day of her life and looks as regal as a priestess.

"I thought you had excused yourself from this particular party," she says. It's what she said to me that morning, meaning Elgin's Papyrus Project, only now I see that she means the party going on around us: women in black veils embroidered with silver stars stand around us in a circle, holding torches. The guardians of Night, I think.

"Are you their priestess?" I ask.

Odette laughs. The full-bodied sound echoes off the rock walls of the grotto we're in and makes the torch flames quake. "Honey, you know I belong to the Greater New Hope African Methodist Episcopal Church, but others aren't so picky about their allegiances. You're still looking at this like a catfish swimming upside down and thinking the mud below is the sky above." She points up, and I realize that what I had thought was a reflection of water on the grotto ceiling is actually the water itself. When I look back down at Odette and the circle of women, they sway and waver and then break apart like reflections in a pool. I'm at the bottom of the grotto looking up through the water and once again I've gotten my shirt snagged in the rock. I look behind me to pull my shirt loose and see that it's not my shirt that's holding me back, but an enormous octopus whose tentacles have encircled my waist.

I wake up drenched in sweat, gasping for air. It's already light out so I decide to get up and shower and get ready for my second, and I hope last, trip to the underworld. What was it Virgil had said? *Facilis descensus Averno.* Maybe so, but I'm beginning to think I've made the trip one time too many.

I spend the boat trip over worried about how I'll make sure that Agnes and I will be able to go our own way in the tunnels, but when we get to the site everything falls into place almost too easily. Maria volunteers to stay aboveground because she has some e-mails to take care of. She heads up to the top level of the villa to make herself comfortable in the field office, so she won't even notice Ely when he enters the site. When I point out that the tunnel outside the Chamber of the God goes in three directions and mention splitting up in pairs, Lyros immediately suggests that Elgin go with him. I see Elgin hesitate, looking at Agnes, but when she chimes in with, "Yes, let's make it girls against boys and see who wins," Elgin shrugs and concedes.

"Make sure you keep your walkie-talkie on," he says. "And stay together," he admonishes Agnes, looking so anxious that I'm pretty sure Agnes was wrong about his intentions, or lack thereof, toward her. Maybe he hasn't made a move for her yet, but clearly he is interested. He can hardly take his eyes off her, even double-checking her backpack to see that she has the right climbing gear, flashlight, and water. He must notice me staring at him, though, because he entrusts me with the walkie-talkie. "Holler if you find anything," he says, and then, lowering his voice for me alone to hear, "or if anything seems fishy to you."

"Fishy? As in mermaids and sea nymphs?" I mean it as a joke, but it reminds me of what Odette said in my dreams about catfish seeing things upside down. What wasn't I seeing right?

"As in anything that doesn't feel right," Elgin says, ignoring my admittedly weak attempt at levity. "Just call my name—"

"And I'll be there." I finish the song lyric for him, recalling too late it was the Mariah Carey song we used to hear all the time driving through the hill country.

"Yeah," he says, smiling now. "I will."

When we reach the Chamber of the God, Lyros takes out a thin steel crowbar and slips it into the crack. The door opens easily. I'm careful to go through first because I want to make sure that Agnes and I get to go in the direction that will lead up. I'm pretty sure that Lyros, without the benefit of reading Phineas's last entry, will want to head down toward the Sirens' Grotto, where he probably thinks the scroll is still hidden, but still, I want to make sure. When I enter the tunnel I find the path marked with a lyre. Well, that's easy enough, I think: I stand in front of the lyre, staking my claim on the upward path.

Agnes comes in next, then Elgin.

Lyros comes in last, and immediately scans the walls with his flashlight until he finds the path marked with the split-tailed siren.

"Okay, then, this path must lead down to the Sirens' Grotto, while this one"—he shines the flashlight directly in my eyes and I reluctantly step aside so he can see the sign on the wall behind me—"that looks like a lyre, doesn't it?"

Elgin steps forward to examine the carving while Agnes and I exchange a glance. "A lyre could symbolize Orpheus," Elgin says, "who led Eurydice out of Hades. This could be a route up. If Iusta stole the scroll she could have taken this route up to the surface."

"But we don't know if Iusta ever got the scroll," Agnes says, "or if she did, whether she made it this far. Shouldn't we check the tunnel to the grotto first?"

I try hard not to stare at her. She seems to be suggesting that she and I take the wrong path.

"Only," she continues, "to tell you the truth, it kind of gives me the creeps to go farther down. I know that seems silly—"

"Not at all," Lyros says, shaking his head. "It's psychological. The descent is always the trickier part."

"If Agnes is really that afraid of being underground, maybe she should go back to the surface and wait with Maria," Elgin says. Maybe he doesn't buy her excuse for taking the upward path. Fortunately the excuse seems enough for Lyros.

"Well, that should be up to Agnes. What about it, Miss Hancock. Are you up for this?"

"Yes, absolutely," she answers.

"Good girl," Lyros says, smiling at her. "It's settled then. Agnes and Sophie will take the path of Orpheus while we take the sirens' path. Then we'll all meet back here in—" He looks down at his watch. "Say an hour? It's half past ten now so let's make it eleven-thirty. Anyone finds anything, or runs into trouble, use the walkie-talkie. And remember what Iusta said about traps. Stay tethered to each other, walk slowly, and watch your footing. Okay?"

I nod as Agnes clips a line to my harness, attaching us together. She starts up the tunnel marked with the lyre and I turn to follow her, but Elgin grabs my arm and holds me back.

"I have a bad feeling about this whole thing," he whispers in my ear.

It's on the tip of my tongue to tell him that maybe he should go up and wait for us aboveground, but then I see the expression in his eyes. He looks really scared and for once it doesn't seem to be for himself. Is he really that afraid of losing me? But then he says, "Make sure you watch out for Agnes," and I realize it's not me he's worried about losing.

"Will do," I say curtly and then, feeling the tug of the line pulling me, I turn and follow her into the tunnel.

CHAPTER 30

"*I*'m sick of everyone thinking they know what's best for me," Agnes says when I catch up to her in the tunnel. "My parents, my teachers, Sam . . . I'm old enough to make my own choices."

"Of course you are. It's just that anyone would be shook up after what happened back in Austin."

"You mean everyone thinks I made such a bad choice with Dale that I can't be trusted to make any other choices."

"That's not what I meant—" I begin, but then stop, wondering if maybe that is why I feel so protective of Agnes. "Maybe you're right," I say. "It's just that I know how easy it is to go from one bad choice to another."

"Is that what you did?"

"It's exactly what I did. I was so upset when I found out that Ely had joined the Tetraktys that I had an affair, with Elgin Lawrence of all people, and I ruined any chance I had of holding on to Ely. I practically pushed him into a cult."

"You shouldn't hold yourself responsible for that." Agnes has stopped and turned to face me. Her flashlight, lowered in front of her, throws a ghastly shadow on her face. "Maybe he had his own reasons for joining the Tetraktys. Maybe you shouldn't have fought it so hard."

I shake my head. "You have no idea, Agnes. This group is really dangerous. You know that Dale was involved with it, right? Did it ever occur to you that the Tetraktys made him shoot those people—" This is further than I'd meant to go. Agnes's face looks pale and stricken in the glare of the flashlight. Her jaw clenches, a blue vein throbs at her temple. "I'm sorry," I say. "This isn't the time or place to talk about it. Let's just go on."

"Which way?" Agnes swings her flashlight in an arc that shows two passages in front of us. We've come to the first fork Iusta referred to.

"I don't see any markings. . . . Wait, here's one." On the right-hand path I find a ship carved into the stone. "It's a boat of some kind. . . ."

"There's a picture of a boat on this path, too. How are we supposed to know which one leads to the surface?"

I swing my flashlight from one picture to the other and then smile. "This one on the right has its sails down and is being poled along by a shrouded figure," I say, "but the one on the left has its sails up and is being pushed by the wind. I'd say the one on the right is Charon's ferry to the underworld and the one on the left is embarking for the isles of the blessed—in other words, the upper world."

"Gosh, I guess so, but it's not as clear as Iusta made it out."

"No, it's not. I say we take the left-hand path, but that we go slowly and carefully."

Agnes nods her agreement and we set off again, carefully sweeping the tunnel floor with our flashlights to watch for any traps. I'm glad in a way that we're concentrating too hard for conversation. I hadn't meant to bring up the shooting or the Tetraktys, or the fact that they might be related to each other. Will it make Agnes feel worse or better to know that Dale was being used as a tool of the Tetraktys? Would she blame herself, as I had, for not trying harder to keep Dale out of the Tetraktys? I'm tempted to ask these questions, but then we find the next fork, the two passes marked with two flowers.

"Okay," Agnes says, "I give up. How are we supposed to tell the difference between two flowers?"

"Well, this one on the left is an iris—"

"Goddess of the rainbow!" Agnes says quickly. "So it must be the right way to go."

"Well, she was also the goddess that came to release the soul at death, but I think you're right. The name means 'eye of heaven.' This one on the right is a poppy, which is associated with the Eleusinian rites, sleep, and forgetfulness. . . ."

"Oh, so definitely that path would lead back to the underworld."

"Or at least to death." I shine my flashlight down the path marked by the poppy. After six feet or so the ground drops away. Agnes inches forward and I follow her, curious to see one of the traps Iusta warned Phineas about, but when I peer over the edge I'm sorry I looked. The pit is lined with jagged rocks that would slice your hands if you tried to hold on and is so deep our flashlights can't find the bottom.

"Man, if Iusta fell into that we'll never find her."

"Let's hope she didn't." I back away from the pit, taking the path marked by the iris. "After all, she was a bright girl and educated in mythology by Gaius Petronius."

"But imagine having to decode these symbols while you're running for your life. It's like a final exam where the wrong answer means you die."

We both lapse into silence again, contemplating that last trip Iusta made through these tunnels. The ground would have been shaking, the air filling with sulfurous fumes. Would anyone have the presence of mind to stay on the right path, to make the right choices? We navigate through the next fork, which is marked with two trees: a cypress, tree of mourning, and the almond, the tree of hope. I steer Agnes up the path marked with the almond tree.

"I get the cypress part—they're gloomy trees—but how did the almond get to be the tree of hope?"

"The story is that a Thracian princess, Phyllis, fell in love with an Athenian prince, Demophoon. He promised to marry her, but first he wanted to pay a short visit back to Athens."

"Oh, let me guess. He never returns."

"Well, he does, but not for many years. By the time he comes back, Phyllis has died of a broken heart and been transformed into an almond tree. Demophoon embraces the leafless tree and it suddenly bursts into bloom, and so it's a symbol of love persisting after death."

"And after betrayal. I wouldn't burst into bloom for any guy who left me for years."

I smile, thinking that Agnes is young and beautiful enough not to have had to make this particular decision. Who would abandon her? What could she do that would require that kind of forgiveness? "Well, it's also a symbol of forgiveness. I wonder if Iusta thought about the story when she came to this turning. Did she consider going back to save Phineas?"

"Oh no!" Agnes wails, breaking into my wishful thinking.

"Look at these two symbols! Two women's faces and they're almost identical. How are we going to figure out which is the right one?"

I step around Agnes and look at the two faces carved into the rock. Agnes is right; they are almost identical, two beautiful women in profile, their hair bound up with flowers. "The one on the left is wearing poppies and stars in her hair while the one on the right is wearing roses and wheat. The one on the left is Night, and the one on the right is Day." I shine my flashlight down the right-hand tunnel and the beam hits a solid wall of tufa. When the pyroclastic flow that covered Herculaneum rolled down Mount Vesuvius around midnight on August 24, it apparently flowed into the tunnel. "It must have been the right way because it was open to the surface."

"Damn. Iusta could be under that," Agnes says. "It could take months of excavation to find out." She sounds close to tears, as if we were trapped under the tufa with Iusta.

I shine my flashlight back on the other tunnel, the one marked by the goddess Night, and take a tentative step forward, but hold my hands up to stop Agnes from following. Two feet from where we stand the tunnel falls away into black space. I crouch down to look inside. Unlike the trap we saw before, with its sharp, jagged stones, this one is a round hole with smooth stone walls, like a well bored deep into the rock. A slab of rock lying next to the opening could have been a lid for it, but clearly no one had to close it to kill the person who fell in. The skeleton at the bottom of the well lies as dropped there, the skull's blank eye holes peering up at us as if waiting for help at last. Next to one skeletal hand lies a long thin object, like a log or . . .

"It's the scroll," Agnes says, her voice reanimated with hope. "It must be."

I nod even though I know Agnes isn't looking at me. I don't trust myself to talk. It's not excitement over possibly finding *The*

Golden Verses and Iusta's diary that makes my throat feel swollen, though, it's grief at finding Iusta like this. Even though she's been dead for almost two thousand years, I can't help feeling bad that I've come too late to help her, and that any change of heart she might have had about saving Phineas came too late for both of them.

"One of us will have to go down to get it," Agnes says. "If you want me . . ."

"No," I say. "I've done more climbing. I can do it."

"Are you sure? I mean, I did go climbing once with Sam . . . only I wasn't much good, especially when it came to going down. I wasn't making up that part before. I actually am kind of afraid of heights."

"I'll go." I look around the tunnel for a stable rock we can use as a belay station and find one just above the pit opening. I unclip my rope from Agnes's harness and loop it around the boulder, tugging hard to make sure it's steady. "I think this will hold fine, just keep an eye on it to make sure the rope doesn't snag. You can keep your flashlight trained on the bottom so I can see where I'm going." *And so I don't land on those bones.*

"Okay." Agnes sounds relieved that she's not the one to go. "Do you think you should leave your bag up here? It might get in the your way."

"Okay."

I hold on to the rope and let myself over the edge, wedging my feet into the wall and leaning out as soon as I can. It's not a bad climb down—only a dozen feet or so—easier than the drop into the Chamber of the God, but still I feel worse going into this narrow pit. The pit of Night, I think to myself. I feel the rock walls pressing in on my chest, constricting my lungs. It's a death pit, designed to trap the unwary. I wonder why Iusta wasn't able to avoid it. Was it because she was rushing to get out? Or because an earthquake jolted her?

When I near the bottom I scan the ground to avoid stepping on the bones. It's hard. The circle is only about six feet in diameter and the skeleton is stretched out across it—arms and legs splayed like the diagram of the Vitruvian man, or like a torture victim stretched out on a Catherine wheel. She must have landed flat on her back and broken her spine in the fall. Had it killed her instantly or had she had time to lie here waiting for help that never came? Had she been alive when the final surge hit Herculaneum at midnight and turned this pit into an inferno? Had she thought she was being consumed by the fires of Hades as punishment for leaving Phineas behind?

I crouch next to the skull, staring into the empty eye sockets as if they held the answers to my questions. I came here—to Italy, to this pit—because I wanted to hear Iusta's voice. I wanted a glimpse of this first-century girl who'd had the gumption to sue her mistress for her freedom, but instead of deepening my knowledge of her I found she became more of a mystery than ever. Elgin was right. I've overromanticized her. I've identified with her too much.

"Dr. Chase? Are you all right? Can you get the scroll?" Agnes's voice brings me back to the present. Perhaps I've done the same with her. I've been reading my own story into hers, believing that she blamed herself for what Dale Henry did and fearing that she'd throw herself into Elgin's arms just like I had. Clearly the girl, even if she did date a crazy boy who turned into a killer, has more sense than I had.

"Yeah, I'm fine. The scroll's right here—charred like the others but intact. I'll need something to bring it back up."

"Here." Agnes tosses down an empty canvas bag. "Put it in this and then attach it to your rope," she says. "I'll pull it back up."

I lift the scroll carefully and ease it into the canvas bag, as gently as though it were a swaddled baby. The image catches me by surprise, reminding me of the one time I held Cory before she died. I feel my eyes filling up, but I don't want to wipe them because my hands are stained with charcoal.

I unhook the rope from my harness and hook it to the bag. "Go ahead," I tell Agnes. I lift my head to watch the bag rise into the air and feel the tears stream down my face. I remember that as light as she was—four pounds, two ounces—I still felt the weight of her when they took her out of my arms. I felt it for months, that weight, like a phantom limb. Like I still felt the half of my lung that was gone and the loss of my mother. So many vacancies inside that it was a wonder I didn't just float away.

I blink and my vision doubles: two Agneses lean over the edge of the hole reaching for two bags. I blink again and the two bags become one, but there are still two heads leaning over the edge of the pit. Agnes and Ely. I think I've conjured him with the force of remembering our daughter, but then I remember that he had the key to the site. It really is Ely. He's come to make sure I'm okay.

"We've got it," I say. "We've found *The Golden Verses.*"

Ely doesn't reply. He says something to Agnes I can't make out and then Agnes says, "No, we can't take the chance."

Ely nods and then looks back down at me. "Sorry, Sophie," he says. Then he leans back so that I can't see his face anymore. I hear a grating noise—stone moving on stone—and a black shadow moves across the circle of light. A cloud moving across the moon. I'm still staring up at it when I realize that Ely and Agnes are moving the stone across the opening. They've sealed me in this pit and left me here to die.

CHAPTER 31

1 don't scream at first. I have this feeling that if I start screaming I may never stop. But then, what choice do I have? My only chance of living is if Elgin and Lyros hear me and come for me.

"Just sit yourself down, and think." It's Odette's voice, calm and authoritative. Even if it's only in my head, I trust it.

I step backward until I feel the stone wall against my shoulder blades and then slide down to the ground, wrapping my arms around my knees and hugging myself into a tight ball so that I don't accidentally touch the bones. I have a feeling *that* would really get me screaming.

"She can't do you any harm," Odette's voice says. "She's dead."

"Well, so are you," I think to myself. At least I'm pretty sure I don't say it aloud. "And you've apparently developed the ability to speak to me now."

I hear a low chuckle that should alarm me for my sanity even further, but instead it makes me smile. "The bit of me that's in your head is more real than any of those old bones, but honey, we don't have time for a me-ta-fizz-i-cal discussion right now." She says *metaphysical* just like she would in life, drawing out each syllable. "You gotta think about what just happened. You gotta think about Agnes. I mean, who'd have thought it! A face like an angel!"

"So you didn't suspect anything, either?"

"I'm not psychic, honey, just smart—though that girl sure played her part to the hilt. Truth be told, I always did think there was something a little off-kilter about her, but I put that down to her being raised up a minister's daughter in a small town. Didn't know she was adopted and spent her babyhood in an orphanage. I don't expect she got held much at all. Now that's a big emptiness to carry around."

I think back to the morning of the shooting and picture Agnes in my office: her chewed nails and ragged cuticles, the dark circles under her eyes. I'd put it all down to nerves over her presentation and worry about Dale Henry, but what if she'd been sleepless and nervous because she knew something was going to happen at the interview? I remember how closely she watched my phone as it flashed its series of coded Pythagorean numbers.

"What if Ely's message wasn't for me?" I say. Aloud this time. "What if it was for Agnes?"

"You think?" Odette replies with a low chuckle.

"But that would mean Agnes belonged to the Tetraktys."

"Think about it: Agnes grows up a God-fearing Baptist but then tosses it aside to study pagan mystery rites. She was looking for something to replace her childhood religion. Why would she stop at studying some crazy old cult when she could belong to a new one?"

"Then she's been the one all along? The one sending Ely the scans of Phineas's journals. She's the Tetraktys member inside the Papyrus Project, not Lyros. How could I be so stupid?"

"Don't feel so bad, honey. She had everybody fooled—although I think Elgin was starting to cotton on to her."

I consider this, recalling Elgin's interest in Agnes, which I had thought was of a different nature altogether. Elgin had watched his sister fall under the influence of a cult; had he recognized the same signs in Agnes? Was he just worried about her, or did he suspect that she was working with the Tetraktys?

"And what will he think when Agnes tells him I'm lost? Will he believe her?"

There's a silence inside my head, whether because Odette—or whatever her voice represents—has deserted me or because she simply has no answer. Will Agnes just leave with Ely, taking the scroll with them? Or will she try to convince Elgin and Lyros that I got lost? She could easily say that I fell into that bottomless pit we passed. She could drop my bag into it and Elgin and Lyros will waste their time looking for me there. They'll never come this far.

"Elgin won't buy it," I hear Odette's voice say. "He doesn't trust Agnes. He'll keep looking for you."

"But he doesn't know how to follow the path we took. No one but Agnes and Ely knows it." I feel despair creeping into my mind, like the blackness that surrounds me. At the thought of Ely, I begin to cry. I've been so focused on Agnes that I haven't let myself think of his betrayal. How can he care so little for me that he'd leave me to die?

"Never you mind, Sophie, some people just lose a piece of themselves along the way and when they fill it up with something else they give themselves up to it completely. There's no room left for love or conscience. That's not religion, it's just hiding from all the emptiness. Don't think about Ely; think about Elgin. . . . I know, you never thought to hear me say a word in Professor

Romeo's favor, but I've come to see things differently. He may not have been the bravest man on earth, but when he saw you were going for Dale he got himself up off that floor and went for him first. He made you come along on this trip because he was worried if you stayed home you'd just brood. He showed up at your hotel 'cause he was worried about you and he's kept an eye on you ever since. He's still looking for you, only you got to give him a little help."

"But how?" I ask.

"Well, let's think about this for a second. This pit you've gotten yourself in—what led you to it?"

"Night," I answer. "The face of Night. This is the pit of Night . . . a trap. . . ."

"But remember, Night always turns to Day eventually, so it makes sense that the pit of Night has a way into the Day—"

"You mean that there could be a tunnel inside this pit leading back to where the path marked by Day . . ."

I don't hear a reply, but I don't need one now. I get onto my knees and feel around the circumference of the pit, cringing when my hands come into contact with the bones, but moving them aside so that I can feel along the bottom where the stone wall joins the floor smoothly, except in one place where I feel a rock bulging from the surface . . . like a boulder that's been laid over something. I run my hands over it, searching for crevices where it meets the smooth wall, something I can get my fingertips into, but the boulder fits so smoothly into the wall there's no space for me to get a grip.

I sit back on my heels, gasping in the diminishing oxygen. Is that how I'm going to die in here? By suffocation? Or will there be enough air to sustain me so that I'll have time to starve to death instead? I remember what Iusta said: her mistress had designed these traps to prolong her victims' suffering. Which meant there were tunnels that let air in.

I force myself to stay perfectly still and concentrate on the air touching my face. It feels like a damp cloth lying over my mouth and nose, smothering me. I resist the temptation to claw at my own skin to get it off my face. Is that how I'll die? Will future archaeologists find my mummified body, my skin torn to shreds by my own hands?

Hush.

It's less a word than an expulsion of air, a mother comforting a fretting child. I turn my head a fraction toward the sound and feel the word tickling my forehead like cool fingertips pushing away my sweat-damp hair.

It's coming from a place just inches above my head. I reach toward it gingerly, afraid of what I'll find. My fingertips graze the smooth wall and then scratch against something rough that peels away in my hand. Iron bars framing a round hole. Frantically, I trace the circumference. It's barely wider than my shoulders. I wonder if Calatoria deliberately had it made just big enough for escape and then barred it to taunt her victims, but it doesn't matter. The iron bars have rusted through from the slow drip of an underground spring. They crumble in my hands, splintering under my fingernails and tearing my skin, but I don't worry about that. I dig toward the air.

When I've cleared away as much of the bars as I can, I scramble into the hole. Shards of the corroded iron scrape at my belly as I pull myself in, but I ignore the pain. I ignore, too, the mean little voice breathing its metallic-smelling breath in my ear. This could lead nowhere, it hisses, you could be digging your own grave. Instead I listen to the softly sibilant whisper of clean air at the end of the tunnel. I concentrate on it so hard it seems to be crooning my name. Sophie. Sophie. Ssssophie.

It is calling my name. At first I think it's Odette's voice again, only fainter and weaker, but then I recognize it. It's Elgin. It takes all the breath in my one and a half lungs to answer him, but it's worth it to hear his reply moving down through the dark tunnel. I crawl forward as fast as I can, the walls of the tunnel so tight I have to keep my arms stretched out in front of me and claw myself upward and forward. There's one bad moment when my fingers graze rock and I think the way's blocked, but then I feel someone grasping both my hands and pulling me out.

Then I'm in the larger tunnel. It feels like a palace compared to what I've just crawled through. In the dim light of Elgin's lantern I can make out the carved head of Day. I feel like kissing her. Instead I kiss Elgin, who's still holding on to both my hands.

He's surprised, but it doesn't keep him from kissing me back.

"Sophie—" he begins.

"You kept looking for me," I say at the same time.

"Agnes said you fell into a chasm a ways back because you took the wrong turn," he says, taking off his jacket and wrapping it around my shoulders. I wonder why and then realize I'm shaking. "We could see your bag hanging from a rock and even hear your walkie-talkie crackling down below, but I just couldn't see you making that mistake. I mean, the tunnel was clearly marked by a poppy and you'd know that had to be a sign of death because of its Eleusinian connections and associations with sleep. I knew I covered that in my Ancient Religions seminar—"

"So basically you thought I couldn't have taken the wrong path because you're such a good teacher?"

Elgin looks down at me sheepishly. "Well, um, yes." A look of genuine embarrassment crosses his face. Although it's hard to tell in this light I could swear he's blushing.

I start to laugh, but the laughter quickly turns into convulsive sobs. Elgin puts his arm around me and pats me awkwardly on the shoulder.

"I know, I know," he says, "I'm an ass, but at least I'm the ass who came looking for you."

"Did you tell Lyros and Agnes what you were doing?" I ask when I'm able to speak again.

"No. It seemed pointless to argue and I felt funny calling Agnes a liar, but, you know, it wouldn't have been the first time I caught her in a lie. I'm pretty sure she cheated on an exam once. She's so innocent-looking I kept thinking I must be wrong, but then I wasn't. I've had an uneasy feeling about her since."

Although I'm curious to know more, I suddenly realize that we can't stand here talking about Agnes. "Well, you were right," I say, heading back down the tunnel. "She and Ely sealed me in here after they got the scroll."

"Ely was here?" He catches up to me at the fork of the two trees and turns me around, holding me at arm's length. "You don't sound surprised that he's here in Italy."

"No," I say, trying not to look away, "I knew he was here. I've seen him twice. He told me that he was working with the FBI."

"And you *believed* him?" I see the look of incredulity on his face and it makes me embarrassed and then angry.

"You told me there was a former Tetraktys member working with you and the FBI. I thought you meant Ely."

He shakes his head. "No, I most certainly did not mean Ely. What else did he tell you?"

"That Lyros was the *magos* of the Tetraktys. You were acting suspicious of Lyros, too, and he had gone down to the tunnels right before Simon was hurt. . . . But that was Agnes, wasn't it? She must have struck Simon in the tunnels and later changed his records in the hospital so they didn't know he was a diabetic. . . . Did you know?"

"I'd begun to suspect—" Before he can finish what he's going to say we hear a moan coming from below. "That sounds like Lyros," he says.

We both hurry down the next tunnel, to the spot where it forks between the iris and the poppy. "This is where I left them," Elgin says. "Lyros had set up a belay right here"—he points to a boulder—"but the rope's gone."

"Help," a voice calls from the tunnel. "Is anyone there?"

I lean over the edge of the chasm and my flashlight catches the terrified face of John Lyros. He's clinging to a rope that is snagged on one of the jagged outcroppings, but I immediately see that the rope is fraying on the sharp edge of the rock. John's hands are torn and bloody—no doubt from trying to climb the razor-sharp rocks.

"I'm going to let down another rope," Elgin tells John, "and set up another belay. We'll have you out of there in a minute."

Elgin goes to attach the rope, but I keep my flashlight trained on Lyros. I know what it feels like to be left alone in the dark.

"What happened?" I ask.

"I was trying to climb down to find you—Agnes was above watching the rope—when all of a sudden the rope came loose. I called for her, but she didn't answer. I figured out then that she'd meant to leave me here. Apparently she also lied about where you were."

"She sealed me in a pit farther up in the tunnel," I say. "She and my ex-boyfriend, that is. They've taken a scroll that I think might be *The Golden Verses*. I'm afraid they've gotten away with it."

"This ex-boyfriend of yours," Lyros says when he's out of the pit, "did he happen to have a boat called *The Persephone*?"

"Yes," I say, wondering how he knew.

"Then we'd better hurry. I have an idea where they might be headed."

When we get to the Chamber of the God we find that the rope has been removed, but luckily Maria is leaning over the opening. Lyros tosses her up one of our ropes and explains how to secure it.

"What's going on?" she asks when we all get up to the stairs. "A strange man came out of the tunnel and then Agnes came out a little later. She refused to explain what was happening."

"She left?" Lyros asks.

"Like a bat out of hell, as you Americans say. I thought there must have been some accident so I came down here."

"She's heading for the marina," Lyros says as we all rush up the stairs. "But she'll have to walk there. I imagine she's supposed to meet Ely there. Let's hope he's waited for her. If we can find someone to drive us we might catch them before they launch the boat."

When we get to the gate we meet the two guards who are arguing with each other, gesticulating angrily in the air, apparently about who left the gate open. Maria steps in between them and demands a car—*Pronto!*—and miraculously they immediately quiet and point to a dusty Fiat listing to its left on the side of the alley. Lyros grabs the keys from the guard before he's got them all the way out of his pocket and we all pile into the Fiat and take off down the narrow streets that lead to the marina.

"The *Persephone* looked pretty fast," I say as we draw closer to the marina.

"Not faster than the *Parthenope*," Lyros says. "But let's hope we can catch them before they put out to sea."

"That's it," I shout as we drive into the marina. "The *Persephone*! It's at the end of that dock." I can see, too, that its engine is running and Ely is on the deck. I spot Agnes heading toward him on the dock.

Elgin has the door open and is half out of the car before Lyros stops it. We all abandon the car and run onto the dock, Elgin in the lead, then me, and Maria. Maria mutters something under her breath—it could be a prayer or a curse. She passes me and catches up to Elgin. They are only a few feet behind Agnes when Ely looks up and sees them from the boat. He has my canvas bag strung across his chest, and I can see him make a quick assessment of the situation, calculating distances and velocities. He steps to the wheel and revs the boat's engine.

Agnes sees what he's doing, and makes a run for it. She leaps for the boat, but just as her foot grazes the edge of the deck it moves away and she tumbles into the water. Elgin, right behind her, stops short, hesitates a split second, then dives in after her. Maria never stops at all. She makes one long fluid leap and lands on the boat, the momentum of her jump carrying her into Ely and propelling them both across the deck. They crash against the bench on the other side and hover there for an instant as the boat, captainless, spins, and then crashes into the dock. The force of the impact knocks them both into the water.

I fall to my knees, searching for Elgin and Agnes in the spume and splinters from the crash, afraid they've been hit by the boat, but Elgin's just a few feet away from the now broken dock, treading water on his back, holding Agnes in a lifesaving grip. I find a rubber bumper hanging from the edge of the dock and toss it to them and only then do I look up and scan the water for Maria and Ely.

"What in the world got into Maria?" I say. "Why does she care so much about *The Golden Verses*?"

"It's not *The Golden Verses* she wants," Lyros says. "She thinks it's a Christian gospel that Phineas was carrying. But she's a fool; they're going to drown each other and anyone who tries to get in between them."

I'm forced to agree with him. We get Agnes onto the dock where Lyros keeps an eye on her. Elgin, though, swims away from the dock toward the struggling pair. He throws an arm around Maria's neck and begins pulling her back toward the dock. It would work, only Maria won't let go of the strap of the canvas bag, which has come over Ely's head but not out of Ely's grasp.

"Let it go," I scream. "The scroll's ruined by now anyway." But even as I say it I can't help wondering what George's spectrograph might still be able to decipher. Perhaps that's what Maria and Ely are thinking, too, because neither will let go of the bag. Maria is holding on with her right hand, and she uses her left to backhand Elgin in the face—a blow so hard I'm afraid it will knock Elgin out. It doesn't, but it does make him release his hold on her. At the same moment, Ely lunges at Maria to wrest the bag away. They both go under. The surface roils and bubbles as if a whirlpool were sucking them under, and then there's a sudden calm and the water goes still.

In the awful silence that follows I stare into the water, trying so hard to see below the dark surface that I don't notice at first that Lyros and Agnes have come up behind me. I turn around to warn Lyros not to let Agnes get away, but when I see Agnes's face I realize that escape is the last thing on her mind. The grime from the tunnels has stained her face the color of bronze, out of which her blue eyes stare at the water like the glass eyes of ancient statues. Then something quivers there—a look of hope—and I turn back to the water to see what's emerged. It's not Ely, though, it's Maria, spitting water as Elgin pulls her back to the dock.

"Ely's at the bottom," Maria sputters. "He won't let go of the scroll."

From beside me I hear a high wild cry—a sound like the screams Persephone's maidens might have made when Demeter turned them into sirens—and Agnes rushes past me. I reach out to grab her—my fingers clasp onto the strap of her backpack—but she peels herself out of it, as easily as if she were shedding old skin, and dives into the water. Elgin is still trying to hold up Maria. I see on his face that he's torn between who he should save. I kneel down on the dock to help Maria up and shout at Lyros to go after Agnes and Ely.

"And get killed myself?" Lyros says, helping me pull Maria out of the water. "After what they've done?"

Before I can tell him what I think of him, Elgin catches my eye. In that moment's look I know that he's thinking about the fight we had under the Porta Marina when I accused him of being a coward. I open my mouth to tell him no, I didn't mean it, I don't want him to risk his life for Ely and Agnes, but he's shouting at Lyros and Maria not to let me follow. He surface dives into the water, disappearing so fast it's like he's been swallowed up by the sea.

We stare into the black water, like children watching a Magic Eight Ball waiting for it to reveal their fortunes. Then I see something white rising up and lean farther over the edge to see if it's his face, but it's only a scrap of paper. A note sent from the underworld. A single word in Ancient Greek: *Nemesis.* Retribution.

CHAPTER 32

*E*very night for the next seven I dream that I am drowning. I feel the weight of sea water pressing on my lungs and watch the bright azure water darken to twilight blue. I awake drenched in sweat, gasping in the airless dark, and for a minute I think I'm still in the pit where Iusta died. I have to turn on all the lights and reassure myself I'm not underground. I'm just at the Hotel Convento where the nuns only pretended that they had been buried alive.

On my seventh morning in Naples, Silvio, noticing the shadows under my eyes and my generally haunted look, takes pity on me.

"Today I send up the mechanic to your room," he tells me as I enter the breakfast room. And then, waving a reproving finger at me: "You should have told me your air conditioner was not working so well."

"Did you hear that?" I ask Elgin as I join him at a table near the edge of the terrace. "I guess the air-conditioning repairmen's union is finished striking."

"Now if only we could get the taxi union to see reason," Elgin replies with a wan smile. It's a nice change from the haunted look he's worn since he brought Ely and Agnes up from the water. He told me later that when he found them at the bottom of the harbor Agnes had entwined her body around Ely's and when he tried to pull her away she had fought him. He had thought that if he saved Ely first, Agnes would follow, but she hadn't. She must have lost consciousness. By the time Elgin went back down, her lungs had filled with water. Later, being loaded in the ambulance, she hadn't regained consciousness.

"Do you have to go back to the excavation police today?" I ask.

He manages another small smile at my name for the Ufficio Sequestri e Scavi Clandestini and also for the waitress who brings him a cappuccino with a heart drawn in the foam on the top.

"Yes," he says, "I have to explain one more time not only how a thousands-of-years-old papyrus scroll found its way out of the Villa della Notte and into the Bay of Naples, but also how it was torn to shreds by the two people who wanted it the most."

"Let Maria explain that part." I dip a lemon cornetto into my foamy coffee. "Or Ely."

Elgin frowns. "How did you know he had regained consciousness? Did you call the hospital?"

"I did not!" I say so vehemently that a German couple on the other side of the terrace lift up their heads from their guidebooks to stare. "No," I whisper, angry at myself when I feel the blood rising to my face. It's shame over looking once again like an ugly American, but Elgin will think it's an admission of guilt. "The hospital called me. It seems, well," I flounder, realizing that I've trapped myself into a worse admission than calling the hospital. Elgin is still staring at me. I look away from him and toward the bright blue bowl of the bay to avoid the recrimination in his eyes. "It seems Ely still had me listed on his insurance as his emergency contact."

I steal a look at Elgin. His jaw is clenched so tight I can see the muscles on the side of his face pulsing. "Really?" he says. "What about his parents?"

"Parent," I say. "His father called me two days ago. Ru— Ely's mother died three years ago." I sip my cooling coffee and look back over the Neopolitan rooftops, focusing on a swag of brightly colored laundry to keep from crying at the memory of Howie Markowitz's voice when he told me about Ruth. "He told me he wasn't coming to Italy. He blamed Ely for Ruth dying."

Elgin nods. "So that's one more death on Ely's head. The hospital didn't ask you to see Ely, did they?"

"No," I say, tossing the rest of my pastry crumbs to a swallow that has alighted on the terrace. "But the doctor who called me said he's been asking for me."

"You're not going to see him, are you?"

"Of course not!" I say, again loudly enough to draw the German tourists' attention. They must think we're a married couple having a fight. The thought makes me blush again and I see that Elgin's face is red, too. Since that kiss in the tunnel, Elgin hasn't touched me. I wasn't even sure if he remembered it. But now the sultry morning light between us ripples with unvoiced longing. Against the backdrop of blue sky and bay, his eyes are the hot azure of the water in my dreams, before it darkens to twilight, and make me feel, for a moment, as giddily breathless.

"I'll never forgive him for everything he's done," I assure Elgin, "but I have to go to the hospital to sign some forms."

"Fine," Elgin says. "Make sure one of them's a 'Do Not Resuscitate' form. I'm still sorry I gave him mouth to mouth."

~~

I have to take a funicular and then a bus to reach the hospital. Silvio offers to find me a private car, but I decline because that seems wrong to me during a strike, and besides, I'm in no rush. On the way to the funicular station I step into the little church next to the Hotel Convento. I come here almost every day to light a candle for Odette. Although she wasn't Catholic, I think she'd approve of this modest little church.

As I light the candle I thank her, as I do every day, for guiding me out of the pit. Today I pause when I'm done, the lit match still in my hand. "I'm going to the hospital," I whisper, "but not to see Ely. Please don't tell me that I have to." I wait another second, but the church, and the inside of my head, are silent. "Good. Then we're agreed on that." I blow the match out, my breath condensing in the air like smoke. Only when I'm outside do I wonder how that could happen in this heat.

At the station, I let the first funicular go without me because it's too crowded, and then when I switch to the bus I feel like even its labored, un-air-conditioned progress through the jammed city streets is getting me to my destination too quickly. When the bus passes the Archaeological Museum, I consider getting out there instead. I could spend an hour in the quiet company of Maria Prezziotti, who is working there in the epigraphic collection on a fourth-century AD calendar of festivals. She confessed to me a few days ago that the reason the Vatican had agreed to help fund the Papyrus Project was because certain scholars believed that the scroll Phineas had carried from the East was an early Christian gospel. "I thought Petronia Iusta was interested in the scroll because she was an early Christian," she told me. The fact that she'd been right about that part gave her little consolation now that the scroll has been destroyed. She'd retreated to the dusty, airless vaults of the Museo Archaeologico to pore over ancient marble inscriptions.

Right now, it seems like a more appealing destination than the hospital for the incurables, but then I remember that John Lyros might be with her.

One of the things I haven't mentioned to Elgin is that while he was testifying at the Ufficio two days ago, John Lyros came to see me. He wanted to make sure I understood that while Ely's claim that he was the leader of the Tetraktys wasn't true, he'd lied when he told me he'd never heard of the Tetraktys. Not only had he belonged to the group at one point, he had donated quite a bit of money to them. "I thought their dedication to Pythagoras was inspiring. I read the sermons your ex-boyfriend wrote on *The Golden Verses*. He believed that if the original writings of Pythagoras could be found, a new world order would come into being. These sermons were so galvanizing that even though they were delivered by one of the *didaskaloi* while Ely sat by in silence, the community made Ely their *magos*. That was a year ago. I began to see how fanatic the group had become and decided to sever ties with them—but I wasn't able to regain the money I'd given them. Apparently, it was enough money to finance Ely's trip to Italy. I should have realized when Simon told me that he'd seen Agnes walking in Pompeii with a young dark-haired man it was Ely. Instead I dismissed him as paranoid. I'm afraid Agnes overheard our conversation that night on the sea steps and decided to silence him. I wouldn't blame you if you wanted nothing to do with me, but if you change your mind, I'll be working at the Archaeological Museum for a few days helping Maria in the epigraphic collection. Come visit me."

Although John Lyros's lapses in judgment are no worse than mine I stay on the bus until it passes the long facade of the museum and reaches the Piazza Cavour. Silvio told me that the hospital was only a block away from the San Gennaro entrance into the old city.

I find the hospital easily enough and miraculously I also find the administration offices, where I sign a sheaf of forms permitting the hospital to do whatever they want with Ely. Each time I sign my name I say to myself, "There! I'm done with you!" but still I walk out of the office with my head bowed, as if I'd just abandoned a puppy at the pound. I'm so reluctant to meet anyone's eye that I bump into the first person I pass in the hall: a thin boy with lank blond hair.

"Sorry," he mutters. "I mean, *scusa*." He brushes the hair out of his eyes as he passes me and I'm startled by an unexpected glint of turquoise.

"Sam? Sam Tyler?" I ask, catching up to him in the hallway. "It's Sophie Chase. I didn't know you were here."

"Yeah, I'm here." He continues down the hall, so I fall into step beside him. "I'm staying until we can take Agnes back to Texas. Her parents are too freaked out to deal with it. I figure it's the least I can do."

"Sam, none of what happened was your fault—"

He freezes me with a look without breaking his pace. "Not my fault? I took her to her first Tetraktys meeting. She didn't want to go—said her parents thought everything New Age was demonic. But I thought it would do her good to let her see that not all religion fit into her parents' narrow definition of right and wrong. You know her father actually used to make her pray to be forgiven for being born a bastard and a Catholic?"

"No, I didn't know that." I have to double-step to keep up with him, his anger fueling his pace. "That's an awful way to grow up."

Sam shakes his head. "I should have known she'd latch on to whatever group offered her some sense of belonging. By the time I realized how bad they were, she was hooked. When I refused to go to the meetings with her, she took Dale—"

"And took him out to New Mexico during spring break?"

"Yeah. When she came back without him, I thought: Good, maybe he'll be the fanatic and she's over it. But I hadn't realized that she'd fallen for your ex."

I nod. I've imagined over the last week that the story Ely told me about the sweeping initiate pausing in the doorway to listen in on the machinations of the *magos* and his *didaskaloi* were true—only the initiate was Dale and the *magos* was Ely. What Dale overheard were Ely's plans to place Agnes with the Papyrus Project as a tool to acquire *The Golden Verses* from the Villa della Notte in Herculaneum before Elgin Lawrence and his Papyrus Project could get it. In other words, Agnes wouldn't be coming back for Dale that summer; she would be going to Italy instead—and with Ely. That was when Dale decided to go to Austin and stop the Papyrus Project in the only way his damaged brain could come up with.

Looking at Sam, it occurs to me that I spent the last five years of my life thinking what he's thinking now—that I should have been able to save the person I loved. I try to think of some way of telling him what a hopeless mission it is, but he stops suddenly at a doorway and I realize that I've followed him not to an exit but to Agnes's room. Beyond the door is a whitewashed room as bare as a nun's cell and a figure swathed in white lying on the bed. A nun in a black habit sits in a chair beside the bed.

"Don't they even have a police guard on her?" I ask.

Sam looks at me as if I were crazy. "Does she look like she's in any shape to make an escape?" He gestures toward the bed as he enters the room and I find myself following him, curious in spite of myself to see exactly what shape she is in. When Elgin had found her and Ely entwined at the bottom of the harbor he'd had to pull Agnes away from Ely to bring him up and he'd inadvertently broken her arm and her collarbone. By the time he went back for Agnes and brought her up she had stopped breathing. Paramedics had arrived by then and they took over the job of trying to bring her back to life, pounding her chest so roughly that they broke all her ribs.

As I move closer to the bed I see that her torso is encased in a white cast and her head is held motionless by a stiff metal collar.

Her face is as white as the walls of the room, but her eyes are burning with awareness. Her lips move to form words—my name, I think—but no sound comes out. Her vocal cords, I heard, were also damaged by all the seawater she swallowed.

"How long will she have to be like this?" I ask.

"The doctors say six months." Sam takes the chair that the nun vacates for him. "It'll be a long haul, but they say it's really a miracle she didn't sustain brain damage from lack of oxygen. She's expected to make a full recovery."

The nun leans over Agnes to adjust her IV tube and I see Agnes's eyes following her motions and then flicking anxiously between me and the nun as if she were trying to tell me something. Remembering how Agnes had felt about nuns the last time we were here I imagine the message is something like *Get me the hell out of here!* I move a step closer to the bed so that Agnes has a clear view of my face. "I'm glad to hear that," I say. "She'll be able to stand trial then."

After I leave Agnes's room, I become hopelessly lost. When I bump into the same nun who had treated Agnes the night we came here with Simon, I almost hug her. I tell her I'm trying to find a way out and she takes me by the hand and leads me through a maze of cavernous hallways full of curious echoes—the ghostly moans and wails, I imagine, of centuries of syphilis patients slowly losing their minds. We finally stop at an open doorway of a patient's room. I turn to her to explain that she's made a mistake, but she only smiles and turns away, her long black habit making a rustling sound like wings beating the air.

Before I can follow her, a voice from the room says my name. It's Ely's voice.

I can still walk away. From where I stand all I can see is the bottom of the bed with Ely's legs covered by blankets. Another nun, this one younger than my guide, is sitting at the foot of the bed. She has a book open on her lap and is reading aloud. At first I think it must be the Bible, but then I realize it's P. G. Wodehouse. With a pang, I remember how much Ely had loved those novels before he'd given them up for books on astral projection and transmigration of the soul. How had the nun known? And where had she come by a P. G. Wodehouse novel?

I pause on the threshold for a minute, stalled by the immobility of those blanket-shrouded legs and the peaceful cadences of the nun's voice.

"To say of anyone's heart that it stood still is physiologically inexact. The heart does not stand still. It has to go right on working away at the old stand, irrespective of its proprietor's feelings."

I recall suddenly something that Ely's mother told me. When his brother, Paul, was sick, Ely had read to him. Wodehouse, maybe, or the Hardy Boys. Who knew? When the young nun sees me she gets to her feet and comes to the door. "Sophie?" she asks.

When I nod, she smiles. "I'm glad you've come. He asks for you day and night. . . . It's okay," she adds when I still don't step into the room, "he's still weak, but your visit will do him good." She thinks that I'm afraid of finding Ely frail and damaged and she's right, but not for the charitable reasons she probably credits me with but because I'm afraid it will make it harder to hate him, and right now hating him is the closest thing I've got to a religion. I'm afraid of letting it go. I summon up an image of Ely leaning over the pit before he and Agnes left me there and, holding on to that image like a talisman, I step into the room.

Ely turns his head toward me. He's so pale that for an instant all I see are those luminous black eyes surrounded by the darkness of his hair, and I think of the skull lying on the floor of the pit. The pit Ely left me in, I remind myself again as I take another step into the room and position myself at the foot of his bed.

"You can have Sister Julia's seat." Ely motions to the straight-backed chair on the other side of the bed. "I've been wondering if she leaves a warm spot when she gets up. She always seems to hover an inch or two above it."

"I'm sure she's flesh and blood like the rest of us, Ely," I say, making no move toward the chair. "We can't all be saints."

His lips, thinner and paler than usual but still curved and pretty, pull back as though in pain, but then he forces a smile. "No, we can't. I'm beginning to see that now."

In spite of my resolve not to give him so much as a smile I laugh. And then I realize when he blushes that he wasn't joking. He'd really thought he was on the road to some kind of enlightened state.

"Is that why you wanted to see me? To tell me that you've finally figured out you're not a god?"

Ely looks down, his eyelashes casting inky shadows on his white cheeks. "I wanted to say that I'm sorry about leaving you in that pit. And also . . . I wanted you to know . . . that time in the grotto . . ." He looks up to see if I'm registering which time in the grotto he means. I'm furious at myself when I feel the blood rise to my face. Then I'm furious at him again. "I just wanted you to know that wasn't part of the plan."

"Oh, so you and Agnes didn't discuss seducing me? What a surprise."

He winces again. "Actually, I did talk to Agnes about what happened. I told her I was falling in love with you again."

"Well, no wonder Agnes wanted to leave me in the pit," I say. "She wanted you all to herself. That doesn't really explain you going along with it."

He shakes his head. "I told myself I was doing my duty, that it was for a higher good. But I see now that any cause that would make me do something so evil couldn't be a good cause."

"Bravo. You must have aced Ethics 101."

"I don't blame you for being bitter. I just wanted you to know that I'm renouncing the Tetraktys."

"That's convenient now that the FBI is investigating them. So what next? Has Sister Julia converted you to Catholicism?"

I've meant it as a joke, but when he lowers his eyes and blushes, I realize I've hit upon the truth.

"She's been a great solace to me. She's even promised to visit me in prison."

Of course, I think, leave it to Ely to find an acolyte wherever he goes. First me, then Agnes, now Sister Julia. "Good," I tell him. "I see you've got everything you need, so I'll be—"

"But I don't have everything I need," he says. "I need your forgiveness."

I'm struck by how young he looks, like the boy who lost his idealized older brother, and it's like I can see the big yawning emptiness that's inside him—a pit darker than the one he left me in—and I realize that I would never have been able to fill that. He needed something bigger to fill that gaping hole.

I sigh. I feel the air moving in and out of my lungs. For the first time since the shooting, they don't feel too small. When the pulmonologist back in Austin told me that eventually my damaged lung would expand to fill my chest cavity, I hadn't really believed him, but now I feel my lung opening up inside me, filling the empty space on my left side. What the doctor didn't warn me about is how much this first full breath hurts. It feels like my chest is cracking open to make room for my expanding lung. It makes me think of that moment in the myth when unfaithful Demophoon finally comes back to Thrace and embraces the almond tree that Phyllis has become and the tree splits open as Phyllis forgives him. Maybe that's what I feel inside my chest, the pain of letting go of all that righteous anger.

I look down at Ely. He seems far away, as if he's in the underground pit and I'm the one who is about to seal him inside to die. I try to summon up the hatred I walked in here with, but it's gone. I don't feel anything for him at all.

He's letting you go, a voice—Odette's voice—inside my head says, *the least you can do is return the favor.*

"Okay," I say, answering Odette's voice out loud. To Ely I say: "If that's the last thing you need from me, you've got it."

I walk back to the hotel, climbing the steep slope of the Vomero like it's nothing, just to feel the power of my recovered lung. I wonder if there's a patron saint of lungs. If so, I should go light a candle to her—or him. I consider stopping back at my room to Google "Patron Saint of Lungs" on my laptop, but then decide to just go to the little chapel beside the hotel. I'm sure whatever saint it's dedicated to will do.

Although I've sat in the church every day in the last week, I've never bothered to see what's it's called. The pantheon of Catholic saints means little to me, since I swore off saints after my mother died. I've enjoyed, though, sitting in the nave held up by its ancient columns and the shadowy shapes on the wall that, no doubt, tell some story in some saint's life. I notice today when I enter the chapel what I've never noticed before: the first paintings on the right-hand side of the nave depict the eruption of Mount Vesuvius. Not totally uncommon in this city, I think. In the Chapel of San Gennaro, vials of the saint's blood are believed to liquefy on the anniversary of the 1631 eruption, and the Napolotani still pray to the saint to calm the furor of Vesuvius. Perhaps this chapel's saint also plays some role in the history of the volcano.

I follow the paintings down the aisle. They show a woman leading a band of shackled slaves away from the erupting volcano. The saint, depicted as a young girl in Roman dress, parts the clouds of volcanic dust with her hands and treads over hot lava, which turns cool at the touch of her feet, enabling her followers to cross to safety. The next painting shows the saint presenting a statue of Mary and baby Jesus to a pagan priest at the steps of a temple. The pagan priest is then shown casting away a pagan statue and embracing the madonna and child instead. I cross over to the left side of the church, noticing that the terra-cotta madonna above the altar is the same as the one in the pictures. On the left side, the paintings show the saint, grown older, healing the sick, founding a convent and then, on her deathbed, rising to heaven where she takes her place alongside Mary—a Mary who has been made to look here much like the statue above the altar. It's only when I come to the last painting that I realize I'm not alone in the church.

"She lived to the ripe old age of ninety-seven, if you can believe the life in this pamphlet."

I turn around. Elgin is seated in the third pew from the front. I leave the aisle and sit next to him, checking to see that we're the only ones in the church before speaking. "I guess she was rewarded for a life of good works," I say. "Are you thinking of following in her footsteps to ensure your longevity? I thought you swore by oatmeal and rowing as your stay-young plan."

Elgin laughs. "I'm sure Santa Justina would approve of good diet and exercise. She was renowned as an herbalist, healer, and marathon walker. She once walked as far as Sorrento to collect a certain herb to heal a Roman magistrate's wife, which convinced the magistrate to convert to Christianity."

"Santa Justina?" I ask.

"Yes, didn't you know that was the church's name? You've been coming here every day—" Elgin stops when he realizes he's given away the fact he's been watching me, but I am too preoccupied to tease him for it. I get up and approach the altar.

"Pretty, isn't it?" Elgin says, following me. "The statue reminds me of Greek Tanagra figurines. A pagan goddess of some spring given new life as a madonna."

"Can you tell which one?" I ask.

Elgin tilts his head to one side and squints at the statue. "I'd have to get a closer look at that crown she's wearing."

I step around the altar and reach up to the statue.

"Hey!" Elgin hisses, "I didn't mean now. Are you nuts? I've just spent the morning testifying to the Ufficio that I would never knowingly endanger a cultural artifact."

"I'm not going to take it." I gingerly lift the clay statue out of its niche. "I just want to take a look. It feels light. Weren't these clay figurines usually hollow?" When I turn the statue over, Elgin gasps and places his hands around mine, cradling both the statue and my hands. Although there's no chance I'm going to drop this statue, I don't object. It feels good to have his hands over mine.

I smile. "And don't they often have a vent in the back so that the clay fires evenly? See, there's a circle inscribed in the clay? It looks like there was a vent that's been filled with wax. Have you got a pocketknife?"

His eyes widen. "Jesus, Sophie—"

"Gosh, Elgin, I didn't know you were so religious. I'm not going to deface Isis, I'm just going to look inside her."

"Isis?" He looks down at the statue's crown. It's made of waves. I see something click in his eyes. "The statue Phineas gave Iusta . . . Iusta? Do you think . . . ?"

"Justina would be the Italian version of her name. Maybe she survived the eruption after all and brought the statue here. I don't know, but maybe if we look inside she'll tell us."

Elgin takes a quick look around the chapel and then pulls a red Swiss Army knife out of his pocket.

"I knew I could count on you to be prepared," I say. "Do you want to do the honors?"

Elgin nods. He slips the tip of the knife between the dark crust of wax and the clay and, with one quick flick of his wrist, loosens the wax plug like he's shucking an oyster. I lift the wax away—

noticing that it smells like incense—and peer inside. And see nothing. Elgin turns the statue over and gives it a shake and a slender cylinder, no thicker than my little finger, slides out and into my hands.

"Jesus," Elgin says for the second time as I unroll an inch of the delicate papyrus. Only when I see the paper flutter do I realize how hard I'm shaking. "We'd better sit down," Elgin says.

I nod and he leads me to the first pew. We both know we should wait to open it, but our hands are already unfurling the scroll. It's so delicate it feels like we're forcing open a rosebud, but nothing cracks or breaks so, with Elgin holding one edge with his left hand and me holding the other with my right, we open the papyrus until it lies flat on our laps. Elgin reads the first four words out loud.

"I, Petronia Iusta, freewoman . . ."

Later, I will realize that the scroll, exposed to the air after so many centuries sealed away, had already begun to fade. By the time we get it to Maria at the Archaeological Museum and she places it under protective glass, the letters will be all but illegible to the naked eye. But for the next half hour that we sit here, side by side, our heads bent over the one page, the words are as clear as day.

EPILOGUE

I, Petronia Iusta, freewoman, do set down this confession of my free will having come to the end of a long, but not blameless, life. We are admonished to confess our sins in church. This is the way of the light, Barnabas tells us. But while I have confessed to many individual sins—idolatry, unlawful copulation, even murder—I have never told my full story. I know that having omitted this duty in life, I have condemned myself to an eternity of darkness, nor do I trust that this accounting in silence and darkness will alleviate my sentence. Rather, I give these words as an offering to the Holy Mother and entrust them to her vessel for safekeeping. Let her, another woman, judge me as she will and hold or disclose these words as she sees fit.

I was born of a freedwoman in the household of her former master,

Gaius Petronius Stephanus, but since I was a child I was told that I was free because my mother had been freed before my birth. In gratitude for her manumission and in the hope that I would gain the advantages of wealth, my mother allowed me to be brought up in the household of the Petronii. I was treated as a daughter by Gaius Petronius, who taught me to read and write in Latin, Greek, and Hebrew, and was given free rein of his copious library. All was well until I was ten years old and Gaius's wife, Calatoria Vimidis, finally brought forth her own children. She began to resent my place in the household and to see me as a usurper of her children's birthright. Quarrels with my mother ensued and my mother chose to leave. She wished to bring me as well, but Gaius and Calatoria wished me to stay—Gaius out of genuine fondness, I believe, but Calatoria out of a wish to thwart my mother and to use me as a nursemaid to her own children. My mother had to bring suit in the courts to wrest me from the clutches of Calatoria and luckily she won.

My mother and I prospered in the business of raising and selling oysters and we lived in peace for seven more years—like the seven years of fat foretold in the Bible by Joseph—but then calamity befell us. My mother grew suddenly ill and died. I have always suspected that she was poisoned, as a slave of Calatoria's was seen leaving our house just before my mother fell ill. Suspicious as well was the fact that Gaius Petronius died soon after. Her husband's funeral pyre was hardly cold when Calatoria Vimidis brought a suit that claimed me as her lawful property—along with the property of my mother, which I had inherited. She claimed that I was born before my mother's manumission and therefore I had been born a slave. As witness she called on a slave of her own household, Telesforus—the same slave whom I suspected of poisoning my mother. He testified that I was born before my mother was freed. Later, I discovered that Telesforus had been given his own freedom in exchange for this lie, as well as a share in my mother's fortune, taken from me along with my freedom. Although I fought this judgment in the courts of Rome, I was eventually returned to the custody of Calato-

ria Vimidis. *I confess that from that time on I harbored in my heart a hatred for my mistress and the determination that I would do anything to be free again.*

I was given an opportunity to gain my freedom by agreeing to take part in a pagan ceremony. I was not forced to engage in this ceremony, but chose of my own free will to play a role in order to obtain my freedom even though my role included tricking and stealing from my mistress's guest, Phineas Aulus, and engaging in lascivious seduction. Phineas Aulus had in his possession a valuable scroll written by the Greek philosopher Pythagoras that my mistress wished to own—but not to pay for. In return for stealing this scroll from Phineas's room, I was promised a document attesting to my freedom, but when I presented the scroll to Calatoria she said I would not have the document until after the rites. Afraid that Calatoria might still go back on her promise, I decided to steal the document, which I knew she kept in the same hiding place as the scroll, and enlisted the help of Phineas Aulus.

When I had obtained the letter and the scroll, I took Phineas back to the chamber where I knew he would be brutally slaughtered. I could, at that moment, have told Phineas the truth and saved him, but an evil thought had come into my head, namely that I could leave with the rare scroll and use it to buy myself a life of comfort. I left him in that chamber to die.

I made my way to the surface by following at each turning the "better" sign and shunning the "evil" one, but at each crossing I could not help but feel I was choosing evil and fleeing the good. When I reached the last crossroads—the one marked by the faces of Night and Day—something kept me from turning down the final path to the surface. I would like to say it was the voice of God that turned me back, but that would be untrue. I heard a voice, but it was the voice of my mother reminding me of what I had been named for—justice—and that I would be betraying my name if I left Phineas Aulus to die.

I hurried back down the tunnels afraid that I would be too late. I could hear the voices of Calatoria and her maenads, wild in their lust for blood, approaching the Chamber of the God. When I neared the entrance to the chamber, I saw a man enter. It was Telesforus, who had poisoned my mother and betrayed me. I knew that his job would be to subdue the victim before the women arrived. I followed him and as he raised a cudgel to bash in Phineas's brains I drew out of my bag the iron bar that I had left for Phineas to open the door to his chamber, and which I took with me when I left him there to die, and brought it down on Telesforus's head.

May God forgive me for the sin of killing that man. Although I told myself it was to save Phineas, I knew in my heart I did it in vengeance for the wrong he had done to me.

Phineas jumped up from his bed and demanded to know what was happening.

"Calatoria and her women are coming to destroy you," I told him. "Quick, change clothes with this man. We'll put him in your place. In this dim light, the women won't know the difference."

Phineas, although trembling with fear, obeyed me. I expected at any moment that Calatoria and her women would come swarming into the chamber, like ants swarming over their prey. And indeed we escaped only moments before they arrived. We ran up the tunnel marked with a lyre in the dark, because, as I told Phineas, we couldn't risk any of the women seeing a light. At each turning I felt along the wall for the mark that would tell me which way to go, knowing always that if we made the wrong turn we would plunge to our deaths. Behind us we could hear the wild cries of the maenads as they fell upon Telesforus. Although I had hated him, I hoped now that I had killed him so that he would not be aware of what was happening to his body. I imagined that I could hear the crack of his bones and smell his blood. So distracted was I by these images of his dismembering that when we came to the last turning I couldn't for a moment remember which way to go.

"Two faces of women," Phineas said after he himself had felt each mark. "One appears to be smiling. Shouldn't we go this way?" He began

walking down that path, but I pulled him down to his hands and knees so that we could feel along the ground for any sudden drops. We had only gone a few feet when I heard a sound behind me that made my blood freeze.

"So you have betrayed me after I raised you as my own. You are no better than your mother."

I turned around and saw Calatoria standing above us—her long hair matted with blood and gore and her dress ripped from her shoulder so that one breast was bare. I thought that it, too, was stained with blood. She held a torch in one hand and a short sword in the other.

I think, though, that what shocked me the most was the look in Calatoria's eyes—not anger or madness, but hurt and disappointment. Had she really thought of me as a daughter? But in the very next instant I saw that her eyes were fixed on the scroll sticking up from my bag.

"That is my property," she screamed. And I realized that while Calatoria might think of me as her own, I was just another piece of property to her—and of less value than the roll of papyrus in my bag.

I withdrew the scroll from the bag before she could reach it and held it over my head. I had realized that the path Phineas and I had chosen was the wrong one. The figure of Night was the one who had been smiling. Just past where we crouched lay the pit.

As Calatoria dropped her torch and lunged for the scroll I let it drop from my hands. For a moment some errant draft caught it and seemed to hold the scroll aloft in the air. As Calatoria's fingers touched it, she, too, seemed suspended in midair. Her foot touched the edge of the pit and she groped in the air for purchase. She spun around and her arms reached for me. I still could have caught her.

May God forgive me for not saving her.

She fell backward into the pit. When Phineas picked up her torch and held it over the pit we could see her staring up at us, her mouth and eyes wide open and her hair writhing around her head like a nest of snakes. A gorgon. When I close my eyes at night it's that face I see. I am afraid that when I close my eyes for the last time it's the face I'll spend eternity with.

"We have to go," Phineas said. His words came as though from a long way away even though he stood at my side and spoke in my ear. "Can't you feel the ground shaking? It's getting worse."

I realized he was right. I turned to him and saw he was still staring into the pit. The scroll. He was staring at the scroll. But then he shook himself like a man waking from a bad dream and looked at me.

"It's caused enough death," he said and then, taking my hand, he led us out of the wrong path and into the right path and up to the surface.

At first I thought we had reached another dead end. There was no light at the end of the tunnel and no freshening breeze. Our torch flickered and gasped in the noxious air. It's just that night has fallen, I thought as we came out of the tunnel, but I had never seen a night such as this one. We came into the open but the air was full of smoke and foul vapors. When I looked up there were no stars in the sky. Instead above us the slope of Vesuvius was covered with patches of fire. The top of the mountain was engulfed in a boiling cloud of smoke. It was what I imagined Hades would look like. Perhaps we really had taken the wrong turning.

"The worst of the cloud is still in the east," Phineas said, "but it is moving this way. We have to find the road to Neapolis. You said it was close."

I turned to him and saw he was covered with soot and I realized that a fine layer of ash was falling from the sky covering everything. I looked around me, but could find no familiar landmarks. Everything had been transformed. I closed my eyes and tried to picture where we were.

"The coast road should be to our left," I said, pointing in that direction.

Then he said, "Listen. Can you hear people?"

It was hard to hear anything over the moans and rumbles of the mountain, as though from a living beast, but I thought he might be right. Footsteps, voices, the frightened neighing of horses—all came through the thick smoke. He took my hand again and we stumbled through the dark until we began bumping into others. I almost wished we hadn't. The people we met looked like the shades of the dead, stumbling along and staring out of their ash-stained faces with wide, horrified eyes. I half expected to meet Calatoria and Telesforus among them and I began to believe that we ourselves were already dead. All night we marched with that legion of the dead. At one point, there was a louder roar from the mountain and turning around we saw a wave of fire moving down the slope toward the lights of the town. A wind blew in its wake, a wind that felt like the breath of Hades himself. I felt the hairs in my nose singe and the spit in my mouth evaporate. Then the lights of Herculaneum were gone.

We turned our backs on the dead city and trudged on through the night, through the smoke and ash. I never let go of Phineas's hand because I was sure if I did I would be lost. When we reached Neapolis, he pulled me away from the crowds and we walked up a steep hill to a temple. When we reached the steps of the temple we turned around and saw the sun rising over the ruined ash-covered land, rising above the coast of Surrentum, touching the isle of Capreae and the water of the bay. I was amazed that the water was still blue and that the swallows were still alive, swooping through the bright air of a new day.

Phineas left me on the steps of the temple to find water. While he was gone, I took out the statue he had given me of the goddess Isis, queen of heaven, and I brought it into the temple. I saw then that the temple was dedicated to Demeter, the mother who was willing to destroy the earth looking for her daughter. I gave the statue to her and prayed to her for forgiveness. I prayed that I might start anew and I prayed for Phineas, too, that he and I might find a new life together.

And this I confess, too, that I still pray to her, along with the mother of our Savior. Even while I have spent my life dedicated to this new re-

ligion I still pray to all of them—Isis, Bona Dea, Demeter, Cybele, Astarte, and even Baneful Night, most dreaded of goddesses, but who carries in her arms Sleep and Death who give us peace at last. The temple that gave us shelter that morning has become a church and Phineas, after living as my husband for many years and converting to the new faith, has been dead these ten years now. The community of women I have lived with will go on and I begin to suspect that they will remember my name, but they won't remember how I came here. How I was saved in the end by one fallible man's love. That is a story I can trust to no man or woman living, so I entrust it to the dark in the hope that one day it might make its way back into the light, as I and my beloved were allowed to do, stumbling along a dark road, holding each other's hand.

THE NIGHT VILLA

Carol Goodman

A READER'S GUIDE

A REGIONAL MUSE

I've long had a penchant for choosing books based on their setting—whether prompted by a certain mood or because I planned to travel to a particular place—and eventually that reading habit translated itself into an obsession with place in the novels I write.

It may have started with *Eloise*. When I was nine years old, my family relocated from Philadelphia to New York. During the year my father was commuting to his new job, he sublet an apartment on the East Side of Manhattan. One of the wonders of this new urban environment (along with proximity to the United Nations and a sixteenth-floor balcony, from which my teenaged brothers threw cherry bombs purchased in Chinatown) was the apartment's library. "Nine hundred books!" the owner boasted (although I have wondered since who would actually count the books in their private library).

Already a voracious reader at age nine, I was looking forward to exploring this immense collection but was disappointed to find that it contained only one children's book. Luckily, that one book was *Eloise* by Kay Thompson, a book that could be read over and over again, pored over for the minute details in Hilary Knight's line drawings. It even had a foldout diagram of Eloise's peregrinations up and down the hotel elevators—especially fascinating to me since I was, for the first time in my life, riding an elevator every day. But what was best about *Eloise* was that its setting, the Plaza Hotel, was just a short cab ride away. We, too, could have tea in the Palm Court, over which Eloise's portrait presided. My mother was happy to indulge my fascination with Eloise and the Plaza because she had a personal connection to the hotel. In her early twenties, she had worked at the information desk in the lobby and had delivered messages throughout the hotel—from the subbasements to the penthouse suites. When she told me these stories, her travels unfolded in my head like the elevator map in the book, her high heels trailing the red dash marks Eloise makes in her journeys. This confluence of book, real life, and personal history became three important narrative elements when I began my own fiction writing.

Meanwhile, this new world of New York was one that I could see mirrored in many books—from *The Cricket in Times Square* to *Freaky Friday*. My favorite, though, was *From the Mixed-up Files of Mrs. Basil E. Frankweiler* by E. L. Konigsburg. The appeal of this classic lies in the escape fantasy of running away from the pressures of growing up and finding a place of one's own. Instead of a secret garden or a magical kingdom, the children in Konigsburg's book take possession of the Metropolitan Museum of Art. I had visited there with my mother and eaten many a cafeteria lunch by the fountain of cavorting fauns where Claudia and Jamie Kincaid bathe and collect coins to maintain themselves. When I was thirteen, I was allowed to take the train into New York City by myself but only to board the Number 4 bus across from Penn Station and go directly to the Metropolitan Museum. Because this was the only destination I was allowed, and because the city drew me—as I would later read in another book, with its "enchanted metropolitan twilight"—I went to the Metropolitan Museum often, sometimes once a week. It became my personal escape valve.

I could never eat lunch by the fountain without thinking of Claudia and Jamie bathing there, or pass the bed of Marie Antoinette without remembering that's where they slept, or slip into the Egyptian tomb without remembering that that was where Claudia and Jamie hid from their schoolmates. Years later, when I entered the cafeteria and found that the cavernous room had been gutted of its fountain—presumably to make more space for diners—I felt like something had been scraped out of my own gut. I stood in the cafeteria line, fighting off tears, stupidly wondering where runaway children would take their baths now and where would they find pocket change. A sanctuary had been defiled—this place that had been hallowed by the strange alchemical mixture of history, imagination, and literature.

Over the years, I've sought out or stumbled upon these happy meetings of place and book. I read *On the Road* by Jack Kerouac while driving cross-country to California and spent the summer in Los Angeles reading Nathanael West and Joan Didion. I spent a sleepless night in the Colorado Hotel that inspired Stephen King's *The Shining*. The year I lived in the southern Adirondacks, I read more James Fenimore Cooper than I ever would have otherwise or ever will again. After a bad skid on the road to Glens Falls, I pulled into a water station and waited out the storm chatting with the clerk about the scene in *The Last of the Mohicans* where Hawk-eye and Uncas hid in a cave below a waterfall. He pointed out the exact spot described in the book from where we sat. I read Larry McMurtry's *Lonesome Dove* in a U-Haul bound for Austin, Texas. This turned out not to be the best idea, though, because by the time I arrived in my new home, I was terrorized by the snakes, scorpions, and poisonous spiders that populate McMurtry's Texas. Better was Billy Lee Brammer's *The Gay Place,* which made 1950s Austin sound as glamorous as Paris. For the next seven years that I lived there, whenever I smelled mimosa I thought of Brammer's phrase "the heavy honied air." When circumstances compelled me to return to Long Island, I was grateful to Alice Hoffman's *Seventh Heaven* for transforming that most mundane of suburbs, Levittown, into a magical place. If she could find magic in Levittown, surely I could put up with living in Great Neck, which, after all, had its own literary lineage as Gatsby's and Nick Carraway's home.

Certainly I knew by the time I started writing short stories and novels that setting was important to me, but I didn't find my fictional country right away. When I began *The Lake of Dead Languages,* there wasn't even a lake yet, just *Dead Languages*. For two years, I carried around this idea of a story about a Latin teacher living at an isolated boarding school with her young daughter before I knew where the story was set. Then, on a vacation to Mohonk House in the Shawangunks, while I was swimming in Mohonk Lake, I suddenly wondered what it would feel like to swim in that cold, cold water if you had lost someone you loved there. I knew then that the reason the teacher I had been trying to write about was so lost and lonely was that she had lost someone she loved in the lake and that when she swam there, she felt the pull of the cold water as the pull of that lost love.

I followed *The Lake of Dead Languages* with a few other Upstate New York settings: a remote hotel in the Catskills in *The Seduction of Water,* a college much like Vassar for *The Drowning Tree,* and a premier artist colony in *The Ghost Orchid.*

After that, I was determined to venture forth from the safety of home and set a novel outside my beloved New York. However, I'm not the kind of writer who can spin the globe and pick whatever place my finger lands on. For *The Sonnet Lover,* I needed a place with which I had history, that I wouldn't mind getting to know better, one that would also resonate with the themes I'm most interested in. Luckily, my research for *The Ghost Orchid* had already paved the way. I'd fallen in love with the Italian Renaissance gardens I had studied to create the setting in that book, and during college I had spent a semester abroad in Rome studying the classics. I decided to set my next book in Italy.

I had trepidation about setting a book on foreign soil, especially because I had neither the time nor the money (or child care) to go live in Italy for a year. Would I be able to absorb enough atmosphere from short visits supplemented by memories and reading to create a believable Italian setting? I decided to hedge my bets by setting the book at an American school housed in a Renaissance villa—an enclosed environment that I thought I could handle better than Italy at large. Then I booked a trip for my husband and our two daughters to go to Rome and Sorrento.

I learned many important things on this trip (the first of three I took to Italy over the next two years). One was how very difficult it is to research a book while escorting two girls on their first trip to Italy without getting the Bad Mother of the Year Award. It was a constant balancing act between visiting a site I needed to research and finding the best gelato, between buying souvenirs and mapping out a route to the next important sight we needed to see.

However, I did get to see Italy through the excited eyes of two young girls viewing its splendor for the first time. This brought back vivid memories of my junior year abroad and helped me realize the narrator of my new novel would be someone who went to Italy when she was young and who was forever marked by that experience.

After *The Sonnet Lover*, I fully intended to scurry back to New York for my next book, but then I happened upon an interesting idea. This is the problem, I think, with setting out on an odyssey: you don't always return home as quickly as planned. A friend of mine, Ross Scaife, professor of classics at the University of Kentucky, mentioned he was trying to get a grant to use MSI technology to read charred scrolls from Herculaneum, and I realized this provided a fictional way for me to "do" Herculaneum. I'd been there when I was a student in Italy, and I'd gone back to Pompeii on a family trip the year before. My own journey to *The Night Villa* had begun without my being aware of it.

There should probably be an early warning system for writers—something equivalent to the slave who stands behind the Roman general in his chariot whispering "Remember you are mortal." The trip to the Bay of Naples started badly, with a missed connection that turned an already brutally long flight into a twenty-four-hour ordeal. Still, I had in my mind a picture of the hotel I'd booked on Expedia.com as a welcome haven. I'd picked it because it was in an old convent overlooking the city, and it had a rooftop pool. How romantic! I thought. And what great material to stay in an actual fourteenth-century convent, and wouldn't that pool feel delicious after twenty-four hours in the same clothes?

When we arrived, though, we learned that the rooftop pool closed at five o'clock. And when we were shown to our room, I realized why they were called cells. Our room had been tastefully decorated, but there was no getting away from what it had originally been: a tiny, sealed, claustrophobic little cell, with one window overlooking a street so loud with motorcycle traffic that opening it only introduced the fumes of a Dantesque hell into the atmosphere. When I put my hand to the "air conditioner," I felt something that might have been the dying breath of the last nun who lived and died in this airless cell, this Hell . . . well, you get the idea. Granted, I was jet-lagged at the time.

We decided to make do with the hotel. This was a research trip, not a vacation. The important thing was to get to Herculaneum to see the Villa dei Papiri, where the charred scrolls had been found. I'd already begun to formulate a story in which a scroll is lost in the villa in the days before Vesuvius erupted. A cast of ancient characters would search for it in the villa, while in the present, my archaeologists and papyrus scanners also wander the villa's ruins. I saw it as a kind of English manor house mystery, with better food.

The morning we had planned to go to Herculaneum, a taxi strike was declared. We managed to get there, however, using a funicular and bus and train. At last—the Villa dei Papiri! On the tour were just my husband, myself, an Italian archaeologist, and our guide: an old man with the keys to the site and who didn't speak a word of English. That was all right, I thought, as we descended into a pit carved out of tufa and crossed a weed-choked underground stream alive with croaking frogs reminiscent of the Styx; I was really doing research now! I was getting the inside dope.

With my limited Italian and a little help from the archaeologist, I understood about one-tenth of what the old man said, but the little I did understand was still amazing. Our elderly guide showed us the tunnels where eighteenth-century excavators had retrieved the scrolls, and then we climbed up to the third level. We walked through rooms with dust-covered mosaic floors and traces of paint clinging to fragments of walls, and out onto a peristyle that would have once faced the sea, but which now faced a wall of tufa that some Americans had carved strange shapes into. (No wonder they don't like us.) Then we moved on to the baths.

I turned back as we left the villa and suddenly realized that that was it. The Villa dei Papiri hadn't been fully excavated. There were only these few rooms and a private bath a few yards away.

After traveling thousands of miles in a cramped economy seat, suffering intestinal discomforts, sacrificing the comforts of home and the company of my child and my pets, having spent too much money to stay in a room that would have been a penance to Renaissance women only to find, as T. S. Eliot puts it, "That is not what I meant at all. That is not it, at all"; I couldn't possibly have my narrator come and stay in this city where it was too hot and there weren't taxis and besides, the villa wasn't excavated enough to support the shenanigans of my characters. An entire trip pursuing my fictional muse had been a terrible mistake.

Later that day, however, I wandered into a quiet room in Herculaneum, a room that had been dug from solidified lava but was now open to the sunlight—like the glimmer of an idea rescued from the dark. My eyes filled with tears. I'd come across the household shrine. For a moment, I felt the presence of the men and women who had knelt to pray at this spot every day of their lives. I experienced the sadness of a place where so many people had died unexpectedly and painfully. At the shrine, I felt the first seeds of inspiration.

More such moments followed in the coming days. The shadow of painted wings, barely visible, on a red wall in another room in Herculaneum; the strangely enigmatic figures performing rites that still have no explanation at the Villa of the Mysteries in Pompeii; the echoing Cave of the Sibyl at Cumae; the empty, sun-filled rooms of the Villa Jovis on Capri.

It was on the way from Capri to Sorrento that I realized what I had to do. I didn't have to write about the real Villa dei Papiri; I could create my own ancient Herculanean villa. Even better, I could give my Papyrus Project a rich benefactor who'd built a replica of the villa (like the Getty Museum) somewhere nearby—like Sorrento, maybe, or the Isle of Capri.

That's where my heroine and the rest of the crew would stay while they deciphered a rediscovered scroll, one lost in the days just before the volcano erupted. As I watched the swallows careening over the bay, I felt my imagination set free and take flight. I had caught up with my muse once again.

Carol Goodman and her husband, Lee Slonimsky, chat about writing, Italy, and good tomatoes.

Lee Slonimsky: Like your last book, *The Sonnet Lover*, *The Night Villa* is set in Italy, but this time in the Bay of Naples. What drew you back to an Italian setting, and why a different part of the country?

Carol Goodman: Having made numerous trips to Italy while researching *The Sonnet Lover*, one visit I found particularly memorable was to the Bay of Naples. This breathtakingly beautiful area has fascinated me since I first visited Pompeii and Herculaneum as a classics student in college. I think any writer strolling the streets of Sorrento would find inspiration there.

LS: Certainly many have. Sorrento's town square is even dominated by the statue of a native poet, Torquato Tasso. So was Italy your main inspiration for the novel, or did something else lead you to this story?

CG: More than most, this book had a very precise moment of origin. My friend Ross Scaife is a professor of classics at the University of Kentucky, and he told me of a grant he'd been given to use multispectral imaging to study the charred manuscripts found at Herculaneum's Villa dei Papiri. I thought this was just about the coolest thing I'd ever heard of and immediately wanted to base a book's plot around a similar exploration. Ross was generous with suggestions and explanations, and he directed me toward a fine book by David Sider, *The Library of the Villa dei Papiri*. As I constructed my story, though, I realized I had to fictionalize the villa as well as give my characters someplace to relax. I also took many liberties with the scientific process of scanning ancient manuscripts, for which I apologize to Ross and his colleagues.

LS: One of the most remembered and tragic events in history, the eruption of Vesuvius in A.D. 79 is an interesting choice of subject matter for a novelist like yourself who often works with themes of memory and loss. Has Pompeii long been a subject of fascination for you?

CG: The first time I saw Pompeii and Herculaneum, I was twenty years old. Spending a semester at the Inter-Collegiate Center for Classical Studies in Rome, I visited a lot of ancient sites. Still, nothing prepared me for walking down an actual street in Pompeii or entering an authentic house in Herculaneum.

LS: Were Iusta and Phineas real people?

CG: Phineas is fictional; Iusta is based on a real person. I first read about her in Joseph Jay Deiss's book *Herculaneum: Italy's Buried Treasure*. Her story is much as I describe it in chapter five of *The Night Villa*, with a few details changed about the lawsuit. All that is known about Iusta comes from eighteen wax tablets. We don't know whether she was even in Herculaneum when Mount Vesuvius erupted. Everything Sophie finds out about Iusta from Phineas is, of course, fictional.

LS: All your novels have been filled with classical references of one sort or another, but *The Night Villa* is the first to contain a literal, if fictitious, ancient manuscript, a real character and voice from the ancient world. What was writing in that voice like for you?

CG: I was worried I wouldn't be able to capture Phineas's voice or tell Iusta's story. For Phineas, I reread a number of classical authors: Pliny, Tacitus, Suetonius, Aulus Gellius, and Livy. When writing those sections, I tried to think about how it would sound in Latin, so while composing in English, I used words with Latin counterparts.

As for Iusta, I was immediately drawn to her story, but it wasn't until the end of the book that I felt I heard her voice. I could have written much more about her, but at least she has the final word.

LS: Was there anything else that inspired you in the course of writing the book?

CG: Your book of sonnets about the life of Pythagoras [*Pythagoras in Love*] suggested to me the nature of the modern cult in *The Night Villa*. I had no idea how important and profound a historical figure Pythagoras was—even more than a mathematician or philosopher.

LS: *The Night Villa* includes two of my poems, one written in this plot-oriented manner, and the other a recent poem you liked and thought would fit your plot. That's the Wilhelmina F. Jashemski poem, which had actually been inspired by reading *The Night Villa*.

CG: It wasn't until the second draft that I realized it would work perfectly as the poem Sophie wrote for Elgin. You know, you've adopted a persona of Pythagoras for your poems and are so adept at writing from the personae I've "assigned" you over the years [Zalman Bronsky in *The Ghost Orchid*, Ginevra de Laura in *The Sonnet Lover*], I sometimes wonder if you ever write from your own point of view. I know I sometimes give my fictional characters pieces of myself. For instance, I give Sophie my old Austin bungalow and, of course, my love of classical authors.

LS: Were there any particular books you read during your research for *The Night Villa*?

CG: I read a lot of nonfiction books for research. For those interested, the most useful were *Herculaneum: Italy's Buried Treasure* by Joseph Jay Deiss, *The Library of the Villa Dei Papiri at Herculaneum* by David Sider, *The Cults of Campania* by Roy Merle Peterson, *The Cults of the Roman Empire* by Robert Turcan, *Romans on the Bay of Naples* by John D'Arms, *Earthly Paradises: Ancient Gardens in History and Archaeology* by Maureen

Carroll, and *Vesuvius A.D. 79* by Ernesto De Carolis and Giovanni Patricelli. For the history and atmosphere of Capri, I read *The Story of San Michele* by Axel Munthe, *Siren Land* by Norman Douglas, *Capri and No Longer Capri* by Raffaele La Capria, and *Greene on Capri* by Shirley Hazzard. It was fun but also hard work. The next book is going to be set in New England.

LS: No more trips to Italy?

CG: Not for a little while, but I was thinking we could go hiking in New Hampshire.

LS: Sounds good to me.

1. *The Night Villa* continues the intersection of past and present narratives common in Carol Goodman's other novels, but with a much-greater expanse of time between the two threads. Does this make for a more dramatic narrative? What other effects does the gulf of time separating the two stories have?

2. Part of the plot is tied to a historical event: the eruption of Vesuvius in 79 A.D. What kind of shadow does this famous event cast over the novel?

3. How sympathetic a character did you find Agnes? Does her background fully explain her behavior?

4. Do you see Phineas as fundamentally decent, a pompous ass, or somewhere in between?

5. Cults play a significant role in this novel, past and present. How do you define a cult? Have you ever known a cult member? Why do you think people join them?

6. Who is your favorite character in *The Night Villa*? Least favorite?

7. The multispectral imaging technology used in *The Night Villa* has the potential to revolutionize the study of ancient manuscripts. What exotic or ancient world would you like to know more about?

8. Do you think Sophie was right to complain bitterly about conditions at the Hotel Convento? Or was she acting like a "spoiled American"?

9. What genre of writing do you think *The Night Villa* falls into?

10. Like previous Carol Goodman novels, *The Night Villa* brings its geographic setting vividly alive. Is there a place you have visited that has artistically inspired you?

11. Sophie is horrified in *The Night Villa* by the loss of her boyfriend, Ely, to a cult. Have you had a similar experience of distance developing in a relationship—perhaps if not because of a cult, then because of an addiction or an all-consuming hobby? If so, how did you handle it?

12. One characteristic of literary fiction is that characters are not static and may undergo genuine changes during the course

of a narrative. What character or characters undergo transformations in *The Night Villa*?

13. Certainly Sophie's impression of Elgin changes during the novel. Did yours? If so, do you think Elgin changed, or was it simply that you got more information about him?

14. When ex-lovers reencounter each other after years have passed, the results can range from animosity to the flame being resparked. Have you ever had such an encounter? What happened?

15. How do the issues in Iusta's life relate to problems faced by contemporary women? Are they drastically different?